Robin Reeves

—BACK TO—
RETURN

First Edition 2015. Reprinted 2023

ISBN: 978-1-910719-07-7

Published for Robin Reeves by Verité CM Limited
Web: www.veritecm.com

British Library Cataloguing Data

A catalogue record of this book is available from The British Library

Design and Typesetting by Verité CM Ltd

Printed in England

ACKNOWLEDGEMENTS

I would like to thank a few people for their help and advice in the writing of this story. The Admiral, (Mick) my strongest critic.

Jessica Grace Coleman for her work on my atrocious grammar.

My Daughter, Belinda, for the technical and computer work carried out.

And most of all to my wife Mary-Jane who encouraged me to finish the story over the past twenty years.

THE AUTHOR

I, Robin Reeves was born on the 29th August 1941 in Horsham, West Sussex, to Dorothy and Len. I now live in Worthing with my wife Mary-Jane.

I had a very happy childhood and teen years, leaving school at fifteen serving a five years apprenticeship as a Painter and Decorator.

Whilst working at Forest Hospital, Roffey, Horsham, in the late 1950s I first came into contact with Down's Syndrome and those years still hold fond memories to this day.

These special people inspired me to write this story. I hope that anyone who reads this book enjoys it as much as I did writing it.

CHAPTER ONE

I ran across the playground towards the group of children encircling the two boys fighting. I hated playground duty – I was a teacher for goodness' sake, not a prison officer. In the classroom I could hold some semblance of control, but in the playground I had nothing. I should be enriching the lives of the kids, not breaking up fights. As I drew closer I recognised the two boys in the middle of the throng: Jenkins, a boy of fifteen, about five feet tall in his socks and must have weighed all of nine stone and Rawlinson who was almost six feet tall and at least twelve stone, despite being the same age as Jenkins.

As I pushed through the howling mob, I could see that Rawlinson held Jenkins by his left wrist, preparing to punch him in the face. Before I could get through I could only watch as Jenkins pulled his head back and with a BANG head-butted Rawlinson in the face. The action clearly had the desired effect: with a scream Rawlinson released his grip and brought his hands up to his face, blood pouring from his nose and his eyes watering so much that he could hardly focus. Before Rawlinson knew it, Jenkins had kicked him in the testicles and as the boy fell to the ground clutching his groin protectively, he landed another kick to the boy's ribs. Finally through the throng of students, I hauled Jenkins away by his shirt, his next kick inches away from Rawlinson's face.

"Jenkins! Headmaster's office!" I barked, holding onto his collar and frogmarching him towards the school, not caring that I was being booed by the observing teens for breaking up the fight, Rawlinson still groaning from his position on the ground, clutching his groin and rolling to and fro in pain. "And someone take Rawlinson to the First Aid room!"

"But he started it, sir!" Jenkins complained as we continued on our path towards the school building.

"Shut up."

"But he's bigger than me, sir!"

"Shut up."

I rapped on the head's door and briefly explained the situation before retreating, leaving Jenkins with the headmaster to face the repercussions of his actions. The thwack of the cane followed me down the corridor as I headed back to my classroom. Jenkins was right; Rawlinson was bigger and known to be a bully, but rules are rules: fighting is unacceptable. It didn't matter that I felt that caning was somewhat harsh for the situation, this was the 1950s and we lived by the saying: *Spare the rod and spoil the child.*

I'd just got everything settled in the classroom and was ready to teach when Jenkins walked in, to the cheers of the rest of the class, a broad grin spread across his face.

"Quiet!" I shouted. "Jenkins, sit down."

"Yes, sir."

Even a good thrashing couldn't wipe the smile off of his face. I found myself staring at him for the remainder of the lesson – what was it that made this boy tick? He fought all the time but even when he got a beating, he still came up with a grin on his face. Maybe it was simply because he was from a rough family. I'd once had to speak to his mother about the fact that he was acting up in class – she'd pinned me to the wall and punched me in the mouth for my trouble. It hadn't been until she'd left that Jenkins kindly informed me: "Next time, talk to my dad. At least he will listen to you and *then* punch you in the mouth."

As the final bell rang and the lot of them rushed for the door, unwilling to stay another minute in the classroom, I called out for Jenkins to wait back.

"Why are you always fighting?" I asked as I walked over and perched on his desk. "Even when you lose, you still go ahead and do it."

"Well, sir," he beamed, "some of the bigger lads think they can

6

push me around. I'm five feet nothing and under nine stone, too small to fight by Queensbury rules, so I cheat a little. If I can kick 'em in the nuts first they come down to my size, if you see what I mean. Remember sir, the first blow is 90% of the battle won."

I considered him for a moment. "Alright, Jenkins, get off home and try to stay out of trouble."

"I don't hold it against you for dobbin me in, sir," he said as he reached the door, turning back to speak to me, still smiling. "See you tomorrow!"

As I gathered my things and started my walk home I couldn't help but think: "There's a prison cell waiting on him when he leaves school."

The next day, inevitably, followed a similar path – the kids were a pain and shouting was the only way to communicate.

"Quiet, please! Settle down!" I shouted, waiting as they did so. Afternoon registration was always the worst. "Jenkins, why on earth have you applied for A-Level History? You don't have the slightest bit of interest in historical events."

"Cause they don't do A-Levels in stock car racing, and that's what I wanna do sir."

I hummed, disbelievingly. "Jenkins, if you don't stop fooling around and start taking an interest in your future, you'll be in for a big -"

A tap-tap-tap on the door sounded and it opened slowly. The bald head of the Assistant Headmaster – Mr Wiltshire – peered around the frame.

"Mr Cross," his voice was sickly, "the Headmaster would like to see everybody after school in his study."

He disappeared as slickly as he'd arrived, closing the door behind him.

"Right you lot, homework for the weekend: What formation did the Romans take up in battle against the invading marauders? What was their favourite method of execution? And Jenkins, if you don't know the answers, apply for an A-Level in Boxing."

The 3 o'clock bell rang and with it the end-of-the-day stampede for the door. If only they had the same passion for history as they had to go home. Remembering Mr Wiltshire's summons to the Headmaster's study, I packed up and made my way to the meeting. On my way I spotted a boy, about 14 years old, coming in the opposite direction. As he drew closer, he lifted his head and smiled at me. To my absolute horror, he was a Down's Syndrome child; I changed my path to make a wide birth around him.

"Who are you smiling at?" I snapped at the boy.

His face changed to expressionless in an instant and he stood there, staring at me as I passed. Mongols. I wasn't sure if I hated them or feared them – maybe it was both. All I knew was that they made me cringe and I needed to put distance between us. I tried to put it aside as I reached the Headmaster's study. Clearly I was the last to arrive – the room had quietened as I knocked and entered.

"Ah, Mr Cross, come in and close the door. I've requested this meeting to inform you that, as of next term, the Board of Governors, the PTA and the Council have decided to introduce children into our school from St Julius in order to help them into the community and hopefully lead a more normal life. Each class will take at least one pupil with the help of teaching assistants."

"Excuse me, Headmaster," I interrupted, "but who, exactly, are these children, and what is St Julius?"

I could feel everyone staring at me; the Headmaster looked over his glasses. "It's a home for children with Down's Syndrome."

"What!" I bellowed, "I'm not bloody teaching Mongols!"

The Headmaster raised his hand. "Please, Mr Cross, keep your voice down; they are next door waiting to view the school.

8

Besides, the Board has passed it."

"I don't care if the *Queen* has passed it I screamed. I am not teaching Mongols in my class. I give my notice verbally now, and you will have it in writing first thing on Monday!" I spun on my heels and stormed out, slamming the door as I left.

That night I lay in bed, thinking about my actions but unable to bring myself to even contemplate teaching those children. As promised, I put my written notice on the Headmaster's desk on Monday morning; he didn't even look up at me, but simply grunted as I left. It was as I was picking at my lunch that my thoughts were broken.

CHAPTER TWO

"Penny for them."

I looked up – Dave, my best mate, stood over me. We had met at teacher training college and soon laid a path of drinking together, pulling birds together and even ended up teaching at the same school. He taught Maths and Science whilst I taught History and English. The only thing we didn't do together was marriage – he found a wife and I was still single at 25 years old.

"I hear you threw a wobbler," Dave smiled. "I wish I could have been there to see the Head's face – I had to leave early to see the dentist. You don't like Down's Syndrome, do you?"

"No, I don't!" I snapped, my brow furrowing into a scowl. "They should be kept behind locked doors and not let out in public."

"Hey, calm down, I'm not here to judge – just to invite you to dinner," Dave brought his hands up in front of him in surrender. "Tracey told me not to take no for an answer. Be warned, though, that you'll be interrogated – forewarned is forearmed and all that."

My shoulders slumped. "Sure, I'd love to mate. It might take my mind off things. I'll bring the wine."

"Sure – see you about eight," Dave lifted a hand in farewell as we parted.

I stopped off at the supermarket on the way home for the wine and a bottle of Scotch. It wasn't until I was in a bath that what I had done hit me: I'd just thrown away the best job that I had ever had. I'd even been shortlisted for an Assistant Head post at a secondary school in Sussex. Now, in one month, I'd be out of work and on the dole. I'd thrown it all away – but I was damned if I would stay at the school with the changes they were bringing in.

I caught sight of myself in the mirror as I headed to my bedroom to dress. It was like looking at an advert for famine relief. All of nine stone and seven pounds, I was a human wreck. Regardless, I'd promised Dave that I would go to dinner, so I'd just have to put on my only jacket and best trousers. Another passing glimpse in the mirror and I figured that it's the best it's going to get. It's almost eight and, grabbing the bottle of wine on my way out, I thanked God for the invention of the automobile – two miles down the road and I'm pulling up outside Dave and Tracey's house.

I rang the door bell. Through the obscured glass I saw a movement of red. The door opened and there stood Tracey. Flowing red dress, red high heels and earrings, red lipstick on her gorgeous pouting lips.

"Robbie!" she beamed, throwing her arms around my neck and kissing my cheek. *Dave was certainly one lucky bastard* I thought. Her perfume was completely intoxicating and, in the haze of overwhelmed senses, I vowed that I would one day marry a woman like Tracey. Pulling back, she took the wine from my hand.

"Come in and make yourself at home – I'll put this in the fridge. There's Scotch in the lounge… pour me one while you're at it? Dave will be down shortly. I mean, he's worse than me at getting ready for dinner."

I chuckled, heading into the lounge. "Maybe, but he doesn't do half as good a job as you."

"You know, it's about time you got married and settled down, Robbie. Are you still seeing Jane?" Tracey called from the kitchen.

Jane. I paused in pouring the Scotch. Oh hell. I was supposed to take her to the pictures tonight.

"Hello mate!" Dave strode in, beaming, all dressed up like the dog's dinner. "Ah, Scotch – pour me one of those, will you? Thanks."

Tracey called to us then, and we finished our drinks as we

headed to the dining room. The table was set with serviettes folded like roses and candles giving the room a warm, homely light, flickering off of three glasses of wine. Dinner passed in a haze of good food and good conversation. I sat back holding my stomach.

"That was the best meal you've ever cooked, Tracey. I've never tasted food so succulent. It's even better than last time I was here."

"You smoothie she said you say that every time. I wish my husband would say it now and then."

Dave looked at her like a child that had been scolded. "Oh come on! You know I think you're an amazing cook."

"I'm not a mind reader," she smiled, quirking an eyebrow at her husband. "It's nice to be complimented now and then."

As we moved to the lounge, Tracey took my hand and urged me to sit next to her on the settee leaving Dave to take the armchair.

"Right then, let's have it," she squeezed my hand. "What's it all about?"

"I can't help it. There's just something about *them* that I can't abide. I feel uncomfortable around them. They're non-productive, good for nothing and they cost the country millions of pounds"

"Surely everyone has a right to live," Tracey said in a soft voice. "It could be one of our children, or even yours when you marry and settle down."

I scoffed. "I would sooner not have children at all if I thought they would be born like that."

"Robbie, I'm a barrister, and in court I've seen murderers sent to prison for life with less hate in their eyes than you have. I feel sad for you – to hate a person for something that is not their fault? It must be eating your heart out. Learn to come to terms with it or it will destroy you."

13

"So what?" I snarled. "It's got nothing to do with you, so mind your own bloody business."

Dave and Tracey shared a glance before changing the subject.

"Have you got any plans for the future?" Dave asked.

"I haven't even thought about it yet – I've got some job hunting to do."

"Well I have a National Union for Teachers magazine you can have – there's lots of jobs advertised in there."

I nodded my acceptance and thanks to Dave. "I'm sorry Tracey – I wouldn't upset you for the world."

"Robbie, you couldn't – we love you too much for that."

We spoke for a while about old times, finally parting ways at close to 2am. It didn't matter that I'd been drinking – I'd had enough to think I could still drive. Despite that, I got home safely and headed straight for bed. I stopped as I spied something white in the middle of my dimly lit living room. A bra? I looked further and spotted a stocking; further still, a pair of red knickers. My alcohol-fuelled brain slowly connected the dots as I reached the bedroom. Jane.

I attempted to slip into bed without waking her, but just as I settled, her arm slipped around my waist and held me tightly.

"Where have you been, bunny wabbit?" she purred sleepily. "I've missed you."

I could hear the pout in her voice. "I had some business to attend to."

"Business," she said, disbelief heavy in her voice. "You could have rung me, you bastard. I've waited all evening for you – we were supposed to go to the pictures, remember?"

"I'm sorry – it was important and I forgot; that's all."

"That's all?" Jane protested. "I spent hours having a shower, doing my hair, make-up, and got all dressed up just to sit on my fat arse waiting for a thoughtless bastard who forgot he was supposed to pick me up at eight? And all you can say is that's all?"

"Well," I stammered, "if you must know, I've lost my job and I'm sick with worry over it. I completely forgot about the pictures. I am sorry."

Jane paused. I could feel her taking this information in and hoped she didn't figure out that I was bending the truth just a little.

"Oh you poor bunny wabbit," she purred eventually. "What happened? Tell pussycat all about it."

"Can I tell you tomorrow when I'm not so upset over it?"

"Of course you can. Come here baby, let me make you feel better."

We made love and Jane fell asleep in my arms. For a long time afterwards I couldn't get the rest I craved – thoughts about what I had done and what the future might hold plagued me.

CHAPTER THREE

The following morning as I sipped at my coffee, my eyes wandered across the NUT magazine that I had discarded the previous night. For the lack of anything better to do, I tugged it towards me and flicked through the pages towards the job advertisements. I begrudgingly picked up the phone and starting calling around.

A few weeks later and I had gotten nowhere. I stared vacantly at the page in front of me, wondering whether I was ever going to find a job. Then I noticed the words that I had been staring at.

Teachers wanted in war-torn Africa.

Africa – that would be a challenge, I thought as I phoned for an application form. I thought nothing more of it until a week later when I received a reply asking me to arrange an interview.

*   *   *

So there I was, having taken a train and a taxi to the city of London, standing on Warwick Street outside a huge Victorian building with sash windows to match and solid oak doors one morning in late June. My heart skipped a beat in mild apprehension as I made my way up the steps, the door creaking as I pushed it open. Inside, where the stifling summer heat of the city was forgotten in a moment of cool relief, a beautiful girl with ebony skin sat behind a desk, her hair perfectly done and her smile radiant.

"Good morning, sir," she said, her voice lilting with a slight African accent. "May I help you today?"

"Hello, I'm Mr Cross… I have an appointment with Mr Mabatto," I said, my palms slightly sweaty with the anticipation of an interview that could completely change my life.

"Of course – please take a seat and I will let him know that you have arrived."

I turned, the plush sofa enveloping me as I sat, looking around at the reception area. A low coffee table sat in front of me, a selection of magazines on the top broadcasting the latest occurrences at home and in Africa. It was only a few minutes later by the clock on the wall, despite feeling like hours, when the buzzer on the receptionist's desk sounded and she told me that I could go through the single door and into Mr Mabatto's office. I had to stop myself from gasping – the office was the biggest I had ever been in, with one of the large sash windows I had admired outside letting in a wonderful stream of sunlight that lit the room beautifully. A huge ornate desk made of mahogany – sat to one side, and there was a Victorian fireplace on the opposite wall with a small collection of comfortable chairs in front of it. I focused eventually on the man walking towards me, hand outstretched. He was short, fat and dark-skinned.

"Mr Cross," he smiled, "glad to meet you. I am Mr Mabatto. Please, sit!" He gestured to one of the chairs by the fireplace, and placed a stack of folders on the small coffee table that I hadn't been able to see before. "Can I get you a cup of tea?"

I could only nod in acceptance.

Stepping away briefly, Mr Mabatto spoke through the intercom: "Tea for two please, Miss Boetoo." Swinging his broad smile back to me, he continued: "Now, let us get down to business. I've been reading through your C.V., Mr Cross, and I feel you could be just what we are looking for." He settled back into his chair. "I represent my country: Africa. With all of the unrest and fighting that we have endured in the past few years, poor people have been scattered for miles in all directions. We now want to get them back to their villages and towns, build new schools and educate them – especially the children – to bring them back into the twentieth century.

"It will be a long, hard slog, Mr Cross, but we feel education is the answer. Do you agree?" He paused, and handed me one of the folders. "Read through this folder – the terms and conditions are laid out in here. If you accept them then feel free to sign the contract and send it back to me. I'll arrange your flight and accommodation. It won't be the Savoy hotel I'm afraid, but it will be comfortable and rent-free. Remuneration is £1,200 a month and all work will be found for you.

"All of the information that you might need is in the folder – please read it thoroughly and contact myself or Miss Boetoo if you have any questions. If you don't accept, please put it in writing in the next fourteen days so that we may offer the position to another candidate."

I nodded dumbly, flipping through the folder and hoping that I looked as though I knew what I was doing. He paused momentarily as the receptionist brought in the two cups of tea.

"Just one last thing," Mr Mabatto said, "you aren't racist, are you? If you are, you won't like the position."

I looked at him. "No, Sir, I'm not."

"Excellent," he said, beaming. "Then I hope that I may hear from you soon!"

We spent a while finishing our tea whilst he talked at length about his country. It was clear that he was passionate about helping to get Africa back on its feet. Once we had finished our tea and parted ways, I headed back to the station to head home. As I went, I realised that I was actually quite excited – a new job in a new country. It would be a huge change, but the prospect of the challenge thrilled me. I started to think of what I needed to sort out before I left: I had to sell the flat and the car, as well as tie up all loose ends. As I got back home I had formulated a plan, but I needed to talk it through with someone. Tracey would be perfect. A quick telephone call and we'd arranged to meet up in a few days on the Saturday evening. This time, I'd supply the Chinese takeaway. I made sure to call Jane to invite her along to our get-together too.

I passed the time studying the folder that Mr Mabatto had given me. Saturday came soon enough and we were all sitting around Tracey and Dave's dining table, drinking wine and eating our

Chinese. I broke the news just as we were heading into the lounge to settle down.

"You'll miss a good Chinese in Africa, Robbie," Dave said as he sat down.

Tracey laughed, "I expect there's already a take-away out there, Dave; they've opened up everywhere else in the world!"

"Well I haven't signed the contract yet," I said, picking up the folder that I had brought with me. "I wondered if you could have a look at it for me, Tracey?"

"Sure." She smiled.

We made our way through the folder, discussing the pros and cons of what was outlined there. Eventually, Tracey spoke up about the contract.

"Well, I see no hidden meanings to catch you out – it's actually a good contract."

"That's good," I said. "I think I'd already made up my mind that I was going anyway."

Silence descended and Jane spoke quietly after a moment: "I don't want you to go."

I could hear a catch in her voice, and as I turned to look at her I could see the tears rolling over her wine-reddened cheeks as she burst out sobbing.

"Oh, pussycat, come on – don't cry." I reached over and put a hand on her knee. "It's only for a while. Once I'm settled I'll call you to come out to me."

"But I don't want to go to Africa! I thought we'd get married, settle down and have children like normal people."

"We will – I promise Africa is only for a little while, and then we'll do all of those things."

She stared at me for a few seconds, sniffing intermittently. "Promise?" she pouted.

"I promise."

"How did the send-off go at the school? Did they have a whip-round?" Tracey jumped in, spotting an opportunity.

"Yeah," I said. "Well, the children and teachers did."

"But not the headmaster," Dave chipped in.

"No, that's true. Not even to wish me good luck."

"Eurgh, what a pig," Tracey commented, pulling a face.

Slowly, as we consumed more wine, the conversation turned to light-hearted chatter.

*   *   *

Over the next couple of days, I re-read the information, signed the contract and sent it back to Mr Mabatto. Three weeks later I got a confirmation back with a ticket for a flight on the 29th August. Only one month and three days to go! Time started to fly past with the preparations for my leaving for Africa coming thick and fast – selling the car and putting the flat on the market at the top of the list, closely followed by cancelling all of my insurances. As the day of my departure drew ever closer, Tracey agreed to handle selling the flat and my car and banking the money for me. With four days to go I decided it was time to treat Jane to a romantic dinner out.

I took her to a little Italian restaurant that we visited often. We knew the food was good and that we could walk there and back, allowing us to enjoy a bottle of wine. The evening couldn't have been more perfect – a warm night, the sky was clear and it was easy to see the stars twinkling beside a full moon. All in all, it was a lovely romantic night for us both to hold on to until we met again.

At least it would have been if, as we turned the corner, a somewhat intoxicated man hadn't walked straight between myself and Jane as though we were invisible, hitting Jane with his shoulder so hard that she hit the wall of the building and fell to the ground with a scream.

"Hey!" I shouted after him, "Watch what you're doing!"

The man turned. "Who're you talking to, you little maggot?" He snarled.

"You!" I snapped.

He strode forwards and grabbed me by the collar before punching me in the face. Stunned, I fell to the ground and he started to kick me in the ribs. Luckily, three men were passing on the pavement across the road and ran over to stop him. He looked down at Jane and said:

"If you want a real man, get rid of this maggot and come see me. The name's Gordon, Gordon Stemp." He smiled, what he supposed was a flirtatious grin before walking off.

"Jane?" I rasped.

"I... I'm okay, Robbie," she stuttered, horrified at what had happened to us.

I winced as I tried to push myself up. I knew she said she was okay, but I wasn't going to believe it until I'd seen her with my own eyes. I tried to hide my grimace as I turned to look at her – she seemed okay; one of the men who had run over to help was crouched down next to her, checking what had happened.

"You alright mate?" Another of the men asked and I nodded.

"Yeah, I just want to get to my girlfriend."

He helped me across to Jane as a paramedic turned up. He assessed us quickly, establishing that neither of us were seriously hurt by the inconsiderate bastard who had knocked us down; Jane was simply shaken and a bit bruised, whilst I had three cracked ribs and had a wonderfully black eye starting to form. We were sent on our way pretty quickly and thanked the men who stopped before we headed home. After all of that unwelcome excitement, we decided to spend the next few days simply relaxing at home.

*   *   *

Those days flew past and soon I was making the trip to the airport with Jane, Tracey and Dave for my flight out. My ribs were still sore, but the pain was tolerable. It was the two black eyes that had developed since the attack that made me look like a panda. I tried to ignore Jane's crying as we waited – not out of meanness, but rather because I knew that if I saw her cry much more I might just not get on the plane. As my flight was called I pulled her into a hug and kissed her, promising to write to her every day. I kissed Tracey and shook hands with Dave.

"Look after yourself, old mate! See you soon!"

"I will, Dave, don't you worry." I reassured him.

The final boarding call rang out from the tannoy system. I kissed Jane once more.

"I love you," she whispered. "Make sure you come back to me."

"Of course I will, Jane. I love you." I started to make my way to the gate, turning half-way and calling back: "You've got my address – don't forget to write! Love you all; bye!"

I kept looking back to them until I had turned a corner and couldn't see them any longer. I really was going to miss them. I smiled at the air hostess who checked my ticket as I boarded the plane and hoisted my backpack more securely onto my shoulder as I prepared to navigate the narrow aisle. After finding my seat and shoving my bag into the overhead locker, wincing as I stretched my ribs, I settled down and started to think about what the future held for me. I was heading from a concrete jungle to a real jungle – the city boy dumped in the middle of nowhere, miles from any civilisation and completely out of my depth. Before long, it was far too late to change my mind and my stomach flipped as the doors closed and we taxied our way to the runway to take off. I watched out of the window as the land below grew smaller and the houses disappeared. It must have been hours later that my attention was diverted with the arrival of the in-flight meal, and limp and questionable as it was, it was

23

still food. The next thing I knew, I was being awoken by the Captain's voice.

"Ladies and gentlemen, this is your Captain speaking. If you would care to look out of your windows you may see that we are approaching the coast of Morocco."

I tuned him out as I stared at the sight below. The sun sat low in the sky and dusk was quickly falling, the shimmering reflection of the sun on the water fading into the glorious splash of colour on the land. Excitement bubbled up within me at the realisation that in only a few more hours, we would be landing in Africa.

"Can I get you anything, sir?" A stewardess asked, leaning over to me, the drinks trolley in front of her.

"A double scotch please." It slipped down easily and before long I had drifted back off to sleep.

BANG!

I woke with a start, my heart pounding and my body full of adrenaline. I had no idea how long I had been asleep, but things had clearly changed – the plane was juddering violently and then suddenly banked to the right.

"Ladies and gentlemen, we are experiencing some turbulence. Please stay calm and remain seated." The Captain said over the intercom.

"We've been hit by lightning! I saw it!" one man shouted out.

Women were screaming and children were crying. People were undoing their seatbelts and running up and down the aisle, with nowhere to go, in panic. The stewardesses were doing their best to get everyone back into their seats and put their seatbelts on.

The Captain's voice rang out again, but this time with less confidence to it. "Please take your seats and take the emergency position!"

The plane started to nosedive, shuddering violently as the engines roared. I looked around me at the other passengers, many now praying out loud.

"Please stay in your seats. The Captains voice again. We'll be making an emergency landing."

In the jungle? I thought. *There's no bloody runway in the jungle.*

"Please lean forwards and place your head between your knees!" One of the stewardesses shouted.

"And kiss your arse goodbye," I muttered as I did as they had instructed. I stared down at my feet and wondered if I would ever see them again.

I waited.

And I waited.

Time seemed to slow as the nose pulled up and we seemed to pause in the air. There was a loud crash as I was thrown about like a rag doll. The safety belt cut into my stomach like a cheese wire. I could hear rocks and trees hitting the plane as we fell, and cool air hit my face as we bumped into something, making the fuselage open up. People screamed as they were suddenly being sucked out into the darkness in their seats. One seat missed me by inches and wedged in the open side of the fuselage. I glanced up and came face to face with a screaming woman who reached out for me.

"Please! Help me!"

I blinked and she was gone, now just a brief dark shadow moving outside of the craft. A metal bar hit me in the chest with such force that my first thought was that it had gone straight through me. I was jammed in my seat and all I could do was close my eyes and wet myself in absolute fear.

All of a sudden, everything stopped.

CHAPTER FOUR

I cracked my eyes open, slowly opening them wider and wider. It was pitch-black. I tried to scream, but all I could do was make a funny gasp. I tried to get out of my seat, but the bar was pinning me – under my arm and heading down between my legs, it had somehow missed me altogether and was simply keeping me in my seat. I took a breath. I had to stay calm. I wasn't hurt any more than before, but I just needed to get out of the seat. I managed to unclip the belt and slide up the back of my seat, and finally escape the confines. My ribs were protesting like mad after everything that had happened as I made my way towards the hole in the fuselage. There was a strong smell of fuel in the air... I hoped it wouldn't ignite. I'd definitely be a goner if it ignited.

"Help!" I shouted. "Help! Is there anybody there?"

All I could hear was my own breathing. I had to move – I scrambled over the carnage that was left of the plane and tried to see how far it was to the ground. All I could see were little flecks of light like fireflies dancing in the darkness. I couldn't see the ground, but I knew that I had to jump. As I started to lean forwards, my trouser leg caught on something. I tried to tug it free – right now my trousers weren't my main concern – but it wasn't working. I bent down to try and work out just what I was caught on, and came into contact with another hand. As our hands touched, the other person grabbed my wrist, making me jump. I traced the arm back and found the belt keeping them in their chair. At least there were two of us alive. I could hear him breathing as I released his seat belt and lifted him up.

"Come on," I muttered to him. "We have to get out of here."

Together we made it back to the side of the fuselage and jumped from the plane. We landed heavily, but the drop couldn't have been more than about 6 feet to the ground. Scrambling upright, I took a step and tripped immediately. Whatever I'd tripped on groaned. I reached out and touched a torso – the person groaned again.

"Hey!" I shouted to the other survivor. "I've found someone else – come and help me."

Together we lifted the man, but I could tell he was clearly badly injured from the screams as we moved him. We got further away and decided to rest. As my eyes adjusted to the dark, I looked over at the aircraft – it had broken into three pieces with debris all around. I shook my head as I took it all in.

"Hello?" I yelled out. "Is anybody there? Can anyone hear me?"

There was nothing – just the two three of us. I couldn't believe it: only three survivors from 138 passengers and eight crew members. Suddenly I saw a flickering light... two... three... all coming from the trees on the other side of the craft. *It must be a rescue team*, I thought. I moved to ready myself to call out to them, but I hesitated. How long had we been down? Would someone have come so quickly out here in the jungle?

I watched as they emerged from the trees and approached the plane. It was completely bizarre – almost like a scene from a *Tarzan* film or something. There were about 50 men, all with skin like ebony, wearing leopard skins and carrying flaming torches and spears. Even from our distance, the whites of their eyes and teeth shone in the flickering torch-light. With the illumination, the crash site was clearer; bodies lay all around, many still in their seats. I jumped as they started to chant and howl, working themselves into a frenzy. The next second they were thrusting their spears into the bodies on the ground. If anyone had been alive, it was certain that they would be dead after that. Suddenly aware of the danger that we were in, we stood, grabbing our more seriously injured companion, and fled into the trees.

We ran – it seemed like forever – and our compatriot had fallen silent. I hoped beyond hope that he had simply passed out from pain and not died. Something kept hitting my leg, almost tripping me as we carried on. Reaching down I grabbed hold of a briefcase handle, tugging at it to try and throw it away into the trees that we were passing, but although it was out of his hand, it still wouldn't come away from our grip. I felt something then – a chain? Was this man's briefcase really chained to his wrist? Soon enough the exhaustion started to creep in, so we found a clump of trees under which we could rest. I remember briefly wondering exactly what we were going to do, before my eyes drifted shut.

*   *   *

I woke slowly, the sound of foraging animals and birdsong lulling me from my sleep. As I blinked my eyes open I realised that the sun was already high in the sky. Momentarily, I revelled in the serenity of the situation before my memories kicked in and the horror of the crash came flooding back. I sat up, trying to orientate myself and noticed that the other survivors were still asleep. Now that I could finally see them, I looked them over more closely.

The injured man was lying on his back, the briefcase still chained to him, his chest rising and falling with each breath, reassuring me that he was still alive. That was good; I hated the thought that I could have been carrying a dead man all of that way. A frown creased my brow as I looked over at the other survivor: a woman? She must have been around five feet tall, somewhat tubby and was lying on her side with her blonde hair draped across her face. I suppose that, when you're recovering from the shock of a plane crash and trying to run away from native people who are trying to kill you, taking note of whether the other survivors are men or women does tend to escape you. Deciding to leave them both sleeping for the moment, I crept past them and took stock of our location, picking a direction to walk. We didn't want to meet the natives – savages, really, I mused – again. We'd been lucky that they hadn't found us overnight. After a few minutes of walking, I stopped at a small stream. At least we would have fresh water if we stayed here. I could still only hear the animals, so I was fairly confident that we were still alone. Satisfied for now, I made my way back.

The man with the briefcase was awake when I returned, propping himself up on his elbows and looking around in bewilderment.

"Hey," I said, as I came into his line of sight. "How are you feeling?"

"I've felt better," he winced, his voice scratchy from sleep and pain.

"What hurts?"

"Mainly my leg – I think I've broken it," he nodded to it. "I think I cracked a few ribs too."

I knelt down by him – there was a long tear in his trouser leg, so I took hold of each side and looked back up at him.

"Am I alright to look? I'll have to tear your trousers…"

"Yeah, just do it."

I assessed his leg as I ripped the material: the lower leg looked okay, but his thigh was swollen and a large purple-black bruise was forming.

"Shit," I breathed. "Er, right, I think you've broken your femur. It's not an open wound, so if I can find something to splint it with, it might help you a little until we are rescued."

A groan and movement from the woman distracted us then, and I turned to look as she sat up. I stared, dumbfounded, as I struggled to take in what I was seeing. A mongol. Of all the people I had to rescue, it was a bloody Mongol. I'd come out here to get away from Down's Syndrome and here I was stuck with one. Not to mention that it now complicated things even more – I had to look after an injured man and nanny this woman, all whilst trying to hide from a murderous tribe of savages. We all stared at each other for a moment when my stomach growled loudly.

"What's your name, mate?" I asked the man whose ripped trousers I was still grasping in my hands.

"Reg," he answered.

"And yours?" I asked the woman somewhat coolly.

"Mary," she smiled.

I had to grit my teeth to stop the shudder that threatened to surface, and stood. "Right, Mary, stay here and look after Reg. I'll head out and try to find some food. And stay stay quiet."

As I walked back through the trees, I started to feel fear like I never had before. The noises had changed since earlier, the animals seemed to have quietened, but there was still something rustling around in the undergrowth somewhere. No matter where I looked, all I could see was a sea of green – it was very disconcerting. I could feel the sweat trickling down my back as I carried on forwards. As I cast my eyes around, I felt a tug on my foot and the world tilted. I'd caught my foot on something in the undergrowth and I was now sprawled out on the ground, my face in the very undergrowth that had tripped me. Just as I was trying to push myself up, a noise behind me made me freeze. I felt like I wasn't breathing – it was almost like when you're caught in a dream where you're being chased by something unknown and just before it catches you, you startle awake in a sweat. But this time, I was awake and this was no dream. Ever so slowly, I turned my upper body, peering through the undergrowth, desperately trying not to make a noise, hoping that whatever was chasing me would kill me quickly if that's what it was going to do...

There, crouched down in the undergrowth was Mary, giggles now rocking her body as she looked at me on the floor. I scrambled up and grabbed her by the arms.

"Shut up, you stupid cow!" I whispered harshly to her, pulling her back to where I'd left Reg.

"Sorry," Reg said the moment he saw us, "she ran off before I could stop her."

I nodded an acknowledgement to him as I sat Mary down. "Stay there, and don't move until I get back."

I set off once more, this trip uneventful save for finding berries and another fruit that looked like an apple. Using a large leaf folded over into a makeshift pouch, I collected what I could and carried it back to the others. I offered the fruit to Mary first, muttering something about serving the ladies first. She wolfed down the fruits she had taken, and I watched carefully to see if there was anything untoward occurring. After a couple of confused minutes, Reg looked at me.

"That was a dirty trick – testing it out on her first," he admonished.

"What else could I do?" I shrugged, as we both reached into the pouch, finishing off what I had brought back. "We can afford to lose her. If we all ate it and it was poisonous, none of us would be rescued."

"More."

I looked up at Mary, her mouth smeared with the juices from the berries. "More what?"

"Hungry. More berries."

"There isn't any more, Mary…"

Before I could finish what I was saying, or stop her, she had jumped up and run out into the trees, the undergrowth rustling and snapping as she barrelled through.

"Shit, she'll be heard for miles!" I exclaimed wildly, throwing my half-eaten fruit down.

"You'd better go and stop her before she gives away our position," Reg said as I jumped up to chase after her.

After ten minutes of trying to move swiftly through the foliage to catch up with Mary, but not make any noise, I was ready to snap. Surely she knew that we had to stay hidden. Did she not realise that there were savages out here that would sooner kill us than ask us to tea? A noise stopped me in my tracks – the foliage muffling the sound so I had no real idea of where it was coming from. There, to my right; I parted the leaves of the trees and caught a flash of a group of men, talking quietly amongst themselves as they moved. The sunlight glinted off their darkened skin, the casual way that each of the broad men held a spear loosely at their sides hinting at the inherent danger they represented. I turned and hurried along the path that I had been following, hoping that my rapid movements sounded more like a large animal and not a human. As I rounded a bend, I spotted Mary, crouched down, picking the berries from a bush and stuffing them into her mouth as fast as she could. I let my momentum carry me forwards, rugby tackling her, both of us crashing into the undergrowth.

"Quiet!" I hissed, clamping one hand over her mouth. "Please, just be quiet."

Mary's eyes were like saucers, the whites of her eyes clear to see around the blue irises, as the men came into view. I glanced back at them – going by their spears, shields and painted bodies I hazarded a guess that they were a war party. One of the men smiled, his white teeth a stark contrast to the glimpses of dark skin that I could see – they were pointed, as though they'd been filed into that shape, lending a terrifying edge to a man who was already intimidating. They paused, a couple of feet from us, resting from their trek. I could feel Mary whimpering quietly beneath me, and willed myself to breathe softly. They moved on after a moment, their chatter fading as they moved further away. When it was silent, I released Mary.

"Come on," I said after peering out to check the coast was truly clear, "let's get back. We need to find a safe hiding place."

I found a couple of sturdy looking branches and something that would substitute for twine and, with my ageing first aid knowledge, splinted Reg's broken leg. It was clear that he was in a lot of pain, but the splinting helped somewhat in the absence of proper pain relief.

"You two stay here," I said, finishing off the last knot, "I'm going to look for a safer place to hide until we're rescued – hopefully we won't be waiting too long."

I glanced up to see Reg's eyes closed – I hoped he was just asleep out of exhaustion and not passed out from pain. I looked at Mary, sat crossed legged and smiling at me.

"Stay. Do not move until I get back. Do you understand?"

She nodded an affirmative at me, and I moved to take my handkerchief from my pocket. I folded it and tied it around her mouth, making it into a makeshift gag.

"Shhhhhh," I said, holding a finger to my lips as she nodded. "Stay hidden and very, very quiet."

I headed out, walking in ever increasing circles from our current hiding place. I'd travelled probably around one hundred yards when the trees suddenly thinned and I stepped out onto the shore of a huge lake. It was beautiful – the water shimmered in the sunshine, looking more like a giant mirror than a pool of water, the far shore barely visible in the distance. I was just contemplating how peaceful and quiet it was when a low growl made the hairs on the back of my neck stand up. I could feel my heart racing into overdrive as adrenaline kicked in.

Turning slowly, I found myself staring in dawning horror at dozens of large crocodiles basking in the sun on the lake shore, their bodies flat against the sand, legs splayed to the sides; mucky-green pointed snouts open and their teeth glinting white. I couldn't stop a gasp of horror, and felt my eyes widen as every muscle in my body tensed. As I stared, one lumbered along the shore towards me, its body twisting slightly as it's short legs propelled it forwards. I took a step backwards, and forced myself into a run as it started to move faster towards me.

It suddenly went up on all fours and at the speed it was travelling I swear it could have won the grand national?

Running in the soft sand slowed me down, and I could tell from the sounds of the crocodile's breathing that he was gaining on me. I nearly tripped over as another crocodile that had been well camouflaged by the foliage lunged at me. I felt the wind as its jaws came together with a crack! Quite how I managed to avoid losing my leg to that beast I have no idea, but the one that had been chasing me crashed into him and they both rolled over in the sand.

Feeling more solid ground beneath my feet I took off like a rocket: if I had wings, I was sure that I would have taken off. I realised that I couldn't hear anything but the sound of my feet hitting the foliage underfoot and my panting breath. Slowing down, as the area became rockier, I realised that I didn't really know where I was in relation to the others. In my panic, I must have covered about a mile… maybe more. I clambered up onto a boulder, figuring that if the crocodiles were still following me, it might slow them down a fraction. As I tried to slow my breathing down, I took the chance to assess this new area.

The rocks led to what seemed like a sheer cliff face; I could see what looked like a cave about ten feet up. There was a tree close enough that I immediately scrambled off the boulder and put my mind to climbing it. I'd never been amazing at climbing trees, but I knew that we had to find somewhere else to shelter. As I climbed I hoped that it would lead to a large enough space for us to hide in. It would be easily defensible; the only issue would be working out a way to get in and out for food.

I could see the shadows starting to lengthen as I climbed, the sun setting: I hoped I could get this checked out and get back to the others before nightfall. Finally reaching the same height as the cave, I could see that its entrance was large enough for two people to get into side by side. There was a branch that extended towards the opening: I hoped it was sturdy enough to hold my weight as I edged away from the safety of the trunk. Reaching the end, I paused. There was six feet of nothingness between me and the floor of the rock face opening. I tried to peer in, but the darkness inside made it impossible to see anything from here. I chewed my lip anxiously. I could jump across, but I had no idea if there was an animal living in there. The fact that the only entrance that I could see was ten feet up held no reassurance for me – there could quite easily be another entrance somewhere in the depths.

There's only one way to find out, I reasoned with myself. Before I could have second thoughts, I had launched myself forwards.

CHAPTER FIVE

I lay there, breathing hard. I'd made it. My legs might have been sticking out over the edge, but I wasn't lying in a crumpled heap at the base of the rock face. It was dark in here – enough that I couldn't see if there was anything lurking further back. Clicking my tongue against the roof of my mouth I listened to it echo back. Surely any animal that was here would have made a noise by now.

Figuring it was safe to move; I pulled my legs in and pushed myself up off of the floor. Being careful not to hit my head on rock, I moved further into the cave. Past the entrance way, it seemed to open up. Finding the far wall, I looked back, letting whatever sunlight there was left show me the area that I had found. It was a cave, about twenty feet in diameter. I stretched my hands above my head to feel where the ceiling was. About seven feet high, I reckoned. If I could find my way back, I was sure that we could make this place work for us.

I moved back to the entrance. The sun had set by now, the moon lending its eerie hue to the canopy, making it seem as though I was in some sort of ghostly place. Casting my gaze upwards the sky was inky black, and I let myself stare in wonder at the millions of stars that I could see. It was certainly nothing that you would ever see back at home. Coming back to the task at hand I wondered just what my luck would be like trying to get down. I had to aim for a branch illuminated only by the moonlight. Gritting my teeth, I stepped back a bit to take a running leap.

I hit the branch sideways, scrambling to get an arm hooked around it to stop myself from falling. Pulling myself up with a few choice swearwords, I managed to hook my leg over it and scramble back to the trunk of the tree to begin my descent.

The noises of the jungle were different now, and I only hoped that there was nothing evil lurking in the darkness. I had no real idea where I was heading now that the sun had set – I hoped that the direction in which I was going was the right one. A few hours passed and I could suddenly hear the sounds of the crocodiles lazily moving in and out of the lake and spied the moon's reflection in the water. At least I was back to a familiar place.

I kept walking, parting bushes as I went, looking for Mary and Reg, hesitant to call out lest there was anything that would be attracted by the noise. I was starting to lose hope of finding them when I finally parted the branches of one bush and smiled in relief. Mary, sat exactly where I had left her, she was staring at me with wide eyes. It was then that I saw why.

All around her, to my horror, were snakes. Curled up, with their heads on their coils, they were illuminated by the moonlight reflecting off their scales and their eyes. I recoiled thinking what to do next. Finding a dead branch I thrust it into the bush shaking it violently.

The next time I parted the branches there was not a snake in sight.

"Come on," I whispered loudly, "we need to get out of there."

She grabbed my hand and I pulled her out onto the path. I moved towards Reg. Holding him around the chest I helped him out.

"Shit, that was intense," he said as I helped him to lean against a nearby tree.

"You're telling me." I replied.

I moved to Mary took the handkerchief from her mouth. "You okay?"

"Don't like snakes," she mumbled.

"Well, hopefully we can go somewhere where we won't get snakes," I told her. "I found a cave. It's about a mile away – do you think you could make it if we helped you, Reg?"

"Yeah, I reckon so, if you both help me."

So we set out – Reg had one arm about Mary's shoulders, and his other – the one with the case attached – around mine. It was awkward to move – Reg was slightly shorter than I was and he couldn't put any weight on his splinted leg, and the fact that Mary was smaller than I was also didn't help that much. Every step we took, the case swung with our momentum and hit me on the arm.

"Reg, can't you get rid of that damn case?"

"No, I can't. It's chained to my wrist and I haven't got the key."

"Well, as soon as we get settled I'll break the chain somehow. It's in the way and it could cost you your life."

"It is my bloody life," he snapped, and we continued moving in strained silence.

We got to the rock face as the sun was coming up.

"How the hell am I supposed to get up there?" Reg asked, staring up at the entrance that I'd pointed out to them.

"We'll find a way. There must be something that we can do. After all, where there's a will–"

"There are relations," Mary piped in.

I chuckled, and Reg smiled. She did sound funny.

We settled down in a shady area and left Reg briefly whilst we went on a hunt for fruit and water. During our search, I stumbled across some thick branches, and suddenly had the thought about fashioning a ladder of some sort. If we could get that set up, and find something that could be a stretcher, we could pull Reg up into the cave.

As the others ate, I worked on collecting the branches and some vines that would hopefully be strong enough to hold them all together. A large piece of bark from a dead tree made a perfect makeshift stretcher. Another thick creeper vine made a decent rope alternative.

First I made a crude but strong ladder.

"Reg, let's get you laid down here," I said, gesturing to the stretcher as I moved towards him.

"Is this going to work?" He asked, looking at the entire contraption dubiously.

"Sure it will," I said, hoping that my voice conveyed optimism and not the possibility that this could be disastrous.

I sent Mary up the ladder first with the vine attached to the stretcher after tying Reg into it. With Mary pulling and me pushing, we slowly managed to get Reg up into the cave. Pulling the ladder up, we collapsed, exhausted and fell into a deep sleep. When I woke, the sun was high in the sky. As the others were still asleep, I took the chance to look around our new home.

On the far wall, the sand that covered the bottom of the cave seemed to dip, and a depression in the base seemed to hint that there was something more to be found. Kneeling down next to it, I started scooping away the sand; sure enough, it seemed to be some sort of tunnel. Just as I was trying to clear more of the sand, I felt something touch my shoulder. Jerking my head around, I saw Mary – her head cocked to one side as she watched what I was doing.

"If you have nothing to do, why don't you help by digging out this tunnel?"

She nodded and immediately continued what I had started. Satisfied, I went back towards the cave entrance. The sun was streaming in the entrance, and I sat down in its rays. As the warmth hit my skin, my thoughts drifted back to England and Jane, Tracey and Dave: I wished I was with them. Did they even know that we hadn't arrived where we were supposed to? Surely they must have realised that something was wrong. I'd lost all sense of how much time had passed since we'd crashed. As I stared out across the canopy, I wondered just how long the three of us could survive here. We were woefully unprepared for roughing it like this, and with Reg out of action there was only myself and Mary to make sure that we all made it through. I don't know how long I was staring out, lost in thought, but another touch to my shoulder brought me back to reality with a start.

Looking round, Mary was pointing at the tunnel. She'd managed to clear all the sand from it and I could see another area beyond and heard what I thought was running water. The opening looked barely large enough for me to crawl through, but it was worth trying to get to the other side.

"Stay here, Mary, and don't go near the entrance," I ordered, as I started to move through the gap on my belly.

On the other side, the tunnel opened up into another cave, much larger than the previous one, with a stream running across the middle of the cave floor into a large pool off to the left. I moved close to it; it had to be six feet wide and probably only about eighteen inches deep, but it was fast flowing. The pool that the stream drained into was a fluid vortex, the centre depressed and calm in a way that reminded me of the way that water drains through a plughole. I could only imagine that the water went through the rocks beneath and somewhere into the jungle.

Spotting a ledge over the pool, I followed it to see a vine covered opening. Seeing daylight through small gaps in the vines, I decided to investigate. The ledge was only about a foot wide, but there were a few decent hand holds on the wall that went some way to reassuring me that I wasn't going to be heading for a swim in the pool any time soon. The vines were thick at the edges of the opening so I moved towards the centre, where they thinned, to be able to part them and look out.

I immediately wished I hadn't. I dare not move as sheer terror overcame me and my heart threatened to jump out of my chest. On the other side of the vines the cliffs dropped away, the ground a dizzyingly vertical two hundred feet down. Forty feet blow my feet, I discovered where our stream of water was draining to – it was jetting out from the cliff face and plummeting down into the trees, terrifyingly fast.

I slammed myself back against the rock my heart was hammering against my ribs and my fingers were gripping anything to steady myself. – It must have taken me at least twenty minutes to get back to the safety of the cave. Where I collapsed in a heap. As soon as everything settled down, I made my way back to the others.

Mary was sat cross-legged, rocking to and fro, humming to herself. Blinking in the acceptance of this somewhat bizarre behaviour, I switched to look at Reg who was now awake.

"What did you find?" he asked, looking interestedly at the tunnel that I'd emerged from.

"We have our own fresh water source and a flushing toilet," I told him as I moved towards the ladder, "though I wouldn't recommend looking at the view. I'm going to head out and look for food. Don't let Mary near the entrance; she could give away our hideout."

At Reg's resigned nod, I lowered the ladder and made my way down.

CHAPTER SIX

I wondered briefly about where exactly we were as I walked. The section of jungle that I had known since we had landed here must be on some sort of plateau considering the drop on the other side of the cave that we were hiding in. I kept glancing back at the cave entrance as I searched for food, hoping that Mary would stay out of sight. Finally I found a tree bursting with fruit that would provide us with a good crop of food. I could see the cave from here, so it would be a bonus for staying out of the sight of the natives that we were still hiding from.

I lost myself in the repetitiveness of picking the fruits and placing them on a large leaf, and only glancing up at the cave entrance now and then. I felt a prickle of apprehension in my gut. I looked up. Mary was in full bloody view waving her arms above her head like a lunatic.

Stupid bitch, I thought, gesturing at her to get back inside. She can be seen for miles.

I relaxed when she disappeared, only to swear again when she came back to the cave entrance, this time with my handkerchief tied around her mouth like before and started pointing determinedly up the path.

I suddenly realised what she was trying to say – I wasn't alone on my forage. I dropped the leaf where I stood and scurried swiftly into a shallow depression amongst the roots of a nearby tree, pulling some of the undergrowth to shield myself from sight.

I held my breath and tucked my head down as six native men appeared on the pathway. I hoped that the fruit just looked like it had randomly landed and not been collected. I couldn't tell if one of them had slowed, but my senses were screaming at me to stay put.

Their footsteps died away but I stayed hidden – listening to the sounds of the jungle – until I was sure that they were gone. Slowly, I emerged from my hiding place and headed back to pick up the fruit.

I was bent over, hurriedly trying to gather them together, when a feeling of foreboding stole through me. I turned my head, looking over my shoulder, so that I could see down the path where the men had disappeared to. Standing there, sneering almost gleefully at me, was one of the natives: he must have been approaching seven foot, weighed about fifteen stone and looked to be constructed out of pure muscle. His spear, once held loosely by his side was now clenched in his fist and raised above his shoulder.

I did what anyone would do when faced with that – I ran like hell. I could hear him running behind me, gaining with every footstep, and I knew that I had very little hope of outrunning him.

If he throws that spear at me, I'm screwed, I thought desperately, suddenly deciding that zigzagging would make me a harder target to hit. I must have looked like a lunatic to him, but if it meant I kept my life, I didn't particularly care.

As I ran around a bend in the path, I felt a searing pain under my chin and saw the shaft of the spear vibrating from its impact with the tree in front of my head. I could feel a soft trickle of warm blood sliding down the underside of my jaw. I realised that I was headed straight for the spear; The shaft caught me under my chin. I did a complete summersault landing flat on my back my pursuer dived on top of me – tussling with him with the extra strength provided by my fear.

I knew that I was no match for him – his eyes barely two inches from mine had a deep set tint of wildness, his foul breath fogging my senses and my breathing restricted as he managed to get one of his massive hands around my throat. I saw a flash of light as he raised a knife over his head, snarling in triumph as his body moved away to allow him to get a better target for a kill. I closed my eyes, preparing for what I assumed would be an initial stab of pain followed by the blissful darkness of death when I felt something wet splatter over my face.

I guessed that it was blood, but there was no pain. Did that mean that I was already dead? I could feel my heart hammering inside my chest – surely that was as good an indicator as any to suggest that I still walked amongst the living. I inched my eyes open to try and work out why I wasn't dead. His face was there, surprise in his eyes now and I gasped in relief as his grip loosened and he rolled off me to the side. His face was replaced by the last person I thought I'd see – Mary was peering down at me, her face hard and determined. As her eyes met mine, she lit up with an instant smile. I tried to gather my wits and work out what had happened.

The spear that was stuck in the tree was now impaling the savage who had been trying to kill me. I could only guess that Mary had seen that I was in trouble and arrived at the precise moment to tug the spear from the tree and thrust it through the back of the savage, the blade exiting his chest by a full foot. I stood slowly, my legs shaking at the realisation that Mary had managed to come to my rescue and had killed a man to do it.

"Mary, we need to move his body," I tried to stay calm, but I could hear the tremor in my voice. I stared at the man who had almost killed me for a moment before reaching out and tugging the spear from his torso, one foot resting on the darkened skin of his back.

Together, we dragged him towards the lake that I had come across the previous day and pushed him into the shallows at the water's edge. I hoped that the crocodiles would come out from their daytime slumber and find him before they found us. It would be hard for his fellow natives, but when you're in a man-eat-man kind of world, you do what you need to to ensure your own survival. That's what I tried to tell myself at least.

I tried to cover the blood with undergrowth – not a perfect

hiding method by any means, but it might buy us a bit of time if they came looking for their missing man. I scooped up his knife, the spear and the fruit that I had been collecting and we made our way back to the cave in silence. It felt reassuring to know that we had two weapons to defend ourselves with.

As we got back I realised that the ladder was where I had left it – I'd pulled it down and hidden it behind the bushes at the cliff base. It wasn't until we both got back into the cave and I explained what had happened to Reg as I pulled the ladder back into the cave that something about Mary coming to my rescue didn't make sense.

"When I realised she was trying to get your attention, I suggested the handkerchief," Reg said, watching me warily as I tried to wipe the dried blood off my face. "The next thing I knew, she'd jumped out of the entrance."

My head shot up, my eyes wide in disbelief. *"Jumped?"*

"Straight out," Reg nodded, "and I couldn't do a damned thing to stop her."

"Mary?" I turned to look at her, waiting until she looked up from the spear that she was turning over in her hands. "Did you hurt yourself when you jumped?"

"No," she shook her head, smiling happily. "Not hurt."

Reg and I exchanged amazed looks and I gestured to him that I was going to head into the back cave to clean myself up.

I thought about Mary's miraculous jump as I stripped off and bathed myself in the cool water. She was turning out to be completely different to the image of the pathetic, dependent person that I had assumed that she would be. I dabbed at the cut under my chin as I contemplated this. It wasn't deep but the cut was oozing blood and clearly needed some sort of bandage – I tore one of the sleeves from my shirt and, after rinsing it in the water, tied it in a knot on top of my head. It wasn't much, but it would stop it from getting infected at least. As I came back

46

into the cave, Mary started laughing and pointing at me.

"Toothache!" She shouted, almost rolling over as she laughed. "Toothache!"

Reg, taken by surprise, took one look at Mary and then me before bursting into laughter too. Seeing both of them almost flat on the floor with laughter set me off – I supposed it did look like I had toothache with the shirt sleeve tied under my chin. We laughed for about ten minutes: the first time we had laughed since we had crashed. When we finally settled down, we tucked into the fruit.

I watched Mary as we ate, realising that since we'd met I had treated her like dirt and now I owed her my life. She was stuffing berries into her mouth, slurping as she chewed with her mouth open the juices running down her chin. I put my finger to my lips, almost unconsciously, and when Mary glanced up she stopped and looked at me.

"Try to keep your mouth shut when you're eating – it helps to keep the juice inside. Look, like this," I picked up a better and ate it with my mouth shut. She watched for a moment and then her face lit up as the penny dropped and she saw what I was trying to show her. Like a child she copied my actions, her head bobbing up and down in time with her chewing. I tried to ignore Reg looking at me approvingly, with a glint of amusement in his eyes.

"How old are you, Mary?" I asked when we'd finished eating.

"Twenty-four and three quarters. How old are you?"

"I'm older than that. You're still only a girl."

"Not! I'm a woman. I wear a bra." She snapped.

Reg chuckled. "You can't argue with that!"

"Mary, who were you on the plane with?"

"Miss Fenshall."

"Where were you going?"

"Don't know." Her face was like stone – her expression had shut down.

"How about you, Reg? Where were you heading?"

"I was on my way to Madagascar," he said, tugging the briefcase against his stomach and closing his hands around it, hugging it closer to his chest.

At a guess, I put Reg at around sixty years old, educated at one of the England's Universities and, from the way he was clutching at the briefcase, some kind of high-powered businessman.

"What about you?" He asked me. "What were you doing on the plane?"

I told him my tale.

"Well, we're a right trio, aren't we? An old businessman, a teacher and a young girl."

"Woman!" Said Mary.

"Sorry, young woman," Reg gave Mary a comforting and apologetic smile.

"The trouble is," I said hesitantly, unwilling to break the genial mood that we were in, "I don't think we'll be rescued for a while. We're going to need more than fruit to survive on."

"We need meat," Reg agreed, "but even if we catch some, how will we cook it? Smoke would give out position away."

Neither of us could come up with a fast solution so we stayed in the cave, venturing out only to collect food. From our high position we kept a watch over the jungle, slowly learning the territory from above and keeping a close watch on the jungle paths in the area for the group of dark-skinned men that passed through at the same time each day. We soon figured out that if we waited until they had passed, it was safe to venture out and explore.

One morning, Mary was sat with her back against the wall when I noted a movement in the sand around her. It seemed to be sinking the way sand in an egg-timer does. Before I could even shout a warning to her the floor went from beneath her and she disappeared.

I scrambled over to the hole and looked down. There she was, sitting in a hole, sand up to her waist, laughing.

"Are you alright, Mary?"

"Yes," she giggled, "all right."

"You aren't hurt?"

"Not hurt."

I carefully swung myself over the edge and down into the hole next to Mary and helped her to her feet. Looking around, I could see that we were in a narrow tunnel – at the far end, daylight glinted through a gap. I held Mary's hand as we crept forwards to investigate. I just hoped that it wasn't going to be another sheer drop like the other opening I found. As we got closer I could see that there was a huge tree trunk covering the opening, the gap where the daylight was coming through large enough to squeeze past.

"Wait here for a moment, Mary – I need to check that it's all clear."

The branches of the tree were hanging down to the ground, providing a good level of cover with the density of the foliage. I pulled some of it back, letting the bright sunlight stream in and looked out. Seeing it was all clear, I beckoned to Mary and took her hand again as we went outside to see where it was. We went about ten yards around the rocks and then spotted the entrance we had been using so far. This one would be much better. From the path it was virtually unseen, and was much easier to get in and out of. It also meant that we didn't have to keep hiding a ladder each time we left the cave. Having seen all of this, I tugged Mary back to the entrance and we headed back to tell Reg of what we had found.

As we waited for the patrol to pass us, I decided to try and find out some more about the people that I was with.

"Where do you live, Mary?"

"Here," she laughed, clapping her hands softly.

"I meant, where did you live in England?"

"Home."

"With your mum and dad?"

"No. Home."

"I think she means that she was in an institution," Reg said softly.

"Oh…" I didn't quite know what to say. I frowned as I realised that it hadn't been that long ago that I had been adamant that all Down's Syndrome children should be in an institution and not mingling with 'normal' folk. But now I was faced with Mary – she was the first person with Down's that I had ever really spent time with and she wasn't harmful. She was vulnerable, yes, but it was sweet – she wasn't completely reliant on us for things. She'd even saved my life. But that this woman had been in an institution – somewhere that she clearly hated from the fact that she had tucked her legs underneath her and was rocking back and forth – roused unsettled feelings in me.

"You got mum and dad?" Mary asked quietly, still rocking herself.

"No," I replied. "They died in a car crash when I was seven."

"What were you doing on the plane, Mary?" Reg asked, trying to steer the conversation away from what were clearly difficult topics for us.

"Don't know. Going somewhere."

"Well…" Reg said, looking at me apologetically, as his starter question failed in opening the conversation up.

* * *

After the patrol had passed by, we ventured out and gathered food. When we returned, Mary started laying leaves that she had collected and set them like a table. Using a smaller leaf, she piled some berries on it and handed it carefully to Reg. She carried on serving us and then herself as well. I was impressed – she was really making an effort.

We ate, making small talk over our meal, before washing up and settling down for the night. Mary moved over to Reg and hugged him, her arms around his neck, kissing his check as she pulled away.

"Night- night Dada!"

She moved to me.

"Night- night Robbie!"

Before either of us knew it, she lay down and fell asleep. I glanced at Reg – there were tears glistening in his eyes and he stared at Mary fondly.

"Do you know, I'm sixty-six, I've never had a wife or children, and I've made work my life. Now I have none of that, but I've gained a daughter. I'm really quite humbled by it all. She's so innocent to what's going on."

"I know, Reg, but remember – innocence could get us killed." Silence settled for a minute. "Look, I've been thinking… we could really do with coming up with a plan as we're not going to be rescued for some time. Maybe I should head back to the wreckage and see if there's anything left that could be salvageable to help us out while we wait."

"That's a bit dangerous, old chap. You could be captured, and I can't be of any help."

"You could look after Mary – keep her inside and don't let her come after me."

With Reg's begrudging agreement, I drifted off and recalled what had happened over the past few days. One day I was teaching and making my way through the modern school system; the next I'm stranded in the middle of the jungle with someone who was the embodiment of what I'd been trying to get away from. Was it truly some kind of random cosmic karma that had left me in this situation or was God – not that I could claim to really believe in one – trying to teach me a lesson?

CHAPTER SEVEN

I was still ruminating on the possibility the next morning as I arose and washed in the stream. I wanted to head back to the wreckage and see if there was anything to salvage. I knew that it had been a while since we crashed, but it would still be worthwhile checking it out.

"Where you goin?"

I turned: Mary was rubbing her eyes, clearly only just waking from her sleep.

"Just to get a few things – I won't be long. You stay here and look after Reg."

"I come with you." She pushed herself up from the floor.

"Mary, it really would be better for you to stay –"

"No! I come."

"It might be danger–"

"No! I come."

"You're not going to win this one, Robbie," Reg chipped in having woken up himself.

I tipped my head back so that I was looking at the ceiling in exasperation. I knew that there was no real way of getting Mary to stay behind, but she would really slow me down… I'd have to look out for her and do what I needed to do.

"Fine," I dropped my head back down and focussed on Mary. "You can come along, but you *have* to do what I tell you to do."

She nodded vigorously. We left the cave through the new tunnel entrance and started heading in the direction of the crash site.

"Mary, listen – if you see *anyone* coming don't shout, just grab me and push us both into the trees so we can hide."

"Grab and push." She echoed.

We walked for an hour and I was just beginning to wonder if I'd forgotten where the crash was when we came across some debris and then the crash site. It was still hard to look at – the ground blackened with rotting vegetation, trees broken and bent from the impact. Clothing and debris were strewn across the area and hanging from tree branches. I could smell the wreckage – the constant sun and heat was clearly having an effect on the bodies of those who hadn't survived, and the stench of rotting, decomposing flesh was almost overpowering.

It was clear as we got closer that the plane hadn't caught fire even after we had escaped, but the sight of the twisted and broken wreckage made me stop and wonder again just how the three of us had managed to escape with our lives. We kept to the undergrowth for a while to make sure that we were on our own but after fifteen minutes of silence, we made our way closer.

"Mary, listen," I pulled her closer. "You hide here and keep a look out. If no-one is coming, do this." I put my thumb up in that well known 'everything is okay' gesture. "If there is someone coming, do this," I turned my fist so my thumb was pointing down.

Mary was focussed on her fist, thumb up and then turning it so it was down. I watched as she repeated the movement over and over, slowly getting a sinking feeling that I wasn't going to be getting the help that I'd hoped I would from having Mary here.

"Do you understand, Mary?"

She turned her thumb up," Okay" she said. Then she turned her thumb down. "Not okay,"

"Just stay here and show me if it's okay or not." I had to hope that she would do what I needed her to do.

As I got to the fuselage, I glanced back at Mary – she was staring back at me. I put my thumb up to her and pointed at it with my other hand in question. She gave me thumbs up in return. There was nothing for it – I just had to trust her. I climbed into the wreckage, close to the cockpit and started to wish that I hadn't had the idea to do this.

In the heat of the days, the cockpit – still completely enclosed – the three crew members were rotting where they sat, slumped forwards from a combination of the crash and the decomposition. The smell was horrific and I gagged for a few moments, desperately trying to not throw up. On the floor, my eyes fixed onto a first aid kit that had tumbled from its moorings on the wall. Before I completely lost my stomach, I grabbed the kit and moved out into the slightly fresher air of the cabin.

There were flight blankets everywhere. It looked like most of the hand luggage on board had been ripped open in the crash, and it was like looking at flashes of people's lives in the chaos of the wreckage. A small item caught my eye – the sun was glinting off of a brooch. I picked it up – a small golden teddy bear, it shimmered with small diamonds that refracted the light coming through the gaps in the fuselage, dark blue sapphires where the eyes would be and golden rims accentuating the belly and paws of the bear. I stared at its innocent face for a moment before slipping it into the pocket of my trousers.

I glanced out at Mary again. She had her tongue stuck out; shaking her fist vigorously like you do when you have a bottle of tomato ketchup and you can't get any of the sauce out, her thumb pointing down. Shit. I scrambled to get myself laid down, covering myself with some blankets that were there.

I tried to slow my breathing down – a breathing corpse would be the fastest ticket to death that I knew. I heard the voices of whoever Mary had spotted and hoped that she had been sensible enough to hide herself. I could just see past a corner of the blanket and the fuselage and spotted the group approaching the plane. There must have been about fifty men, their leader striding ahead, wearing some kind of mask and waving a piece of string with what looked like some bones above his head as he jumped about. They were stood around the wreckage, chanting and dancing themselves into a frenzy. Were they drunk or high?

I lost sight of them after a while, but didn't dare move until I couldn't hear them anymore. I slowly moved from my conspicuous hiding spot. I looked out towards the spot where Mary had been and panicked a bit at the thought that she had been taken by them. Then I saw her. She'd slipped down behind the rock that I had told her to stay on, and had hidden in the bush at the side. She laughed when we caught sight of each other and put her thumb up. I couldn't help but chuckle as I returned the gesture.

I finished up my search of the plane and collected my new findings of a box containing a flare gun and six flares, a roll of packing wire and a toolbox with the first aid kit and a few blankets that weren't too badly damaged. Mary joined me as we headed back to the cave.

"Was I a good girl?"

"Yes – a very good girl."

"Goody!" She beamed.

I shook my head affectionately as she skipped off a little way, clapping her hands together in happiness.

Back at the cave, we told Reg what had happened.

"It was a good job you took Mary with you," he said.

"Yes, alright," I grumbled. "I admit it."

After supper we made up beds with the blankets we'd brought back from the plane and settled down for the evening. Mary gave us both a kiss goodnight and went to sleep as usual.

"I tell you what, Reg," I said. "There's tons of stuff at the wreck we could use. If we make a couple of trips this cave could be quite comfortable."

"Yes," he said, thinking it over. "But sod's law says you will eventually get caught."

"I know," I said. "But we've got to chance it."

*　　*　　*

Over the next few days Mary and I made repeated trips back to the plane, collecting anything we considered useful. A needle and cotton, a mirror, loads of clothes, dozens of toilet rolls, tins of powdered milk, tea, sugar, coffee, matches. The bar boxes were full of drinks – even soft drinks for Mary. We even took three seats up to the cave, one at a time, carrying them between us. We salvaged everything we could and got it all back to the cave without any encounters with our tribal friends.

That evening I looked at our haul and the matches gave me an idea.

"Reg, tomorrow we're going to make one last trip."

He looked up, surprised.

"What for?" he asked. "We have all we need, don't we?"

"Yes," I said, "but I'm thinking about those poor devils at the crash site."

He nodded soberly, understanding.

*　　*　　*

The next day, Mary and I ventured back to the crash site.

The plane had hit the trees about five hundred yards from its final resting place. Keeping a watchful eye open we went back to where the first bodies had been thrown out. They were already well decomposed, the process accelerated in the heat and humidity of the jungle, still strapped into their seats. The stench was terrible.

"Mary, give me a hand."

Mary screwed up her face in understandable horror.

"Urgh, no," she shook her head. "Horrible."

I tied cloth around my mouth and nose and Mary stood still while

I did the same for her. I cut the seatbelts with my knife, trying not to look too closely at the grim remains of our fellow passengers.

"Mary, bring me some blankets," I instructed, while I worked.

I wrapped each corpse in a blanket, though it did little to block out the stench it did preserve a small part of their dignity.

"Now," I said. "Give me a hand to carry the bodies back to the plane."

She shook her head.

"No."

"Mary, we can't leave them like this, it's not fair on them – or their relatives."

Reluctantly she helped me carry the corpses back to the plane and put them in the broken fuselage. By the time we'd found everyone and got them back to the fuselage it was getting dark. There was fuel all around, but I knew we'd need more.

"Mary, can you find me a bowl or something, please?"

She came back with a bucket from the galley. I took a fire axe, hoping there was still fuel in the tanks. I swung the axe into the lowest part of the wing, making a great clanging noise that I hoped no one nearby had heard.

We stopped and listened for a while, but nothing untoward happened, so I pulled the axe back out, letting the fuel gush out. I filled bucket after bucket with aviation fuel and threw it into the plane, over the bodies. Mary looked on, just watching me work.

I soaked some rags in the fuel, lit them and tossed them into the fuselage.

It seemed a long walk back to the cave in the twilit jungle. The three of us watched as the flames lit up the night sky, towering over the trees.

I realised that Mary was staring at me.

"Have they gone to heaven?" she asked.

"Yes," I said, slowly. "They have finally gone."

"Say a prayer."

"But I don't know any prayers, Mary."

"Say a prayer," she repeated.

I shared a glance with Reg and we bowed her heads.

"Father, please forgive them their sins and receive them in heaven," I said, feeling a little silly despite the solemnity of the occasion. "And for pity's sake, send someone to rescue us. Amen."

"Amen," Mary and Reg repeated.

I felt lighter, somehow, as I settled down to sleep that night. Finally, those souls could rest in peace.

CHAPTER EIGHT

I slept soundly that night, and when I awoke in the morning Mary was gone. I checked the other cave, but there was no sign of her. A noise from the tunnel made me freeze. I grabbed the spear, held it aloft and waited, tense. Reg sat up, peering at the tunnel.

If Mary had ventured outside and been captured she might lead them right back here.

There was a sudden hush, as if the world was holding its breath, and then Mary stuck her head through the hole, a large leaf full of fruit in her hands.

"Breakfast!" she cried, beaming.

"You idiot!" I shouted. "You might have been seen – or even caught!"

Mary's face turned to stone. I went down the tunnel to check that she had not been followed. When I came back she was sitting cross-legged on the floor, staring at her feet.

"You could have got us all killed," I scolded.

"Sorry."

"You could have been hurt."

"Sorry, again."

"You don't realise the danger!"

"Sorry," she repeated, rocking backwards and forwards.

"Look, in future, don't go anywhere without telling me or Reg so we know where you are okay?"

"Okay, okay, okay," she repeated, still rocking back and forth.

"Don't be so hard on her," said Reg. "She collected breakfast without supervision. She was only trying to impress you, she doesn't know how dangerous it is out there."

"I know," I said. "But what if she were caught?"

61

*   *   *

Toilet paper; such a simple thing, but heaven after weeks of dry leaves making my bum sore.

I was crouching behind a bush, trying to poo. Mary was standing nearby, talking the hind leg off a donkey. She didn't really care about privacy. She could just squat down, go to the toilet, clean herself up, pull her knickers up and carry on.

Then a thought struck me?

I cut two long poles, along with a shorter length of wood and took them to the other cave, where I banged the poles into the ground to form uprights in the sand beside the stream. With packing wire I fixed the short piece between them, forming a bar we could sit on. I stood back and appraised my work. It wasn't Da Vinci, but it would do: we now had a flushing toilet.

I stuck two more sticks either side of the tunnel entrance and hung a blanket over them as a kind of a door.

Mary came in, curious.

"What you doin?" she asked.

"You sit on the bar, go to the toilet and wash yourself in the stream," I explained. "It's more hygienic."

Mary promptly dropped her knickers and sat on the bar, quickly losing her balance and falling backwards into the stream. I nearly fell over laughing. She crawled out, looking like a drowned rat.

Reg had followed her in and was standing with the aid of a crutch I'd fashioned.

"I will be glad when I can walk properly," he said. "And then I'll be able to carry my corner without you two waiting on me hand and foot."

"You just get better, mate," I smiled.

I noticed he was no longer chained to the briefcase; it was on the floor next to his bed. He noticed me looking.

"I took it off," he shrugged. "What's in there is no good to anyone in this God forsaken place."

                    *   *   *

As the weeks passed the jungle noises became familiar. We learned to identify those animal sounds that meant safety, those that were warnings and – the one audible change that always made us freeze – sudden complete silence, which meant imminent danger.

Reg was walking unaided now, though he still couldn't travel far on each trip, and we put his chair outside the cave under the trees in daytime so he could sit in the shade and get some fresh air. Mary fussed over him like a mother hen, making him comfortable and giving him food and drink.

One morning I left Mary with Reg under the tree.

"Won't be long," I told them, going to cut some wood. "I have an idea."

I had remembered some trees with long, straight branches not far away. Working quickly, I cut what I needed and headed back up towards the cave. When I returned, Reg was asleep in his chair and Mary was nowhere to be seen. She wasn't in the first cave.

"Mary!" I shouted.

A muffled sound from the next cave made me throw the wood on the floor and crawl through the tunnel. As I got to my feet, my eyes fell on Mary – I froze.

She was standing in the stream, water up to her knees, completely naked. Her clothes were folded neatly in a pile on the bank. She was staring at me in sheer terror: wrapped around her left leg, waist, chest and shoulders was the largest snake I had ever seen.

Its head was about two feet above hers and looking down at her with its tongue flicking in and out, tasting the air. The head alone was bigger than mine; the coils around Mary's waist were as thick as my thigh. It moved slowly, tightening the coils around her body, slowly crushing the life out of her.

Without thinking, I drew my knife, waded into the water and slashed the blade across one of the coils about her waist. The snake's enormous head came down at me, sinking long fangs

63

into my shoulder. I slashed again, opening up the flesh. It uncoiled itself from Mary at some speed, trashing violently and knocking us all headlong into the water.

With its jaws still locked on my shoulder, I put one arm over its neck and pulled it to my chest, sawing at its flesh with the blade. We were being dragged towards the vortex, helpless in the death throes of the great snake.

I heard Reg shout – he'd crawled through the tunnel, hobbled across to the stream and managed to pull Mary out.

The snake released its grip on my shoulder as we neared the whirlpool, the water getting faster and faster. I struggled to put my feet on the bottom, grabbing at a jagged rock in my panic, cutting my fingers. Shaking, I pulled myself out. I looked over my shoulder in time to see the snake disappear down the hole in the cave floor.

Reg hobbled over.

"Are you alright, Robbie?"

"Yeah, I'm alright," I said. "How's Mary?"

She was on all fours, coughing and retching. There were dark red marks all over her body from where the snake had coiled around her, but she was alive. I helped her to her feet; she threw her arms around my chest and held me tightly, sobbing.

When we managed to calm her down enough we crawled back into the other cave, where she dressed and dried herself. She sat on the floor, rocking and gently humming to herself. I supposed it must help her stay calm.

Reg tended my wounds as I watched her. She was in a little world of her own.

"Do you know what, Reg? A few weeks ago I could not stand people with Down's Syndrome, and now…"

"Now you just risked your life to save one," he finished. "She's a lovely girl, not an ounce of malice in her. And she thinks the world of you," he added. "Whenever you come into view she lights up."

"Rubbish," I said. "Mary?"

She looked up at us.

"Where did the snake come from?"

"In there," she said, pointing at the other cave.

"Show me."

We crawled through the little tunnel and she pointed at the hole where the stream came in.

"Right," I said. "I'll fix that."

I left Reg looking after Mary and went out into the jungle to cut some long, slim poles. I took them to the other cave and lashed them together to form a lattice, staking some uprights in the sandy ground I staked a sturdy framework over the hole.

I nodded to myself. That ought to do the trick. The water could still flow freely out, but the framework would prevent anything nasty from coming in with it.

Pleased with my work I returned to the wood I had cut earlier, in the main cave. My intention was to make a bow and arrows. I had made them, on a smaller and less deadly scale, when I was a boy, so I thought it should be easy enough to make them now. First I cut the bow stave, about five feet long and two inches in diameter. Then I scraped off all the bark and painstakingly whittled the ends down, so they tapered down to about an inch. This took quite a long time. I cut a groove in each end of the stave.

Next, I cut a length of packing wire about four feet, six inches long and made a loop at each end. With some difficulty, I bent the bow stave and hooked the string on each end; it held taut, which was a good start, but I could barely draw it.

I cut straight sticks of the same length for the arrows, trimming the leaves and cutting a point on the thickest end of each. I cut a notch into the other end, to serve as a nock. About four inches from the point I made a shallow incision around the arrow and shaved off the bark to the top, counting on the weight of the remaining bark to make the arrow fly true. I now had a bow and ten arrows; I stood back and admired my handiwork, feeling rather proud of myself.

Mary came over and handed me a cup.

"Drink," she instructed.

"What is it?"

"Drink."

I sniffed the contents. It was fruity.

"Drink," she said again, pushing the cup to my lips.

I took a sip – it tasted pretty good, so I drank it down.

"I made it!" she beamed.

"How?"

Mary took my hand and led me to one of the buckets we'd liberated from the wreckage of the plane. It was filled with cool water and a variety of crushed fruits. I patted her on the back, impressed.

"Clever girl."

She took the cup and titled the bucket, pouring the liquid through her fingers, using them as a makeshift strainer. I hoped she'd washed her hands.

"Drink!" she laughed.

I had to admit, it was a very refreshing drink.

"Thank you Mary, that was lovely."

She held her hands together in front of her chest, as if in prayer, and patted them together happily, giggling.

The sun's rays were coming in low, now. Mary settled herself on the ground, gently rocking and humming to herself. It was the first time she had seemed happy and contented since the crash.

I glanced over at the tunnel to the other cave; rocks had been piled over the entrance.

Reg grinned; "She's not taking any chances."

CHAPTER NINE

After a night devoid of further reptilian attack, I decided it was time we went hunting. We hadn't seen the natives for some days, so I took Mary with me. We crept out into the morning sun; I carried the bow and Mary the arrows.

We came to a small clearing covered with animal tracks.

"Mary, up that tree," I said, looking around.

I helped her into the branches before following her into the tree. I pressed myself against a branch, waiting.

After a few minutes, she put her face close to mine.

"What we waitin for?"

"Shh," I whispered.

Oblivious to the danger, a small deer tripped into the clearing, nibbling on the new grass. Slowly, I put an arrow to my bow and drew it back.

Mary's face lit up when she saw the deer.

"Look!" she whispered, pointing at it excitedly. "Look, look!"

I loosed the arrow and missed by yards. It fell somewhere in the undergrowth, so far from the deer that it didn't even hear it fall. I put another arrow to my bow, drew back and took aim. This time, I would hit the deer, I could feel it.

Mary, however, had other ideas.

"NO!" she shouted, and pushed me.

Birds squawked and monkeys jabbered at the sudden commotion; the deer shot off between the trees. As I rolled back off my branch, the arrow shot upwards through the forest canopy.

I landed flat on my back, the wind knocked out of me. Everything went quiet. There was barely a sound from the animals, nor even a breeze in the trees. Then a faint noise began to filter through my consciousness, getting louder.

Phit, it went. *Phit, phit, phit, PHIT, PHIT, PHIT.*

Something was coming down through the canopy at great speed. Then it dawned on me: what goes up must come down. Before I had time to react, my arrow came flying back out of the leaves and embedded itself in the ground, not one inch from my neck.

I leapt to my feet, shaking with fear. I had nearly committed suicide.

Mary climbed down out of the tree, waving her finger at me sternly.

"You Naughty," she scolded. "Don't hurt baby."

"But we need meat," I blurted out.

"No," she repeated. "Not hurt baby."

We walked back to the cave, Mary in front, me trailing behind like a naughty child.

"But we need meat," I kept saying, to no avail.

"No."

Back at the cave I told Reg what happened and he couldn't stop laughing.

It was fairly obvious that I needed more archery practice. I crawled into the other cave and stuck an arrow in the sand at one end. Standing at the other end I put an arrow to the string, drew back, took aim and – missed. By six feet.

I shook my head, certain I had been better at this when I was a child.

I kept practising and gradually got my arrows to fall closer to the target, going at it until my arms and fingers burned with the effort. I decided to give it a rest for the day and continue practising in the morning.

As I was collecting my arrows a thought struck me. Snares. As a boy I had helped my uncle catch rabbits on the railway embankment near his house. I could still remember how it was done, and I had plenty of wire.

"I'll make snares," I said aloud.

I cut the stakes, made nooses from the wire and bound them to the stakes, making six in all. I decided to set them that night, leaving Mary with Reg in the hope that what the eye didn't see, the heart wouldn't grieve over.

At dusk I took the traps and headed off into the jungle until I found a clearing with tracks and fresh droppings all over it. I hammered the first snare over a run and carefully opened the wire loop.

"Now," I murmured. "If anything runs down that track the trap should catch it."

I set the others over different tracks and returned to the cave, feeling hopeful.

As I walked in, Mary jumped up and threw her arms around my neck, holding me tightly.

"Sorry!" she said, sobbing.

She must have thought I'd gone out because I was angry with her for stopping me shooting the deer, I realised. I put my arms around her and gave her a cuddle.

"Don't be," I told her. "No harm done. Let's get some sleep."

Mary dragged her bed over next to mine and lay down beside me. Putting her arm around my chest, she kissed my cheek.

"Night-night," she said, and fell asleep within seconds.

Poor girl, I thought. She was a child trapped in a woman's body. I feared she'd have to grow up very fast. I had a feeling that we, along with the rest of the passengers, were feared dead and that there would be no rescue forthcoming.

*   *   *

In the morning I woke with Mary still cuddled against my chest. I tried to move, but she held on tight.

"Wakey wakey," I said, "time to get up."

She opened her eyes and smiled, planting another kiss on my cheek.

"Ello," she beamed.

"Come on," I said. "Let's go and see if we have caught anything."

The first trap was empty, as was the second. My heart began to sink. Perhaps jungle animals were less like rabbits than I'd thought. The third trap lifted my spirits. It held a small rodent – some kind of squirrel, I thought. It was quite dead and I glanced up at Mary to see if she was upset, but she wasn't. I supposed it could have been different if she'd actually seen it die. I took it out and tucked it in my belt. The next trap was empty, too.

The bushes quaked and rustled as we approached the final trap; deep in the vegetation, something squealed in panic.

"Mary, stay here and keep watch," I whispered.

I crept closer to the bushes, my heart racing. Snared by its hind leg was a pig like animal, about the size of a Jack Russell and very unhappy about its current predicament. I picked up a piece of wood; my stomach churned. I had never killed anything before, but we had to eat, and this little pig would be a good source of protein.

Thunk! Thunk! It stopped squealing and I hit it again, just to be sure. As I lifted it out of the snare I heard a noise and turned to

70

discover another pig, about ten times larger than the first, bearing down on me like a steam train. Its tail was straight up, enormous tusks lowered in a deadly charge. It barrelled toward me, emitting unearthly screams and shrieks.

"Oh, shit!" The Mother?

I dropped everything and ran like a man possessed. I don't think my feet touched the ground for the first four paces. I shot out of the bushes – Mary was standing in the middle of the path.

"Get out of the bloody way!" I screamed.

She stepped to one side and I sprinted past her, the pig right behind me and gaining fast. A searing pain shot through my right calf; fear gave me an extra surge of speed. I turned off onto another path. The pig was so close it overshot the turning, but it scrambled around and was quickly back on my trail.

Its mistake gave me time to jump for a low branch, as my legs swung up I felt its cold, wet snout hit my heel. I clung on for dear life. It never had the sense to look up, though I was sure it could still smell me.

It ran round and round the tree, looking for me, then shot off through the undergrowth, crashing about and menacing the other forest residents.

I checked my leg; blood was pouring from a six-inch gouge in my calf where the pig's tusk had ripped into my flesh.

"What you doin up there?"

I looked down. Mary had caught up and was staring up at me, curious.

"Trying to get down," I said, dripping with blood and sarcasm.

Together, we collected the snare and the two animals, and walked back to the cave.

"What happened to you?" Reg said, when he saw my leg.

"I miss all the fun," he remarked, when I told him. "I'll be glad when I can come out with you."

"When you can walk unaided you can help with the trapping," I said.

The blood on my leg had more of less dried, apart for one weepy bit near the middle of the cut. Reg rummaged through the first aid kit and pulled out some antiseptic cream. Mary found a bucket and collected some clean water from the stream. Without saying a word she washed my wound, gently dried it, applied some of the cream and bandaged it up.

I was surprised at her skill and thanked her. My leg felt better already. Reg and I watched her as she tidied up and put things away.

"You know, Robbie," said Reg, after a while. "That young lady is not as silly as you might think she is."

"Yes," I said. "I'm beginning to realise that myself. She carries her corner very well."

"Now," said Reg, rubbing his hands together. "What are we going to do with this meat now you've caught it?"

Well I said. The Native Americans used to burn dry dead leaves and wood to lessen the chance of being detected when they needed to build a fire, perhaps we could do the same. If we wanted to eat meat we would have to take a gamble.

"I reckon I could do that," said Reg, when I explained my idea. "If I take my time. Come on Mary."

While they were gone I set about preparing the meat. I had never skinned an animal before, so much of it was guesswork. First, I cut off the head and legs before slicing up the belly to remove the innards. I gagged. I'd never previously realised just how much the inside of an animal could stink. By the time I had finished it didn't look a great deal like meat, but it was the first time I had prepared it and I was quite pleased with myself.

Reg and Mary returned with armfuls of wood and leaves. We took it into the other cave and dug a shallow pit for the fire. While they were stacking the fuel, I created a crude spit.

I hesitated when it came time to light the fire. What if there was smoke?

Reg took the matches out of my hand.

"Shit or bust," he smiled, lighting a match and putting it to the dried leaves.

The fire crackled noisily into life, burning fiercely. The wood Reg and Mary had chosen was dry and old and there was only a little smoke, which quickly dissipated as the wood caught. By the time it had reached the roof of the cave it had vanished.

I skewered the meat on the spit and put it over the fire. We all sat staring at it. As the flames died down to a pile of red-hot embers, the smell began to make our mouths water. I looked over at Mary, who was sitting with her tongue out, concentrating intently on the meat.

"Mary, give it a turn will you, please?"

Her face lit up.

"Me?" she clapped her hands. "Can I?"

"Don't burn yourself," I warned.

"No, Not burn," she said, getting to her feet. "I promise."

After ten more minutes of that delicious smell driving us half insane with hunger, I decided it might be cooked.

"Let's try it," I said.

I cut a piece off and handed it to Mary.

"Here," I smiled. "You can have the first bit, but watch out – it's hot."

She blew on it and put it into her mouth.

"Mmmmmm, lovely."

I gave some to Reg and cut a piece for myself. Mary was right, it was delicious. We gorged ourselves until we could eat no more. We had some left over, so Reg went and got a plastic bag from the gear we'd brought up from the plane. He put the remains of the meat in it and drove a stake over the stream, some way up from our makeshift toilet. He tied the bag to the stake with packing wire, so the bag was partially submerged in the cold water.

He looked up at us and shrugged.

"I don't know if it'll work, but it might stop it going rotten by tomorrow," he said.

We threw the waste parts of the pig into the stream near the vortex and watched it disappear.

"We must have the biggest waste disposal in the world," I joked.

I needed to practice my archery, so I filled a shirt and trousers with leaves and tied it up like a scarecrow at one end of the cave. I was just settling it in place when I found something in one of the trouser pockets – it was the teddy bear brooch I had found at the crash site. I stuffed it in my pocket.

I took up position at the far end of the cave with my bow, took aim and fired. The arrow hit the target on the shoulder, but bounced off again. It was disappointing, but the fact that I'd actually hit it gave me the confidence to carry on.

I practiced every day – at every opportunity. This was a matter of survival. We caught plenty of food in the snares and Reg quickly picked up how to trap and collect animals.

Together, we taught Mary to prepare and cook the meat, which she did to a surprisingly high standard. She was a quick learner and loved it when we said how tasty it was.

CHAPTER TEN

One evening after dinner, I told Mary to close her eyes and hold out her hand.

"What for?" she asked, looking at me suspiciously.

"Just do it," I said. I put the brooch in her upturned palm. "You can open your eyes now."

Her face lit up when she saw it.

"Oh, a teddy! I love teddies," she exclaimed and held the brooch up to me. "Put it on, please?"

I pinned it to her blouse. Mary kept looking at it and smiling.

"Pretty," she beamed. "Pretty."

By now we were all becoming accustomed to the climate. I had reached a point where all I wore was a pair of shorts, shirts being rather pointless in the endless heat. I had also given up on my trainers and went barefoot instead. I had bad blisters at first, but they soon healed.

Our wounds had all healed up now and the others were beginning to come around to my way of thinking. Reg had taken to wearing a pair of trousers with the legs torn off and a knotted handkerchief to cover his bald head, which could burn quite badly in the sun. Mary had a pair of short-legged dungarees. We were tanned and healthy, doing pretty well considering all we'd been through.

The three of us had become an odd little family: Mary called Reg 'Dada and cuddled up to him whenever she was unhappy. He would tell her stories to make her feel better, making them up as he went along. You could easily mistake them for father and daughter.

Every night, Mary slept next to me, with one arm around my waist. I suppose it made her feel safe. She would kiss me on the cheek, say 'Night-night,' and within thirty seconds she would be asleep. I have no idea how she did it.

Our tribal neighbours hadn't been around too much, which was something of a relief. We'd seen them in the distance – and I assume they'd seen us, too – but we'd had no direct encounters. We had, by now, learned the noises of the jungle. It speaks to you all the time – all you have to do is listen.

We must have been in our cave for about three months by this point. It was difficult to tell, sometimes. Time had a way of stretching out differently in the jungle. There were no clocks or calendars to mark out the hours and days. It had become fairly obvious that no rescue would be forthcoming.

My archery had improved to the point of being able to hit the target within an inch of the mark. It came in handy. I'd taken to studying the footprints of the different animals and following their runs through the undergrowth. It meant that meat had become a large component of our diet – I even thought I might be putting on weight.

One day, Reg came back to the cave with some new fruit that looked like pears and smelled incredibly sweet, like honey. We sat down to eat them.

"Oh, delicious," Reg said, taking a bite. He smiled and took another mouthful.

I tried one too, and I must admit it was very tasty. I was about halfway through my fruit when I came over quite dizzy. I looked at Reg, who I was horrified to discover lying face down in the sand. My vision started blurring; I saw Mary put the fruit to her mouth. I reached over and slapped it from her hand before she could take a bite.

"No!" I cried, as I lost consciousness.

When I came round my throat was sore and full of mucus, my head pounding fit to explode. My arms and legs felt leaden and uncooperative. Sweat was pouring from my body. Through blurred vision I could just make out Mary standing over me, saying something I couldn't make out. My skin felt like it was on fire. All my muscles were taut and I was shaking hard, as if I was fitting. Then I passed out again, surrendering to oblivion.

The next time I came round I was naked. Mary knelt beside me, pouring cold water over my body. It just about turned to steam when it hit me, but it felt good. I had been sick, I realised dimly, my bowels had emptied and I had urinated. I could feel it running away from me, helpless.

How many times I faded in and out of consciousness I don't know, but each time Mary was there, mopping my brow or washing me down with cold water, taking care of me.

When I finally came to myself, my headache was easing and I wasn't sweating. I breathed more easily than I had since eating the fruit. I turned my head to find Mary lying next to me, her head resting on my shoulder and her arm across my chest. She was fast asleep.

Reg, too, was sleeping or unconscious. Either way, he was still breathing, and that was a relief. He had also been stripped naked to keep his temperature down. Around us, the cave was neat and tidy.

Mary must have felt me moving. She woke up and looked at me with that silly smile on her face. I don't know what made me do it – relief at being alive, perhaps – but I held her close and kissed her on the lips. She responded by kissing me back.

"How long have I been ill?" I asked.

Mary held up five fingers.

Five days!

She took my hand and led me to the other cave. By the time we got there I was exhausted and weak. The fire was alight, meat cooking merrily away. Mary cut a piece of it and handed it to me. At first I had a job getting my throat to work, but I managed to swallow it. After I'd eaten a little more and drunk plenty of fresh water from the stream I felt much better.

In the last five days, Mary had been on her own. She had been out into the jungle and picked fruit, set snares, caught fresh meat, cooked it and taken care of both Reg and I without being caught by the natives. She had a lot more sense than I had given her credit for. I owed this young woman my life twice over, now. I slept soundly that night.

The next morning, Reg came round and Mary fussed over him as she had with me. She must have been so frightened of losing us.

"I'm sorry Robbie, I didn't know that fruit was poisonous," Reg said, when he had recovered a little.

"Don't worry, Reg – it could have happened to any one of us. At least we're all alright."

When I told him that I'd been out too and Mary had looked after us unaided for five days he was amazed.

"We owe that girl our lives," he said, wonderingly.

I nodded. It was a debt that would take a long time to repay.

*　　*　　*

Over the next few days, Reg and I got our strength back, eating the fruit and meat Mary brought us, doing gentle exercise. I practiced my archery.

A few days after our most recent brush with death, Reg suggested we had a party.

"We can get dressed up in clean clothes, we have a little booze and we let our hair down," he suggested. "I think we deserve it, don't you?"

"Yes, I do," I answered.

"Oh, please, please?" Mary giggled. "Please?"

That evening we all went into the other cave, stripped off and bathed in the stream. It didn't seem out of the ordinary to be naked around one another anymore, so we simply washed together. We dried off and dressed in clean clothes, the shoes feeling alien on my feet after weeks of going barefoot. Reg and I splashed on some aftershave we had liberated from the wreck, though we both had beards now. Mary put on a dress, combed her hair and sprayed a little perfume on – another gift from the plane. She pinned her teddy bear brooch to her dress. She looked very attractive. It felt nice to put on clean clothes again.

Mary set out some leaves on the floor and set the makeshift table with fruit while I cooked the meat. Reg pulled out the drinks from the crash, along with some glasses.

I set the meat out on a piece of dry bark and we sat down to eat.

After the meal, Reg opened a bottle of single malt scotch; he poured a measure each for me and him, and an orange juice for Mary. It didn't take much and we were quite tipsy. It seemed like a very long time since I'd last had a drink.

"What's it like?" asked Mary, pointing at the scotch.

Reg poured a little of it into her orange juice so she could try it. She took a sip and smiled. "It's nice. I like ."

We talked and drank, and all three of us were laughing when Reg started to sing, his rich, slightly wobbly baritone voice filling the cave.

"You can dance every dance with the guy who gives you the eye, let him hold you tight," he sang, happily.

I got to my feet and held out a hand to Mary.

"Shall we dance?"

"Can't dance," she said.

"Of course you can – I'll teach you," I said, pulling her to her feet. I put my arm around her waist. "Put your left hand on my shoulder and hold my other hand with your right."

As Reg sang we swayed from one foot to the other. Mary's body was as stiff as a board.

"Relax," I said, and held her close so she couldn't see her feet.

Reg sang out of tune; we danced out of step, Mary giggling along with our laughter. The moon was shining in through the entrance to the cave. We danced until Reg ran out of songs. He went quiet almost suddenly and I turned to find him slumped forward, an empty scotch bottle in his hand, fast asleep in a drunken stupor.

We made him a little more comfortable before thinking about turning in ourselves. We got undressed and lay down. Mary cuddled up tight to me. I breathed in her perfume, thinking about how good it smelled. The scotch had made me quite light headed.

I put my arm around her, my hand on her breast. She gazed at me in the moonlight for a few moments before our lips met. I went up on one elbow, looking down at her. She lay there, smiling up at me. We kissed and caressed, tipsy, until I was completely aroused and she was whimpering with pleasure, her head arched back and her eyes closed.

I entered her slowly. She gasped and I realised she was a virgin. Mary wrapped her arms and legs around me as I thrust into her faster and faster, until she rammed her body taut and hard against mine. She cried out as we both reached our climax. She held me so tightly I could barely breathe.

For a while her body was shuddering beneath me, then she relaxed and we kissed gently, falling asleep in each other's arms.

*　　*　　*

When I awoke the sun was up and Reg was still snoring. Mary was not lying next to me. I sat up.

She was sitting cross legged a little way away from me, gazing at me with her chin resting in her hands.

"Love you," she said, and smiled.

The night before suddenly came back to me in full force. What had I done? I had been drunk, but that was no excuse. I had effectively led her on, a vulnerable adult for whom I technically had responsibility. A wave of self-revulsion washed over me. I didn't know what to say to her.

She must have been up early: the breakfast was all set out and ready. I went through to the other cave, bathed and came back. Mary was still smiling at me.

Reg woke up.

"What happened last night?" he asked, groggily. "I feel like a crocodile has crapped in my mouth.

After he had bathed we ate breakfast together. He sensed there was something wrong; he kept looking from me to Mary and back again.

We went out to check the snares. About halfway there, the jungle went quiet, as if somebody had turned the volume off. All three of us dove into the undergrowth and lay, breathing as quietly as we could on our stomachs, peeking out through the leaves. Twelve tribesmen came along the path, carrying weapons: clubs, spears and knives. A hunting party. We waited as long as we could bear it after they'd passed before collecting the spoils of our snares and returning to the cave.

One day, I knew, we might be caught and have to defend ourselves. I had a bow and arrows so blunt you could have ridden bare-arsed to Brighton on them, a knife and a spear. Not enough to defend against a well-armed hunting party – and we were trespassers here. This was their territory.

I stood looking out over the jungle when we got back, trying to come up with a plan.

Mary sat cross-legged beside me, rocking back and forth.

"Talk to me," she said, abruptly.

"Quiet, I'm thinking."

"Talk to me," she said again. Then, "I love you."

"And I love you, too," I replied, surprising myself.

Her face lit up.

"Do you?" she beamed. "Do you?"

"Please be quiet, Mary, I'm trying to think."

She stood up and gave me a wet, sloppy kiss on the lips just as Reg came in. She clapped her hands together, happily.

"He loves me. He loves me."

"What's that all about?" he asked as she moved into the other cave.

I had to tell somebody.

"Last night, after you fell asleep, Mary and I went to bed and one thing led to another," I said, feeling ashamed.

"And you made love to her," he finished.

"How do you know that?" I asked. "Were you awake?"

"No," he said, with a wry smile. "But you could cut the atmosphere in here with a knife this morning."

"Reg, I feel so ashamed of myself for taking advantage of her like that," I said, wringing my hands.

"Robbie, let me ask you this," said Reg, quietly. "If she didn't have Down's Syndrome would you still have made love to her?"

"Yes, I suppose so…"

"Remember, my friend – even the most beautiful diamond has a flaw. Mary's flaw is there for all to see, but she's a woman, with a woman's needs. And she thinks the sun shines out of your backside. Make the most of each other while you can. If those savages catch us it will be 'goodnight, nurse' – and dead is forever."

I held out my hand and Reg shook it.

"Thanks Reg. I know my way forward, now."

When Mary came back in we stood looking at one another for a few seconds. She gazed up at me, uncertain. I held out my arms and her face lit up as she ran to me. We held each other tight for ages.

CHAPTER ELEVEN

"I want to make one last trip back to the crash site," I said. "I have an idea."

"I'll come with you," said Reg. "I feel fit enough. Anyway, I would like to see what we escaped from."

Cautiously, we made our way back to the wreckage. Reg drew a long breath.

"My God, we walked away from *that?*"

I looked at Mary, made a 'v' sign with my fingers, put them to my eyes and pointed up the bank. She understood and went to her lookout post.

"Reg, you stay here," I instructed. "If you see anything, give me a thumbs down and then hide. If it's all clear, give me a thumbs up."

"Got it," he said, and crouched in the bushes.

The fire had taken care of the dead. The lingering stench of rotting flesh had gone entirely. Yards of hydraulic copper tubing was hanging from the gaping hole in the fuselage; it was about a quarter of an inch in diameter.

"That's just what I want," I muttered.

I glanced up at Mary and Reg, who both held their thumbs up. I broke off about five yards of tubing, rolled it up and put it beside the path.

A cargo hold door had been blown off on impact and was lying in the bushes, the jungle vegetation only just beginning to reclaim it. I dragged it over to the path and beckoned the others out of their hiding places.

"Have you got everything you need?" Reg asked.

"I think so," I said. "Let's get back before we have company."

As I turned I noticed a half-broken spear sticking out of the ground near the fuselage, the shaft split in two. We took that, too.

We stacked everything in the other cave, where I could work on my project without anything being heard in the jungle outside.

*   *   *

That night, Reg took his personal belongings and his coveted briefcase into the other cave.

"I'll sleep through there," he told us. "Give you two lovebirds a bit of privacy."

After the daily round of chores the next morning I started work on the fuselage door. I suspected it might be one of the nose wheel doors. It measured about three feet long by two feet wide and curved gently. I cut the rivets out with a screwdriver and a hammer and took off the framework.

I drilled some holes about a third of the way down from the top of the door. Next, I cut a leather belt and bolted it to the inside of the door with some nuts and bolts I found in the toolbox. I put one arm through the strap and held the other. I now had a reasonable shield.

When I had finished with the shield I decided to work on a new set of arrows.

I cut the copper tube into four inch lengths and then flattened them at one end. With the hacksaw I cut each length to a point and filed it until it was sharp. I took the shaft of an arrow and whittled it down until it fit snugly into the end of the copper tube. I pinched my new point on tightly with the pliers.

For flights I collected some parrot feathers from the undergrowth and stripped them down. I tied four feathers to the end of each arrow. They looked pretty damn good when I'd finished and I was eager to try them out.

I put an arrow to my bowstring, took aim at my scarecrow and let fly. It hit it full in the chest and went right through. When I went to pull it out I found the pole that held the scarecrow up split almost in two.

"Jesus," said Reg, when I showed him. "You could kill someone with that."

"That's the general idea," I said. "Let's hope I never have to."

I picked up the spear blade. It was about three feet long, three inches wide, tapering to a point. There was a six inch tube where the shaft usually went. It was made of iron, so either the local tribes could smelt metal, or they knew someone else who could. I cut the broken shaft off.

I now had a sword, spear, knife and shield. They weren't exactly pretty, but they'd do the job. The blades were quite tarnished, so I took up some wet sand in a cloth and polished them until they shone. I sharpened them with a stone, giving them a fine, lethal edge.

Quite pleased with myself, I went back into the other cave. Mary saw me coming and poured me a drink of her fruit concoction. She kissed me on the cheek.

"Love you," she smiled.

I sat down next to Reg and watched Mary pottering about the cave like a contented mother hen. She seemed to enjoy having a purpose in life. She was a good cook and the cave was tidy, with everything put neatly in its place.

"Where did you learn to keep house?" I asked.

"Back home," she said, looking solemn. "Horrible home. They hate me."

"What about your mum and dad?"

"Don't have a mum."

"Where's your dad, then?"

Mary's face lit up and she pointed at Reg.

"Dada."

"Well," said Reg. "It looks like you've gained a wife and I've gained a daughter." He laughed.

"That makes you my father-in-law," I smiled.

As the days ticked by Mary and I lived as a couple. She was insatiable in the bedroom (well, cave) and very adventurous. It took all my strength just to keep up with her. I supposed since love was new to her she didn't want to miss any opportunity. I thought when the novelty wore off a bit she might slow down. I was yet to find out how wrong I was about that too.

I practiced my archery at every opportunity, along with knife throwing and fighting with a sword. I gave the spear to Reg to defend himself, but he never practiced with it. With my bow I could split a melon at fifty yards. I could judge a distance and throw my knife so that it stuck in point first on most throws. It was my skills at swordplay that needed the most work.

Every day I practiced lunging, hacking, cutting, thrusting, under arm reverse thrusts… finally, the thought struck me that I was never going to get any better until I actually found myself in combat. God willing, I would never be put to that test.

We were all a picture of health, our little family. Reg had lost some weight and I had put some on. I actually had muscles. Mary was blooming. Her hair shone and her skin glowed. She was happy.

One morning, Reg and I were talking when we heard noises coming from the other cave. We crawled through to find Mary on her hands and knees, retching into the stream.

"Are you alright?" I asked.

"Sick," she blurted, retching again.

"Have you eaten anything bad?"

"No."

Her eyes were watering and she retched again.

"I hope you're not going to be sick every morn-" I cut myself short.

Reg and I looked at one another.

"No, she can't be," I said. "Women with Down's Syndrome can't

86

– can they?"

After she stopped being sick I helped her clean herself up and took her back to the other cave and laid her on our bed.

"You just rest," I said. "Don't lift a thing. I will do the work today."

"And me," said Reg.

I held her in my arms and kissed her,

"I love you," I said, and really meant it.

She fell into a deep sleep; Reg covered her with a blanket.

"I am going to be a Granddad," he said, excited.

"And I'm going to be a Dad…"

How could we raise a baby out here in the jungle? Its cries might give away our position. I looked at Mary's sleeping form. She must have been at least two or three months gone.

Reg and I decided that we would do what we could so that Mary could have the baby with the least trauma possible. We would face the future as it came.

While she slept, I held her hand and watched the gentle rise and fall of her chest. She really was beautiful.

We hadn't seen any natives for some time, which gave us some hope that they'd moved on to a different part of the jungle and didn't visit the area any more.

That evening, when we had finished eating, Mary patted her tummy happily.

"Baby," she said, smiling.

Neither of us had told her she was expecting, she just knew, instinctively. I leaned forward and kissed her belly.

"I know," I beamed. "It's our baby."

She went to stand up, but I put out my hand.

"No, you sit down – I will do the chores. You rest."

Reg wrapped a blanket around her shoulders and tucked her up. She kissed his cheek.

"Ta, Dada."

One evening, the three of us were sitting, looking out over the jungle at the sunset.

"Mary," said Reg, suddenly. "You can't have a baby without being married. It's not right."

We both stared at him, bewildered. He took off the ring he wore on the little finger of his left hand and handed it to me, expectantly.

"Well, my boy, go on," he encouraged. "Do the business."

I went down on one knee in the dying light of a jungle sunset.

"Mary, will you marry me?" I asked.

She giggled.

"Yes, oh yes, yes!" she said.

I went to put the ring on her finger, but Reg stopped me.

"No," he said, "not until the wedding. I'll be vicar – I think it's time we had another party, anyway."

We set out a table with food and drink before bathing in the stream. Reg and I got dressed up – Reg wore his shirt back to front with his jumper over the top, so he looked like he was wearing a dog collar. Mary got dressed in the other cave, it being bad luck for me to see the dress and all before the wedding.

When she came back through she took my breath away.

She had wrapped a white sheet around her, pinning it in place with the teddy bear brooch. She had tucked flowers in her hair and behind her ears; she carried a small posy of jungle flowers.

Standing there in the moonlight, I knew I would love her forever.

I held out my hand, which she took and came close. She was trembling. I looked at Reg.

"Do you know the words?"

"Of course I do, my son," he said, in his best vicar voice. "I've done it a thousand times. Dearly beloved, we are gathered here tonight to join together this man and this woman in holy matrimony. If anyone should object to this union, speak now or forever hold thy peace."

Mary looked around.

"There ain't nobody here," she pointed out.

"I know that," said Reg, enjoying himself. "But I'm the vicar and I have to ask, or it isn't legal, is it? Can I carry on, now?"

"Yes," she giggled.

"Do you, Mary, take this man, Robbie, to be your lawfully wedded husband?"

"I do, I do," she exclaimed, jumping up and down.

"I haven't finished yet," said Reg, with a grin. "To have and to hold, to wait on hand and foot? To put him to bed when he's drunk, or in sickness and in health? And to forgive him for all the nasty things he's said and done, in the past and from this day forth?"

Mary stared at him for a moment.

"Well, do you?"

"I do, I do!" she grinned, face lighting up.

"Do you, Robbie, take this woman Mary, to love, honour and cherish? To protect her and dote upon her, in sickness and in health, for as long as you both shall live?"

"I do," I said, beaming.

"Have you got the ring?"

I took the ring from my pocket and held her left hand.

"Say after me," Reg instructed: "With this ring, I thee wed."

"So do I," she said.

"With my body, I thee worship."

"So do I," she said again, giggling.

"And all my worldly goods, I thee endow."

"So do I."

I slid the ring onto her finger.

Reg held our hands together.

"I now pronounce you man and wife," he declared. "You may kiss the bride."

We embraced one another and kissed. I will remember that kiss for the rest of my life.

We ate the food and drank the wine – our wedding feast. Mary kept holding out her hand and admiring the ring.

"They told me I wouldn't ever get married," she said, after a while.

"Who told you that?" I asked.

"The home," she said. "I told them I would, and I have!"

We sang and laughed and danced until the early hours. Then Reg said goodnight as he crawled into the other cave. We undressed and lay in the cool, moonlit air. I kissed Mary's tummy, then her neck and lips. We made love tenderly. The perfect finish to the most perfect wedding day.

I watched her sleeping, her chest rising and falling gently with every breath. I put my hand on her tummy and even in her sleep she took my hand and made a contented sound.

The next day Mary and I went out to pick some fruit and on our return Reg was sitting in his chair with a smile on his face looking smug. He held out a piece of rolled up paper tied up with a ribbon. I went to take it. Not for you he said. It's for Mary.

She took it, removed the ribbon and unrolled the paper. While we were out Reg had written a marriage certificate all in posh scroll writing. Dated and signed by The Reverend Reg. It was very impressive.

I read it out loud after which Mary clasped it to her chest with tears running down her cheeks. Then she hugged and kissed Reg then me. Then disappeared into the other cave.

Reg put his hand on my shoulder. Leave her a while he said, It's a woman thing.

CHAPTER TWELVE

Some days after our wedding, the three of us were out collecting firewood. Mary carried the fire axe and Reg had his spear. I had the bow over my shoulder, arrows in my hand and the knife and sword in my belt. I was thinking about making sheaths out of skins to house them in, when Reg tapped me urgently on the shoulder.

He put his finger to his lips and pointed through the trees.

We hid in the bushes. From the undergrowth, we could see three men walking along the path. Two of them we recognisable as part of the hunting parties we saw patrolling the jungle from time to time – the third was different. He was little more than a boy and quite obviously their captive. His hands were tied behind his back and his ankles shackled with a short piece of wood, so he had to walk with his legs apart, shuffling along. He had a creeper tied around his neck and was being led by one of his captors, like he was a dog.

His face was bloodied; it had dripped down his shoulders and chest. His captors were laughing and jerking the lead. One of them smacked him in the face with a club. He fell to the ground, where they dragged him on by the neck. The other tribesman lifted him to his feet and urged him forward with the blade of a spear in his back.

I gestured to Reg and Mary to stay put and crawled through the undergrowth to a point in the path where a jagged rock protruded across it. I put arrow to string as they approached, taking careful aim.

A few feet from my hiding place, the boy was struck again; this time he stood his ground. His captors were talking and not looking in my direction. The young lad saw me first. He looked surprised; I wondered if he'd ever seen a white person before.

I gestured for him to get down. He took my meaning and

dropped like a stone. One of his captors pulled on the lead to make him rise, but he stayed low – the other man raised his club high above his head. I drew my bow, emerged from behind the rock and loosed my arrow.

The arrow hit him full in the throat, coming out from the back of his neck. The man stood stock still for a few seconds, the club still raised above his head, the arrow running through him – he crashed to the ground. The second man saw me and raised his spear. As he drew it back to throw it, Mary hurtled out of the undergrowth behind him, axe raised with both hands, her tongue sticking out between her teeth in concentration.

She brought it down between the man's shoulder blades. He hit the ground next to his companion, the axe buried deep in his back. She put one foot on his shoulder and wrenched her weapon out.

"Strewth," Reg cried, emerging from the bushes. "Robbie, are you sure they're dead?"

"They'd better be," I said. "We're going to feed them to the crocs. Mary, get the arrow out – Reg, give me a hand…"

We dragged them to the lake a short distance away and rolled them into the water.

Mary untied the noose around the boy's neck; I picked him up, put him over my shoulder and we ran back to the cave.

Reg kept a lookout to make sure we weren't followed. The lad sat on the ground, staring at us. He was stark naked, except for a plaited leather belt and a string of coloured beads wrapped around his penis and testicles. I drew my knife. He shut his eyes tightly, expecting to have his throat cut. Instead, I cut his bonds, freeing his hands and ankles. Mary gave him a glass of cool water, which he gulped down greedily.

She warmed some water and bathed his wounds. There didn't seem to be any broken bones or permanent damage. He couldn't take his eyes off her skin. When she had finished, he ran his fingers down her arm and stared at them, as if to see if the colour came off.

Reg looked back into the cave.

"I think it's all clear," he said, glancing at the boy. "I don't think we were followed."

After the lad had eaten, we tried to communicate.

"Can you speak English?" I asked.

He looked at me blankly, which I took as a 'no'. Reg tried in French, but to no avail. We gave up.

I made him up a bed and he sat on it, staring at us one at a time. Eventually, as the sun began to sink over the jungle, he seemed to relax a little and lay down to sleep.

I noticed his back was scarred and on closer inspection the scars resolved themselves into a beautiful picture of a bird, wings open in flight. It looked like it had been cut into his back with a blade. I was very impressed, but I couldn't help thinking that it must have been a very painful process.

Reg was looking at it, too.

"I seem to remember reading something about tribal tattoos," he remarked. "But I can't remember if it was a coming of age thing, or if it was only the chiefs. This lad's no older than fifteen or sixteen."

"Will you be okay with him, Reg?" I asked. "I need to practice my fighting skills – more than ever after today."

"Yes," he said. "I'll watch over him."

As it got dark, Mary came through with a cool drink for me. She put her arm around me and kissed me. We sat listening to the stream as it gurgled by for a while. It was nice – peaceful.

"I love you," I whispered, giving her a bit of a squeeze.

She looked up at me and smiled.

"Love you, too."

We cuddled up together, content. If it wasn't for the savages, this place would be a paradise: no financial pressure, credit cards, vehicle licenses or taxes to worry about. Without the constant threat of death it would be perfect.

Back in the other cave, the lad was still fast asleep – and so was Reg.

I thought back to our encounter. I had picked this kid up, put him over my shoulders and run with him for nearly half a mile. He weighed almost the same as I did. How had I done that? I am and always have been the original nine stone weakling – the one who gets sand kicked in his face on the beach. It must have been pure adrenaline; you can achieve anything if you're scared enough.

I examined my chest and arms and was surprised to find that they'd filled out a bit. I flexed my muscles. *Blimey*, I thought – I actually *had* muscles.

I left Reg to sleep where he was. It didn't seem fair to wake him just to send him back to the other cave. Mary, as usual, was asleep in seconds. I soon followed. It had been quite a long day.

* * *

The next morning, Mary shook me awake and pointed at the lad's bed. It was empty. Our guest had taken his leave during the night.

"Damn it," I exclaimed. "I should never have brought him back to our hideout."

Reg sat up, rubbing his eyes.

"What's going on?"

"He's gone – during the night," I said. "If he comes back with others we won't stand a chance."

"There again," said Reg, looking at the empty bedding, "he could have killed us as we slept, but he didn't."

"From now on, we can't take any chances," I said.

Near to the tunnel to the other cave I stuck three arrows in the sand and laid down my bow and shield. Next to that I left the loaded flare gun. In the other cave I stuck the rest of the arrows in the sand near the vortex and leaned the fire axe against the wall by the tunnel entrance. If anyone came through there it would have to be on their hands and knees, giving us an advantage.

Reg carried his spear and I my knife and sword in my belt at all times.

The days crept slowly by, with no sightings of the tribe we had attacked, or of the young captive and his friends.

After a week, Reg said, "If they were going to attack, they would have done it by now."

He was right. The tension began to ease; gradually, we began to return to our old way of living, though we still kept the weapons ready just in case.

Mary had developed quite a bump by now. I watched her as she pottered about the cave, tidying up. She must have been about six months gone. I wondered whether the baby would be Down's Syndrome, like her, or normal, like me. I had no idea what the chances of either were. I knew I would love them both to bits, either way, forever.

At times my mind would drift back to Tracey, Dave and Jane. It seemed like another time entirely – another era. They must have believed I was dead. How my life had changed in ten short months. I had survived a plane crash, fought an enormous snake and tribesmen – killed game, killed men. I had a friendship with Reg that would probably last a lifetime. I had a beautiful wife who I adored and I was going to be a Daddy.

CHAPTER THIRTEEN

One morning, Reg was out checking the traps. Mary and I had just finished breakfast, when we heard a noise coming through the entrance tunnel.

"Blimey Reg, that was quick," I called.

There was no reply. A prickle of fear crept up my back and I picked up my sword, waiting. A head appeared through the entrance tunnel – a black, bald head, painted yellow, red and blue. Definitely not Reg.

As he climbed up into the cave I flew past Mary and swung the blade, hitting him in the neck, almost severing his head. He disappeared back down the hole. Another head popped up in his place – he didn't look pleased about what had happened to his friend.

"Mary!" I bellowed. "Go into the other cave!"

I caught a glimpse of her running to the tunnel and crawling through before the next one appeared. I drew my bow – the arrow hit him in the chest. He fell back down the hole. Another man had climbed up a log at the other entrance; as he stood up, two more came up into the cave. I aimed the flare gun at the one standing in the entrance, closed my eyes and pulled the trigger.

BANG!

The flare hit him full in the stomach, the force of it folding him in half as he shot backwards out into the jungle, screaming. The light of the flare blinded the other two. I used the distraction to slash one across the ribs and run the other through. Two more heads popped up and another man came in from the cliff face.

"Shit!"

I dived into the tunnel and scrambled through. Mary was waiting, axe in hand.

"Stand there!" I shouted.

She stood next to the entrance, tongue between her teeth, watching in anticipation, the axe raised in both hands. I stood back so the first man could see me.

"Come on, you bastards!" I yelled.

As he came into the cave – *thunk!* The axe took his head clean off. The body was dragged back through the tunnel, gushing blood, but the head just lay there, staring at me.

As the next one came in, Mary swung the axe down hard, but our assailant ducked back into the tunnel and the blade buried itself into the sand. Before she could wrench it back out, he grabbed it and pulled himself into the cave, quickly followed by another man.

The first man pinned Mary against the wall of the cave, where she screamed and struggled; the second came at me. As he lunged forwards with his spear I sidestepped and brought my sword down on the back of his head. His skull opened up like a ripe melon, spilling blood and brains everywhere.

The tenor of Mary's screams changed pitch and I span around in time to see her attacker raising his knife. I ran forward and managed to swing my blade hard before he could bring his down. It took his arm off at the shoulder. Screaming in agony, the man fell to the floor, clutching at the gaping wound in his shoulder, which was emitting intermittent gushes of blood. Mary picked up her axe and plunged it into his chest. She yanked it out when she was sure that he was dead and ran to my side.

The cave was beginning to fill up with savages – there were already too many for us to handle alone and from the sound of it there were more at the other end of the tunnel. We had screaming savages in front of us and a whirlpool behind – the proverbial choice between a rock and a hard place. To stay in the cave would be certain death. The vortex a close second.

I made my decision in a heartbeat. I picked Mary up with one arm and she threw her arms around my neck. We shared the briefest of kisses before plunging in the centre of the swirling vortex.

The power of the water span us around in the centre for a few seconds, whirling us faster and faster until we were sucked down into the vortex. We were spinning so fast now that I could hardly hold my breath. There wasn't time to think, let alone to act.

Whoosh!

Suddenly we were in mid-air, our limbs flailing ineffectually as we fell further and further. I opened my eyes: I had a flash of the jungle rushing towards me until all of it was swallowed by a large circle of blue. We were dropping into the pool below.

It seemed to take forever – *crash*! We landed in the pool feet first. The force of hitting the water knocked all the breath from my body – down and down we went, plunging deeper and deeper into the water. Holding Mary tightly I kicked for the surface, my lungs burning.

Finally our heads came out of the water, gasping and gulping in good clean air.

We swam towards the shore and managed to get to our feet where the water was shallower.

"Are you alright?" I gasped.

"Yes," she nodded.

I put my hand on her belly.

"Baby okay?"

She nodded again. I lifted Mary up in my arms and spun her round and round.

"We made it!" I laughed. We made it!

Mary's face froze; she was looking over my shoulder.

"What?" I said, not wanting to look around. "What is it?"

She didn't move. Slowly, I turned to find about a hundred

tribesmen surrounding the pool, holding spears. I went for my sword before remembering that it lay at the bottom of the pool with the axe. I drew my knife.

One knife against a hundred spears. I didn't stand a chance – but we wouldn't want to go down without a fight.

We faced each other for some time, before the circle opened to reveal the young lad we had saved. Mary's face broke into a wide grin and she waved.

He beckoned us out. I took Mary's hand and walked from the pool. They turned, and in single file walked into the jungle. Mary put her hand on the back of my belt as we followed them.

*   *   *

We walked for several miles through dense jungle until we came to a clearing of about one hundred yards in diameter. The left side of it was taken up by a vast lake; The right side was a rock face at least fifty feet high. The two other sides were jungle.

Around the perimeter were dozens of huts made from sticks and palm-like leaves. Fires were dotted about the clearing, tended by the women of the tribe. Children played everywhere. When they saw us coming they all ran and encircled us, jabbering and pointing. It was obvious that we were the first white people anyone in the tribe had ever seen.

We were led to the largest hut and stood outside. The young lad went in, emerging a few minutes later with an old man. He walked over to a chair made of bamboo and covered in furs, taking a seat. He stared at us, first at me, then at Mary.

It occurred to me – far too late – that these people might be cannibals. If they were, there wasn't a great deal I could do about it now.

The old man said a few words and pointed to a nearby hut. We were led inside, Mary still holding onto my belt. Four young girls greeted us. One of them came over to Mary and put her hands on her tummy,

"Nado," she smiled.

Mary looked up at me, confused.

"I think it means 'baby'," I said.

They undressed Mary and brought in perfumed hot water that smelled of magnolias. They bathed her, gently washing her tummy. She loved every minute of it. When they were done, she was led to a rug on the floor and laid down so they could dry her off.

Then it was my turn. The four girls bathed every inch of my body – even the naughty bits. It was very sensual and I had a job not to show it. After they had dried me we were handed some robes. I must admit it felt very good to be clean.

By now it was growing dark. Around us, torches were being lit and the village had a warm glow about it.

As we gazed out of the hut, two men came over and beckoned us out. We followed them to the centre of the clearing, where a great fire had been built. All around it was a carpet of leaves with food set out like a banquet. There was fruit, nuts, meat, fish and a kind of bread. The entire tribe encircled the fire.

We were led to a gap in the ring, near the chief's hut. Everyone began chanting when we took our places, louder and louder until the chief emerged. It stopped abruptly. He raised his hands and everyone sat down.

On his left sat the young lad, and Mary and I sat to his right. He raised a hand and the tribe began to eat. It seemed to be quite the family affair. Everyone was talking and enjoying the food except for one man, who was staring at Mary. I felt uneasy. After a while he noticed me looking at him, he got up disappeared between the huts.

Dotted amongst the food were jugs made from half melons, containing liquid. Mary picked one up and took a drink.

"Mmm, nice," she said, and drank some more.

I took a swig; it was sweet, but definitely alcoholic.

"Not too much, Mary," I said. "We must think of the baby."

She nodded her head.

"Not too much." She echoed.

At a guess, the meal lasted over three hours. Then the drums started and all the women and girls stood up to dance.

Two young girls came over and took Mary's hand. They led her to the dance, where she soon got into the swing of things. She laughed and giggled, looking over at me and waving. It was just like a dance back home at the drill hall – all the women dancing round their handbags and the men propping up the bar.

The young lad we had saved came to sit beside me. He pointed at the scars on my shoulder.

"Snake," I said.

He looked bewildered.

"Snake," I said again. This time I drew a rough picture in the sand with my finger.

"Ah, Pitoona," He laughed.

He pointed at the scar under my cheek.

"Spear," I said, and pointed to the spear being held by the chief's bodyguard.

I showed him my calf and pointed to the pig's head on the table.

"Ah, pig," he said, nodding.

"What's your name?" I asked.

He looked puzzled. I put my hand on my chest.

"Robbie," I said, and then pointed at him.

His face lit up in understanding.

"Ah!" He put his hand on his chest. "Mbata."

I held out my hand and he stared at it in incomprehension. I taught him to shake hands. We talked in sign language and sand drawings into the early hours.

Mary danced until the drums stopped. Then she sat behind me and put her arms around my chest, kissing me on the neck.

"Love you," she whispered.

It was good to see her so happy. I know the drink helps to break down barriers, but to be amongst friends gave us a tremendous feeling of security. Finally, the chief got to his feet, raised his hand to signal the end of the festivities and retired to his hut. We were shown back to the hut we had bathed in earlier where a bed had been made up for us.

It was raised on legs about three feet high with a flat, wooden top like a table and covered in furs. It looked so uncomfortable I took the furs and laid them out on the floor. Mbata came in and when he saw the furs he went ballistic. Talking fast in his own language, he picked them up and put them back on the bed.

Well, I thought, *there must be a reason.*

Mary and I lay for a while in each other's arms, lost in our own thoughts – then she jumped.

"Baby!" She grabbed my hand and pressed it to her belly. "Baby move!"

"Blimey," I smiled. "He's playing football in there."

We lay with our hands on her tummy until the baby settled down and Mary fell asleep.

My mind drifted to the life we had left behind at the cave. Reg wouldn't have stood a chance against those savages. I prayed that his death had been swift.

I hoped that our luck was changing. I drifted off into a deep sleep. When I awoke, the sun was just rising over the trees. Mary was snoring and I wanted a wee. I swung my legs over the side of the bed and froze. Lying on the ground next to the bed, minding its own business, was a twelve foot crocodile.

I leapt back onto the bed, screaming – Mary woke up and started screaming, too. The croc decided that we were being altogether too noisy and ambled towards the door. Some of the tribe emerged from their huts in time to see the ancient creature disappear into the lake.

They started laughing at the two of us, still standing on the bed. Now we knew why they didn't sleep on the ground. *A lesson well learned,* I thought.

Our food was brought to us. They were treating us like royalty. It turned out that Mbata was the son of the chief, and our saving him had done us a bit of good.

We went to wash in the lake. About twenty yards out were four canoes with men looking into the water, brandishing spears. I thought they were fishing. About fifty children were swimming, twenty to thirty feet from the bank, splashing and giggling as kids do. Suddenly, one of the men in the canoes shouted and thrust his spear into the water. All the children screamed and swam for the bank.

Another man plunged his spear into the water – and into a crocodile. It thrashed about wildly, nearly capsizing the canoe. They paddled for shore as quickly as they could.

The blood from the injured croc attracted dozens of others, which was bad news for him. They attacked mercilessly, tearing it apart. The village children stood on the bank, pointing and laughing. As soon as the water was calm again, they all ran back in to swim, as if nothing at all had happened.

Later that morning we were taken to the chief's hut and introduced to the main man himself. He invited us to sit, smiling. We were given a drink and, with the help of Mbata, communicated by drawing pictures in the sand with twigs. It took hours, but we eventually got our story across – at least, I think we did.

I studied the chief closely while we spoke. He was tall – at least six feet nine inches in height. He wore a white, full-length toga, braided with gold, and a gold sash waistband. Everyone else in the village was naked, so these were most probably his ceremonial robes.

He had an aura about him; he made you feel humbled, but secure in his presence. He pointed at Mary and patted his stomach. I nodded my head.

"Baby," I said.

He smiled.

"Nado."

I looked at Mary, 'baby'.

When we stood to take our leave I held out my hand. The chief stared at it for a few seconds and then took it in his. We shook hands and he realised it was intended as a gesture of friendship. He shook my hand vigorously, laughing out loud.

We came out into the bright sunshine. Mary put her arm around my waist, resting her head on my shoulder. I kissed her gently.

CHAPTER FOURTEEN

O ver the next few days we settled into daily life with the tribe. It had become painfully obvious that rescue was not in our future, so a life here, with these generous and lively people, seemed a happy alternative. We became very close friends with Mbata, who would call every day and help us understand the tribal life. To be honest, I was enjoying myself, and so was Mary. The people of the village never saw her as anything other than another woman; the only difference to them was her fair complexion.

The children of the village were beautiful, with ebony skin, big, dark eyes and were always laughing. Whenever they were nearby, their joyful spirits were infectious and we would soon be laughing along with them.

They followed Mary around everywhere – and she loved it. Kissing and cuddling them.

The men were all over six feet tall, some nearly seven feet and very muscular. They wore nothing but a string of coloured beads wound around the length of their penises and their testicles. The women were the same height as the men, and all had their nipples and labia pierced with gold rings. Their nipples were permanently erect and the glint of the gold against their dark skin was very sensual. Sex was a thing that the tribe took very seriously, but there was a time and a place for it.

*   *   *

One morning we were led to a part of the clearing near the lake. The whole tribe turned out and began to build a hut. We watched as it took shape. When it was finished, the chief arrived and beckoned us in. Then the penny dropped – this was our new home. We had been accepted into the tribe. I was overjoyed.

The door of our new home opened out onto the lake; the ripples sparkled like millions of diamonds in the sun. Just before the dawn, Mary and I could watch the moon slowly disappear into the water and the sun begin to rise for the new day. It was a truly magical place.

There was a canopy over the door, held up by two poles and a hammock slung between them. Mary was in her element here, cleaning and tidying up. She quickly made it into a cosy little home for the two of us.

Every morning, a group of men left the village on hunting trips. They would be gone all day and come back in time for the food they had caught to be prepared and eaten. Apart from ceremonial banquets, all the food brought back was cooked on a fire in the centre of the village and shared out equally amongst the tribe so that no one ever went hungry. An idea that the rest of the world could certainly learn from.

While the women prepared the meat, the men built up the fire. They dug a hole in the ground about two feet deep and six feet in diameter. Then they filled it with rocks and made a large fire on top. The prepared meat was wrapped in wet leaves; they would rake the top layer of hot rocks away and the meat parcels were places on the lower level of hot rocks. The meat parcels would then be covered back over with the rest of the rocks and the burning embers.

While everything was cooking the smell made your mouth water and the taste when it was done was out of this world.

Mary had made friends with a young girl who was also expecting a baby and she taught Mary how to prepare food and cook it.

I had picked up quite a few words of their language and could communicate with a basic understanding. I asked Mbata if I could go hunting with them, wanting to take a more active part in village life.

*   *   *

The next morning I was woken before sunrise and given a spear. Off we went in single file. I noticed that this morning they

108

were all wearing plaited leather belts. I wondered what they were for.

We walked into the jungle for two or three miles before spreading out to comb the area. We went round in circles, but caught nothing. Moving on, we came across some monkeys, scrambling about high in the treetops. The hunters shot three down with their bows. Then we got lucky. Two deer, five piglets and some birds that looked a little like turkeys were added to the pile.

If only I had my snares, I thought. Then it struck me – I could go back to the cave, get them and salvage anything else we could find.

We returned to the village and when Mary saw me coming she ran into my arms.

"Missed you!" she said.

"And I have missed you," I said, giving her a squeeze.

I noticed a man staring at Mary from the other side of the clearing; it was the same man I had seen the day we arrived. He had an unpleasant countenance, was about seven feet tall with a long scar across his right cheek. He had a very strange look on his face.

There was something sinister about him, it made me feel uneasy. I stared back. His gaze shifted from Mary to me; our eyes met and he turned and disappeared into the jungle.

I told Mbata about my plan and he agreed to come with me. I rose early the next morning. It was still dark; the sky to the east was a deep indigo as the sun approached the horizon.

Outside, Mbata and another five lads were waiting for me. As I got to the door, Mary was right behind me.

"No, you stay here," I said. "The baby is due soon."

"I come," she smiled.

"No, you stay here."

"I come," she said, more firmly, and went to stand with the others.

I followed, resigned. With Mbata leading the way, we walked through the jungle in single file. Mary tucked her hand down the back of my belt as she had done before. It did feel good to have her near me.

We walked for miles – it was further than I remembered. Finally we came to the pool. I looked up; the water was gushing out in a torrent from the cliff face. how we ever survived that fall I will never know.

The water in the pool was crystal clear. At the bottom, I could see the fire axe and my sword, about ten feet from it. I wondered if I could dive that deep and retrieve them.

I climbed up onto a rock, hanging about twenty feet above the pool, took a deep gulp of air and dived in. The water was much deeper than I had anticipated, but I swam down to the bottom and grabbed the fire axe. I had to swim for the sword next and my lungs felt fit to burst. My fingers closed around it – I kicked my feet against the sandy bottom of the pool and headed for the surface.

The extra weight of the axe and my homemade sword made the return journey slow and laboured. My lungs were on fire. I was about to lose my grip on the weapons when Mbata and his friends jumped in and helped me reach the surface. I gulped at the air as my head broke the surface of the water.

Mary was laughing and clapping her hands together. We swam to the side and she hugged and kissed me as if she hadn't seen me for years. She took the axe and held it up.

"Mine," she said. "Mine."

After I got my breath back we made for the cave. We had to walk a few more miles to get around to the higher level and the entrance to the cave.

Under the branches of the tree at the entrance to the tunnel, the lads kept watch for us as Mary and I went in. The place had been utterly ransacked. Lying in the sand was the marriage certificate Reg had made for us; I picked it up and handed it to Mary, who looked very solemn.

She had a good look around the cave for her brooch, but it was nowhere to be found.

"Teddy gone," she moaned, clawing her fingers through the sand. "Teddy gone!"

I gave her a hug.

"Don't worry, love, I'll get you another one."

It was only a brooch I had picked up at the crash, but to her it was a treasured gift.

The corpses of our attackers were rotting where they fell and the stench was overpowering. In the other cave my bow lay broken and the arrows were gone, but the packing wire and copper tubing was still there, so I comforted myself in the knowledge that I could make some more. I found my shield in the stream, still in one piece.

We salvaged anything worth taking – which wasn't a great deal – and rejoined the others. We searched the neighbouring jungle, but I could find none of the snares we usually set. They must have caught Reg before he even had time to set any. At least we had plenty of wire – I could make more snares, too.

We gathered everything up between us and headed for home. By the time we got back to the village the sun was setting over the lake, looking like an enormous orange. Everyone came out to greet us. Despite the dangers of this place, it really was a heaven on earth.

We ate a hearty meal and went to bed. As usual, Mary was asleep in seconds. I lay there thinking about the future while she slept, and all that it held for us. At least I had my sword and shield back, and Mary her axe. I decided to make a new bow and set of arrows in the morning.

*　　*　　*

The next day, Mary got up and went to the lake to bathe. When she returned she was naked. She looked radiant, with a huge tummy and smooth skin. Her eyes shone like diamonds. I wondered how I could ever not have loved this woman. I held out my arms as she approached and she walked into them, smiling up at me.

"I love you porky," I said.

"You stink," she replied, screwing up her face. "Go wash."

Well, that's romantic, I thought. *How do I follow that?*

I entered the water to bathe; the children were swimming happily in the shallows. Someone shouted and they all ran out, screaming and laughing, myself included. It was a false alarm, so back in the water we all went. In England, mothers wouldn't let their kids play in the street these days, let alone in a lake full of crocodiles.

I noticed that not many crocs visited this part of the lake. Maybe they had learned that few lived to tell the tale if they passed the line of canoes, but now and then a chancer would try his luck.

I didn't bother to put my clothes back on and went back to our hut naked. I felt a little self-conscious at first, but nobody took a blind bit of notice. I must admit that it felt good not to be wearing my cumbersome clothes, and a lot cooler. It was liberating.

CHAPTER FIFTEEN

I spent the rest of the day making a new bow and arrows, along with new snares. There was a small clearing in the jungle behind our hut and I set up some targets there to practice my fighting skills. I would spend at least two hours a day there from then on. I didn't know if I would ever need to use them, but with a wife and a baby on the way I wanted to be prepared for every eventuality.

That evening, Mary and I went off and set our snares in the jungle. In the morning we checked our handiwork to find five animals caught. I tied their hind legs together with a piece of twine and carried them over my shoulder back to the village. With a cocky smirk on my face, I laid my modest catch on the ground while our tribe looked on.

Fully expecting them to be taken aback in wonder at my hunting skills, I was a little despondent when all they did was fall about laughing.

Right, I thought. On the next hunting trip I would set the snares for larger game and show them just how clever the modern white hunter was. They would be laughing on the other side of their faces then.

That evening I tied the snares to my belt, took the fire axe to bang the stakes in and walked through the village. I must have looked quite a sight with about thirty wire snares and stakes hanging from my belt like a wooden skirt, clonking about like a wind chime.

The whole village turned out to watch, pointing and laughing at me. Even the chief came out of his hut, a smirk on his face. As I walked into the jungle, my pride wounded, I turned back and shouted, "He who laughs last laughs longest!"

It took me about three hours to set the traps. By the time I'd finished banging the stakes in place the entire jungle knew I was there. When I returned the tribe was still laughing. Tomorrow, I thought, I would wipe the smiles off their faces.

"Just you wait and see."

Early the next morning we set off and after a mile or so a man left the party and went into the undergrowth. I thought he was going for a wee, but he beckoned me to follow him. In the bushes he pointed at a well-used track and fresh animal droppings. Then, from his belt, he pulled a single strand of leather and made a noose with it. He set it across the track and tied it to a root.

As he worked it slowly dawned on me what a fool I had made of myself. He wore his snares as a belt. He tied it off silently, without any need for the noisy banging in of stakes, telling the whole jungle what he was about. He worked fast and efficiently, setting dozens of traps in half the time I had set thirty.

From that day on I decided to watch and learn instead of trying to teach my grandmother to suck eggs. After all, their hunting and fishing skills had been perfected for this environment, honed over hundreds, if not thousands, of years.

One morning I was crouched in the bushes having a poo when a thought struck me. I took a flat piece of bark and, using it as a shovel, dug a hole in the ground behind our hut about four feet in diameter and six feet deep.

Over this, I constructed a framework of poles and covered it with leaves. Then I tied a thick branch across it to act as a seat, fixing a deer skin across the front to act as a door.

Mary came out to examine my handiwork.

"What you doin?" she asked.

I pulled back the deer skin to show her.

"Our own, personal toilet," I smiled.

"Oh goody!" she giggled, clapping her hands together. "I want a go."

"Okay," I said, "but mind you don't fall in."

Well, I thought, *at least going to the toilet is going to be a bit more civilised from now on. All I need now is a morning newspaper delivered and a cup of coffee and it will be a home from home.*

Suddenly, drums started beating in the village. Mary came out of the toilet and took my hand. People were running about the clearly; the whole village was buzzing with excitement. At the centre of it was Mary's young friend, who was sitting on the ground and holding her belly, Mary ran over as soon as she saw her and held her hand.

Two men picked the girl up and carried her to a nearby hut, laying her gently on a bed. She was well into labour by now, beads of sweat covering her body. The rest of the village – including the chief – stood outside the hut, waiting in anticipation.

Of course, birth is not a swift process. We were waiting outside for several hours until finally, with a muffled scream, the cry of a newborn baby was heard. Everybody cheered as the father emerged, proudly holding the child aloft. Mary and some of the girls bathed the mother and stayed with her until she slept.

That evening a feast was laid out and everyone celebrated the arrival of the new addition to the tribe. I wondered if they would treat Mary with the same care, as we were outsiders. I supposed I would find out in due course.

I hardly saw Mary that evening. She stayed close to the mother and babe, fussing around them, keeping mum cool and holding the baby when needed. The father was getting drunk with his friends, being praised for his part in the conception. The mother had done all the work and he was getting all the praise. I smiled slightly. Apparently some aspects of childbirth were the same the world over.

*   *   *

The next morning, Mary bathed in the lake and she walked back to the hut. She was huge now, but she was radiant. He skin was smooth and her eyes sparkled with happiness. I wondered how she would cope with childbirth. Would she struggle with it, or would it come naturally to her.

Whatever happened, I knew I would be there to help as best as I could.

I didn't know how long we had been here, but it must have been over a year. My thoughts drifted back to my friends in England and my old life. I wondered what Dave and Tracey were doing, whether Jane had married. I thought of the school, an image of Jenkins and Rawlinson fighting in the playground resurfacing. How everything used to be solved with the cane. Here, of course, it wasn't pain from a cane but death from a blade for breaking the rules.

I caught a movement out of the corner of my eye. The big fella who always made me uneasy was standing a little way away, indulging in his favourite hobby: staring at Mary. I stood and walked towards him.

"Bugger off, you weird bastard!" I shouted.

He stalked off into the jungle, scowling.

I went back to my wife, wrapped my arms about her and kissed her neck. She turned and returned the embrace, her head resting on my shoulder.

"I love you very much," I whispered.

She squeezed me even tighter.

I picked up my bow and went to the little clearing for some target practice. Mbata joined me, bringing his own bow and arrows.

I wedged a melon in the fork of two branches and asked him to shoot at it. He took aim and fired; the arrow penetrated the melon, with about four inches of it sticking through the other side.

I took aim and let fly. My arrow went straight through the melon and lodged in a tree about twenty feet beyond.

Mbata stared at my bow, wide-eyed. I handed it to him, with one of my improved arrows, and pointed at the melon. He took aim and loosed – the arrow slid through the melon as if it was made of butter and lodged in the distant tree, next to mine.

I explained that it was down to the design of the bow, not my skill. We went to the lake.

"Now shoot your arrow as far into the lake as you can," I said.

His arrow travelled about forty yards before hitting the water. Mine, loosed a minute later, sailed on for about one hundred and twenty yards. Mbata was excited, so I offered to make him a bow like mine.

We had really settled into the tribe, now. We could speak their language with reasonable ease, but were still learning something new every day. It was a lot easier to communicate verbally instead of drawing pictures in the sand and waving our hands in the air.

*   *   *

One morning, the children were swimming and splashing about in the lake when a shout went up.

"Croc!"

Everyone made a dash for the shore. A man in one of the canoes plunged his spear into the water, but it missed its mark. He shouted and pointed at the dark shape heading straight for the children.

Mary and I were close to the water and both of us ran into the lake until we were waist deep, screaming at the kids to swim faster. As they reached us we grabbed them and literally threw them up onto the bank.

Three of the children were still in the water, swimming like mad – about ten feet behind them the eyes and nostrils of the croc slid beneath the water. We caught hold of two of the children and threw them out – Mary grabber the last one by the wrist and lifted her clean out of the water.

Before she could turn, in a moment that seemed to stretch on for an eternity, the lake seemed to open up. Two thirds of the crocodile's body came out of the water. Its jaws snapped shut around the little girl with a resounding "crack". She must have died instantly. As it crashed back into the water, all I could see was the child's arm sticking out of the great creature's mouth, Mary still clinging grimly to it.

As the crocodile went for deep water, Mary went with it. I was screaming at her to let go – she was dragged about ten yards through the water when the child's arm was wrenched from her grasp. I swam to her and with all our strength we swam hard for shore. There was a splash right next to me that made my heart leap to my mouth – for a moment I thought it was the croc, or one of his friends, back for more, but it was Mbata. He helped us towards the bank.

The men in the canoes were rowing hard after us, pointing and shouting. Just a few feet to go – another splash behind us made the water swirl around our legs. I felt a searing pain in my left calf. Limping, I helped Mbata drag Mary out of the water; she was crying hysterically.

"Is everyone okay?" I shouted, still panicked.

Apart from one little girl, I thought. Somewhere in the village, her mother screamed.

The lake was churning with crocs.

Mbata pointed at my leg. Blood was pouring from a long, deep gash. We went back to the hut and dressed it. Mary couldn't stop crying. I tried to comfort her, but it did no good.

We found out later a man in one of the canoes had speared the croc at the last second. He had saved our lives.

After that, life got easier. The tribe were even more friendly towards us than ever – though we hadn't been able to save all the children, our bravery had made an impression. The chief invited us to sit and talk with him again. He wanted to know about our home. When I told him about cars, busses and trains he just laughed and laughed. I'm sure he didn't believe me.

*   *   *

One morning, I cut two posts and dug them into the ground about ten feet apart, just outside our hut, overlooking the lake. I fixed a cross member at the top, from pole to pole. On this I built a framework and covered it with long, wide leaves for shade.

I made a crude hammock from creepers and lined it with furs. We now have two hammocks, one each

"Mary, come out here," I shouted.

"What you want?" she answered.

"Just come here."

She looked out of the hut.

"Ooh, a new bed," she giggled.

"It's a hammock, not a bed," I told her and lifted her up in my arms, laying her gently in it.

The motion rocked her gently to and fro and she smiled up at me.

"Nice – I like." She smiled.

I lifted her out and climbed in it myself. Mary gently rocked me for a little while, but she suddenly stopped.

"Oh," she gasped, looking down. Her hands flew to her belly.

"What's up?" I asked.

"Baby coming," she whispered, awed.

"What?" I shouted, stunned.

"Baby coming," she repeated.

I rolled out of the hammock and fell flat on my face in the dust. My brain went blank. I knew I was supposed to do something, but I had no idea what. In my panic, I ran around the village, shouting the baby's coming, the baby's coming!

Mary laughed at me, running around like a headless chicken. Drums started beating. The village came to life around us; Mary's friend came over and took her hand, as she had done for her.

As my blind panic subsided I lifted Mary up and carried her into our hunt, laying her on the bed. Some of the village girls came in with cool water, bathing her naked body while they chattered excitedly.

As before, the rest of the village began to assemble outside the hut, including the chief.

I held Mary's other hand; she looked up at me and smiled. The smile turned to a wince as another contraction came.

One of the girls handed me a cup of liquid and indicated that Mary ought to take a drink. I gave her a sip of it, giving her a little more after each contraction. They were coming quicker now. Sweat was pouring from her body and her breathing was getting heavier and more laboured.

I felt utterly helpless. I wanted to ease her pain, but I just had to stand there and watch as the woman I loved went through the greatest and most painful miracle that God ever created.

"I love you," was all I could say, over and over, as I mopped her brow.

"Love you *too*," she said, caught by a big contraction.

With a scream she pushed and out came the baby's head. She relaxed again.

"Big breaths," I said. It was all I could think of.

I gave her another drink and watched in amazement as the baby's head turned slowly sideways. Mary growled with the effort of pushing and suddenly there lay the tiny body of a little girl.

For a moment, I panicked. Both mother and baby were motionless.

One of the girls picked the baby up and wrapped her in a cloth. Another took a straw and used it to suck the mucus out of the tiny girl's mouth and nostrils. A third girl dipped a cloth in cold water and began to wash the baby down. As soon as the cool water touched the child's body she gave a sharp intake of breath, letting out a loud, indignant cry at having to start her life in this world. The cries echoed through the village and our tribe cheered and clapped.

At the sound of her baby's cries, Mary opened her eyes and held out her arms to hold her child, running on pure instinct.

I was handed two pieces of twine and told to tie them about three inches apart in the middle of the umbilical cord. I cut between the knots with a knife. While the girls bathed and cleaned Mary, I was ushered outside to present our daughter to the tribe.

I have never felt so proud as I did that day, holding our tiny miracle in my arms and sharing her with the rest of the tribe.

I took her back into our hut, where Mary was sitting up and smiling, resting after her ordeal. I placed the little mite in her arms and she held her gently, as only a mother can. The baby's eyes were open, staring up at her mother; Mary rocked gently to and fro, humming softly.

It made my heart flutter to see mother and child bonding so sweetly.

*　　*　　*

That evening, another feast was prepared in honour of our new arrival. Mary and the baby came out for a while, but she soon tired and went back to the hut to sleep. I stayed out drinking, popping back every now and then to check on her and the baby. The next morning I awoke with a bit of a hangover. Some kind soul had put me in the hammock to sleep it off. I fell out and went into the hut.

The sight that greeted me nearly moved me to tears. Mary was sitting up in bed with our baby at her breast, humming gently.

She looked up as I came in.

"You drunk," she smiled. "You sleep outside."

I went over and kissed her.

"You are a very clever girl. Look what you have given us – a beautiful little baby, who looks just like her mum."

She put her arm around my waist and we watched our little miracle suckling at her breast.

CHAPTER SIXTEEN

Over the next few weeks I looked after Mary and the baby until they were both fit and well, keeping my hand in by practicing my fighting skills when I could.

We named the baby Jawana, meaning 'beautiful flower'. I didn't know if she had

Down' Syndrome or not, I couldn't tell at this age. Even if she did I didn't care, I loved her with all my heart.

I was bringing my weapons back from the clearing one day when another shout of 'Crocs' came up from the lake. I watched the kids screaming and running from the water. I couldn't imagine letting Jawana swim in the lake when she was a little older, it was far too dangerous. Yet Mary would take her to the lake and sit in the water to wash, without a second thought about crocodiles.

Then a thought struck me.

"A swimming pool!"

If we built a swimming pool the kids could swim and play in relative safety, away from the crocodiles. I put the idea to Mbata, who asked the chief and he agreed to the idea. I took the fire axe and, with the help of some of our neighbours, found a large clump of bamboo.

I cut down a couple of dozen lengths, about eight feet long by six inches in diameter. Making a point at one end of each stave. Back at the lake we banged the first stake into the ground at two feet from the water's edge, and put in a second stake three feet from that. We drove in stakes every two feet and out into the lake, making a semi-circle stretching about thirty feet into the lake, all the way back to shore.

We had to go back and cut dozens more stakes until the semi-circle was complete. Then we cut short cross pieces and bound them with twine. On these we tied long lengths of bamboo to walk on. Now we had a jetty down to the bottom of the lake and three feet above the platform to act as a fence.

To finish it off we dropped boulders into the water at the base of the fence so that the crocs couldn't get underneath. The water in the inner circle was about six feet deep at the jetty, getting shallower towards the shore.

The whole village watched as I walked out onto the jetty, dived in and swam to shore. The children, laughing with glee, hurled themselves into the water. I felt rather pleased with myself.

I walked back to our hut, where Mary was lying in the hammock, cuddling Jawana. The big fella was standing a little way away, staring at them again. He moved away when I walked towards them.

I practiced my archery, knife throwing and swordsmanship every day. My confidence was growing, though I did wonder whether I would still be so confident in a real fight.

The only thing I was not very proficient at was the spear. I couldn't hit the inside of a barn with the doors shut. One day I was practicing throwing at a tree and missing by miles. Mbata came up behind me – he started laughing.

Taking the spear, he aimed at a slim branch about twenty yards away. It left his hand at a terrific pace and split the branch in two. Now it was his turn to gloat. He gave me a few pointers and I started to practice in earnest.

That evening, after Mary had fed Jawana and put her to bed, we climbed into the hammock together and lay watching the sun set into the lake. Mary had her head on my chest and was humming softly to herself, content.

"Do you miss home?" I asked.

"No."

"Not even a little bit?"

"No," she said again.

The hammock rocked gently back and forth as we dozed in each other's arms. Living here, I was the happiest I had ever been in my life.

As the sun disappeared at one end of the lake, the moon rose at the other, as if it had slipped right out of the water itself. It was magical.

*   *   *

I had noticed an old lady in the village. She was a bit of a loner. She kept doves – hundreds of them – in and around her hut. Wherever she went, they flew all around her, landing on her arms, head and shoulders. She was quite a character. I don't know if she bred them for food, or kept them as pets, but she never went anywhere without them.

The children would run up to her and scare them off, but the doves would fly up around and landed back on her again.

One afternoon, some women and children came into the village. They were carrying sacks of seed that resembled wheat, which the village made bread from. One of the women was covered in blood.

They told us they had been attacked; A women and two children had been killed.

The men gathered their spears. I ran into our hut, put on my quiver and sword, and grabbed my bow and shield. As I came out, Mary picked up the axe and followed me.

"You stay here," I said.

"I come," she replied.

"Stay, and look after Jawana," I said, gently.

Mary hesitated.

"Okay," she said. "I stay."

I left her at the door to our hut, still holding the axe, watching me run into the jungle behind the others. After a couple of miles we came to a stream. The grain the women had been harvesting was growing on either bank. We followed the stream for about fifty yards and came upon a sight that made my blood run cold.

Three bodies – or what was left of them – were lying in the grass, their hands and feet cut off and their stomachs slit open. They had been disembowelled and decapitated. We never found their heads.

Lookouts were posted around the periphery and we wrapped the bodies in large leaves, carrying them carefully back to the village.

"How could anyone get pleasure from this inhuman slaughter?" I murmured, aghast.

On our return, the chief was waiting for us. He raised his arms in the air and said a few words. The drums started beating and people were crying. Mary came out and held my hand, tears running down her cheeks. I realised then that these people were not members of a warring tribe, but a gentle people who just wanted to live in peace. An easy target for sadistic bullies to prey upon.

Behind the village was a strip of land near the cliff face. A hole was excavated, about ten feet in diameter and five feet deep. In this a funeral pyre was constructed. The three bodies placed on top and the fire lit.

As the flames rose into the air, everyone stood around, watching silently as the fire consumed the dead.

"Rest in peace," I said, softly.

The three were a mother and two daughters – a teenager and child. It took many hours for the bodies to burn. As the flames died down, one man sat cross legged, staring into the embers, his face twisted into a mask of horror. One by one, the mourners left, leaving him sitting there motionless. I took him to be the husband and father.

As the last flame died, I put my hand on his shoulder. He got to his feet, picked up one of the wooden shovels and started to fill the hole with earth. I did the same and we toiled together until the grave was filled. Then Mary placed some flowers on it and we left the man to grieve in peace.

*   *   *

The next day the chief invited me to his hut. He seemed glad to see me when I arrived. He gestured for me to sit. Seated behind the chief were ten exquisitely beautiful young girls and one middle aged woman. All his wives, I guessed. The older woman was the matriarch, acting as a sort of manager and housekeeper to keep her husband and the other wives in check. How he could keep eleven women happy I will never know! I had enough of a job just keeping one.

On the chief's command, food and drink were laid out for us to eat and we had a good, long natter.

I asked him why the women went out into the jungle to collect grain, with all the dangers that they faced out there from wild animals and the other tribes. The chief explained that the grain was plentiful in the wild, but none of it grew close to the village. I told him about farming in Europe, how we cultivated land and grew our crops by sowing and reaping in controlled fields.

I suggested that we could try a similar system near the village so that the women wouldn't have to leave and face the dangers of the jungle alone. They were going to be much safer near the village than out of it.

The thought of what seemed like needless work in fields when the plants grew naturally didn't appeal to the chief, but he agreed to let me try anyway.

Dotted around the village were little grassy areas, each about twenty yards across. I made myself a set of primitive tools from materials harvested from the jungle and around the village and began to clear one of them. I began to attract a small audience of women and children, who stood and watched what I was doing for a while. It wasn't long before they joined in and started helping me, quite without being asked. After the first area was cleared we dug the ground over.

I paused when we had finished – this was hard work, particularly in the close humidity of the jungle. I knew that planting usually happened in the springtime in England, but I had no real gauge of the seasons here. There seemed to be one long, hot, balmy season, all year round. This was as good a time as any to experiment. I hoped that the seeds I was about to sow would grow.

I watched the women of my village dusting themselves off and hurrying away to prepare the evening meal, thinking about the way things were back in England. Back home, the men were the basic bread winners and most of the women stayed at home to look after their families, but things were beginning to change. There had been so much social upheaval in the years preceding the 1950s, and England was on its way to becoming a place of social equality. The way I felt it should be.

Things were very different out here in the jungle. Here, the women waited on their men, raised the children, did most of the heavy lifting, prepared the meals – and the men took all the credit for their work. I shook my head sadly, doubting that the people of this village would ever enjoy the gender equality I had come to expect back home.

After making sure that the land was well-prepared for sowing, I stood up at the evening meal and asked for volunteers to come out into the jungle with me and collect grain for our new, small fields. Every last woman and child raised their hands – again, I was impressed by their courage and their willingness to work for the good of the village. I selected ten single women and no children – there was no point in taking undue risks.

*   *   *

With fifteen men as guards, we set out the following day, carrying sacks. The journey to the stream was uneventful, but on arrival I asked Mbata to send two men down each path as lookouts. The rest of the men helped the women to fill the sacks with grain.

After about five hours of hard work, the sacks were beginning to mount up. We were quite enjoying the work, it was pleasant to be out in the sunshine together as a community. Our work was cut short when two of our scouts came running back, pointing along the trail behind them. Men were coming.

Mbata and I barked orders, while the other men hid the sacks and got the women into what cover they could find. The two of us concealed ourselves in the trees where we had an unobstructed view of the path. It was only a matter of minutes before we heard voices: along the path came six men, walking in single file.

"Are they the same tribe as before?" I whispered to Mbata, and he nodded.

My heart began to pound in my chest. I wasn't afraid anymore, I was filled with a blind fury at what our women had gone through. The first man was walking straight towards me, and none of them had spotted us. I put an arrow to my bow, stood up and let fly – the arrow shot through the leaves of my hiding place and hit him square in the chest. He dropped like a stone.

The rest of the party were taken by surprise – they obviously hadn't expected any resistance. Screaming abuse I drew my sword and charged at the second man. He raised his spear; it glanced off my shield. At the same time, I slashed him across the chest.

The rest of our attackers spread out across the path, their spears raised and ready. Mbata's spear whistled over my shoulder, taking out the third man. Our men ran out, yelling and brandishing their weapons. Realising they were outnumbered, the other tribe retreated, scattering back into the grass. Two of them fell before they reached the jungle, spears sticking out of their backs.

Only one man made it into the cover of the trees; we chased him for a little while, but he escaped.

"Is everybody alright?" I asked Mbata.

"Yes," he replied. "No injuries."

We rolled the bodies into the stream, which began to carry them onwards. I watched them go with a sour taste in my mouth. If they got as far as the lake the crocs would find a use for them.

We gathered our sacks of grain and the women carried them on their heads back to the village. It was funny watching them walking ahead of us, their bodies moving to and fro while their heads stayed perfectly still. I couldn't fathom how they did it. Balancing such heavy weights aloft and maintaining such a fast walking pace was amazing. I supposed that part of their focus must be a fear of the man who escaped bringing his friends along the trail towards us.

Back at the village, we laid out the wheat to dry. When the grain and husks started to separate in the hot sun, the women and girls beat it with twigs, blowing away the husks and leaving the grain behind.

I showed the children how to make drills in the fields with sticks. They were pleased to help out – they seemed to see it as a great game.

Together, we planted our seeds and covered them over with leafy branches to protect them from the birds and wildlife. The women and I watered them every night with water from the lake. Even Mary came out and helped. She enjoyed the company of the other girls. It was great to see her happy.

Jawana was getting bigger every day. There were no signs of Down's Syndrome in her. Mary was an excellent mother; it came to her as natural instinct, and she took to it like a duck to water. Often, I felt a bit left out, but I accepted it as part of a mother and baby's bonding. After all without me she wouldn't feel safe to do so.

At the end of each day when Jawana was asleep, Mary and I would cuddle up in a hammock and discuss the events of the day. Through the daytime we spoke our new language, but in the evening we spoke to one another in English. We had already decided to teach Jawana both languages. It was always possible that we might get rescued one day.

*   *   *

In the weeks that followed, the wheat grew tall and strong. We had no reprisals from the other tribe, which came as something of a relief. Maybe they had thought better of attacking villagers who were prepared to defend themselves. But we stayed vigilant, all the same.

One sunny morning, we rose and went to the lake to bathe. Mary sat in the water with Jawana, enjoying the cool water lapping around her waist. For a second I glimpsed the reflection of myself in the water and went back for a better look. I had actually put on weight – I now had muscles where there had never been muscles before.

"It must be the fresh fruit and meat," I thought, out loud. *"It's been a long time since I had a carry out or fast food."*

I walked up onto the jetty and leaned against the fence. I allowed my mind drift back to my life in England while I enjoyed the morning sun. I watched Mary as she bathed and played with our beautiful daughter in the shallows. She noticed me watching and gave me a little wave.

In many ways, Mary and I were both happier and healthier than we had ever been back in England. We were accepted by and played active parts in the community around us.

As I smiled fondly at my Mary, my eyes lighted on some marks in the sand on the shoreline. I frowned. It looked like something had travelled from the pool, around the jetty and into the lake. No... from the lake and into the pool.

I felt my heart clench in my chest. I scanned the water – I spotted a ripple and a dark shape below the surface, heading

131

straight for Mary and Jawana.

"Mary!" I screamed. *"Get out of the pool!"*

Mary sprang to her feet, carrying Jawana with her; I watched, horrified, as the dark shape began to pick up speed. They would never get out of the pool in time.

I drew my knife, ran round the jetty and dove into the water, as high and as far as I could. As luck would have it, I came down right above the crocodile. I opened my eyes as I plunged under the water. I took the great animal by surprise, landing on its back. I locked my arms around its neck and my legs over its back legs.

The power of the creature was immediately obvious. I could feel it surging beneath me, lifting us both out of the water, towering above Mary and the baby. I glimpsed the look of sheer terror on her face before we came crashing back down into the pool. As we plunged back down, all I could think was, 'Don't drop the knife, don't drop the knife, don't drop the knife'.

I held on tight as the croc headed for deeper water, spinning round and round, trying to dislodge me. I pressed myself tight to its scaly body my cheek pressed against its head, between its eyes. Together, we rushed in and out of the water, the pressure of holding on and profound dizziness from all the spinning making me lightheaded.

The next time we surfaced, I held on tightly with one arm and stabbed the knife into its eye. It was thrashing about and I was getting weaker. I didn't know how much longer I would be able to hang on. I tried to stab it in the throat, but I couldn't get a good swing under the water without being thrown off. Spinning round and round I could feel the gravel on the bottom tearing at my skin but I felt no pain.

We surged back up out of the water. With my strength waning I knew I had to do something – and fast. In a last, desperate frenzy I stabbed at its throat over and over again. The croc and I crashed back into the pool, my body underneath his. The impact knocked all the breath out of me and then everything went black.

When I came round, I was lying on the bank, looking skyward. Mary was sitting next to me, crying. I felt hollow; numb. She must have seen me open my eyes, and put her arms around me and held me tightly.

As my vision returned, so did the pain. Everything hurt. My skin felt red hot where I had been tolled across the bottom of the lake. Every bone in my body felt broken.

Our fellow villagers were standing around us, pointing and jabbering. Slowly, I got into a sitting position and testing my limbs. Although I was in a great deal of pain, it didn't seem as if anything was broken. A few feet away lay the crocodile. He was a huge beast, at least fourteen feet from nose to tail. My knife was still sticking out of its neck, only the handle visible.

I blinked stupidly at it for a moment, unable to believe what I'd managed to do.

I looked at our daughter, safe and sleeping innocently next to her mother, ignorant of all the ruckus. I thanked God that they were both safe

Slowly, I got to my feet and pulled the knife from the crocodile. Around me, people were cheering, but it was difficult to hear over the strange buzzing noise that had taken up residence in my brain. Mary helped me stagger back to our hut.

The blood had dried now, embedding dirt and grit into my flesh. On the chief's orders, four of his wives appeared with warm water and a strong smelling green paste. They spent hours bathing me and cleaning my body, before gently rubbing the green paste into my wounds. It stung at first, but after a few seconds I could already feel it doing me good – apart from the horrible smell, that is.

When they were finished, Mary gave me a cool fruit drink and I climbed wearily into the hammock. I fell into a deep, dreamless sleep.

I slept all day, and all the next night. When I awoke, the sun was shining again.

134

CHAPTER SEVENTEEN

I climbed out of the hammock, feeling very stiff indeed. My wounds appeared to be healing – they weren't even painful anymore. When Mary saw that I was awake she took my hand in hers and led me to the lake.

"Wash," she instructed. "You stink."

Just for a second I hesitated by the edge of the pool. The children were swimming and playing in the water so I supposed it must be safe. I sat in the shallows, aching and still tired, while Mary washed me all over.

My wounds looked pretty good, all things considered. I wondered what was in that paste – it had worked on me so fast I might almost be prepared to swear it had magical properties.

The hospitals back home would probably kill for something like this!

With a sweet smile, Mary took my hand and looked into my eyes.

"You very brave," she said. "Very, very brave."

I looked at her and felt my face form an answering smile. I couldn't help it.

"I love you," I told her, and watched her face light up.

"Love you to, she smiled."

I spent the next few days doing as little as possible, just eating, sleeping and playing with our daughter until I was fully recovered.

One morning, there was a bit of a commotion in the village. Mary stuck her head out of the hut – then she screamed.

"Dada!"

She ran out into the sunshine and I followed. There, in the

135

middle of the village, stood Reg, still holding that blasted briefcase. He was staring about wide-eyed and looked a little afraid.

I couldn't believe what I was seeing, but it was definitely him. He had a leaf tied onto his head, a dirty old white shirt on, all torn up, and a pair of very ripped shorts. When he saw Mary running towards him, he dropped the case and held out his arms.

"Mary!" he gasped.

She ran to him and they hugged each other, Reg swinging her to and fro, overjoyed. When she finally stood back, he looked at me and held out his hand. I just put my arms around him, and we hugged each other, too.

"I thought you were dead!" he exclaimed.

"We thought you had been killed back at the cave!" I told him.

Mbata made his way over to us, through the growing throng of villagers.

"Reg," I said, "I'd like you to meet Mbata. This is the lad we saved back at the cave before we were attacked."

Reg held out his hand and Mbata shook it.

After Reg had been introduced to the chief, he was taken to a hut and given the same treatment as we were when we had first arrived at the village. That evening, another big feast was prepared in honour of his arrival, and Reg sat between Mary and myself in the circle.

"You've got a good set up here," he smiled. "While you two have been living it up, I've spent weeks dodging here and there in the jungle. The day of the attack I was emptying one of the snares when I heard voices approaching. I hid in the undergrowth and waited until they had passed me by. The trouble was, they headed straight for the cave, so I had no way of warning you.

"I know the two of you put up a good fight," he continued. "I saw one of them fly out from the cave, clutching at a flare in his stomach. After they had all left, I waited a few hours and then went back to the cave. I saw the carnage and you two were nowhere to be seen, so I took you both to be dead or captured."

I told him how we were outnumbered and had had to jump through the vortex and into the pool, and how the tribe had taken us and made us welcome. Reg, Mary and I sat up until the small hours, catching up on the last few months. Mary kept hugging and kissing him, happy to have him back.

Eventually, we wandered back to our hut.

"You can sleep in our hammock tonight," I said. "But before you do, we want to show you something. Come inside."

Mary held his hand and led him over to the bed where Jawana was sleeping. He looked in.

"Oh, bless!" he whispered, so as not to wake her. "A little girl – she is beautiful."

He put his arm around Mary.

"You clever girl."

Mary went all coy and shy, though Reg and I could both tell she was very proud. She smiled up at him.

Reg climbed into the hammock.

"Whatever you do, don't get out of bed without looking," I laughed, "Or you might learn the hard way, like I did."

Mary put her arms around his neck.

"Night- night, Dada."

"Goodnight, gorgeous," he said, patting her head. "I'll see you in the morning."

The next day, the village gathered together and we built a hut for Reg. When it was finished, he stood looking at it with tears in his eyes.

At last he spoke, "A place of my own," he said, happily.

*   *   *

For the next few months, the village settled down into everyday jungle routine. Everyone went about their business – hunting, fishing, tending the wheat fields – with great success and no interruption. It became obvious that in time we would need bigger wheat fields, but the idea was proved sound, particularly as the women and children felt safer.

Every day we practiced with our weapons, the whole tribe together. I still hoped we would never need to use them, but in my heart I knew we would have to, one day.

Jawana was about eighteen months old now, and still growing fast. Proudly, I had watched her first steps, felt her first tooth, heard her first words. Any chance I got I spent time with Mary and Jawana. We went on jungle picnics. I made a swing from vines and pushed them on it. I would put Jawana on my back and swim about the pool. She held her arms around my neck so tightly she almost choked me.

She was becoming quite a daddy's girl now, cuddling up with me and falling asleep in my lap. Whenever she hurt herself it was always 'Dada' she called for; she had her mother and I wrapped around her little finger, and we loved every second of it. It was now obvious that she didn't have Down's Syndrome, or any other developmental issues, and I was pleased about that.

One day, Mary and I were working in the wheat fields when we heard kids laughing and screaming behind our hut. We ran round to find the children pointing at the back of our toilet. Jawana had tripped and fallen feet first into the pit, up to her neck deep in excrement.

I lay flat on my stomach, grabbed her hand and pulled her out. Our daughter was surrounded by a magnificent pong. Mary pushed her towards the lake with a stick, holding her nose.

She told her to splash about in the water to get the muck off, then she scrubbed her over and over, until her skin turned red. Still, she couldn't get the smell off her, even by rubbing perfumed oil into her skin.

138

I smiled to myself. The little monkey!

Standing behind a tree, watching us, was the big fella who seemed intent on Mary and Jawana. I crept up behind him and as he turned, this time I punched him on the jaw. He went back against a tree, but otherwise he barely flinched.

For a few moments we faced each other. He was over a foot taller than me, and a few of stone heavier.

"Stop leching over my wife, you bastard," I shouted.

At this point, Mary ran out of the hut with the fire axe in her hand. She stood next to me and glared at the big fella. He looked at her and then back at me, turned and walked off. We watched him disappear between the huts. I kissed Mary on the forehead.

"Don't like him."

"No," I said. "Me neither."

*   *   *

One morning I was lying in the hammock, minding my own business. The air was hot and still. Mary and Jawana were in the hut out of the hot sun. A man ran into the main clearing, shouting. I looked up in time to see a spear strike him full in the back. He fell face down in the dust.

Behind him, fifty warriors streamed out of the jungle, brandishing spears and shields. I recognised them by their painted bodies. This was the same tribe that had killed our women at the stream, nearly a year before.

In moments, the village was in uproar. They took us totally by surprise. Our men ran for their weapons, though some didn't make it. All around, children ran back and forth in the confusion, the women chasing them, trying to keep them safe.

I grabbed my sword and my shield; with all these people running about, my bow was useless – I couldn't risk hitting members of our own tribe. I raced across the clearing as the chief emerged from his hut, ready to face his enemies, flanked by his bodyguards.

The attackers were so intent on killing the chief that they didn't see me until I was among them. I ran in screaming, hacking, cutting and jabbing any painted savage in sight. I felt my heart plummet as I turned. Mary had Jawana in one hand and the fire axe in the other. She ran over to the chief and stood Jawana next to him – without looking, he put his hand on her shoulder and held her close. She wrapped her arms around his leg and held on.

Mary lifted the axe high above her head, her tongue out in concentration, and ran into the melee. I felt a pain across my shoulder as a spear glanced off; leaving a gash. I turned to face my attacker, who rushed towards me, armed with a knife. My sword found his stomach and he fell. Now our men ran back to us, fully armed.

One savage sprinted past me, screaming, closely followed by Mary, axe up and tongue out. As she brought it down, she lost pace and he gained it. She missed her target by a hair and he disappeared into the jungle. Lifting the axe she looked around for another target, and off she went again.

We were stronger now, and the battle was beginning to go our way. Our enemy retreated back into the jungle. One man, breaking away from the others, made a final attempt at the chief. He ran through our ranks, spear raised. As he was about to throw it, the chief lifted his head in defiance, looking his enemy dead in the eye.

Crack! The savage hit the ground hard. Mary stood over him, her axe blade buried deep into his back. She looked up at the chief, grinned widely and pulled the axe out, charging after the retreating attackers.

They were disappearing into the jungle now; the last man turned and hurled his spear at me. I raised my shield and it glanced off, passing behind me. I watched him disappear into the trees, beyond my reach.

I turned and froze. It felt like my heart had turned to stone. Mary had followed me as we chased our attackers off. She was on her knees, looking up at me in confusion, her axe lying on the ground beside her.

The spear had glanced off my shield and hit her in the stomach at a right angle. I could see the blade sticking six inches out of her back.

"MARY!" I bellowed.

I picked her up, my heart pounding. She put her arms around my neck. With my mind blank I carried her back to our hut. Mbata ran over, a look of horror on his young face, and guided me inside. I laid Mary on the bed and just stood, staring at the spear sticking out of her, my mind racing. I had no idea what to do next. I could barely think at all.

The chief came in and put his hand on my shoulder. I felt numb. Drums were beating all around the village, slowly, like some kind of death march. The witchdoctor danced around our hut, shaking his rattle.

Mary's body was drenched in sweat. Two of the chief's wives bathed her, soothing her fevered brow. The old woman with the doves came in and placed a pot on the floor. The witchdoctor danced around, shouting and pointing his rattle at the pot. Then the chief's wives held it aloft.

The old woman put her hands in it and drew out the foul smelling green paste and slicked it over the shaft of the spear. The witchdoctor was still chanting. The old woman told me to grasp the blade. Outside the hut, as if responding to some unknown cue, the drums stopped, leaving the entire village eerie and silent.

The chief met my eyes and nodded. I looked down at Mary, my heart in my mouth. I knew what I had to do.

As gently as I could, I pulled the blade through her body, dragging the green paste through the wound. Mary didn't move a muscle as the old woman plugged the wounds with some mashed up leaves. Everybody went to leave; I looked around, lost and faintly nauseous.

As the chief reached the door he turned and looked at me.

"Jungle medicine is very strong," he said.

My mind was in overdrive as I was left alone. I couldn't think. I put my hand on her shoulder – her skin felt cold and clammy under my fingers.

I pulled myself together. I had to think of Jawana and look after Mary. I wondered if I would be strong enough to help her through this. Would I crack under the pressure? Was I going to lose my wife?

After a while, my whirling mind began to slow down and I could think a little more clearly. I bathed Mary with cool water and patted her dry. She was still sweating profusely, her breathing slow and shallow. As I stared down at my wife, watching her struggle to survive, I felt a small hand take mine. It was Jawana.

She looked at her mother, then back up at me, her eyes brimming with tears. I lifted her up.

"Well, my beautiful little flower, your mummy needs us to look after her now," I told her, gently.

"Yes," she whispered, frightened. "I love you daddy."

My heart gave an uncomfortable clench. Mary must have taught her to say that before…

We stood, watching over her until Jawana fell asleep in my arms. I laid her gently on her bed and kissed her goodnight. The loss of a parent was such a traumatic thing to happen to a young child. I only hoped it wouldn't come to that. Whatever happened, I knew I would be there for our daughter.

I went back to Mary. I sat beside her, stroking her hair. She meant the world to me, if I lost her…

The thought had never crossed my mind before – Mary and I had been constant companions for so long now. I sat beside her through the night, holding her hand gently in mine.

CHAPTER EIGHTEEN

When I awoke, Jawana was standing next to our bed, staring at her mother. We both looked up when the chief's wives came in to bathe Mary. Conscious of her distress, they let Jawana help in her own little way. The old woman returned to redress her wounds.

As I watched her work, Reg came in and put his arm around my shoulder.

"I'm sorry, mate," he murmured. "If there is anything I can do, just ask."

For eight days every hour I moistened her lips with water. Finally, on the ninth day, she stirred. She managed to take a few sips of water and went back to sleep. At least she had drank some fluid. I sat watching her with Jawana settled on my lap. Mary lay covered in perspiration, the dim moonlight outlining her labouring body, her chest gently rising and falling as she breathed.

From the corner of my eye I caught a tiny movement near the doorway, followed by a muffled noise. I drew my knife, suddenly fearful. What the hell was it? It was too small to be a croc – I tensed. My heart was beating so loud you could almost hear it. As it came nearer, I lay Jawana on the bed next to her mother.

Something fell over in the darkness – it was too clumsy to be a leopard; too quiet for a boar. I peered into the patch of shadow by the door, breathing softly, ready for anything.

Then something wet and cold touched my leg, catching me off guard. I cried out, leaping in one bound onto the bed and dropping my knife.

Hearing the noise, Mbata ran in with a torch, followed by our neighbours. As the flame filled the hut, my eyes fell on my tormentor. Sitting on the ground, looking up at me, one ear up, one ear down, its tongue lolling out of its mouth, was a tiny puppy. It wagged its tail, enthusiastically.

Everyone started laughing. I must have looked totally stupid, standing on a bed, screaming, afraid of a little puppy. Reg joined the small crowd around the doorway and shook his head, grinning.

That said it all.

Jawana had awoken in the commotion and was laughing so hard that tears were running down her face. I looked over at her mother, but she was still out cold. God I hoped there would be a change soon.

I jumped down from the bed and approached my adversary. His head bowed immediately, expecting a beating. I picked him up and he went mad with excitement, licking my face and hands, desperate to be my friend.

I handed him to Jawana, who already had her arms outstretched. She took the puppy and held him close.

At least she would have something to take her mind off her mother's condition, I thought.

* * *

For the next three days things stayed the same with Mary. The old lady came and redressed her wounds and the chief's wives bathed her. I gave her sips of water. It was hard to watch her lying there, silent and still. I began to wonder whether I would ever hear her voice again.

On the fourth day, I had dozed off and awoke to find Mary staring at me, her eyes strangely expressionless. For a horrible, nearly endless second, I thought she had died with her eyes open. Then her face lit up and she beamed.

"Ello, it's me," she said.

I ran over and threw my arms around her.

144

"Oh Mary, I have missed you so much!"

I held her close and burst into tears. She cupped my face in her hands.

"Don't cry," she said. "I love you."

"And I love you, so much."

Jawana ran in, hearing her mother's voice.

"Mummy! Mummy!"

I picked her up and put her on the bed beside her mother. They hugged and kissed, holding each other for some time.

I sat down totally drained. The little dog padded over to me and pawed at me, standing on his hind legs looking up at me. I lifted him onto my lap and stroked him. Watching Mary and Jawana made me feel good. I was so tired that my eyes closed and I quickly drifted off into a deep sleep.

When I woke up next it was just getting dark. Reg was sitting next to me.

"Hello mate," he said. "They've been taking care of Mary while you slept and I'm babysitting. Mary looks great," he told me. "It's nice to have her back. See you tomorrow, mate," he smiled, and left.

I lay on the bed beside Mary. She opened her eyes, smiled and kissed me.

"You lazybones," she smiled. "You sleep all day."

I was relieved to find that she was no longer sweating and her skin was a normal temperature. For the rest of the night we lay talking and kissing. I never wanted to go through the trauma of the last few days again. The thought of losing her had nearly destroyed me.

*   *   *

Over the next few weeks she got stronger. The wounds healed, leaving two nasty scars, but it wasn't long before she was her old self again. From that day on, whenever we parted or met, went to bed or woke up, Mary and I kissed and said 'I love you'.

In this precarious way of life, I wanted to make sure that if anything happened to either of us, the last words we spoke to one another would be 'I love you'.

My mind drifted back to the battle. We were taken completely by surprise. Plans had to be made so it could never happen again. Our village needed to be able to defend itself.

Jawana and the puppy were, by this point, inseparable. When she was asleep I tried to train him. This was more difficult than I had expected. In fact, it was a bit of a joke. When I told him to 'sit' he just stood there, wagging his tail. If I threw a stick and told him to 'fetch', he would sit down, as if to say 'you want it, you fetch it'. When I told him to 'heel', he would lollop off into the jungle.

One morning while out hunting, the most beautiful bird I had ever seen landed in a nearby tree. It had feathers in a riot of colour – red, white and yellow. While I was admiring this wonder of nature, Mbata drew his bow and felled the bird. I felt sad that a magnificent specimen like this had to die so that we could eat.

That evening, after the bird had been plucked, a thought struck me. When I told Mary and Jawana they both clapped their hands with glee.

The next day I took a piece of hide, cut out a circle about eighteen inches across, then cut out a wedge at its centre. Mary sewed the edges together to make a bowl.

"Jawana," I said, "we need an old bird's nest, can you find me one? There are plenty in the trees," I told her. "Just find a small one, about as big as my hand."

Jawana ran off happily and came back a few minutes later with three nests, all different sizes. I picked one.

"This will be the finest Easter bonnet ever made," I laughed.

"What's an Easter bonnet?" asked Jawana.

"I'll explain later."

Mary sewed the nest to the underside of the bowl. I cut a thin length of hide, cut a hole each side of the hat threaded the hide through and tied it off as a chin strap. We pierced holes all around the brim and pushed the coloured feathers through them, into the nest in the middle.

Then we went to the lake shore together and found three egg shaped pebbles to fit the nest. Jawana painted them different colours and then painted black spots on them. When they were dry I stuck them into the nest with tree resin.

"There," I said. "Finished."

Mary put it on Jawana's head. She looked so pretty and it brought a lump to my throat. She reminded me of my childhood when all the girls wore Easter bonnets and ate chocolate eggs.

"Right, let's go and surprise someone," I said.

As we walked through the village, our neighbours stared at this wondrous garment and began to follow us. By the time we reached our destination the entire tribe was behind us, even the chief.

We approached a hut at the bottom of a rock face at least a hundred feet high, peppered with holes where hundreds of doves had made their nests.

The old lady came out of her hut, her shoulders garlanded with doves. She had a face like stone, peering around at the crowd. The whole village went quiet, waiting to see what would happen. Mary held out the hat.

"We made this for you," she said. "To say thank you for all you have done for us." I smiled.

The old woman stared blankly at the hat, a look of clear incomprehension on her wrinkled face.

Mary put it on.

"It's a hat," she explained. "To keep the sun off."

She took it off again and offered it to the old woman. She bobbed down and allowed Mary to set it on her head. The old woman stood up, looked at everybody and then burst out laughing. The whole tribe cheered, jumping up and down and clapping their hands. She flung her arms around Mary and kissed her.

From that day on we never saw her without it. I think she even slept in it.

That night Mary was very quiet.

"What's the matter," I asked her.

"You don't love me anymore," she sniffled, tears welling in her eyes.

"I do," I said, surprised. "I love you more than anything in the world, you and Jawana."

"Don't," she pouted. "I would give my life for you I said."

Her face lit up. She grabbed my hand and led me to the bed. We had not made love for a long time, not since her injury, and she thought I didn't want to. I had wanted to make sure she was well enough – I didn't want to hurt her. It turned out she was well enough that night.

*   *   *

Some days later I was sitting in the shade, working out a plan against another attack when I noticed the village was buzzing, an air of excitement all around us. A feast was being prepared. I wondered what it was for, this time.

I heard a noise and looked around. The puppy was chewing on a bone. He was growing quickly, over a foot tall now with paws like dinner plates. He ate anything we ate – fruit, fish, meat. He was more or less a living dustbin and when he passed wind – phew! I'm sure he knew when he was going to drop one and would purposefully sit next to me. I would then be forced to

148

flee out to fresher air while Mary and Jawana laughed until they cried.

He stopped chewing for a second, aware of my scrutiny, and looked up at me. He always looked like he was trying to work out what I was thinking, one ear up and one ear down. He returned his attention to his bone. I threw a stone at him. The puppy yipped and scrambled across the room to Jawana.

"Don't throw things at him, Daddy."

She cuddled him and he licked her face. I watched them, chastened.

That puppy is going to be trouble, I thought.

As the sun sunk into the lake, the drums started beating a slow, soft rhythm. Mary was combing her hair and I had Jawana on my lap.

Mbata appeared in our doorway and beckoned us outside. Two lines of the chief's bodyguards stood waiting, wearing their robes and carrying torches. They led us to the clearing. I held Mary's hand and carried our daughter in my arms.

As we approached, the chief came out of his hut, dressed in his royal robes, the witchdoctor doing his usual bit and dancing around the chief, shaking his rattle. We entered the clearing together, but two bodyguards held their spears before me. The chief waved Mary forward. She looked at the chief and then back at me. I nodded that it would be okay and she carried on.

Laid on the ground in front of the chief was a brightly coloured mat. Mary was escorted to it and made to sit down, facing the tribe. She had her legs crossed, her hands in her lap like a school girl at assembly.

Jawana went off to play with the other kids, taking the puppy with her.

The tempo of the drums began to pick up, beating faster and louder until the noise became almost a living thing, filling the air above the clearing. Everyone was swaying and chanting, led by the witchdoctor who had worked himself into a real frenzy. Mary clapped her hands, happily, giggling every time he raced past her. Then a man came into the clearing carrying her fire axe. He placed it reverently on the mat in front of her.

I leaned over to Mbata.

"What's going on?" I asked.

"She is to receive the highest honour."

"What for?"

"For saving the chief's life," he told me. "She will become a chief and sit by his side."

I sat there speechless, mouth open, watching a young woman who had spent all of her life being told what to do and how to live, in a position to take or grant life with a wave of her hand.

I was so proud of her. Her innocence could be so childlike, so beautiful. She knew and cared nothing for the responsibility she was about to take on, she was simply enjoying the party atmosphere.

The drink was flowing now and Mary was getting a little tipsy. A cloak was placed around her shoulders, the axe cradled in her arms like a mace. They tied an armlet about her upper arm. Jawana was taken to a hut, along with the other children, to sleep the night.

The drink was beginning to get to me now and I was feeling quite woozy. Now the party really got going. It wasn't long before I passed out, drunk and content.

When I awoke the sun was high and the light hurting my eyes I was lying on our bed, head pounding and my mouth tasted foul.

Mary was lying next to me, her head on my shoulder. I kissed her forehead and she murmured her approval. I looked down and recoiled. There was blood everywhere.

"Mary! Wake up!"

She sat up and rubbed her eyes.

"Is it me or you?" I asked, panicked. I climbed off the bed and checked myself. "It must be you – you're bleeding, you're –"

I stopped mid-sentence. Mary's chest was cut to ribbons.

"What have they done to you?" I gasped.

I span around to find the chief and his wives, bearing water and more of the smelly green paste. They washed her down and covered the cuts with the paste. Mary didn't seem to be in any pain.

"Don't hurt," she told me. "Don't hurt."

I felt uneasy. The tribe had been good to us so far, and I trusted my wife's judgement, but her chest looked awful.

For the next few days, the women came and dressed her wounds. Mary seemed happy enough in herself, so I decided to wait and see what would happen.

CHAPTER NINETEEN

One morning, Mary and Jawana were bathing in the lake. Her chest was almost healed now and for the first time I could appreciate what they had cut into her. It was the axe. The blade was above her left breast and the handle diagonally between her breasts, ending on her stomach, just above her right hip. It was a form of scarification – like a tattoo, but made with cuts rather than ink. It was quite impressive.

As I watched her I thought about what her life had been like back home. There she was considered a mentally handicapped girl, here she was a woman of stature – a tribal chief. There I was an educated man, a teacher – here I was just one of her followers. I smiled.

Later, I found out that her tribal name was Jimaju, meaning 'White Death'.

She told me afterwards that she had seen Jawana in danger and killed the man. The fact that the chief had been standing next to her hadn't even crossed her mind. If that's not being in the right place at the right time, I don't know what is.

"Mbata," I said. "Talk."

I grabbed a jug of jungle juice to share with my friend and we sat by the lakeside in the shade.

"I want to know everything about the tribe that attacked us," I told him.

Mbata told me that the tribe attacked the village every year, killing and looting. They had heard the same stories from other villages, too.

"They take all the young girls they can, about twelve and fourteen years old," Mbata said. "They know we are peaceful. It is easy for them. They use them as slaves – we never see or hear of them again."

I stared at my young friend, horrified.

"They took my sister last year and my father has never been the same since."

He told me that they were called the 'Butata' tribe and were known for their sadistic practices, feared by all the neighbouring tribes.

"How far is their village?" I asked.

"A day's walk," Mbata said, pointing across the lake. "Six of us went to see if we could free her, but we were ambushed. I was the only survivor – thanks to you, Mary and Reg."

"Can you take me there?"

Mbata hesitated.

"I have a plan," I assured him.

"Okay. When?"

"Tomorrow – before the dawn."

* * *

The next morning I crept out of bed, leaving Mary and Jawana in a deep sleep. I thought it was best not to wake them, or Mary would insist on coming with us and I couldn't refuse a chief. I donned my sword and bow and left them both sleeping.

Outside, Mbata was waiting with seven others. We set off into the jungle, a long trek ahead of us. After a few miles, we came to the deep pool below our cave. I gazed up at the water cascading from far above us and wondered yet again how in heaven Mary and I had survived a fall like that.

Mbata pointed to a hole in the rock face. It was a tunnel leading up through the cliff to the top. We emerged into the sunlight and fresh air.

"Is that the only way back down?" I asked.

"Yes," he said. "Unless we walk around the lake – a two day

journey."

As we walked I recognised some of the paths from when we lived in the cave. We had spent all that time there without finding the path down to the pool.

One of our men raised his hand and pointed behind us. We dove into the undergrowth. I was lying on my stomach looking up the path, my heart pounding.

Something wet touched my ear and I jumped. I turned, terrified, to find that damned puppy staring back at me. He must have followed us – and now he might give our position away. I picked up a rock and threw it at him. He scampered away into the undergrowth.

"You will have to kill him," said Mbata.

"I can't do that," I said. "Jawana will never forgive me. Maybe he'll find his own way home…"

We set off again. We had been walking all day with no one in sight. As the sun began to set we left the main path and walked through the trees.

Mbata whispered, "It's just over that ridge."

Nearing the edge of the ridge we could hear voices. We crawled forward on our stomachs and looked over the edge into the ravine. It was about a hundred yards long by fifty yards wide, one end opening onto the lake. The only way in or out was along an exposed path running by the lakeside.

The tribe outnumbered our at least five to one. Their huts were ranged in a circle, with a large fire burning in the centre. There was no laughter or children playing in their village – the only sounds were screaming and shouting.

I heard Mbata gasp – he pointed. A young girl emerged from a hut, carrying a pot.

"Rowana!"

He jumped up and I had to pull him back down.

"Not now," I hissed. "If they see us we will all be killed! We must plan a rescue attempt and come back when we're ready."

Just then that blasted dog came bounding out of the trees and decided that, since we were lying down, we must want to play. He ran round and round us, barking. I tried to grab him, but he was too quick. Looking back at the village I knew our cover was blown – they were all peering up at the ridge and pointing. Shouts went up around the lake.

"Let's go!"

We ran like the wind, all the way back to the cave. The moon was full and visibility was good, but it didn't seem like we were being followed.

"We can rest here until dawn," I said, and we made ourselves comfortable in the cave. As the others slept my mind drifted back to Mary, Reg and my time here. How Mary and I had fallen in love and Reg had married us. She was always so happy. I could barely remember a time when I hadn't been in love with her. Even though I had only been away for a day I missed her like hell.

For the rest of the night I pondered our situation. If we attacked directly to rescue the women it would be at our cost – we were greatly outnumbered.

As the sun rose and slivers of light shone into the cave, a noise from the tunnel disturbed my thoughts. Everyone rose and surrounded the hole, spears raised. Then a head popped up. It was that blasted dog again.

Mbata and the others burst out laughing. I locked eyes with the puppy and he must have seen something there because when I lunged forward to grab him he bolted back out of the tunnel and into the jungle.

"That dog has got to go," I said. "He's a threat to everyone's safety."

Maybe I could tie him up before I left the village – but Jawana would only untie him again.

Next morning we returned to the village and everyone came out to greet us. I crossed the clearing and made for our hut. As I approached a hot blade of rage struck through my heart.

The big fella, Mamooto, was lying in my hammock and Mary was handing him a drink. I ran over and tipped him out, leaving him face down in the dust. As he tried to get up I dived on him and we scuffled about in the dirt until our neighbours pulled us apart.

"He was trying to seduce my wife when I wasn't here!" I shouted.

Mary stood watching, her mouth open, the drink still in her hand.

"He was thirsty," she said. "He asked for a drink."

Mbata ran over.

"He's after my wife!" I told him, pointing in Mamooto's face.

"But she is not your wife," said Mbata. "Not until your union is blessed by the chief."

I stared at him.

In a sudden movement, Mamooto drew his knife and threw it. The blade stuck in the ground between my feet.

Mbata looked at me.

"He has challenged you to combat," he told me. "If you refuse he will claim Mary by your cowardice."

"I accept!" I cried, angrily. "What now?"

"Pick up the knife and throw it flat on the ground."

This I did.

"The chief will summon you and Mamooto to combat," said Mbata. "The winner lives and takes Mary and Jawana, the loser dies."

I held my wife and daughter close. They seemed happy to see

me. Mary couldn't see anything wrong in her actions, even though it could cost me my life.

We were part of the tribe now and had to abide by their law.

*   *   *

Later that afternoon the chief's bodyguards came to our hut to escort me to the central clearing. When we arrived, the tribe was sitting in a circle. Mamooto and I were given a spear and knife each. The chief stood up and raised his arms.

"To the death!" he shouted.

Mary grinned, laughing as if she was at the circus. It was obvious that she didn't really understand what was going on. Jawana had run off to play – thank God.

Mamooto and I turned and faced one another. He was a very big man, over a foot taller than me. He was all muscle. There wasn't an inch of fat on him. He stared at me, expressionless. The drums suddenly stopped.

We both crouched, side stepping round and round, circling each other. He thrust his spear at me and I knocked it away with mine. We changed direction, almost synchronous with one another, and began pacing again, looking for a gap when the other's guard was down.

He lunged at me again – I side-stepped and thrust my spear at him. The blade slid between the shaft of his weapon and the palm of his hand. He dropped his spear, the blood dripping from a wound on his palm.

I raised my spear, but he was too quick. He ran under the blade, crashing into me, knocking the spear from my hand. We only had our knives now and he was a powerful man. His arms were longer than mine so I stayed out of reach, waiting for the right moment.

He thrust at me. I stepped back and brought my knife as hard as I could, up under his arm. The blade went through his

158

forearm to the hilt.

He dropped his knife and turned and ran for his spear, my blade still in his arm.

I now had no weapons and he was closer to his spear than I was to mine. I raced after him. I rugby tackled him as he stooped to pick it up and we crashed to the ground, rolling over and over. He reached for his spear – I wrenched my knife out of his arm. He yelled out in pain, pushed me off him and ran for his knife.

I was right behind him when he dived for his knife, rolled head over heels and stood up to face me.

I thought he was at a disadvantage – he had to use the blade in his other hand. I was wrong. He thrust and slashed at me, cutting into my shoulder and stomach. We rushed at each other. I grabbed his knife hand and drew my blade up to his chin. He turned his head away, the blade opening his face from chin to ear.

We both stepped back, our bodies drenched in blood. After a moment to catch our breath we ran in again, grabbing each other's knife hand. He was still much stronger than me. Our faces almost touched – his eyes were staring, unblinking, into mine. There was an evil sneer on his face as he slowly forced his knife closer to my throat. He knew he was winning and the sneer transformed into a twisted grin.

The tribe were jeering and shouting, and my strength was waning. A distant image from another life flashed into my mind – Jenkins fighting Rawlinson on a cold playground, thousands of miles away.

I have to fight dirty, sir – if I didn't I'd lose every time, sir.

I drew back my head and BANG! I head butted him right on the bridge of his nose. He let go, dropping his knife and trying to focus. I brought my foot up and kicked him in the groin. He roared in pain and dropped to his knees, holding his balls.

I stepped forward with a crashing right uppercut to his jaw.

Dazed, Mamooto hit the ground like a ton of bricks. I picked up my spear and stood over him. He looked up at me, waiting for the cold steel of my blade to end his life. There was a deathly silence as our audience waited for the end.

Looking into the eyes of this defeated warrior, I lowered my spear. I knew that I couldn't kill this man. I would have been turning my back on my own morals. I broke the spear over my knee and threw it to the ground. I held out my hand.

Instinctively, he took it and I pulled him to his feet. He stood staring at me, bewildered. I turned my back on him and went to our hut. Mary caught up with me.

"You shouldn't play with knives," she scolded.

I bathed in the lake and Mary dressed my wounds, then Mbata came to our hut.

"The chief wants to see you."

"I thought he might," I said. "I will come now."

The chief wanted some answers – mainly why I hadn't killed my opponent. I explained, if we are going to do battle with the Butata it is better to kill them, not each other.

"Mamooto is a brave warrior – we need him alive, not dead."

After a few drinks, the chief mellowed and I explained that where we came from the women decided which man she would marry, not forced into a marriage she may not want to marry a man she doesn't love. He didn't understand. In his world, men were dominant in everything.

Mbata had told him about his daughter still being alive. When I told him of my plans to rescue her he readily agreed. I wasn't exactly sure how to achieve it, but I had a couple of ideas to sleep on.

I walked back to our hut. The moon was full and as bright as day, the animals were making their night sounds and the jungle was at peace. The flowers in the warm night air gave off a perfume that made me feel good.

I was so relaxed that I lay next to Mary and we started kissing. I rolled her underneath me and trailed kisses down her neck, across her breasts and lower, across her belly.

Out of the corner of my eye I saw a movement by the entrance. I looked up. It was Mamooto, he sat down in the doorway and bowed his head as if to sleep.

"Oy! What's your game?" I shouted. "Get out!"

He didn't move. I jumped to my feet as Mbata came into our hut.

"What's he doing in our hut?"

"You defeated him in combat and chose not to kill him," he says. "The chief rules that his life belongs to you. He is your bodyguard for life. If you don't accept this he will be executed according to our laws. It is your choice."

"No, he can't eat and sleep with us – how am I supposed to perform with him watching me all the time?" I demanded. "What's he going to do, give me marks out of ten for style? Tell him to sit outside."

"You tell him, he belongs to you."

"Sit outside," I said, pointing at the door.

Wordlessly he rose and went out. Mbata walked off laughing. Needless to say our night of passion was off.

CHAPTER TWENTY

The next morning I went to the lake to wash. Mamooto was still on the ground, head low. As I passed him he rose and followed me. It was unnerving – a man who only a few hours earlier had tried to kill me, was walking just three feet behind me. When I went to the toilet he stood outside – I could not go because I knew he was standing not a foot away from me.

I called Mbata.

"I can't have this," I told him, frustrated. "Tell him to go about his business and let me go about mine."

"You are his business," said Mbata. "He will carry out his duty to you until the day he dies. If anything happens to you, he will die. He will be your shadow until that moment."

Over the next few days I thought over a battle plan against the Butata. With Mbata and the other members of the tribe I planned our movements carefully, making drawings in the sand in preparation for the attack. If everything went to plan I thought we could get in and out again without too many casualties. The chief agreed.

"We need to dig a trench around the village, from the left cliff face behind us to the right cliff face beyond," I told the men. "About five feet in from the jungle – it needs to be about ten feet deep and ten feet wide, so no one can enter without crossing over it. Another trench should run four paces in from the first, about two feet deep by three feet wide."

Everyone mucked in without question. After three days of hard toil, the trenches were finished.

"Now," I said, "we must build a log bridge over them so there is only one way in or out of the village."

In the trees around the village we tied long vines about ten feet apart, hanging down to the ground and suspended large logs between them. They hung three feet from the ground, like big swings, all around the perimeter of the village. Everyone looked a bit bewildered at this, but they carried out my instructions anyway.

We tied more vines to the centre of each log, pulling them back towards the jungle, out of sight, high in the branches of the trees. The vines were secured with stakes driven into the ground.

"Once the vine is cut, the log will swing out of the tree, knocking anyone in its way into the trench," I explained.

Next, I made a scarecrow from bamboo and grass and stuck it in the ground on the other side of the trench. Everyone was pointing and laughing. They thought I was mad. I cut the vine with my sword – it lashed into the air as the log was released, swinging down out of the tree. It hit my scarecrow in the back and sent it flying into the trench.

Mbata looked puzzled.

"But won't they just climb out on our side?" he asked. "They will attack and there will be no escape."

"Right," I said. "So we dig a narrow gully from the lake to our trench and fill it with water – about eight feet deep. Then we trap some animals, cut them up and leave a trail from the lake into our trench."

"But won't the crocs come out of the lake and eat it?" Mbata asked.

"Yesssss," I said.

His face lit up as the penny dropped.

"We have a croc filled trench, the logs knock the Butata into the trench and..." he grinned.

"Give that man a coconut!" I cried.

"We fill a second trench with dry grass – anything that burns, and top it with green leaves to make smoke," I explained. "This side of that we cut bamboo poles, sharpened at the top, dug into the ground at an angle, so the points are about waist high, pointing towards the trenches. If they get past the smoke then they'll run on – straight onto the stakes.

Mbata nodded.

"Finally, a row of archers beyond, that should give them a run for their money." I clapped him on the back. "Four defences – crocs, fire, stakes and archers. That should be enough."

I went to see Najeet, the dove lady. I took flowers, fruit and some of Mary's cool berry juice. Najeet took them and looked at me suspiciously.

"I need to borrow nine doves," I told her.

"What for?" she demanded, eyeing her birds with jealousy.

"I want them in case the Butata attack." I explained what I wanted to do, and that their feathers needed to be coloured. "Red, blue and yellow – two of each colour."

Najeet nodded and offered to colour them for me. The next day she sent a message for me to collect them from outside her hut. There were three baskets made from reeds, containing the nine coloured birds.

Three main paths led into our village. I picked six children of about twelve years old to help, two to a basket. About half a mile down one path I told the children with the red doves to climb a tree and hide – they weren't to show themselves to anyone until one of us called them down.

"Now, wait for my signal," I said.

We did the same down the second path with the yellow birds and then down the third path with the blue birds . A man was left standing sentinel at the base of each tree. The rest came back to the village with me.

"Mbata," I said. "Go and tell the man on the first path to release the birds."

Off he went. We waited about five minutes before sending

another man down the second path, then another five for the third path.

Everyone still in the village stood looking up, waiting. Then, from the direction of the first path, in flew the red doves. A few minutes later, the yellow birds arrived and shortly after them, the blue. Everyone seemed to be having a great time – but really this was a serious business.

Once the children had returned safely, we relaxed. I looked up at the rock face behind our huts. About ten feet up there was a cave, running into the rock for about fifty feet. We stored food in it. I thought we could use them for other purposes – if we made some kind of door we could put the children and the elderly in it in times of threat.

I asked Mbata, "How can we get to the top of that rock face?"

"We climb up," he said. "I'll show you."

There was an area to the side of the cave with jagged bits sticking out.

"This was cut many moons ago to see if hunting was better up there than down here," he explained.

"And was it?"

"No," he said. "It's just flat rock – the game doesn't go up there."

We climbed up to the top. It was easier going than I thought. We looked back down over the village.

"If we put ten archers with spears up here they could fire over the village onto the enemy," I said. "We could leave the weapons up here ready, so they can climb up and start firing."

Mbata agreed.

I thanked Najeet and went back to our hut. The dog was getting bigger now, about two feet high. He was lying on the ground, chewing his own tail.

"Good for nothing mutt," I grumbled as I walked. "Just as long as he stays out of my way."

*   *   *

For the next few weeks we all trained hard for the coming fight. Even the women learned to use their weapons skilfully.

I didn't see much of Reg. He spent half of his time with the chief, drinking and laughing. We could hear him all over the village. The rest of the time he was with the kids. They loved him – he would chase them and play hide and seek. At least he wasn't carrying that blasted briefcase anymore. If he saw us he would wave and shout a greeting. He did look relaxed and happy. I felt glad for him.

One morning I decided to spend some quality time with Mary and Jawana.

"Let's go for a picnic," I said.

Mary giggled.

"Oh yes," she said. "I love picnic's."

"What's a picnic?" Jawana asked. "You'll see – come on."

We set off into the jungle, Mamooto tagging behind. All I carried was my sword and knife – Mamooto his spear. We weren't expecting trouble so close to home.

After a while we came across a clearing with a little stream running through it, surrounded on all sides by fruit trees. Mary and Jawana picked fruits and berries while I cut some large leaves and laid them out like a picnic blanket. Mamooto did nothing, just stood on guard. It was a beautiful day. Sitting in the shade we finished our meal and drank from the stream. Jawana was picking little flowers and making a chain of them humming to herself.

I turned and noticed Mamooto peering into the trees.

"What is it?" I whispered. He pointed through the trees. I drew my sword.

167

Out from the jungle ran seven Butatas. They must have been watching the village and followed us. As they ran into the clearing, Mamooto let fly his spear. It passed through the first man's chest. Mary didn't have her axe with her, so it was six against two. I ran at the next man and brought my sword down on his shoulder, splitting his chest in half.

The next man ran at me. I turned my back to him, put my sword under my arm, point backwards and thrust. He ran onto the blade.

Mamooto was hand to hand fighting with knives. Mary ran over to Jawana. As she reached her one of them grabbed Jawana and held Mary around the neck. The Butata were screaming and fighting. The next man ran at me.

Then, from the jungle, came the roar of a beast that made my blood run cold. A beast I had never heard before – the very sound filled me with horror. For a few seconds, time stood still.

Then that dog came charging into the clearing, snarling and growling – but it wasn't the dog I knew. He came in low, hackles raised from the back of his head down to his tail. His eyes were stretched wide, the whites bloodshot, his red lips curled back to show the meanest set of fangs I had ever seen, saliva dripping from his mouth. He was not a puppy anymore.

He sprang at the man holding Mary and Jawana, launching himself straight at his head from about ten feet away. The man released his grip and went for his knife – too late. The dog hit him full in the chest, bearing him backwards. Those terrible jaws closed around his neck and before they hit the ground he ripped his throat out.

Then he stood between the girls and the next Butata, who raised his spear and let fly at the dog. It went past his neck and opened a gash from his shoulder to his hind leg. The man turned and ran into the jungle, the dog hot on his heels.

The screaming and snarling only lasted a few seconds, and then all was still.

Mamooto slit the throat of his opponent, then ran after the remaining two who disappeared into the jungle. He never caught them.

I ran over to Mary and Jawana. They were not hurt, just shaken. Into the clearing came the dog – no longer a terrible beast, just bounding about like a puppy, tremendously pleased to see us.

I will never say a cross word against him again, I thought. From that day on we seemed to have a better understanding of each other.

We returned to the village, which was buzzing with activity. As I tried to enter our hut, Mbata stopped me. Mary and Jawana were allowed in.

"Come with me," he said.

I followed him to his hut. The moment I got through the door, six girls pounced on me, lay me down and washed me from head to feet.

"What's all this about?" I asked.

"You will find out soon," smiled Mbata.

The girls trimmed my beard, cut my hair and dressed me in a leopard skin loin cloth. The water they used was highly scented. When they had finished and I got to my feet, Mamooto was eyeing me up and down.

"What do you think?" I asked, but he didn't respond.

The more I thought about it, the more I realised I hadn't heard him speak a word since I had entered the village.

As he turned to leave, the girls pounced on him, too, and gave him the same treatment. I went outside. The drums were beating low and slow, they were gentle, almost soothing. Mbata came out and joined me, as did Mamooto. It was the first time I hadn't seen him carrying his spear. I thought he looked quite impressive.

A grand feast was set out – the whole tribe was there. The chief emerged, dressed in his white robe with gold trimmings. I was taken and stood in front of him, Mamooto stood behind me.

The girls from our hut came across the clearing and when they reached us they parted, revealing Mary. She was breathtaking. She wore a short white skirt with flowers in her hair and about her throat and waist. Her breasts were bare, showing her pert, pink nipples. There were flowers around her wrists and ankles, and she was carrying a posy of orchids.

As she came near I smelled her perfume. She was smiling at me. She was the most beautiful woman I had ever seen.

I held out my hand to her – she took it and stood close to me.

"Love you," she whispered.

"I love you, too."

Mbata leaned over.

"The chief wishes to unite you."

We stood in front of him, Mamooto towering above us. I looked up at him.

"Go," I told him. "Sit down and enjoy yourself."

He looked at the chief who nodded his approval. Mamooto went and sat with the rest of the tribe, but stayed within striking distance.

The chief raised his arms and the unmarried men and boys led me to the centre of the clearing. We stood in a line. The unmarried women and girls line up across from us, with Mary and I facing one another. I felt someone push in next to me – it was Reg.

"I'm single," he laughed. "I'm not missing out on this."

A bowl of jungle juice was passed down both lines and each time it passed us we drank. The drums picked up and as the drink kicked in we all started dancing.

Mary was really into it, looking at me with a sideways grin, her breasts bouncing and swaying. She was very sensual.

Abruptly, the drums ceased and the two of us were carried bodily to the chief. The witchdoctor was in a frenzy, shaking his rattle and feathers. I'm sure he had been drinking something stronger than jungle juice – rocket fuel, perhaps. Then everything went quiet except for the crackling of the fire.

The chief took my left hand and Mary's right hand. The witchdoctor handed him a blade which he then drew across our palms. As the blood flowed he bound our hands together with twine. I didn't feel any pain, which must have been the juice.

Now the festivities had really got going, everyone ate and drank. It wasn't long before the dancing got started. Mary and I sat it out. We talked and kissed one another for hours. The boys and girls were up in lines again, the girls dancing sensually, moving their bodies erotically. The boys were showing off, trying to impress the girls.

I looked at Mamooto and nodded towards the dancers, but he shook his head and sat tight. All of a sudden, the drums stopped and the girls sprinted off into the forest, the boys in hot pursuit. Even Reg fancied his chances – last seen running with his arms outstretched and his tongue out, chasing a girl who seemed to be egging him on.

Mary was so beautiful. I had eyes only for her. I picked her up in my arms, our hands still bound together, and carried her back to our hut. Jawana had a sleepover with her friends so I knew we wouldn't disturb her.

Mamooto stayed outside and fell asleep in the hammock. I lay Mary on our bed and cut the bonds from our hands. I lay down beside her.

The light of the moon shone dimly through the door onto us, illuminating the tiny beads of perspiration that trickled down her body. She smelled good enough to eat. I kissed her neck, her ears, her eyes, her mouth before exploring every inch of her beautiful body.

She lay with her head back, low gurgling noises of pleasure

hummed in her throat. She shook gently and I thought she was going to explode with pleasure. She put her arms around me.

"Now," she said. *"Now."*

We made love. We were both in such a state of arousal that it didn't last long at all, but it was the greatest feeling I had ever had in my life.

"I will remember this night forever," I murmured.

Mary and I fell asleep in each other's arms.

CHAPTER TWENTY-ONE

When I awoke the next morning the sun was already high. It must have been mid-afternoon. Mary had her head on my shoulder, staring at me. We kissed and said, "Love you."

"Let's go and bathe," I said.

As we emerged into the sunlight the whole village was outside our hut. They leapt to their feet, cheering and clapping. Mary beamed, but I felt my cheeks glowing red. I was so embarrassed. I ran and plunged into the lake, Mary close behind.

We spent the rest of the day in each other's company, lazing around, kissing, cuddling and whispering sweet nothings to one another.

The next morning I was standing on the lakeside, looking into the water when I noticed fish had swum into the bathing pool from the lake. There were hundreds of them, motionless in the clear water. They must have come through the framework because it was safer there, away from the crocodiles.

It struck me that we could build more pools around the lake with built-in nets that could be pulled in after the fish had entered the pool, rolling the fish onto the bank. It would save men from standing waist deep in water to cast their nets and being eaten alive by crocodiles.

I talked to some of the fishermen and asked them to make a net big enough to cover the floor of the swimming pool. That evening we laid the net on the pool bed and pegged it along the edge of the water. We tied vines to the far edge of the net near the platform framework and sank it to the bottom of the pool.

The following morning at first light I went out to the lake to find most of the village was already there, looking into the water. The pool was full of fish of all sizes. Big ones, little ones – the nets would be teeming with them.

I got the fisherman lined up. They took the lines and told them to pull on my command.

"One, two, three – pull!"

The net folded over the fish. The small ones escaped through the holes in the net while the bigger ones were dragged out onto the bank. There were thousands of them. Everyone was grabbing fish and running them back to the huts. Then ran back for more. This method of fishing would save us losing good men to the crocs.

"Now we must concentrate on our enemies, the Butata tribe," I declared. "We need a battle plan to fight them on our terms, not theirs."

I thought of a Roman ploy, using shields to cover warriors while they went to battle on the field.

We cut bark from dead trees about five feet by three feet wide to make shields – thirty of them. I stood five women in a row, holding five shields in front and five more women behind them, holding their shields above their heads. Behind them walked five archers, then five more women, then another row of archers and another row of women, and so on.

I asked them all to stoop down with the shields over their heads and walk forwards, like a giant, many-legged tortoise.

At first they kept tripping over and when one went down the others tripped over them and they all fell about, laughing. With a little practice they soon got the hang of it.

I got the children to throw rocks at them. One woman stuck her head out to look and was hit. Another was hit on the leg. They all soon learned to stay close and protect themselves – and the archers.

"In battle it won't be rocks, but spears and arrows," I told them. "Now, on my command lift the front top row of shields upright at the same time. The front row of archers should loose and then duck, while the women lower their shields again. You can use that time to reload.

"On my next command, the second row should raise their shields," I continued. "Like before, the archers behind them should stand and shoot, and so on. When the last archers have shot we'll go back to the front and start again.

"We do all this while walking towards the enemy," I instructed them, "so a constant barrage of arrows are raining down on them and they don't have a chance to return fire."

It seemed like a lot of fun for them, but we had to train hard to get it right. I wonder if the Romans had this much trouble training.

"We need two more groups like that," I said.

Everyone came forward to volunteer. For the next few weeks they trained very hard. A door was made of bamboo and fitted at the entrance to the cave to keep the elderly and the children safe. Reg said he would take care of getting them into the cave and closing the door.

Finally, the time came when we felt we were ready.

We dug a deep channel from the lake to our trench and filled it with water. The fire trench was prepared and ready to light. The bamboo stakes were sharpened and put in place. Finally, we laid a trail of meat from the lake into the trench. The sides were steeply cut – we needed to ensure that when the crocodiles got in they could not get out.

*   *   *

We woke early the next morning to find the trench writing with crocs. We filled the channel to the lake in, trapping them.

We then dropped our bamboo bridge over the trench. We positioned a man at each stake, each with a shield. When the time came, they were to cut the vines to the logs in the trees. At this point, the chief emerged from his hut with Mbata.

"My father will lead the village into battle!" he declared.

175

Good, I thought. I could think of no better man for the job. With the chief leading them, they would fight to the death.

"Now," I told them. "Cover your bodies with bright clay paints. Try to make yourselves look as hideous as possible. When you attack you must shriek and scream as loud as you can. Put the fear of the gods into them."

I found Mary painting herself with the others.

"No," I frowned. "Not you. It's far too dangerous. You must stay here and look after Jawana."

"I go ." She said.

"No," I said. "You stay here."

"No, I go," She argued.

I gave in. She was a chief after all, and where she wanted to go she would go.

The children took the doves and hid in the trees. My last instruction was for everyone to 'be prepared' and wait for the coloured doves. That would tell them from which direction our enemy would be coming from.

"Is everyone ready?" I shouted.

They all screamed 'YES!'

Reg took Jawana with the other children. Mbata and I took fifty men with Mary and headed for the Butata village.

We set off at a steady pace. I felt something brush against my leg. I looked down as Jekyl the dog (that's what I named him after our last episode with the Butata) ran past. It seemed I couldn't stop him coming either.

When we reached the tunnel that went up through the cliff we stopped.

"Find some dry grass and dead wood mixed with lots of green leaves," I commanded. "Line the tunnel with just enough of a gap for our men to pass through. We'll leave two men waiting here – when you hear the Butata coming down, light the fire before they get to the entrance then get back to the village. They will need you there."

The rest of us set off again. About three hours later we stopped for a rest and to discuss tactics.

"Mbata will take ten men and distract the guards while the rest of us hide," I said. "Hopefully they will chase them and leave the village unguarded."

When we reached the ridge overlooking the village Mbata and his men set off on their quest. Looking down, we could see no guards; they weren't expecting an attack – we had the element of surprise.

"I want ten men to go to the other side of the clearing," I ordered. "Try not to be spotted."

We watched them go.

"Mary, stay close," I said.

She looked at me and smiled. Jekyl must have known that something was up. He had made no noise at all and was staying very close to Mary. We crept down the steep slope without detection. At the bottom we crouched low, about ten feet from the huts when I spotted our other men on the far side of the clearing.

So far, so good, I thought.

We were in position. Now it was up to Mbata.

Suddenly, a bloodcurdling scream came from the top of the ridge and a body rolled down into the clearing. The village came alive like ants from an anthill. At a guess there must have been three or four hundred people.

We haven't got enough men, I thought.

More screams emanated from the ridge. The Butata grabbed their spears. Mbata and his men were jumping up and down, screaming abuse and rolling rocks down at them. Then they sprinted off into the jungle with the enemy hot on their heels. As the noises faded into the distance I scanned the village. There were about fifty people left, mostly the elderly, the women and some children.

We ran into the clearing, the others saw us and came in from the other side. The old men stood their ground in defiance. Some younger men, probably guards, put up a fight but they were easily disposed of.

This should be easy, I thought.

Then a woman picked up a fallen spear and plunged it into the chest of one of our men. It took us by surprise. Other women grabbed spears and joined the fray. A woman lunged at me, her spear glanced off my shield. As she went to lunge at me again, Mary ran past me and took her down. Our men ran in and slaughtered the others.

"Get everyone in the centre!" I yelled. "Hurry in case they come back!"

Our men surged into the huts and what came out was sickening. Young women and children –nearly all girls – their limbs bound. Some were so badly abused they could barely walk, cuts and sores all over their bodies. Some of them had broken bones.

Mamooto came out holding the hand of a young girl.

"Is this the chief's daughter?" I asked.

He nodded. I looked around. One young girl of about fourteen cowered before us, clearly terrified. Looking at her back she had taken a few beatings.

"Do you want to stay here or come with us?" I asked.

"With you," she replied.

There were about thirty young girls and women, some carrying babies.

"Anyone who wants to stay here, go back to your huts," I called, "If you want to come with us, come now."

They all followed us except for the young boys, who went back into their huts.

I picked out five of our men.

"I want you five to take this lot back to the caves above the waterfall and barricade yourselves in," I instructed them. "When it's safe we'll send someone for you. Don't take the main path in case the Butata come back before you get there."

The tribe's canoes were tied at the lakeside. We took the ones we needed and smashed the others up. We set off and paddled like mad. After an hour or so we could hear the sound of battle.

We moored the canoes and ran the last five hundred yards. The sight that greeted our eyes at the village was utter carnage. The logs hidden in the trees had done their grisly work and pushed the attacking Butata into the trench. The water was crimson with blood, almost boiling as the crocodiles thrashed about, ripping their bodies apart.

The Butata had cut the logs from the trees and used them to bridge the trench. The fire trench was well alight with thick smoke. Some of them had jumped through the smoke only to impale themselves on the bamboo stakes.

I drew my sword and ran over a log into the fray, the others followed, all of us screaming abuse at the top of our voices.

It took them by surprise and for a crucial moment they dropped their guard. The battle that followed was hard fought and bloody.

Arrows, spears, knives and my sword flashed in the sun. All around me were the screams of dying men, I cut and thrust, slashing and piercing human flesh. Men and women lay dead or dying all over the clearing. Three men rushed at me, spears raised. Before we clashed, Jekyl the dog leapt forward and ripped one man's face off. My sword found its mark in another's chest and Mamooto's spear found the third. The ferocity of our fighters won through and the enemy turned and fled into the jungle.

Their wounded were all slaughtered, not a single prisoner taking. I turned as the last man fell and there in the centre of the clearing stood the chief, his white robes stained in blood, a knife sticking out from his shoulder. Spear raised, he finished off the last man. He looked magnificent and the tribe cheered in triumph. He was a great chief and I was proud to be one of his tribe. Three of his bodyguards were dead, but they died doing their job.

I looked round. I could not see Mamooto. For a second my heart sank. I had grown used to him always been there. Then I saw him coming out of the jungle. I raised my thumb and he nodded.

Their dead were taken out into the lake and fed to the crocodiles. The trench was unblocked and the crocs were driven back to the lake. They had done their job and eaten well for it. They showed little interest in eating us.

Mary was dispatched to the cave to check on the children and Reg. They were, much to our relief, all okay. She came back to the village alone; the others would join us in the morning. Some of our children had lost mothers or fathers, or both.

We had a count up of our dead. Eleven women and thirty-two men. The Butatas, on the other hand, must have lost dozens. With any luck, this battle might make them think twice before attacking us in the future. But I doubted it. They were so very warlike and we had humiliated them. We had to stay vigilant.

The chief summoned Mbata, Mary and I to his hut. While his wounds were treated we discussed the battle, our dead, what to do with the orphaned children and the captives we had rescued from the Butata.

It was decided that so many of our tribespeople had died that we would build a large funeral pyre on one bank of the lake with a joint ceremony to say goodbye. The injured would be nursed back to health and those that were more seriously injured would be cared for for the rest of their lives. The orphaned children were to be fostered in families who would raise them as their own.

The trenches was filled in and you would not think a battle had been fought there.

The next morning, five men went with Mbata to escort the women and children down from the cave. The rest of us constructed the pyre and laid our dead upon in. Then a vast banquet was prepared. The village was buzzing in preparation to welcome them home.

Mbata walked into the village later that day, hand in hand with a young girl, the others close behind him.

The chief emerged from his hut and stared at the girl, who had tears streaming down her face. He held out his arms and she ran to him. They embraced one another for ages. Mbata approached me.

"Thank you Majumi," he said. "We are a family again."

After all this bloodshed, at least something good has come out of it, I thought to myself.

The rescued women and children were taken to huts where their matted hair was cut and combed. They were bathed and their wounds were dressed.

That evening as the sun set, the funeral pyre was lit and we all said farewell to some very brave friends. The flames rose a hundred feet in the air. They must have been seen for miles.

Then everyone sat down to feast. The new arrivals looked around wide-eyed, they didn't understand why they were allowed to eat with the rest of the village. After months or even years of slavery and abuse it would take them a long time to feel secure again.

Mary sat next to me; I had Jawana on my lap, her head on my chest and her arms around my neck.

"I love you Daddy," she said.

"I love you too, Jawana."

The events of the last few days had understandably unsettled the children, and most of them were suddenly more clingy than we had been used to.

Mary took my hand, kissed it and then held it to her cheek. She looked up at me and smiled. I kissed her gently on the lips.

"I love you," I whispered. She put her arms around both of us and held us tight.

The drums started beating and some young men took up spears and started to dance around, re-enacting the battle. Then a woman painted white danced around, carrying Mary's fire axe. She mimed slaying twenty men. Next a man painted white leapt up and slayed five imaginary men with my shield and sword. Finally, a warrior dressed in white came over, carrying a spear. The 'chief' fought like ten men, slaying fifty Butata. Well, he was the chief and so was Mary. I was just one of the ranks.

CHAPTER TWENTY-TWO

I lay in my hammock with a cool drink. Mary came over and put something around my neck. It was a necklace made from the leather thong the chief had tied our hands together with at our wedding. She had also made one for herself and asked me to put it on her.

"You look gorgeous," I said.

"Thank you," she beamed. "I made you something else." She smiled and held out her hand. It was a string of beads.

"Thank you."

I took them from her and put them around my neck.

"No, silly," she giggled. "They are for your thingy."

"What thingy?" I asked.

Then I realised that it wasn't a necklace at all. They were willy beads. Someone must have shown her how to make them. She helped me to put it on and then she looked at it.

"They look nice," she laughed, and gave it a kiss.

When I saw Mbata I asked him if the women and girls we had rescued came from the same village.

"No," he said. "From six different tribes. The very tall one is from the Tunta tribe. She is the daughter of the chief."

"I have an idea," I said. "We can bring all the girls out and sort them into their own tribes."

"Why?" he asked.

"If we can get them back to their villages we may be able to lessen hostilities between the tribes."

We went to see the chief and I explained my idea. He was very cautious.

"Our tribes have hundreds of years of mistrust of each other," he said. "They may simply kill you on sight."

"Can I at least try?" I asked.

He agreed, reluctantly, "But be careful."

The tall princess was called Oomi and her tribe lived about a half a day's walk away.

*   *   *

We set off the next day at sunrise with twenty men, led by Mbata. We sent scouts ahead in case of hostiles. With Mary holding my waistband we left at a steady trot. After a couple of hours, Mbata called a halt.

"The path to the village is up ahead," he whispered. "We will wait until the scouts come back."

"All clear, no one has passed yet."

"Mbata take half the men and spread yourselves along one side of the path and hide," I said. "We will do the same on the other side. On my order, show yourselves, but do not attack unless they do first."

About ten minutes later, down the path came seven men carrying spears and shields. Their bodies were not painted and they didn't seem aggressive like the Butata. In fact, they were chatting and laughing like they were on a pleasant morning stroll.

Mary, Mamooto and I jumped out in front of them. They stopped in their tracks and raised their spears, but our men stood up and surrounded them. Realising they were outnumbered, they lowered their spears and dropped them to the ground, followed by their shields. I think at this point they thought they were going to die.

They were staring at Mary and me.

They had never seen white people before. I walked up to the lead man, picked up his spear and shield and handed it back to him. He looked bewildered. We did the same with the others and beckoned for them to follow us, which they did, still unsure of their fate.

When we arrived back at our village the chief ordered food and drink for our guests.

After they had been refreshed, Mary went to the chief's hut and came out holding Oomi by the hand. She looked beautiful, dressed in fine white robes with flowers in her hair. She looked every inch a princess.

When our guests saw her they fell to their knees, foreheads to the ground. She walked over and told them to rise. Each took her robe and kissed it. Then she sat with them and told her story, how we rescued her and the others. They heard how a great battle was fought led by a white warrior and a she devil.

"No," I interrupted. "The battle was led by our chief – we fought under his command."

The Chief looked at me and smiled his approval.

While we were away the chief had explained our ideas to Oomi and she did the same to her tribesmen.

It was time for them to leave. The chief ordered twenty men to escort them safely back to where we had found them. Oomi kissed Mary goodbye and held her tightly. Then she kissed my cheek, before turning to the chief.

"I will put your ideas to my father and hope to see you again soon," she said.

Over the next few weeks we returned all the girls back to their tribes in the same manner and waited for any feedback.

*   *   *

Early one morning there was a crack of thunder and the rains came, it poured and poured. It was nothing like the rain in England. It was warm and poured down for days at a time without stopping. You had to be careful where you trod because there were holes in the ground, and in those holes lived some very scary things, like poisonous snakes, lizards and spiders.

Mary and I lay in our hammock with the rain hitting our bodies and turning to steam. Just such a creature emerged from one of the rain filled holes nearby. A spider the size of a saucer crawled out and climbed up a tree. Jawana pointed at it laughing. Back in England if I saw a spider in the bath I would have ran a mile, but out here it didn't seem nearly as worrying.

A few days later the rain stopped as suddenly as it had started and the sun came out. Everything smelled fresh and clean, as though mother nature had spring cleaned the jungle.

Weeks went by without any sign of the Butata. We all hoped we had scared them off for good.

We were checking the fish nets and Jawana was picking some flowers for her mother. Mamooto was keeping watch. Mary was looking at me, a strange look upon her face.

"I love you," she said. That was unusual she usually only said "Love you" not I love you.

"And I love you too," I smiled.

She patted her tummy.

"Are you hungry?" I asked.

"No," she said.

"Have you got a pain?"

"No," she snapped.

"Well, what then?"

She patted her tummy again.

"Baby," she said.

"What?"

"Baby," she said again.

I stood there, staring at her with my mouth wide open. We had never taken any precautions. The only contraception in the jungle was saying 'no', and that had never been said. It had never entered my head that she would get pregnant again.

"I'm going to be a dad!" I shouted, jumping up and down in excitement. I picked Mary up in my arms and kissed her. "I love you!"

"I love you! I love you!" she giggled.

Mamooto looked at us as though we were quite mad. I grabbed his hand and put it on her tummy.

"Baby," I shouted. "Baby!"

He smiled. I think he was happy for us, but it was hard to tell.

When Reg heard he came over and shook my hand. He gave Mary a big hug.

"Congratulations, my old mate," he beamed. "Congratulations."

The tribe continued to train in case the Butata returned. Like a schoolyard bully, once they got a bloody nose they stayed away, their tails between their legs. However, we heard they were still attacking other villages.

*   *   *

One day, Robin Hood and Little John came to my mind.

I wonder, I thought to myself.

I cut two poles about six feet long and as thick as my wrist. Mamooto watched, totally uninterested as usual.

I shaved off the bark and let the poles dry in the sun while I had a cool drink. When they were dry I threw one to Mamooto.

"Defend yourself," I said. Then I swung a blow at his head.

Instinctively, he blocked it and squared up to me. I swung another he blocked it again and pushed his pole into my stomach, knocking all the wind out of me. I fell flat on my back.

He smiled down at me, held out his hand and helped me up.

Three times he laid me down and three times helped me up. It occurred to me that he always swung his pole the same way. The next time he swung at me I sidestepped and brought my pole underneath his chin. He went down like a ton of bricks.

This time *I* smiled down at *him* and held out my hand to help him up.

Some of the other villagers came over to watch with interest. We cut some more poles and they joined in. To them it was a game, but the idea was to train them to fight with staffs, so if they were caught without weapons they could take a branch of a tree and have some means of defending themselves. Or though they were not used to close combat.

One day a man came running in, shouting that some tribesmen were approaching the village. We prepared for battle and waited.

Then, from the jungle and into the village came about forty men and women, carrying bundles. They were from the Watiti tribe and their chief came with them. Four of the girls we had rescued from the Butatas ran in, screaming and giggling like young girls do. Our girls hugged and kissed them and they all chattered and laughed together.

Their chief had agreed to take us up on our offer to trade: clothes for fish and grain. The two chiefs sat talking and drinking, putting old hostilities behind them. Then the bartering began. It went on for the rest of the day, by which time it was getting dark and they were invited to stay the night.

They agreed. A fire was lit and another banquet laid out. We sat up most of the night talking, mainly about the difference between black and white skin. By the time we slept they knew everything about us.

In the morning we brought out baskets for their fish. Because they were empty, the Watiti all looked a bit puzzled, but then some of our fishermen pulled in the nets and filled the baskets with live fish. They were still laughing when they left to return to their village. Fish kept jumping out of the baskets and the young girls picked them up and threw them back in.

It was decided that if they were attacked, they should call for assistance, now that our tribes were friends. The coloured doves method would be best. Najeet agreed, colouring ten birds orange and putting them in a basket for them. We explained that if the birds were released they would fly back to us. If they were attacked they should have released two birds, so that at least one or both will come back.

"Then we will send warriors to fight with you."

Najeet put another ten white doves into a basket.

"These young birds have never flown," she told them. "So look after them in a hut, feed them and let them out every day."

We showed them how our children cared for the birds. They were still a bit confused, so Mbata asked if two men could go with them and live in their village until they understood the new system. A young husband and wife volunteered. They took the baskets and returned to their new village escorted by some of our men.

As time passed, other tribes made contact: the Nimwas, who bred cattle; the Raato, who made pottery; the Manooti; the Bawani; and the Tunta.

They all took different coloured doves back to their villages and were taught how to manage them.

One day, this new system was put to the test. Najeet sent word that two orange birds had just flown in. The Watiti were in trouble.

We took up our weapons and ran to their aid. As we approached we could hear the familiar sounds of battle in the distance. We spread out. It was our old adversaries, the Butata – and they were getting a beating. Three other tribes had arrived before us, driving them back.

We came in behind them and they fled into the jungle. In the confusion of battle, with different tribesmen fighting one another at close quarters, one or two instances of friendly fire took place. Subsequently we agreed that each tribe would wear an armband of feathers the same colour as their birds. That way they would know which side they were on.

From then on, things went quiet, and a brisk trade emerged between all the local villages. We still kept an eye out for the Butata, but they didn't show their faces.

Mary was getting big now. She had short little legs and a pot belly with huge breasts, but I thought she looked radiant. Her eyes sparkled and her hair shone. I watched her pottering about, humming to herself. She was a wife, a mother, a lover and a warrior.

In this environment she was a natural. She fit in and was highly respected in our village and among the other tribes. Back home she would have been shoved in an institution with no prospects or future at all.

CHAPTER TWENTY-THREE

One day we were sitting by the lake in the shade, playing with Jawana when Mary gave a start of surprise.

"Ouch," she winced.

"What's up?" I asked.

"Baby coming," she said, holding her tummy.

"What? It can't come yet, I'm not ready!" I shouted.

In a panic I jumped up, but didn't know which way to run.

"The baby's coming!" I shouted.

Mamooto casually walked over, picked Mary up and took her to our hut. Some girls followed her in with hot water and bathed her, ready for the birth.

Unlike me, Mary was calm, taking it all in her stride as before. Najeet arrived and took charge.

I held Mary's hand and told her that I loved her. She looked up at me with a smile, which quickly turned into a grimace. She screamed. Sweat was running down my face and I was only watching.

Najeet poured some oil on Mary's loins and told her to push on the next contraction. As she took a breath and pushed.

"Push!" I shouted.

She squeezed my hand so tightly that she nearly broke my fingers.

The baby's head appeared and then Mary relaxed. Najeet told her to pant until the next contraction. When it came we all shouted, 'Push!'

The baby's body slid out into Najeet's hands. She looked at me and smiled.

"It's a boy," she cried, and at about the same moment he took a break and wailed.

Everybody outside the hut heard his first cry and cheered. Najeet tied the umbilical cord and I cut it before handing me my son. Mary, exhausted, was smiling up at me.

"You clever girl," I said. "He's a little beauty."

I kissed his little head and then handed him to his mum.

Jawana sat on the floor, legs crossed, staring at her little brother. I wondered what she was thinking. Was she jealous?

I needn't have worried. Mary called her over and let her hold him. Jawana's face lit up.

"Will you help mummy look after him?" I asked.

"Yes please!" she beamed.

"Well, I am relying on you," I said. "Mummy is going to need all the help we can give her until she's back on her feet again."

"What shall we call him?" Mary smiled.

"I don't know yet," I said. "We will think of some names after you have rested."

The girls bathed Mary and the baby, and they both fell into a deep well-earned sleep.

As the sun went down I sat outside and wet the baby's head with Mamooto. I thought to myself how lucky I was to have a beautiful wife and two lovely children.

We named him 'Lani', which meant 'handsome warrior'.

*   *   *

Over the next few years – how many, I am not sure because time moves differently in the jungle – we lived a happy and reasonably quiet life. The Butata tribe raised its ugly head now and then, but they were beaten by the newfound partnership of the neighbouring tribes.

Jawana was growing into a young lady and My handsome warrior followed me around everywhere. Living in the jungle with all the dangers that threatened us, I still felt safer than I had in my concrete jungle back in England.

CHAPTER TWENTY-FOUR

Meanwhile, back in England, two men and a woman were standing in the library at Lodden University, studying some maps. The door opened and in walked a distinguished looking man with a white, neatly trimmed beard.

"Ah, Professor Jenkins," said one man. "We have something here that will interest you. Your theory on that area of jungle in Africa – Doctor Price here has acquired some aerial photographs, taken a few days ago."

The Professor raised an eyebrow and studied the photos carefully, comparing them to his maps.

"You see these little white dots?" said the man. "We think they might be aircraft that have disappeared without trace in recent years."

"Thank you Baines – and the lady."

"Oh, sorry Professor," he said. "This is Miss Melanie Pointer. Her father was the late Doctor Pointer of the Pointer Foundation, who died last year."

"I knew him well," said the professor. "He was a good man and a brilliant explorer. I was sorry to hear of his death."

She held out her hand, but the professor ignored it.

Pompous arse, she thought taking her hand back.

"If," she said, "you intend an exploration in this region I would like to come with you, in my father's name."

"No," replied the professor, without looking up.

"Why not?" she snapped, indignantly.

"For two reasons," answered the Professor. "One, I think it's too dangerous for a woman. We don't know what we might find. This is uncharted territory. They could be uncivilised tribes and

193

even cannibals. Two, we already have a team, all of whom are male. To put an attractive woman amongst them could be disruptive."

"I can take care of myself," she said, affronted.

"The answer is still 'no'."

"You pompous old fart!" she shouted and walked out, slamming the door.

Without batting an eyelid the professor carried on talking.

"Do you realise, Baines, if this area has never been explored, just think of the natural treasures waiting to be discovered," he said, a lust for scientific glory in his eyes. "Flowers, insects, plants, animals – we could find cures for incurable diseases. And what happened to the passengers in those aircraft? Some of them could have survived. I'll see the board of governors to finance the expedition at once."

When Baines came out of the library, Melanie was waiting with a face like thunder.

"Who the hell does he think he is?" she snapped. "I'm not a child!

"He's old school. Said Baines He thinks exploration is a man's job."

"Well, let me tell you, Mr Baines, I will be going on this expedition whether he likes it or not!"

*　　*　　*

The following week, Professor Jenkins went to see the board of governors, bundles of papers tucked under his arms. After a short wait, the door opened and a man said, "Come in, Professor."

"We have read your report on this expedition," said a member of the board. "And we want to know why the University should finance you."

The professor explained.

"This could be one of the last places on earth where civilised man has never been," he said. "Who knows what we might find. There could be plants that can be used to cure diseases – even cancer. Maybe creatures the world has never seen before."

"But Professor," said the member of the board. "This is all 'maybe', 'might be', 'could be'. This is a big financial gamble that the University can ill afford."

"But gentlemen," the Professor argued. "This is what expeditions are all about. If I am right – and I think I am – then the University will become the world's leading authority on my findings. Students will flock from all over the world to enrol."

The members of the board exchanged glances.

"Professor, will you wait outside while we discuss this matter, please?"

After about ten minutes he was called back in.

"Professor, we feel that this venture is too big a gamble for the University to finance, so I'm afraid we will have to decline at this time."

The professor's face dropped.

"But surely," he stammered.

"On the other hand, Professor, an offer has been made to finance the whole expedition," said a board member. "By Miss Pointer of the *Pointer Foundation*, on condition that she is a part of the expedition team."

"But gentlemen," said the professor, aghast, "I can't take a woman on an all-male team – there will be no washing or toilet facilities. Men are only human," he added, darkly. "She would be exposed to all sorts of embarrassing situations. How on earth will a woman cope?"

"We are sorry, Professor," said the board member. "I'm afraid you'll have to take it or leave it."

"Okay," he sighed, defeated. "I accept."

"Call in Miss Pointer," said the member of the board, nodding at the student acting as an usher.

"Melanie, my dear," said the board member as she walked towards the table. "The professor has agreed to accept your generous offer."

"Only on one condition," said the professor. "She must realise that I am the head maggot in this cheese and my orders are to be carried out unquestioned."

"Agreed," she said with a sweet smile, and held out her hand.

This time, without much choice in the matter, he shook it.

"You will still be representing the University," said the member of the board.

"Oh, I see," said the professor. "You don't want to finance me, but you still want to reap the benefits."

He stood for a while, considering the members of the board. Then he spoke:

"Gentleman and lady," he said. "The expedition is off. Get someone else – I will not represent a cheapskate bunch of misers with no imagination. I resign."

As he walked out and shut the door behind him, he could hear the board and Melanie shouting at each other. Although he was very disappointed he felt some satisfaction at resigning.

I think I'll go fishing, he thought to himself.

He returned to his flat, packed a few things and got out his fishing gear. He loaded it all in the car, ignoring the landline phone, which was ringing almost continuously. He did not answer it. Before he left he phoned Baines and told him the news.

"What are you going to do now, sir?" Baines asked.

"I'm off fishing for a few days," he said.

"I'll come with you, if you don't mind Sir," said Baines. "Where are you going?"

"My old shack in Taunton," said the professor.

"I will see you there tomorrow," replied Baines.

"Okay," he said, "but don't tell anyone where we will be."

*   *   *

For the next few days the two friends went fishing. They fished all day, drank scotch all night and reminisced over all the adventures they had been on.

"How long have we been together, Baines?" the professor asked.

"Twenty-seven years, sir," he replied. "And I have enjoyed every minute of it. If I had another twenty-seven years I would do it all again."

"Thank you Baines, I appreciate that," said the professor. "Have another scotch."

They were enjoying their self-imposed exile so much that they ended up staying in Taunton for two whole weeks.

Returning to his flat, the professor unplugged his phone, which was still going off continuously, and sorted through the post that had built up on the carpet. He picked out the important ones and binned the rest without reading them.

He had a shower, put on his pyjamas and dressing gown, and then sat down to watch television.

"What do I do now?" he wondered aloud. "An out of work professor... Money is no problem but I am bored already."

Just then, the doorbell rang. As he opened the door, the professor was already saying, "Can't stay away Baines?"

But it wasn't Baines. It was Melanie Pointer.

"Can I talk to you?" she pleaded. "Just for a moment?"

"You'd better come in," he said, and opened the door wide. "Drink?" he asked.

"Please – scotch, if you have any."

He poured them both a drink and they sat down.

"I have been trying to reach you for two weeks," she said, with an air of admonishment.

"We went fishing," the professor said. "We enjoyed it so much we decided to stay. It's not like we had any reason to come home."

"Who's 'we'?" she asked, interested.

"Baines," he replied.

"No wonder I couldn't get hold of him, either." She frowned. "Look, we didn't get off to a very good start, so can we try again? I really want to go on this expedition. When you resigned I contacted the rest of your team – I even offered to double their salaries, but they all said that if you weren't going, they wouldn't go either. I admire them," she said. "They are very loyal to you."

"Well," he said. "We have been together for a long time, through good and bad times."

"Let me put a proposition to you," she suggested. "The *Foundation* will fund all your expedition costs if you and your team will let me tag along. No conditions other than that," she added. "I promise."

The professor considered her offer carefully, trying to fathom what she was up to. After a few drinks, Melanie and the professor agreed to resume the plans for the expedition where they left off.

"I will inform Baines and the rest of the team," said the professor. "In fact, I will ring him now."

There was a brief interlude where the professor made a call and Melanie tried not to appear too nosy in peering around his flat. He put the phone down.

"He's on his way round now," he smiled.

Ten minutes later the doorbell rang.

"It was Baines."

"It's on then?" he beamed. "Good."

The professor poured his old friend a drink and topped up his and Miss Pointer's glasses.

"I want to show you something," he said.

He put a video in the recorder, turned the lights down and pressed play. It was a recent documentary on the potential of untouched jungle ecosystems.

"This piece of jungle is most probably the last unexplored land on earth – at least in Africa," he said, when the documentary had finished. "We hope to discover all manner of plants and animals not currently known to the scientific community."

The doorbell rang again and in trooped the rest of the exploration team. The professor groaned. As much as he appreciated his team, when this lot got together they cost him a fortune in scotch. He wouldn't mind so much if they reciprocated.

"Miss Pointer –" he began, but she interrupted.

"Call me Melanie – or Mel," she said.

"Melanie," "Let me introduce you to our expedition team. There is me and Mark Baines you already know – he's second in command. Then there's Woods, who handles botany, Barns, who runs our audio visual section, Price, who is our resident zoologist, and Briggs, our etymologist."

Melanie nodded at each in turn.

"Then we have Abbott, Philips, Greaves, Taylor, Jones and Jackson, general dogsbodies and camp specialists," Jenkins continued. "They handle the cooking, carrying, tent maintenance and so on, but each one is trained to take over in an emergency. With you, that makes thirteen. I hope you're not superstitious!" he smiled.

"Not at all," she laughed.

"We generally call one another by our surnames," he explained. "That way, two people with the same first names don't get mixed up."

"Except you," said Baines, amused. "You're the only professor, after all."

"They all know how I work," he said. "And I'm sure you'll get used to it. I do have a few idiosyncrasies, so I'll trust Baines to fill you in on my expectations."

CHAPTER TWENTY-FIVE

A week later they all met at the corn exchange hall hired by Professor Jenkins.

"Right," he said, clapping his hands. "Everything is arranged. We leave Gatwick at 06.30 a.m. on October the 17th for Jarras. From there, by light aircraft to Lawinda, where we will refuel, and then fly on to Gitac, then refuel again. There is no runway in the jungle, but there is a clearing about one hundred yards square."

"Who's the pilot?" asked Woods.

"Lex."

Everyone groaned.

"Oh no, not *Lex*," Woods complained. "He's a kamikaze pilot! During the war he flew thirty-eight missions!" for Japan?

"But if he's a kamikaze," said Melanie, "then how –"

"Don't ask," the professor laughed. "It's a joke."

"Oh," she said, dubiously, still not understanding.

"He will fly over the clearing a few times, dropping our supplies, and then we will parachute down ourselves," Professor Jenkins explained. "We will parachute in tandem to save Biggles flying to and fro too many times. Right, lady and gentlemen," he continued. "Baines will keep you informed of any changes as we get closer to departure. I would like you to keep quiet about our plans, please. No press – the less who know about it, the better. We don't want any rivals getting wind of this."

As they were leaving, Baines approached Melanie.

"Would you care to join me for lunch?" he offered. "I'm hungry, so you must be!"

"Yes," she said. "I would like that, thank you."

"Excellent," he said. "I know a nice little restaurant not far from here."

After a pleasant meal, Melanie and Baines enjoyed a glass of wine. She looked at him.

"Do you mind if I call you Mark?" she asked.

"Only when we are not with the Professor," he said. "He's a bit of a stickler for the rules."

"He does seem a bit bombastic," she said.

"He does appear that way," he replied. "But don't judge him before you get to know him. He knows what he's doing and he puts the safety of everyone else before himself. Most of us owe him our lives, one way or another."

She moved to the edge of her seat, interested.

"Pray tell," she said, "how did he save yours?"

"We were exploring a lake in Ragooa," said Baines. "It was said to be an ancient burial ground for tribal chiefs who were lowered into the water, laden with gold."

"Did you find any gold?" she asked.

"No," Baines shook his head. "The silt was too deep and we couldn't get through. It was an expensive trip with no results – that's probably why the University won't fund this trip."

"Well," said Melanie, impatient. "How did he save your life?"

"I tripped in the boat," said Baines. "Hitting my head and knocking myself out. I fell into the crocodile infested water – they told me later I sank like a stone. The professor dived in after me, swam down and pulled me out. As we got to the boat, a croc grabbed his leg. Woods spotted it and hit the croc in the eye with an oar. The croc let go and they pulled us out – when he wears his shorts you will see just how lucky he was. He may not look like much, but he's a tough old bird."

"You seem to hold him in high esteem," said Melanie.

"We all do," said Baines. "That's why we sign up with him time after time. We trust him and he trusts us. You will too, when you get to know him."

"I doubt that," she said. "He's not my kind of person."

Baines frowned slightly, finishing his drink.

*   *   *

As the day of departure came closer, Mark Baines telephoned her.

"A taxi will pick you up on the 16th of October at 16.00 hours," he said. "Have everything packed and ready to go. You will be taken to a hotel near Gatwick Airport. We will stay overnight and fly out on the 17th at 08.15 a.m."

The taxi arrived on time and took her to the hotel.

That evening, over dinner, the professor addressed her, "Make the most of tonight. It will be the last time you will sleep in a comfortable bed for months."

She was so excited that she hardly slept a wink all night. The next morning she showered and dressed, meeting the others for breakfast. A minibus collected them and took them to the airport. The equipment was quickly stowed and they boarded the plane.

As they sped down the runway she wondered whether she had done the right thing. Would she be able to cope with the coming adventure? Would she regret going?

Still, it's too late to change my mind now, she thought.

It was a long flight and after a couple of drinks she fell into a deep and dreamless sleep. She awoke with a start as the plane shuddered violently. Immediately, all those possible wreck sites came to mind.

"Please fasten your seatbelts," said the captain. "We have run into a little turbulence."

She looked at her watch and was astonished to discover she had been asleep for six hours. She had slept through lunch so the

203

stewardess brought her a sandwich. She slept again, then. The plane landed with a jolt as the wheels hit the runway. She had slept through most of the flight.

The equipment was unloaded at Jarras and packed into a lorry with wooden bench seats running down either side. The drive for the next two hundred miles was particularly hard on the bum. They arrived at Gitac airfield as the sun rose.

"They call this an airfield?" Melanie mumbled to herself.

It was just a mud track with a tin shed for a hangar. The so-called aircraft was little more than a beat-up pile of junk held together with duck-tape, glue and string. It looked like it wouldn't get off the ground.

Sitting on the ground, smoking a cigarette and drinking a can of lager was a scruffy looking tramp.

Melanie turned to Baines.

"Look at that old tramp, drinking at this time of the morning," she whispered.

"That 'old tramp' as you call him," Baines whispered back. "Is our pilot."

Melanie cringed.

"Never!" she exclaimed. "We're all going to die!"

The tramp got up, walked over to the professor still drinking his lager and shook hands.

"Nice to see you, Prof!" he said.

The Professor turned to Melanie.

"This is Lex," he said, our pilot. "He's an American, wanted in most parts of the world for gun running, smuggling, slave trading and lots of other things you don't want to know about."

Lex took her hand gallantly, and kissed it.

"Nice arse," he grinned. "Come to think of it, the rest of the equipment looks pretty good, too!"

Melanie snatched her hand away, wiped it on her blouse and stomped off in disgust.

A tarpaulin was tied to some trees as a shelter, under which Briggs was making a nice cup of tea and preparing a meal. Everything he made came out of tins.

Lex and Professor Jenkins were working out the final details of the flight when a figure appeared at the far end of the runway. They watched as he got closer, and eventually they realised he was an elderly tribesman. His skin was the colour of ebony and he wore a bright red cloth around his body, tied at the waist with a leather thong. He had a spear in his hand.

Lex welcomed him and led him over to the others.

"This is the man I told you about, Prof."

He invited him to sit in the shade and was given some fruit and water. Watching him eat and rest, Melanie admired his skin. It was as black as coal and as smooth as silk.

I'd pay a fortune for skin like that! she thought.

With Lex translating, the old man told stories of a big demon bird falling out of the sky and crashing down into the jungle like thunder.

"That sounds like a plane crashing," said Baines.

He told of a white warrior they called the 'crocodile slayer' and his woman, who they called 'Mary'.

"Mary?" said the professor. "That's a Jewish name, isn't it? Not African?"

"It's possible she could be related to a centre of missionaries," Baines suggested, but he looked doubtful.

The old man told of great battles, and how the birds would speak and warn of enemy attacks.

"Talking birds," said Baines. "That's different. Parrots only mimic – they can't hold a conversation."

205

"Ask him if this white man is a chief," said the professor.

"No," said the old man, via Lex. "The white man is not a chief, but the white woman is."

"Way to go women's liberation," Melanie laughed. "At least it's reached the jungle!"

After the old man had finished they gave him some salt, food and water, and then he disappeared into the jungle.

"What do you make of that?" the professor asked.

"Sounds like a load of old codswallop," said Baines. "If the stories are true then it means people are going in and out of that part of the jungle all the time, and we will be wasting our time."

"Why parachute in when we can just walk?" Barns piped up.

"Hmm," said the Professor. "I don't know."

Over the next two days, preparations were made for the drop. The equipment loaded onto the plane.

"When we get over the drop zone I will drop a marker to find the wind speed," said Lex. "Then you'll unload the equipment, and after that you'll fly."

Melanie looked a little apprehensive.

"Don't worry," said Baines. "I'll look after you."

The professor looked at her.

"You can still change your mind if you want to, you know," he said.

"No way," she snapped, affronted. "I'm in it for the duration."

All the last minute checks were made. Everyone paired off and put their parachutes on. They checked and double checked their equipment.

"Everyone on board!" shouted Lex.

The engines came to life with a roar and the little aeroplane taxied to the end of the runway. He opened the throttle. The plane was vibrating so much that Melanie wondered whether it might simply tear itself apart.

The brake was released and they moved down the runway, slowly gathering speed. The wingtips just missing the trees on either side of the runway. The end was getting closer and closer. Lex was yanking on the joystick with all his might.

"I'm going to have to lengthen this bloody runway one day!" he shouted.

Now he tells us! thought Melanie.

The moment the runway vanished the plane lifted off the ground. With the engine at full throttle, the trees were coming up fast.

Whoosh!

The wheels brushed the tops of the trees, missing catastrophe by inches.

"Crikey!" shouted Lex. "I didn't think we were going to make it!"

"You didn't, and you're the pilot!" Melanie yelled back, over the roar of the engine. "How do you think we felt?"

Around her, the rest of the expedition all looked a bit white; finally she understood why they had all groaned at the mention of Lex's name.

As they flew over the jungle, the team looked down. There were trees as far as the eye could see in every direction, flocks of birds rising in places from the vast green carpet. Little sparkling lights like diamonds reflecting off rivers winding through the trees.

After a few hours they could see mountains in the distance, rising up from the jungle proper. The peaks actually had snow on them. Lex pulled on the joystick and we rose above them. On the other side there was jungle again, trapped in what must have been the crater of an extinct volcano. The mountains formed a complete circle, hundreds of miles across.

207

"It's no wonder this area had never been explored," said the professor. "No one could get in or out without a parachute."

They flew on for another hour or so, with the Professor carefully reading his map and compass.

"The clearing should be up ahead," he shouted. "There – there, that's it!"

Lex's marker was a lump of rock with a bright piece of rag tied to it.

Professor. "When I get over the middle of the clearing, I will shout 'now' and then you drop the marker," shouted Lex. "If the wind takes it fifty yards past the clearing I'll drop you fifty yards before the clearing – that way you should land in the clearing, yeah?"

The plane banked around and levelled up. Over the centre of the clearing, Lex shouted, *"Now!"*

The professor dropped the marker. They watched it land about thirty yards into the trees. He flew around again.

"Now, when I give the signal, drop the first piece of equipment," shouted Lex.

After several passes, all the equipment was dispatched safely.

"Now, hook up your static lines," the pilot instructed. "I'll fly round again and you jump, two at a time on my signal. Good luck!"

As the plane banked around, Baines and Melanie, kitted out to jump in tandem, and stood in the door of the plane.

Lex gave the signal and Melanie squeezed her eyes tightly shut as Mark pushed her out. She froze in terror at the sudden plunge. The fear and the wind speed were such that she couldn't even scream.

When she did open her eyes they were about a hundred feet from the ground, directly over the clearing. She cast around – the professor and Briggs were on target, too, but the others had overshot into the trees.

Baines pulled hard on the rigging lines and they landed safely in a heap. They quickly unbuckled their harness and went in search of the others. Melanie shaded her eyes against the hot sun in time to see the plane disappearing over the trees.

Some of the party were hanging in the trees, but others had landed less elegantly in the undergrowth. Most were bruised and battered, but luckily there were no serious injuries.

A roll call was made and all were accounted for.

"Let's get the equipment together, hide the parachutes and move out in case there are hostiles about," Baines barked. "Can you handle a gun?" he added, to Melanie

"Yes," she said. "Pistol and rifle."

"Put this in your belt," he said, handing her a pistol. "I hope you won't need it, but just in case."

A path led from the clearing into the jungle; they peered along it.

"From now on," said the professor. "Keep your mouths shut and your eyes open."

CHAPTER TWENTY-SIX

They headed off into the into trees, the professor in front and Baines at the rear as a sort of tail gunner.

After a couple of hours they came to a clearing. The sun shone down in streaks and the rising steam making eerie patterns of cloud and shadow, like ghosts hanging in the trees.

The professor raised his hand.

"We will make camp here," he said. "Briggs, make us a nice brew, would you? I'm parched."

They set up camp and enjoyed a nice cup of tea and a jam sandwich.

Woods got to his feet.

"I'm going to look for any unrecorded plants," he said. He had clearly been bursting to do this all through their lunch.

"Not on your own," said the professor. "Abbot, you go with him. If you run into trouble, fire a series of shots – one every ten seconds – until we find you."

"I could do with a bath," Melanie reflected. "I smell terrible."

"Okay," said the professor. "We will try to find a rock pool. Whatever you do, don't bathe in a river or lake. You'll make a tasty meal for a croc. Baines, come with us."

They walked for about ten minutes through the dense undergrowth until they came across a little stream. They followed it up to a waterfall cascading into a crystal clear pool about twenty feet across.

"You should be safe enough to bathe in there," said the professor.

He and Baines sat on a rock on the edge of the pool, talking.

"You don't think I'm going to strip off in front of you two, do you?" Melanie stormed. "Turn around!"

The two men looked at each other, raised their eyebrows and turned their backs.

She didn't trust them, but it was worth the gamble. She stripped off and entered the cool, clear water. It was heavenly, washing the sweat and dirt off her body. When she had finished, she came out and walked towards her clothes.

Baines turned instinctively at the movement. He drew in an appreciative breath and turned away again.

"Thank you, gentlemen," she said, and they walked back to the camp together.

After she had gone into her tent, the professor raised an eyebrow at his old friend.

"Well, Baines, was it worth a look?"

"Strewth, yes!" he exclaimed. "She has a body to die for!"

Later, the others returned to camp having had a fruitful rummage about in the jungle, and they all settled down for the night.

Woods rattled on for a while about the unidentified plants he had found.

"We saw no sign of life," said Philips.

"It's a big jungle," said the professor. "I expect there are villages out there somewhere."

The next few days were spent exploring the area, logging new species of plants and trees. Flower seeds and nuts were picked and dried, and put into packets to be taken home for further study. Price was delighted to encounter a lizard he had never seen before.

"Right," said the Professor. "I think we have exhausted this area. Tomorrow, we move on."

* * *

Early the next morning they packed up camp and moved off. After a couple of hours or so the path opened out, making

212

progress much easier. The trees on either side were black for about five hundred yards.

"There has been quite a fire here," said Philips. "It must have been some time ago, because the undergrowth has re-established itself."

They walked the full length of the scar to the end, where they came across the burnt out fuselage of a large passenger aircraft.

"Blimey," Abbot exclaimed. "I wonder if anyone survived that…"

"If they did, they didn't get far," said the Professor, pointing a little further along in the grass.

Melanie put her hand over her mouth, horrified.

"Oh my God," she exclaimed.

In the grass lay a skeleton with a broken spear through its chest.

"So the natives are hostile," said Baines. "Keep your eyes peeled."

They took some photographs and moved on. From then on, nobody spoke a word. They all looked around, wide-eyed.

"When we make camp," whispered Professor Jenkins, "we'll stay well off the beaten track. Only light a fire in daylight – and only use dry wood and leaves. We don't want to give our position away."

After they set up camp the professor asked Melanie if she wanted to bathe again.

"No thank you," she said. "I'll have an all-over wash in my tent."

"Abbott, try the radio and see if you can contact anyone," said the professor.

Abbott turned the radio on and moved all over the camp trying to get a signal, but to no avail. He even climbed up a tree, but it didn't work.

"The mountains are too high," he announced. "Nothing can get through – we're on our own."

"Right," the professor barked. "We will pair off and post lookouts, changing over every hour. Baines, you and Pointer take the first watch, then me and Abbott, then Woods and Briggs, and so on."

After everyone had turned in, Baines and Melanie kept lookout. She looked at Baines.

"I have an uneasy feeling," she said. "I get the impression we are not alone."

"Me too," he said."

"Have you ever been in this position before?" she asked.

"Yes, may times," he nodded.

"What happened?" she asked.

"I'm still alive, aren't I?" he chuckled.

"That doesn't fill me with confidence, I have to admit," she grumbled.

"No," he said. "This is uncharted territory. A lot of these tribes might be warlike – even cannibalistic."

"You're scaring me," she said, quietly, staring out into the night.

"Well, you forced your way onto this expedition," said Baines, giving her a hard look. "The professor did try to warn you."

*   *   *

The next few days were spent exploring and finding new plants and animals. They were all drawn and logged, and their particulars recorded. Seeds were put in packets as before, but now the entire team was on edge. There was an air of urgency about their every activity. Four men kept watch at all times.

One morning they had packed up camp and were walking along a path when, all of a sudden, Philips stopped and put his hand up.

"Listen," he said.

Everyone stopped.

"I can't hear anything," said the professor.

"Exactly," said Philips. "It's too quiet."

"Quick," whispered the professor. "Get off the path."

They dove into the undergrowth and lay as still as they could. Only a few seconds later a dozen or so tribesmen came around a bend in the path carrying spears and shields. Their bodies were painted.

They ran past and disappeared into the jungle. After a few minutes, Baines got up.

"Stay down," he said. "I will check and see if it's all clear."

They waited, tense, until he came back.

"They've gone," he whispered.

"Do you think they were looking for us?" Abbott asked.

"Well, with that war paint and those weapons, I don't think they were going on a picnic do you?"

"Right," said the professor. "We wait here for an hour to see if they come back."

Baines set out again after an hour, to make sure the coast was clear.

"All clear," he said when he came back.

"We will travel on the less used paths from now on," the professor ordered. "No talking, only whispers or sign language. Have your guns ready."

They travelled on for about three hours without stopping, trying to put enough distance between them and the natives. As the sun started to set the path opened up into a clearing about fifty yards wide and two hundred yards long.

The jungle stretched along three sides of it, and on the fourth was a sheer rock face. At the base were some caves, with some boulders before them.

"We will camp here in one of the caves," said the professor. "As before we need two lookouts, changing hourly. I think we have enough daylight for a brew up, but we must put it out before it gets dark. These white rocks will reflect the flames like a mirror and give our position away."

The cave looked like it would be easy to guard. Everyone took their turn on watch and the night passed peacefully.

As the sun rose over the trees, Abbott was sitting on a rock, dozing, and Woods was sitting on the ground by the cave entrance. He looked up.

"A noise came from the jungle," Woods whispered. "What was that?"

Abbott jumped to his feet, staring out into the trees.

"Nothing," he said, slowly.

The noise came again, and this time they both heard it. Abbott took the safety lock off his rifle. He leaned forward to get a better look. At the same time a head appeared on the other side of the rock, face distorted into a scowl and slathered in war paint.

Abbott jumped back in surprise, but before he could pull the trigger an arm wielding a knife came over the rock and slit his throat. The rifle went off with a crack, the bullet hitting the savage in the chest. They both fell, either side of the boulder.

The commotion woke the others, who struggled to their feet and grabbed their guns. When they emerged from the cave Woods was already firing across the clearing. About twenty natives were running towards them.

"Shoot at will," the professor shouted. "Make every bullet count!"

As the first wave came close enough, all the guns let loose; ten of the enemy hit the dirt. Another wave ran in, the rifles cutting them down again and again. The natives began to turn and run back into the jungle.

"Cease fire – don't waste ammunition!" the professor yelled. "Fire again when you see the whites of their eyes!" He took a breath and looked around. "Are there any casualties?"

"Abbott's dead," said Woods, "And Taylor. Everyone else is okay."

"Good," said the professor, focussing on the task at hand. "Be ready for the next onslaught."

Melanie was standing in the cave entrance, shaking. She held her pistol up in front of her in both hands, but she hadn't fired a shot. Baines took the gun out of her hands.

"Stay in the cave," he said. "We'll take care of this."

"No!" she shouted, and took the gun back. "I said I would hold my own and I will."

She nearly dropped it when they came out of the trees again, shrieking like banshees. Another volley of bullets sent them retreating again. This time, a hail of arrows flew out of the cover of the trees. Briggs, Greaves and Philips all died with arrows in their chests.

"Get down!" Baines roared, but the professor was too slow and an arrow struck him in the shoulder.

Price turned to run and he was immediately struck down by an arrow, passing right through his heart. He was dead before he hit the ground.

Melanie started screaming uncontrollably.

"Shut up!" shouted Baines, but she was beyond listening to him. "Shut up!"

He grabbed her arm and slapped her around the face. It did the trick; she stood there, looking stunned. They took defensive positions and waited for the next attack.

CHAPTER TWENTY-SEVEN

Back at the village, Jawana was playing with Lani and Mary was going about her chores, happily talking to herself. She was funny to watch, walking about the village without a care in the world. She looked after our little family and any other waifs and strays that needed love. Lani was about three years old now, and was living up to the meaning of his name: 'handsome warrior'.

He was handsome alright – he got that from his father.

From the corner of my eye I saw a movement: two yellow doves flew in over the trees. The Raato tribe were in trouble.

Our chief summoned everyone to arms. The Raato village was about twenty miles to the south – it would take some time to get there.

I felt a hand in the back on my waistband. Mary stood there, smiling up at me with her axe in her hand. I wanted to tell her to stay in the village, but I knew it would be a waste of breath.

Reg held Jawana and Lani's hands and nodded at me. I knew they would be safe.

I led the tribe out of the village, followed by Mamooto and about half of our warriors. Mbata took the other half down a different track in case of an ambush.

After a few hours of running we could hear gunshots in the distance. I knew of no tribes with that kind of firepower. We entered a clearing full of Raato warriors, who greeted us warmly.

"The Butata are fighting with white people," they told us.

"White people?" I exclaimed.

We crawled through the undergrowth and observed the fighting. To the left, behind some rocks were a handful of white people and to the right were a horde of Butatas.

Hastily, we made a battle plan. At that moment there were only two tribes – us and the Raato.

"We will have to do something before the Butata overrun them."

*   *   *

"Professor! We're running out of ammo'!" shouted Baines.

"Keep firing!" the professor roared back. "If we are going to die, we'll die fighting!"

Suddenly everything fell silent. The Butata froze – they stood like statues, staring at the end of the clearing, their spears raised.

"Baines, what's happening?" asked the professor.

"I don't know sir!"

Cautiously, the few remains of the expedition team watched the Butata square themselves up, shoulder to shoulder with their new enemy.

Then, from the trees, a white man and woman ran into the clearing, followed by an enormous dog.

"I don't believe it!" the professor exclaimed. "So the stories are true!"

Behind them, two groups of people moved forward in ranks under shields, like two great tortoises. The Butata regrouped and raised their bows. As they fired I pushed Mary in front of me and knelt behind my shield. Jekyl sat behind Mary.

*   *   *

A hail of arrows rained down onto the shields. Our archers put arrows to the strings of their bows, ready to return a volley.

"Fire!" came the order. The shields went up and a barrage of arrows flew at the Butata.

They must have lost about twenty men. They fired again as our shields went down.

"Fire!" Came the order again.

Another volley of arrows took out another twenty of their warriors. They decided to rush us; I drew my sword.

"Charge!" I bellowed.

The dog shot off like a rocket, Mary and I hot on his heels, wielding our weapons. The rest of our men came out of the trees behind us, yelling and screaming. There was a crash like thunder when we met in the middle. The dog let fly and took out the first man. I went in next, then Mary, her axed raised above her head.

"I don't believe this is happening!" shouted the professor. "It's like nothing I have ever seen before"

As they watched the battle taking place, a Butata warrior jumped up onto a rock. He scowled down at the professor and raised his spear. Before he could throw it he crashed face down onto the rock. And there stood Mary, she had buried the axe into his back. She put her foot against his shoulder and wrenched the blade out. Grinned down at the Professor.

Then with her tongue stuck out in concentration she ran back into the affray.

In close combat we were gaining the edge. Then, from behind us, two of our friendly tribes joined the fight. The tide really began to turn – we outnumbered them about three to one.

Melanie was standing with her back to the rock face, petrified; two Butata grabbed her and ran into the jungle, followed by the rest of the tribe.

They fled, leaving their dead and wounded strewn around. I scanned the battlefield: Mary was standing with the axe raised above her head. She was drenched in blood, but alive. Mbata was checking our fallen for wounded, but I couldn't see Mamooto.

Mary started walking back towards me when she dropped her axe and fell to her knees. For a moment I thought she had been hurt. She looked up at me, a pained expression on her face. Frantically, she beckoned me over to her. Mamooto was lying on the ground with a spear in his back.

"Mamooto!" I shouted.

He opened his eyes.

"Stay with me," I told him. "We will get you back to the village."

Mary held his hand, tears streaming down her face. I snapped the lance off as Mbata ran over.

"Make up a stretcher and get him home," I told him.

I ran over to the shell-shocked group of strangers.

"Stay here until I call you."

The man who looked like he was in charge nodded. We made up stretchers for our wounded and sent them home first. Next we tended to our dead; they had fought and died as heroes. The Butatas had lost about one hundred men. Their wounded were slain and all the bodies were carried to the lake to be disposed of.

As we prepared to move out I called the leader of the bedraggled looking group.

"Have you lost anyone?" I asked.

"Yes," he said, sadly. "Ten men dead and one woman missing."

He shook my hand vigorously.

"Thank you for – " he began, but I stopped him.

"We haven't got time," I said. "They may regroup and come back. You have about a twenty mile walk ahead of you – I will leave some men to guide you, but you must not stop for anything. Keep moving. I have to get back urgently."

Mary grabbed my waistband and we set off at a fast pace. All the way back to the village I prayed that Mamooto had made it back alive. We must have covered that twenty miles in record time.

* * *

When we got to the village, Mamooto was lying on his side in his bed, the witchdoctor dancing and chanting around him. As he had with Mary, Najeet covered the broken shaft with green paste. Mary held Mamooto's hand and I stood with my hand on his shoulder. His other hand came up and covered mine, but he didn't open his eyes. Najeet grabbed the shaft and pushed it hard; the blade came out through his stomach. Then she gripped the blade and tugged it right through his body. He didn't even flinch.

After dressing the wounds, some girls came in with water to bathe him.

"No," said Mary. "I do it."

I watched as she gently bathed him from head to toe. When she had finished, I picked him up and carried him to our hammock. He was a part of our family, after all.

Mary sat next to him, his hand tucked into hers. I went outside and sat down. Before now, I hadn't realised how much this man meant to us – to me. He was closer than a brother. I started to shake, forcing my tears back.

Mbata came over and sat beside me.

"He can't die," I stuttered. "He can't."

Mbata put his arm around my shoulder.

"Have faith in jungle medicine," he told me.

One day our luck had to run out, I mused. Although the battles are fewer, sod's law said that one of us would have to die sooner or later. That's the way of the jungle.

Just then, Jawana and Lani ran past me and into our hut. They stood next to their mother, staring at Mamooto. She put her arms around them.

"Mamooto is asleep," she whispered. "We will look after him."

Both children ran out crying. We all loved this man, despite our past differences. I was glad, then, that I hadn't killed him.

I went to the lake and bathed, trying to get a handle on my emotions. I returned as the rest of our tribes came back with the survivors of the expedition. The chief welcomed them in. The leader of the group came over and introduced himself.

"We heard stories of a white man and woman, but we didn't believe them!" he told me.

"First," I said. "You clean up and have your wounds dressed. Take some refreshment and then we'll talk."

"Good idea," he said. "But what about Miss Pointer?"

"Forget about her," I advised. "There's nothing anyone can do for her now."

"But surely we should try – not just give up –"

I shook my head.

"Then pray that she is already dead."

The expedition party bathed and Najeet dressed their wounds. After they had eaten, we sat and talked, filling one another in on our histories.

It was pleasant to hold a conversation in English again, though Mary and I often spoke it together – we had taught it to our children in case we went home.

"If you hadn't arrived when you did," said Professor Jenkins, "I don't think any of us would still be alive."

"No," I agreed. "The Butata take no prisoners, unless they find women or children to enslave for their own sadistic pleasure.

"Do you think Miss Pointer is still alive?" the professor asked. "If she is, what will they do to her?"

I sighed.

"First the chief will abuse her, then she will be handed around the rest of the tribe to do with her what they will. Before they have finished with her she will beg them to kill her – and eventually, they will."

"Good God," the professor exclaimed, aghast. "It doesn't bear thinking about. There must be something we can do to save her."

"I will talk to the chief," I promised.

CHAPTER TWENTY-EIGHT

The next day, the professor and I approached the chief and he agreed that we could check out the Butata's village – but only with the help of the other tribes. Messengers were sent and they all agreed to help.

Two days later we all met at our village. There must have been over five hundred warriors, fully armed and battle ready, just to check over a village.

The plan was to reach the Butata tribe after dark and watch for any signs of Miss Pointer.

"We'll come with you," said the professor.

"No," I said. "We have to run miles and you won't be able to keep up."

I looked up as Mary came out of the hut, axe in hand.

"No," I said again. "You stay here and look after Mamooto and the children."

For once, Mary didn't argue. She simply nodded and returned to our hut.

We set off in small groups, taking different paths. Five hundred men and women running together would have sounded like a herd of elephants trampling through the jungle, giving our position away. Before we reached the village we stopped and worked out a final plan. If there was any sign of Miss Pointer the Watiti, Nimwa and Munooti would circle the village, taking out the guards without alarming the other villagers.

The rest of us were to position ourselves in the trees surrounding the huts. The other warriors set off to take out the guards while the rest of us crawled up to the edge of the ridge to wait. It was a cloudy night with no moon, which gave us an advantage.

The village was lit up by fires, which were dotted around the clearing. The Butata tribesmen were sitting in a circle, eating a feast and drinking heavily. If we had to attack then they were in no fit state to fight. We would have the edge of surprise.

In the centre of the circle was a table – like an altar. From one of the huts two men dragged a white woman. She was naked and screaming, struggling to escape. They put her on the altar and held her down. We had to act now, or it would be too late.

I gave the signal and we climbed down the slope into the trees.

In the village, a cheer went up as the chief came out of his hut and walked over to Miss Pointer. He positioned himself at her feet and leered down at her, saliva dripping from his lips. Roughly, he grabbed her hips and pulled her towards him.

We moved in closer, hidden by the huts. We were looking at the top of her head and down her body towards the chief.

He entered her with such force that she screamed and passed out, which was probably for the best. I stood up and drew my sword, ready to give the order to charge. Mbata stopped me.

"He is mine," he signalled.

From the darkness on the other side of the village came a blood curdling scream – one of their guards had managed to raise the alarm before he was taken out. There was a moment of silence as Mbata let fly his spear; our men ran in, screaming. The chief opened his eyes to see Mbata's spear not ten feet in front of him. Before he could move out of its way the spear hit him full in the chest. The force of the impact threw him backwards horizontally. He was dead before he hit the ground.

The rest of their tribe were caught off guard and ran around like headless chickens. It was a massacre. I ran forward in the confusion and picked Miss Pointer up and carried her into the trees.

I could hear the killing behind me until I was out of earshot. I rested then, and checked Miss Pointer. She was still unconscious and as limp as a wet rag. I waited until our men caught up with me, then I put her over my shoulder and started running for our village. About halfway home, Mbata took her from me and carried her the rest of the way.

She was still unconscious when we arrived back at the village, but still breathing.

The women bathed her and put her in a hammock to sleep. I looked in on Mamooto and Mary, but there was no real change in his condition. His eyes were open, though, and he held out his hand.

"I'm glad you're back with us," I smiled.

Jawana and Lani jumped up and down, clapping their hands and laughing in excitement. They were as glad as I was to see him back.

"Outside, kids," I told them. "Let him get some rest."

Mary gave him some water and he went back to sleep. Each day he got stronger and stronger.

"We have lost ten good men," the professor lamented, "and maybe Miss Pointer if she doesn't pull through. I don't want to lose anyone else before we go home. Our radio was smashed in the ambush so we have no means of calling for help. We will have to walk," he added, "when we can leave."

"We have been here for so long I had almost forgotten the thought of going home," I admitted. "Civilisation actually frightens me."

"But you must, man!" the professor declared. "You owe it to your wife and children. They need a proper education – and Mary needs the benefits of modern living. You need to mix with your own kind again."

That night I lay awake, thinking about England. Mary could tell I was restless.

"You not sleep?" she asked.

"No, I'm not sleeping."

"Why?" she smiled.

"How would you and the kids like to go home?" I asked.

"I am home."

"No, England home."

She gave me an odd look.

"Don't know," she said, and fell asleep.

"I suppose it would be nice to wash with soap and hot water," I reflected, quietly. "Use a flush toilet, drink a glass of wine and drive a car instead of running everywhere…"

The next morning, Mary helped Melanie stand up. She was covered in cuts and bruises, but they would heal in time. Mary bathed her in the lake, dried her body and sprinkled her with oils. She combed her hair until it shone, entwining flowers into it. Then Jawana led her outside and sat with her.

*   *   *

One morning, Baines and the professor came to our hut.

"Have you thought about going home?" they asked.

"Yes, I have thought about it," I said. "But there is no way out of here that I know of, and neither does the chief. His people have lived here for thousands of years."

"We don't have a radio," said Baines, "but we do have these."

He held out some papers.

"These are aerial maps of the area – and I think they might show us a way out of here."

We studied the maps over a drink. We were in the centre of a vast jungle, with hundreds of miles of dense trees, lakes, rivers, swamps and mountains, with no visible signs of an exit.

"There might be a way," said Baines, pointing to the charts. "This river here flows to that mountain, where it disappears. It must flow somewhere – eventually, all rivers lead to the ocean."

"But that could be miles from where it disappears," I said. "It could go anywhere. What if it does flow through the mountain and the channel is smaller than the boat? We would all be crushed to death! Or, if it exits the mountain three hundred feet up we would never survive the fall."

After a heated discussion we decided to let the subject rest for a while.

"How is your shoulder, Professor?" I asked.

"Great," he smiled. "What's in that cream she put on it? If I knew the formula we could give it to the world and save millions of lives."

"Professor," I said, carefully. "Have you thought about what might happen to these people if civilisation invaded their world? They would end up like the American Indians or the Aborigines, their way of life wiped out completely."

"Nonsense," he snorted. "Their way of life as it is, is prehistoric. We would bring them out of the dark and into the light! There would be no more fighting and killing each other."

"Yes, like the civilised world," I said. "After thousands of years of religious fighting in the name of God. Country against country, fighting over oil or gold. These people only call to arms if they're threatened, not for greed or for power."

He stared at me for a moment.

"Point taken," he allowed. "But I do believe that it would be to their advantage."

"Well, I don't," I said.

"Okay," he replied. "We will just have to agree to disagree. If you don't want to return home yourself, will you at least help us to get back? My team have families that don't know if they're alive or dead." He paused before continuing, "I think it's our duty to let the families of the deceased know so they can at least grieve and not live in the hope that they will be returning home."

"Okay," I agreed. "I will help you, but only on the condition that you do not bring civilisation back here."

"In that case, I don't have a choice," he said. "Deal."

"Shake on it."

I shook his hand, but I didn't entirely trust him.

*   *   *

Over the next few months, plans were drawn up and a boat was constructed. The professor learned to speak the basic native language and spent hours talking to the chief, learning the history and laws of the tribe. They became close friends and, by the way they laughed together, they were like two old friends having a pint down the local pub.

I sat gazing at Mary and the children. When we first crashed in the jungle, I would have given anything to go home, but now I have the chance to, I was no longer sure I wanted to. But did my reluctance to go home give me the right to deprive the children of a modern education, or to keep Mary living in a hut with no mod cons, running twenty or thirty miles, wielding an axe – fighting and killing, then running back home again to take up her duties as a wife and a mother? One day she might not come back – what then? My heart jumped. I could never live without her.

Mamooto was back on his feet now. I was glad to have him as my shadow again. Melanie never left Mary's side, but she still wouldn't speak. I suppose she was still pretty traumatised.

*   *   *

One day the chief sent for me.

"You are troubled," he said. "Why?"

"I have been asked to take my family back to England," I explained. "Part of me wants to go, but part of me wants to stay. I don't know what to do."

The chief looked at me and smiled.

"You have lived with us here for many moons and in that time have proved yourself to be a leader of men and a fine warrior, and Mary has proved herself to be a noble chief," he said. "I love you all as my own. If you have a yearning to go back, you must take the opportunity. Sleep on it and give me your decision in the morning."

All that night I lay awake thinking: go or stay?

Mary never had a care in the world. She slept like a rock from dusk until dawn. In the morning I felt her stir beside me. She opened her eyes and smiled.

"Love you," she beamed.

"Mary…"

"What?" she asked.

"How would you like us all to go home?"

"Okay," she said.

"Do you really want to go?" I asked again.

"I go with you," she answered, then got up and made breakfast.

Later, the chief welcome the professor and I into his hut and I agreed to go with them.

"Good man!" said the professor. "Without your help, I doubt we would make it to the mountains, let alone back home."

The boat was completed now. It was about forty feet long, six feet wide and clinker built – like a Viking longship. Shields lined the sides of the vessel; broad, oblong shields that could be raised above our heads to protect us from arrows. Considering the primitive tools the tribe had used, it looked magnificent.

The boat was loaded with supplies for our departure the next morning. That night, a great feast was prepared to bid us farewell. The chief sat in his usual place with his daughter and Mbata at his side, Mary sitting next to him in her ceremonial robes. I shall never forget that scene for the rest of my life. Mary was every inch a chief.

I hadn't seen much of Reg lately. He kept mostly to himself. He didn't say it, but I don't think he was sure about going back home. I thought perhaps that the unknown dangers of the river scared him. When we did meet he just said 'hello' and carried on with his business, but he always gave Mary and the kids a kiss and a hug.

During the feast the professor came and sat with me.

"I don't wish to be rude," he began, "but you and Mary – you two do seem to be an unusual match."

"Yes," I said. "A few years ago I would have agreed with you, but if you could only see her through my eyes…"

"Oh, I can see you are both very much in love," he said. "And when the rest of the world sees what she has achieved it could change people's views on Down's Syndrome."

"That's what scares me," I told him. "Not knowing which way the rest of the world will jump."

"Can you tell me why she sits with the chief and you sit with the tribe?" he asked.

I told him our story over a couple of drinks, how she had saved the chief's life and was rewarded for her courage by being made a chief.

"Amazing," he said, when I had finished. "I have seen her in battle. She doesn't lack courage and shows absolutely no fear."

After the feast the drums started. I noticed Melanie had drunk quite a bit of jungle juice and was swaying to and fro. The girls got up and started dancing. I nudged the professor.

"Look at Melanie."

"She's drunk," he laughed.

"Don't worry," I said. "She's safe enough and it will do her good to loosen up a bit."

She stood up and walked over to the other girls. Mary had wound flowers into Melanie's hair and around her neck and wrists. She wore a tiny leather thong and nothing else. She seemed like she was in a trance. As the drums got louder she danced faster and faster. Her body was covered in a sheen of perspiration.

Beads of sweat ran down her body as she danced; then the drums stopped. Her hair was stuck to her face and her whole body was covered in sweat. It was one of the most sensual sights I have ever seen. I heard the professor go 'phew'!

CHAPTER TWENTY-NINE

That night I held Mary tightly. I fell asleep wondering what the future will hold. In the morning the chief invited us to sit with him to eat. When we had finished he asked for thirty men and women to row the boat for our journey.

Without exception the whole tribe stepped forward. I felt humbled. They were willing to risk their lives for us. I looked up to see Reg walking towards us carrying that briefcase.

"Are you ready?"

"No," he replied. "I am staying here. I don't want to go back to the rat race. Take this with you," he said, holding out the briefcase. "Take it to my old business partners. Their names and addresses are inside. Give them my regards and they will work out a fair price for the contents. Do what you like with the money."

He put his arms out and we hugged.

"Do me one favour," he asked.

"Anything."

"Give me your penis beads."

"Why?" I asked.

"Trust me," he smiled.

I took them off and gave them to him.

"You'll understand when you open the case," he smiled again. "Oh, and I will look after Jawana's dog."

He hugged and kissed Mary and the kids, tears running down his face.

I took Mamooto to one side.

"Thank you for being a good friend," I said. "But now I release you from your bond. You must stay here. Take a wife and have a family."

"I go with you," he said. That was the first time I had heard him actually speak.

"No," I told him. "You have served me and the chief well and it is time for you to stand down and make a life for yourself."

"No. I go with you," he repeated.

"Alright," I said, sensing I was losing this battle. "You can come as far as the mountains and then return to the village with the others when we leave."

As we made our way to the boat, the tribe lined our way, banging their shields with their spears. The women and children waved and cheered. At the cast off I turned to see Mbata climb on board. He smiled at me as he sat down; it felt good to have him on board. We cast off, waving at our friends. We kept waving until we could no longer hear or see them.

As the village slid out of sight beyond the trees I felt my heart sink in my chest. Mary felt it too; she squeezed my hand.

We had ten men rowing, changing every two hours. On the third change I took my turn, with Mary sitting opposite me. Everyone cheered as we started rowing.

We travelled the lake for four days, stopping only to collect food and for toilet requirements. We saw signs of life, but there were no hostilities.

Melanie sat looking out across the lake. I joined her on the deck.

"How are you feeling?" I asked.

"Much better now, thank you," she said, quietly. "This place is so beautiful. It's like paradise." She put her hand on mine. "Thank you for not telling anyone about – well, you know…"

"I didn't think it was anyone else's business," I said.

"Thanks anyway," she smiled.

Mbata was rowing now; he looked back at me and smiled. I thought back to the day we rescued him from the Butata. He was only been a boy then, now he was a strapping warrior – a young chieftain. His father was very proud of him.

In the distance the lake was narrowing into a river. Mamooto kept lookout: if the river got too narrow we would be open to ambush. Mbata told everyone to keep quiet.

"We don't want our presence known."

The river was about a hundred yards wide and narrowed down to about sixty. It stayed like that for the next three hours, making us feel enclosed. Darkness was falling now. As we rounded a bend a wide open bank came into view.

"There," I pointed. "We'll make camp for the night."

After a quick check of the area all seemed well, so we posted guards and prepared a meal. We bedded down for the night, changing guards every hour to give us all a chance to sleep. The night passed without incident.

*   *   *

The next day we boarded the boat and set off. The river narrowed down to about forty yards. Then, after a couple of hours it narrowed even further to about thirty yards, then twenty. The water was travelling quite fast now.

All of a sudden there was a *ffffffffthunk!* An arrow embedded itself into one of the shields.

"Everybody down!" I shouted.

A hail of arrows hit the side of the boat.

"Stay in the centre of the river!"

We were a fast moving target, which was to our advantage.

"Raise shields!" shouted Mbata.

The shields were raised above our heads, forming a roof. A second volley of arrows hit the shields and I gave the order to prepare to return fire. I looked out to see a row of men preparing their bows for another volley.

"Wait for it –"

Their arrows hit our boat.

"Now!"

The shields were lowered and our men stood up and let fly. They were trying to reload again and were taken by surprise. Our arrows hit true and the rest ran into the trees. In the jungle, everything went quiet.

"They know we are here so be watchful," shouted Mbata.

Every now and then a movement in the trees told us we were not alone; they were following us. As we took a bend in the river the cliffs on either side towered up over a hundred feet, with no banks.

Soon we were rushing through a ravine about ten yards wide.

Baines gave a shout, "Oh my God – look at that!"

About five hundred yards downstream an enormous tree had fallen or been felled across the ravine, and lining the full length of the trunk were two rows of men, all brandishing bows and spears.

Right in the centre was a gigantic boulder about ten feet in diameter.

"They're going to bomb us!" shouted the Professor.

We were like rats in a trap.

"Shields up!" shouted Mbata.

"I'll take the tiller," I said. "I'll try to zigzag – it might lessen their chances of hitting us."

Mbata gave the order to arm, "When I give the signal, lower shields and fire!" he bellowed. "We might take them by surprise."

"If they drop the boulder late it might give us a chance to get past them."

The river was flowing faster and it was all I could do to keep hold of the tiller. Another pair of hands closed over mine – it was Mary.

"Get back under the shields!" I yelled.

I might as well have been talking to the cliffs.

We had about twenty yards to go and the men on the tree were pushing the boulder. As we got within range I shouted, "Now!"

The shields went down and the arrows flew up. By the time they realised their mistake it was too late. At least fifteen of their men were hit and fell off the tree into the river, but they still managed to push the boulder over.

I was looking straight up at it as it began to fall. I pushed the tiller hard to the right – the boat veered to the left and the boulder hit the side, ripping a large gouge in the wood. It rocked and nearly turned over, but luckily stayed afloat. Those of us who hadn't fallen with the rocking of the boat fired another volley at our attackers. In their panic to get off the tree it dislodged and rolled over, coming crashing down into the river behind us. Fifty of their men plunged into the rushing water and were lost.

Beyond the ravine the river opened up into the jungle again.

"Have we lost anyone?" I asked.

"No," said Mbata. "Two injured, but nothing serious."

After a few hours we began to hear an ominous noise like thunder.

"Rapids!" shouted Baines, from the prow.

As we got closer, we could see the white water breaking over the rocks ahead. To the left was a narrow bank.

"Pull over there and tie up!" I called.

We walked down to the rapids and realised the water was too shallow to sail down. The rocks would rip the bottom of the boat out. The rapids covered about half a mile of river before opening out into a vast lake.

"We will have to manhandle everything including the boat down the path," said the professor. "If we widen and level the path we could cut trees to make rollers and roll the boat down, then refloat it in the lake below."

*   *   *

After two days of hard graft we were ready to pull the boat out of the water. On the third day we emptied the boat. Pushing the stern out into the water we placed the first roller under the bow and dragged the boat onto the bank, pushing roller after roller under the boat to keep it moving. Once it was straight it was easy enough to roll it down next to the lake. By the middle of the afternoon we were ready to give it one final push. The boat was refloated and our gear reloaded.

As we boarded it, I noticed hundreds of eyes and nostrils peeking up above the water.

"Don't anyone fall in," I warned everyone. "The water is full of crocs. Keep your hands in the boat."

"I can't believe we did that," the professor remarked. "It was a real team effort."

As I turned, I saw Mary smiling. She gave me a little wave. I had neglected her and the children for far too long. In the distance we could see a ridge of mountains. I wondered what we would find there.

We rowed for an hour or so until we found a flat mooring spot.

"We'll camp here for the night," I said. "A meal and a good night's sleep will do us good."

Throughout the night we heard noises and movement, but there didn't appear to be anything threatening.

In the morning we rose and went to board the boat. From out of the trees came tribesmen brandishing spears – about four hundred of them. Our men instinctively raised theirs.

"Lower your weapons," Mbata yelled.

They did as they were ordered; forty men against four hundred was no contest. Anyway, if they were going to kill us they would have done it while we were sleeping.

They didn't seem hostile towards us. Their ranks parted and an old man dressed in a red and gold robe, with a headdress of feathers and a crocodile teeth came through. Mbata walked up to him and bowed his head. The old man held out his arm and we followed him into the trees.

They didn't take our weapons, so we knew we weren't captives. We walked a few hundred yards until we came to a large clearing containing over a hundred huts. There were women going about their chores and children playing all around. It reminded me of our village, only it was much bigger.

We were escorted to a large hut where we bathed while a banquet was being set up.

The chief and the elders of the tribe sat in a line with Mbata, Mamooto, Mary and I sat between them. I introduced Mbata as our chief, Mamooto and I as his bodyguards and Mary as – but before I could finish they bowed their heads to her.

"A fine chief and a great warrior," said their chief.

Mary sat chewing a piece of meat off the bone without a clue about what they were saying about her.

The feasting went on all day and into the night. Fires were lit and the drums started. As in our village the girls started dancing. The professor and Baines were quite drunk and when some girls held out their hands they quickly got up and joined in. They never had a clue how to dance, but thoroughly enjoyed themselves. Melanie never moved or smiled, just sitting on the edge of things, staring into space.

I thought it would take her a long time – if ever – for her to come to terms with the past.

Mary stood up and beckoned me over to dance. I glanced at Jawana and Lani, who were happily playing with the other children. As I got to my feet to join Mary the drums changed beat. The girls ran to one side of the clearing, the boys to the other. The girls' dancing was very sensual. Marry cupped her breasts in her hands and made thrusting movements with her hips, all while looking me straight in the eye.

I got the message.

Abruptly, the drums stopped and all the girls ran into the jungle screaming and giggling, followed hotly by the boys. I ran after Mary, but she disappeared into the trees. I kept looking until I came to a clearing with a stream running through it.

The moon was full and bright, but I couldn't find her. As I went to leave, a voice went, 'Cooeee!'

I looked around the clearing. 'Cooeee!' It came again. As I crept around a boulder; Mary grabbed me pulled me to the ground, embracing me tightly. We made love under the moon beside the babbling brook. It was magical. Later, we fell asleep in each other's arms.

CHAPTER THIRTY

In the morning we bathed in the brook and returned to the village. We breakfasted with the tribe and explained our intentions to the chief. He shook his head.

"There is no way through," he told us. "Only the water knows a way."

"Can we see the ocean?" I asked.

Some of his men took us up a mountain pass to the top – about a two mile trek. When we arrived, we looked over the edge. The sight took our breath away; it was a sheer drop of over a thousand feet. In the distance we could just see the water cascading out from the cliff face. It was impossible to tell whether it was a twenty feet drop to the sea or a two-hundred feet drop.

"Well, that way is out," said the professor. "Let's try plan B."

Back at the boat we walked across a flat area of rock that the water flowed through. On one side about twenty feet down it entered a large hole in the rock face. It flowed under our feet and came out the other side into a chasm about a hundred feet down and two hundred feet across.

The spray from the waterfall was creating a rainbow. It was like a vast bowl with a lake in the bottom. The water disappeared into a hole in the mountain.

"Can we get down there?" asked the professor.

The chief pointed out a narrow ledge that ran around the cliff face. Baines, the professor and I climbed down.

"The rest of you wait up here – we won't be long," I told them.

It was quite an easy climb, but it was difficult to see how we would get the boat down. At the bottom we walked around the ledge to the hole where the water entered the rock face. It was fast flowing and the gap between the water surface and the cave roof was about two feet.

"The boat will never go through there," said the professor. "We'll have to find another way."

"Not necessarily," said Baines. "Let me think about it."

Later that day he emerged from a hut.

"Let me run this past you," he said. "If we dam the flow of water through the rock into the pool, I estimate it will take about two hours to rise the twenty feet to flow over the rock. So, if we get the boat down into the pool then dam the flow, allowing the pool to empty, we should have about three minutes to spare to get to the ocean – with no hiccups.

"Now, assuming the flow of water is travelling at speeds of up to forty plus miles an hour," he continued. "We must be at least halfway through before the waterfall starts again, or it will catch up with us and it'll be goodnight nurse. This, ladies and gentlemen, could be the biggest gamble of our lives."

"Okay," said the professor," all in favour of giving it a try, raise your hands."

Without hesitation, the four men and Mary put our hands up.

Over the next few days, vines were cut, the boat emptied and taken to the edge of the waterfall.

The ends of three vines were tied round the boat on the bow, the middle and the stern, so we could lower it down to the pool. Three more long vines tied to the hull and across the waterfall to pull it away from the rock face on its descent. It took over a hundred men to lower the boat into the water. The equipment we needed was loaded and tied on and secured.

"We need the boat to be under control – and to be ready to go on command," said Baines. "Every second will count."

A long pole was cut to measure the depth of the water at the entrance to the cave – about fifteen feet. Boulders were placed over the entry point, ready to dam the flow.

The shields were discarded from the boat and torches soaked in animal fat lashed to the sides. We were ready.

*   *   *

The next morning everything was explained to the chief who told his men to dam the flow with rocks. We said our goodbyes to our tribesmen and women, and thanked them for all our help. I held out my hand to Mbata, who ignored it and put his arms around me; I did the same.

"I will miss you, old friend," he said.

"And I you."

I went to shake Mamooto's hand.

"No," he said. "I come with you."

"My world is not your world and you will not like it there," I warned him.

"I come with you," he repeated, unmoved.

Mbata interrupted before I could argue further.

"The chief ordered him to guard you until death, and guard you until death he will," he said. "You cannot change that."

Mamooto climbed down to the boat, carrying Jawana in his arms. The others followed him down. I thanked the chief for his hospitality and we boarded our vessel. The water was slowing down now, the hole in the side of the mountain was about five feet deep now, and getting bigger. Eight feet. Ten feet...

"The boat will go through now," said Baines. "Light the torches."

"Cut the vines!" I shouted, holding onto the tiller.

A fat lot of good that did! The tunnel was only three feet wider than the boat and it could only go one way: forwards and downwards. All I had to do was prevent it from crashing into the walls.

The torches lit up the roof but not the way ahead. We were racing into a black hole; at every bend we hit the wall, bouncing us to and fro. We must have been travelling at about thirty miles an hour and increasing. Grown men were screaming in panic. The Kids joined in for fun.

245

My heart was pounding like a steam train. I looked over at Mary: she had Jawana in one arm and Lani in the other. She looked at me, laughing fit to burst. You would think she was on a waterslide at a fairground, not a death ride through a mountain. We were racing along at breakneck speed, still going downward, being tossed helplessly about like a twig on the torrent. We rolled side to side, nearly tipping over every time we hit the wall.

The bow dipped dangerously low, beneath the water, and some of the torches went out.

"We can't take many more like that, or we're done for!" I muttered.

There was over a foot of water in the boat now, splashing to and fro. We rounded a tremendous bend and the narrow tunnel opened up into a vast cavern. On the left side was a low, flat area of mud. The boat couldn't take the sharp bend and grounded itself out of the water on the mud, the river rushing past on the right hand side.

"Quick!" I shouted. "Get it back in the water!"

Mamooto and I leapt into mud that came up to our knees. Mary joined us. We heaved, but the boat was just too heavy. The Professor and Baines just sat there, waiting for us to save the day – as usual.

"Get out and bloody well push, or we will all die!" I bellowed.

They seemed to come out of their trance then and jumped into the mud beside us. As we all pushed, the boat started moving. I stepped forward; my foot got stuck in something in the mud. I looked down: in the dim light lay a half buried skeleton, around its neck was something bright on a chain. Without thinking I grabbed it and threw it into the boat.

"Everybody get back in!" I screamed.

Mamooto and I were the last two to swing back in. We gave the boat a final shove and as the bow entered the water once more Mamooto's foot slipped in the mud. He managed to grasp the stern with one hand. I dove forward and grabbed his wrist, but it was wet and slippery – I was losing my grip.

The boat picked up speed as we headed for the tunnel. Two people, one on either side of me, leaned over the side and grabbed Mamooto's arms: I turned to find Melanie and Mary helping to pull him in as we reached the end of the cavern.

This tunnel was much lower, and as we entered it the prow hit the roof.

God, I thought. *If it gets any lower further in we'll be pushed underwater with no hope of ever getting out!*

"Stay down and lie flat in the bottom of the boat!" I shouted. "And don't sit up for anything!"

At that moment what sounded like a huge explosion went off high behind us.

"The dam has burst!" I yelled. "If you believe in a god, now is the time to pray!"

The tunnel was much steeper now and getting narrower about a foot either side. Every time the boat bounced the prow hit the roof. I hoped it was strong enough to withstand the pressure.

"Stay down!" I yelled.

Mary was trying to hold onto the children. They were crying with fear. I crawled to them. The roof of the cave was only inches from our backs. Mamooto joined us. We held one another close; abruptly, all the torches went out.

We hurtled down the tunnel in complete darkness; it felt like we were going over a hundred miles an hour. A great crash behind us told us that the water had reached the cavern and entered the tunnel we were still in. It sounded like a volcano had erupted, the lava gaining on us fast.

The boat seemed to be screaming as it hurtled down the tunnel, scraping against the sides of the rock wall.

"Stay down and don't move," I screamed, but I doubt that anyone could hear me.

The noise behind us was getting louder and louder. All sorts of thoughts were racing through my mind: the dangers had I put Mary and the children in, flashes of my past life, of Tracey, Dave, the boys at school, Jane...

Then, in an instant, a pure white light hit us as we shot out of the tunnel like a rocket. Our eyes stinging, we found ourselves hanging in the air for what seemed an eternity, then the boat pancaked onto the sea.

"Paddle!" I screamed. "Paddle for your lives!"

We all grabbed our oars and paddled for all we were worth. I glanced back at the tunnel entrance – it was about thirty feet up. We were about twenty yards away when, with an almighty crash, an extraordinary torrent of water belched out, going over a hundred feet into the air. It hit us, nearly sinking the boat – we clung to it as hard as we could. Around us, the sea boiled with foam for a few moments before everything went quiet.

We all sat stunned for a while, then suddenly, as if a spell had broken, everyone cheered. We all shook hands and embraced. I kissed Mary and the children, and we all hugged Mamooto. That had been close.

"Let's get the water out of the boat before we sink," said the professor.

"What now?" Baines asked, while we worked.

"If we follow the coastline around we must finally come to civilisation," I said.

We rationed our food and water to the minimum, letting the tide take us by day, paddling by night to save water. On the sixth day we saw a speck on the horizon; as it came nearer, we waved and shouted until they saw us and turned our way.

Baines looked at me.

"I think you ought to put something on," he smiled.

Mary, the children, Mamooto and I were still naked. Mary found the cloth we had packed and we draped it over our shoulders as togas, tying them at the waist with leather thongs.

"I hope they are friendly," I said, "and not pirates."

As the ship came closer I noticed the metal object I had found in the cavern. I turned it over in my hands – it was a medallion about three inches across on a gold chain. It had been cast with a man's head at the centre. He was wearing a feather headdress.

"What have you there?" asked the professor.

I handed it to him.

"I found it when we grounded in the cavern," I told him. "It was on a skeleton."

"My God!" he exclaimed. "Do you know what this is? It's a funeral medallion adorned with the face of a chief when they die. That must have been a burial ground we passed through. I bet there are hundreds of these in that cavern!"

"Well, if you think I'm going back in there to look you've got another thing coming," I said.

He looked at me for a moment.

"Quite," he smiled. "Quite." He handed me back the medallion.

It turned out that the boat we had hailed was a fishing vessel on their way home and were happy to give us a lift.

We loaded our meagre possessions on board their craft and cut our boat adrift we left any weapons we had on board, except Mamooto's spear. A wave hit it sideways on. It rolled over and slowly sank.

Rounding the headland we saw a village with a jetty jutting out into the sea.

The fishing boat was tied off and we trod on terra firma at last. It took some time to walk without losing balance. It felt like the ground was still moving like the sea. It's funny how the brain can play tricks. Villagers stood staring at us as we walked towards the huts, but there were no smiles or a welcome for us here. Then, from one of the huts came a white man he was fat with a bald head and a big smile on his face. He held out his hand and the professor shook it.

I am "Reverend Bales," he smiled.

"Professor Jenkins," the professor gestured at the others, "and my team – we are trying to get back to England. Can you show us the way?"

"Well," said the reverend. "England is that way by about two thousand miles, but first let's have some refreshment and rest a while, then we'll see if we can help you. I am a missionary," he told us. "I have been here, spreading the word of God for eleven years."

Over the meal, the reverend asked us, "So, what are you doing in these parts?"

"We've been exploring the jungle –"

"For plants and insects," I cut in.

"Yes," the professor agreed, "for plants and insects."

The reverend looked at me.

"You are obviously a white man, but you are dressed as a native," he observed. "So, what's your story?"

"We like this part of the world," I answered, "and feel closer to God by being part of it."

"What about this lady?" he asked, pointing at Mary.

"My daughter," the professor said, quickly. "I take her everywhere with me."

He looked at us and I could see the old-fashioned prejudices reflected in his eyes.

"Oh, I see," he said slowly. "Daughter."

"How can we get to a port to board a ship for home?" Baines asked.

"Well," said the reverend, "a boat comes here once a month to deliver supplies to our village. You can catch a ride on that if you cross the captain's palm with silver. That will take you to Verno, where you can get a ship to begin your voyage back to England. It will be here in four days."

"Wonderful," said the professor.

CHAPTER THIRTY-ONE

O ver the next four days I spent every minute with Mary and the children. The reverend kept staring at us, but he didn't say anything further.

On the fourth day there, we heard the low drone of an engine in the distance and spied blue smoke rising above the trees. Then, around the headland she came: the most beat-up wreck of a rust bucket you could ever have seen, with a wood burning steam engine rattling away. She sat low in the water, either overloaded or sinking. It chugged over to the jetty and a man tied it off.

Jawana and Lani hid behind Mary. They had never seen a steam boat before.

Forty-seven people got off the boat, some carrying live chickens, others leading goats on ropes; the women carried bundles on their heads. Out of the wheelhouse came an immense, dirty white man, wearing an oily *'Kiss me quick!'* hat that had seen better days. He wore a filthy roll-neck jumper that stank of sweat and stale whiskey.

"'Ello Rev'!" he shouted. "I've got your gear and some English newspapers, a couple of weeks old, but readable.

The reverend introduced him.

"This is Davy, a scurvy rogue, but a fair man," he said. "If you cross his palm with silver he will take you to Verno."

"How much," the professor asked.

"Five hundred pounds sterling," he replied.

"That's a bit steep, isn't it?"

"Take it or leave it," he shrugged.

I opened the bag and held out the money we had collected from the crash site. We had enough. Davy and his mate stared at the bag as I handed him the money.

"What else've you got in that bag?" he asked.

"Nothing to interest you," I said.

We loaded our gear and said our goodbyes to the reverend and his village. As we made to board the reverend grabbed my arm.

"Watch yourself," he whispered. "Davy is a nice enough bloke, but he would slit his grandmother's throat if he thought there was money in it – if he hasn't already."

"Thanks reverend, I will keep that in mind."

When we were out to sea, Davy and his mate were in the wheelhouse, talking in whispers and glancing out at us. I gave Mamooto the bag and asked him to keep it safe.

"– and watch your back."

He glanced at the wheelhouse and nodded his understanding.

Davy came out.

"Not long now," he told us. "About an hour or so until we reach Verno."

As we got nearer to the port we could see little houses nestled in a cove, a backdrop of jungle rising high above it. Jawana and Lani stared wide-eyed at the ships moored at the docks as we pulled into port. Mamooto didn't seem to take any notice, taking it all in his stride.

We moored up and disembarked with the others.

"Right," said the professor. "Let's get you some clothes."

I thought we might look out of place here, but white and black went about their business together without batting an eye. Tribesmen carrying shields and spears walked beside suited gentlemen. This port must exist somewhere on the border of past and present, I reflected.

We found a general store; the owner was a rough looking

character, a white man with skin parched like leather, deep lines scored in his face. He had the look of a man who had smoked too many Cuban cigars. He looked a lot older than he probably was.

"What can I do for you?" he smiled, eyeing us up and down.

"Do you take sterling?" I asked him.

"Yes, but with a fifteen percent surcharge."

"Okay," I said. "We want clothes for two men, two women and two children."

"All I do is trainers and t-shirts to fit anybody, or army surplus," he smiled, taking a puff on his cigar.

"Okay, that will do fine," I said.

Melanie, Mary and the children went off to rummage through the small range of clothes on offer. Even after spending time in the jungle, it seemed like the women never forgot how to shop. They were laughing and giggling, trying things on, taking them off and trying something else.

I took Mamooto over to the army surplus rail, where I found a sweatshirt and a pair of camouflage trousers to fit me. I also picked out a pair of trainers. I looked critically at Mamooto. He was an enormous man and I doubted I would find anything that would fit him. Surprisingly, a sweatshirt fitted quite well and I found a pair of trousers that were right in the waist, but the legs were about a foot too short. I tore them off at the knee to form shorts. I thought he looked good, but I could tell he didn't like wearing clothes and he flatly refused to wear trainers. He tied a knot in the laces of the pair we bought him and hung them around his neck. But no way was anyone going to take Mamooto's spear from him. We paid the shopkeeper and left.

"Let's find a hotel," the professor suggested.

Right on the dockside was a rambling, colonial looking building with rotten windows. The whole thing was badly in need of repair and decoration. A sign on the wall read 'rooms'.

We opened the door and found ourselves in a large entrance hall. The inside of the hotel was nearly as derelict as the outside.

Standing behind a desk was a woman of about sixty years old, wearing a black basque and a bright red tutu. She was caked in makeup of the cheapest kind. The whole effect was like something out of an old Western.

Eyeing us up and down, she snapped, "Yeah, whadya want?"

"Rooms," said the professor. "How much for all of us?"

"How long for?"

"A week," I said.

"That will be a thousand dollars," she snapped.

"How much is that in sterling?"

"A thousand pounds," she barked, with a sneer.

"Are pounds worth the same as dollars?" I asked.

"They are in here," she sneered. "In advance."

We paid her the cash, somewhat reluctantly.

We must have looked a very odd bunch, but she never questioned it. A little wizened old man showed us to our rooms.

"We will meet after we have washed up" said the professor.

As I went to close the door, someone pushed it back open. It was Melanie.

"Can I sleep in here with you?" she asked, clearly nervous. "I fear being on my own in a place like this."

Mary took her gently by the hand and led her inside. The room was about fifteen feet square with six unmade beds. The mattresses reeked of urine and a cracked mirror hung on the wall; there was hardly any reflection from it.

Mary looked at me, an unusually solemn expression on her face.

"Don't like it here," she said.

"No, nor do I," I told her. "But hopefully it won't be for long."

Later we all met up and found a greasy spoon café. After a reasonable meal we set about looking for a ship to carry us further, but to no avail.

"We'll try again tomorrow," said the professor wearily.

I bought a bottle of scotch and went back to the hotel. We stacked all the mattresses on top of each other and sat on the floor. The children were so exhausted that they fell asleep straight away. I opened the scotch and passed it around. After a few swigs we all began to relax a little. Mamooto still had the bag over his shoulder, protectively.

"Give it here," I said, and took out Reg's briefcase.

He had unlocked it before he had given it to me, and we were all curious. The catches opened with a couple of loud clicks.

"Now, let's see what he's been guarding all these years…"

I gasped as I lifted the lid: the sight of the contents stopped me in my tracks. The top tray was full of sovereigns and half-sovereigns, all in sealed plastic packets. The second tray was full of Krugerrands, also in protective pockets. Underneath that was a third tray, covered with a scarlet cloth. When I pulled it back, Melanie nearly fainted: it was full of diamonds of all sizes.

"There must be millions of pounds worth of gear here," I exclaimed.

A crudely written note from Reg read, *'Received from Robin Cross, one string of penis beads for my collection of coins and diamonds. Signed, R. Bond.'*

It also gave his old partners' names and address.

"We can't keep this lot in the case," I said. "It would be too easy to steal."

I tore off a piece of rag from one of the old togas, emptied the contents of the case into it and then tied it up like a kid's marble bag. I put the bundle back into Mamooto's bag, then hid the case between the reeking mattresses.

"Guard that with your life," I advised.

It was far safer on Mamooto's back than in any bank in the world. I lay on the floor for a while, wondering how Lani and Jawana would find living in a house with flush toilets, electricity and "sweets". How would they do in school? We were heading for an entirely new way of life.

I finally drifted off to sleep.

Clonk!

I sat up; so did Mamooto. The noise had come from outside the window. The sash was open and a cool breeze gently ruffled the filthy net curtains. Fleetingly, a shadow passed across the light shining up from the street.

Mamooto stood by the window and I went to the door, gently holding the knob with my fingertips. After a few seconds of silence I felt it turn and slowly begin to open. At the same time, a man's head and shoulders came in through the window.

Mamooto grabbed him by the hair and smashed his face down on the windowsill. I wrenched opened the door, grabbed another man by his lapels in one hand and his testicles in the other. Lifting him clear over my head I ran across the room, throwing him out of the window, where he collided bodily with his mate. They both crashed headlong into the street, screaming all the way down. There were two distinct thuds and the screaming stopped.

No police came and nobody asked any questions. It was as though nothing had happened. The children never even woke up. Mary opened her eyes.

"What happened?" she asked softly.

I kissed her gently on the forehead. "Nothing," I said. "Go back to sleep."

*   *   *

We all met downstairs the next morning.

"Did anyone hear the commotion last night?" the professor asked.

"We had visitors," I said. "They didn't stay long."

"Oh, is that what it was?" the professor said, amused.

We toured the docks again that day, but there were no ships going to England. Finally, we found a skipper who knew of a cargo ship that was heading to a port in the south of France, from where we might find passage to England. He pointed it out to us.

"Let's go and see the captain," the professor suggested.

As we climbed the gangplank, the ship was being loaded with timber. The captain was a large man, over six feet six. We explained our intentions.

"Have you got passports?" he asked.

"Well, no," the professor began, "but…"

"No passports, no go," said the captain, firmly.

"How much to take stowaways?" I asked. "We'll leave the ship before we reach France."

He stared at me for a few seconds, assessing me.

"You couldn't afford it." He quipped.

"Can we talk?" I asked.

He nodded, leading us below to a private cabin. I took the bag from Mamooto, opened it and took out a handful of the diamonds. I laid them on the table for the captain to examine. After a few moments, he picked one up, took it over to the porthole and scratched a deep groove in the glass. He knew then that the jewels were real.

"We sail this afternoon at 16.00 hours," he said. "Don't be late, or I will sail without you. I can't afford to miss the tide."

I gave him four more diamonds.

"That's five," I said, "and I'll give you another five when we get there."

At 15.00 hours we boarded the ship. The captain met us with one of his crew.

"Stay out of sight until we are out at sea."

The sailor showed us to a cabin next to the engine rom. There were hammocks tied onto pipes and across the cabin, so we had a nap before departure. Without warning the engines roared into life, the sound rumbling through the deck. It was deafening. It took Mamooto so much by surprise that he fell out of his hammock, face down on the floor.

We waited about an hour and then came back up on deck; we were surrounded by water. Far behind us lay the coastline. I felt relieved we had left that place.

When we caught sight of the captain, I asked if we could sleep up on the timber as it was too hot and noisy down below.

"I don't care," he said. "Sleep where you like."

That night we climbed up onto the deck, which was covered with tarpaulins. The air was warm. We lay on our backs, looking up. The sky was jet black, decorated with millions of twinkling stars.

Without turning her head, Jawana said, "Daddy, what are all those little lights?"

"Well," I said, "when it's time for little girls and boys to sleep, God pulls a big curtain across the sun."

After a few seconds of thought, she said, "There are lots of holes in the curtain, aren't there Daddy."

CHAPTER THIRTY-TWO

The next day we took the children to the stern so they could see the trail left by the propellers, when I noticed a ship on the horizon. I told the captain.

"It's most probably another cargo ship," he told me. "It's too far out to be the coast guard.

"It could be pirates," I suggested.

"They are rife in these parts, but they shouldn't bother us since we are only carrying timber." The captain looked at me sideways. "Unless you have something they want."

"We might," I said.

"Then I advise you to lose it before they catch up," he replied.

I called the others together.

"Mamooto, hide that bag somewhere safe," I instructed. "There is a ship following us and it could be pirates. If they are then they will make their move soon, so let's be prepared."

"Pirates," scoffed the professor. "What planet are you on? Can you see the skull and crossbones on the mast?" he smirked. "Can you hear the cannon?"

"Professor, we have lived in a hostile environment for years and learned to be prepared for anything," I said. "Most of the time, the least likely dangers are the ones that happen."

Later that afternoon the ship caught up with us.

"Mamooto, take Mary, Melanie and the children and hide them in the timber," I told him. "Professor, you and Baines get out of sight."

"I will not," he snapped. "This is preposterous. I will stay on deck – pirates, indeed!"

The only weapon we had between us was Mamooto's spear. I kept out of sight on the freight deck. As the ship drew level a man's voice came over the loudhailer.

"Ahoy! Captain. Can you help us, ? We have an injured man aboard and our radio has packed up. Can we use yours to call for assistance?"

"Aye, come aboard," shouted the captain.

We cut our engines and a dinghy with three men in it launched from the other ship; a net was lowered and they climbed on board. None of them looked to be armed. We had one man with a rifle standing by the bridge door.

"You two wait here," said the captain, as he took the third one down into the radio room.

I stood on deck watching the other two. They seemed a bit edgy.

Then, without warning, the radio room door burst open. Out came the captain with the third man behind him, one arm around his neck and the other hand holding a loaded pistol to his head. At this point, one of the other two drew a gun from under his jumper and shot our rifleman at point blank range.

Another dinghy left the other ship, this time with six men on board. As it came closer I peered between the timbers and recognised our old friend Davy. They climbed on board.

"Right!" he bellowed. "I want everyone on deck, now!"

The rest of the crew came up from below.

"Where are the rest of them?" he shouted. "If they are not here in one minute I will kill the captain and scuttle the ship!"

The man holding the captain dragged him round to the front of the wheelhouse and stood next to him, still holding the gun to his head.

"If he tries anything, shoot him!" bellowed Davy. "You have ten seconds to get out here! Ten! Nine! Eight!"

At that point, I walked out from behind the timbers.

"Well," Davy sneered. "So, you come out of hiding like a bilge rat. Where's that freak of a woman and the brats."

"You don't need them," I said. "I'll give you what you want."

Mary took the decision out of my hands. She emerged from behind the timber with Melanie, holding Lani and Jawana's hands. Davy swung around and pointed his gun at them.

"Well, lookey here," he sneered. "The whole family. Where's the bag?" he barked. "bring it here!"

I went below and found an old sack. I put a weighty rope in it and tied it closed at the neck. While I was gone, Davy pushed his face near Melanie's. She could smell his foul breath.

"When we have finished our business here," he said. "We will take you along with us for a little fun."

I came back on deck and threw the sack down in front of him. Davy shouted for one of his men to open it. The man knelt, put his gun on the deck and untied the sack.

Our captain was standing in front of the wheelhouse looking forward over the timber. His assailant was examining his face, holding the gun steady at his skull. It was the captain who caught a movement on the timber about fifty yards away. It was Mamooto, spear raised. He ran forward and let fly. The captain just stared as the spear came closer and closer.

His jaw slowly dropped and his eyes got bigger and bigger. His captor, seeing the captain's face change, turned to see what he was looking at. The spear hit him full in the chest, the impact carrying him through the bridge window. The gun slipped from his fingers and went off with a bang as it struck the deck.

The man undoing the sack went for his pistol. I pounced on him and we wrestled, tumbling over and over.

Davy roared over the confusion, "Shoot them! Shoot them!"

He pointed his gun at me. I rolled over, turning his mate with me. The bullet hit him in the back. As he pointed the gun at me again there was a bang. I opened my eyes and Davy was lying face down next to me on the deck. The captain had picked up his assailant's gun and shot Davy through the head.

The rest of them threw down their guns and raised their hands over their heads. The pirates on the other ship gave up without a fight. They say, if you cut the head off the snake the body will give up; cowards are the same the world over.

Davy and his dead mates were thrown over the side to the sharks and the others taken below. Our crew bound and locked them in a storeroom, before turning their attention to their fallen shipmate. They wrapped him in a shroud and sewed it together, placing him in the cold store to return him to his family for burial. When they boarded the pirate ship they found guns, booze, cigarettes, gold and at least one thousand kilos of cocaine.

Everything was stowed on our ship except for the cocaine. That was opened and thrown into the sea.

"I don't do drugs," said the captain.

Their ship was tied astern.

"Start engines!" bellowed the captain. "Let's go home."

When the professor emerged, Baines gave him a look.

"Pirates, cannons, skull and crossbones – preposterous, huh?"

"Alright," said the Professor. "I was wrong, I admit it."

*   *   *

That evening we were sitting on the timber, watching the sun go down when one of the crew approached us.

"The captain would like you all to join him for dinner at nine o'clock," he said. "If you want to use the washroom, it's below deck behind the radio room."

"Tell him we would be delighted," said the professor.

Mary, Melanie and the children washed first, then us men. It was pleasant to wash in hot water with soap, even though it was carbolic, and shampoo as well. Mamooto turned up his nose at the soap and just washed in water.

We arrived at the captain's cabin. It was small with a table laid out, boxes and cushions made up to resemble seating. He welcomed us in, shaking our hands. Mamooto had to stoop to get through the door.

"This is the man I want to thank," said the captain, shaking Mamooto's hand vigorously. "I have never seen anything like it. That spear, and at that distance – fantastic! Brilliant!"

Mamoot looked at me, puzzled.

"Good throw," I translated, in the tribal language.

He nodded.

Wine was served and orange juice poured for the children. It was nice to taste a fine wine again. Mamooto took one swig, winced and spat it out.

"Sorry captain," I said. "He's never had wine before."

I poured him a scotch.

"Try that," I said.

He took a sip, nodded and drank it straight down. The captain laughed.

"Leave the bottle with him."

As the drink took hold, everyone relaxed and began to feel good. The door opened and in came a little man wearing a black and white striped t-shirt, jeans and an apron.

"Ah, Cookie," smiled the captain. "I hope you are all ready to eat"

The first course was soup, followed by roast chicken and three veg', and ended with upside down treacle pudding. Mamooto and the children ate the whole meal with their fingers, not being used to knives and forks, but they did seem to enjoy it.

After the meal, Cookie came in to see if there was anything else we needed. The professor raised his glass.

"My compliments to the chef on a magnificent meal."

"Hear, hear!" we all agreed.

"Well mateys, it's been a pleasure cooking for 'ee!"

The table was cleared and we sat back. Our glasses were replenished and another bottle of scotch was brought for Mamooto.

"So, what's the story?" asked the captain.

"It's a long one," I said.

"That's alright," he answered. "It's a long voyage, we have plenty of time."

We told our whole story while he sat back, not saying a word.

Soon, the children were nodding, so Mary and Melanie took them out to sleep. The rest of us sat talking and drinking until dawn.

*   *   *

Over the next few days we spent time with the children. They were quite grown up now. Jawana was about ten and Lani about five years old, but really I could only guess I had lost all track of time.

One morning, the professor asked me, "What are you going to do when you get back to England?"

"I don't know," I said. "I will most probably go back to teaching. I'd like to give the children a good education and an easy life for Mary. She's been through a lot in the jungle over the last few years."

"You could write a book on your adventures," the professor suggested. "I think it would sell pretty well. You could make a fortune."

"I have a fortune in diamonds and coins," I told him. "Mamooto is my only concern."

"It will be a job teaching him to speak English – what will he do for work?" the professor asked. "I don't think there is much call for bodyguards in England."

I got to know the captain quite well. His name was Mick and under that hard exterior he was a well-educated man. On numerous occasions if he saw me sitting on my own he would bring out a bottle and a couple of glasses, and we would sit and natter for an hour or two. He was married to a woman named Sue, who stayed back at port, and had eleven children. He could speak six languages.

"That man, Mamooto, deserves a medal for saving us and the ship," he said. "I am very grateful. He threw that spear from at least fifty yards and he missed me by inches. I nearly pooed myself."

CHAPTER THIRTY-THREE

One morning he called us to the bridge.

"We're going to dock tomorrow," he said, "at a little port in France called Bergea to unload the timber. Then we go on to Dusseldorf to load another cargo. We'll make a detour and call in at Shoreham Harbour in England. I'll put in the log that I rescued you when your ship sank, or I will be arrested for transporting illegal immigrants."

The professor shook his hand.

"That's okay with us," he said.

"In France, stay below decks until customs have disembarked," the captain advised.

Customs officers came on board when we docked, along with the French police, who arrested the pirates and took them away. Then arrangements were made for our dead man to be returned to his family for burial. Legal procedures were began to sell the pirate's ship. After all reports were in order and the timber had been unloaded, we set off again for England.

Once we were out at sea I spoke to the captain.

"What are you going to do with the contraband?" I asked.

"I have my contacts," he told me. "With that and the sale of the pirate ship I'll make sure that Bernie – our dead crewman's – family are set up."

In the distance we could see the English coast. I gazed at it, wondering how much had changed while we had been away. As we got closer I handed the captain a packet with a dozen diamonds in it.

"You have paid more than enough," he said.

"Please, take them," I smiled. "A little contribution to you and your crew – and give something to Bernie's family."

"Very much appreciated, thank you," the captain grinned. "I hope to see you again someday, and we can spend a few hours reminiscing over a bottle."

"I would like that," I told him.

We turned against the current into the English Channel, passing the Isle of White. Rounding the island, we pulled hard to port, heading for Shoreham Harbour. We moored up, disembarked and waited for the coast guard.

When they arrived, the captain told them his story, how he picked us up adrift in a lifeboat and brought us into Shoreham. The professor, in turn, told his side of the story – leaving out the bit where he met us in the jungle. We were all taken to the Coast guard's office and questioned. Everyone was allowed to go except for myself, Mary, the children and Mamooto.

Melanie kissed us goodbye and the professor and Baines shook our hands before leaving. We sat there until a man and woman arrived, carrying briefcases. They were escorted by the police. After another hour's questioning the man spoke to me.

"I'm afraid we are going to have to take the children into care and the lady into an institution until we can sort things out. And you are under arrest for taking advantage of a Down's Syndrome woman."

Mary pulled the children close and held onto me.

As the police moved in to take them away, Mamooto stepped forward, grabbing the policemen by the throat, one in each hand. He lifted them clean off the ground.

"Mamooto, no!" I shouted, and he lowered them to the ground.

In our tribal tongue I told Jawana and Lani to go with the lady and be good until I came for them. They nodded. I told Mary to do the same.

"Promise?" she asked, clearly frightened.

"I promise."

The professor came in and calmed things down a little.

"Is there anything I can do for you before I go?" he asked.

"Yes," I said. "Contact a barrister called Tracey Reece. She used to work for Butler and Coombs of Whitechapel."

"Right," he said, "consider it done. Where are you taking him, officer?"

"Brighton Police Station."

Mamooto and I were put in a police car and driven to the station. I was ushered into a room with nothing but a table and two chairs. Mamooto went to follow me, but he was held back by a police officer. A huge right fist sent him crashing to the ground. More officers came in, and one after the other they were sent tumbling to the floor. I ran between them.

"Don't antagonise him," I shouted at the police. "He doesn't know our laws and he is only trying to protect me."

A senior officer came in and ordered his men to stand down.

*   *   *

At the chambers of Butler and Coombs, the phone rang.

"Mrs Reece, would you come to my office, please?"

Tracey walked quickly to Mr Coombs' office and tapped on the door.

"Come in," came the voice of her employer.

She opened the door, closing it behind her.

"You wanted to see me Mr Coombs?"

"Yes, Miss Reece, take a seat," he said, gesturing to his patent leather chairs. "We have a situation in Brighton. A man has been charged with having unlawful sex with a mentally handicapped woman and he has asked for you, specifically – by name – to defend him."

269

"Why me?" she demanded, shocked. "You know what I think of those sickos. Get someone else to do it."

"He wants you and nobody else," Coombs shrugged.

"Is he pleading guilty or not guilty?" she stormed, feeling trapped.

"Oh, he's guilty alright," came the answer. He has two children by her.

Tracey gaped at him.

"How on earth can I defend a man whose guilt is proven by that kind of evidence?"

"I told the police you will be there at ten a.m. tomorrow. Let me know the outcome – and close the door on your way out."

Tracey was mulling over the case that evening when Dave came in. He poured himself a drink and sat down.

"Penny for them," he said.

"Oh, sorry," she said. "I am not with it at the moment. I have been asked – no, told – to take a case I don't want and I can't get out of it."

"Well," said Dave, "just go out there and do your best."

"But the man is guilty," she complained. "Everyone knows that, even before the case even starts. How can I defend a man when I know he's guilty?"

"Well," he said again. "You've done it many times before, so what's different with this case?"

"He is guilty of a crime I detest," Tracey explained, annoyed. "My heart just won't be in it."

"Oh, difficult," he said, sympathetically. "I wish you luck."

*   *   *

The next morning, she caught the train to Brighton. On the way she wondered why in the hell this man had picked her. She didn't even know anyone in Brighton. The train pulled in, bringing an end to her thoughts. She walked out of the station, trying to be professional and having a hard time pushing her negative expectations to the back of her mind. She found the taxi rank fairly easily.

"Where to lady?" asked the taxi driver.

"The police station, please."

It was a short ride to the station and she used the time to set her thoughts about the case in order. By the time she had paid the taxi driver and reached the front counter, she felt she was ready to face whatever the case threw at her – however she felt about it.

The sergeant looked up from his paperwork.

"Can I help you madam?" he asked.

"Yes, I'm Tracey Reece, the barrister for Mr Cross," she told him.

He nodded.

"Sign the book please, Madam," he said, and offered her a pen. "Parker," he called, to another officer. "Take this lady to interview room three and bring Cross through."

"Yes, Sarge."

The second officer led her to a room.

"Please wait here, madam, and I'll bring him through," he said.

She sat down and opened her briefcase. A few minutes later the door opened and the police officer led a man in. She looked him up and down, puzzled. His skin was bronzed, his hair uncombed and he looked like he hadn't shaved for weeks. He sat down opposite her.

"Would you like me to stay, madam?" asked the officer.

"No, I will be alright, thank you," she said.

He let himself out, politely.

"Now," she said, "let's get started. Why did you specifically ask for me to defend you, Mr Cross? Personally, I think you should reconsider and choose another barrister. I have read your notes and feel I cannot give you my best attention."

"Hello Tracey," I said. "How are you? And how is Dave? Is he still working at the school?"

Tracey gaped at him.

"Do I know you?"

I smiled up at her.

"If I bought a bottle of scotch and picked up Jane, came over to your place for dinner, would you wear that little red dress – and those scarlet high heel shoes? Put on that perfume and bright red lipstick that drove me wild?"

Tracey watched him for a moment, looking puzzled. Then something stirred in her memory.

"Oh my God," she gasped, as the impossible truth sunk in. "Robbie!" she shrieked. "Is it really you?"

"In the flesh," I said.

She ran round and threw her arms around me, squeezing me so tight I could hardly breathe.

The door burst open, admitting two worried looking police officers.

"It's alright," she said. "I know this man, he's a friend of mine."

They retreated, content to let the conversation continue, and Tracey sat down.

"Robbie, where have you been?" she asked. "What's all this about sex with a mentally handicapped woman? You detest them, for God's sake!" She shook her head. "I can't believe it's you after all these years. What happened to you?"

I told my story of the plane crash and Reg and Mary. Leaving out the Down's Syndrome bit.

There was a long silence after I had finished speaking. Tracey nodded mutely. It had been a lot to take in.

"Right, the first thing to do is to get you bailed," she said. "I'll be back later."

CHAPTER THIRTY-FOUR

A couple of hours later Tracey returned with bail paperwork.

"You are bailed to me until the hearing, so don't do anything stupid," she said. "Have you got anywhere to stay?"

"No," I said.

"Good, you can stay with us," she said. "Dave *will* be surprised."

"I have one small problem," I said. "Mamooto."

"What's a Mamooto?" She asked?

"Not what," I said, chuckling. "Whom. He's a friend of mine."

"Okay," she shrugged. "We have plenty of room – he can stay, too."

After explaining to the police officers that Mamooto couldn't speak English and had felt threatened in detention, and that he would be applying for asylum, they relented.

"Okay," said the Chief Superintendent. "But if he attacks another police officer he will be charged. Miss Reece, as a barrister I'm holding you responsible for him."

"Alright," said Tracey. "I will look after them."

"Parker, release the gentleman from cell two," he called.

The door opened and Mamooto appeared, filling the entire doorway. Tracey stared up at him, he towered nearly two feet above her head.

"He's your friend?" she said. "It's a good job he's not your enemy."

If only she knew, I thought to myself.

He still had the bag over his shoulder.

"Did they look in it?" I asked, in our language.

He shook his head.

"I expect they were too scared to ask you."

"What did you say?" asked Tracey, watching us closely.

"I asked if he slept well" I lied.

"You can't go out of the main door," said the sergeant. "It's crawling with press."

"But we have to get to the train station," said Tracey.

"Go out of the back door and a car will take you to the station."

Mamooto showed perfect indifference to the train, but then again, he never seemed to care about his surroundings under any circumstances. Tracey never stopped asking questions. I couldn't really blame her.

"Dave will have a fit when he sees you," she declared.

We took a taxi from the station to her house. They still lived in the same place and the sight of the front porch brought back memories. Stepping inside was like stepping into my own past. It even smelled the same.

"I'll show you to your rooms," she said.

"Mamooto will sleep in my room," I told her.

Tracey stared at me for a moment, surprised.

"Oh!" She gave me a very old-fashioned look.

"I will explain everything later," I promised.

"Oh, well – there are clean towels in the airing cupboard. I'll leave you to freshen up," she smiled. "You know where the bathroom is."

Gratefully, I ran a hot bath, stripped off and climbed straight in. Mamooto stood staring at me. He had never seen a bath before. I wondered why this, of all things, was the thing that should shake his composure.

When I had finished I got out, refilled the bath and told Mamooto to get in. He flatly refused.

"Why not?" I asked.

Apparently, when he heard the bath water going down the plug hole he thought it was a demon that would drag him to his death.

"Get in," I ordered.

Reluctantly, he stripped and gingerly climbed in. He was so tall he had to lie with his head, arms and legs hanging over the sides of the bath. He looked like an upside down tortoise. I started laughing so much that it started him off. It was the first time I had really seen him happy.

We were making so much noise that Tracey burst through the door, worried.

"Is everything alright? I heard all the noise and…"

Without thinking, I turned and faced her. She gaped at me, her mouth and eyes wide. Her eyes went from head to toe and back again.

"Strewth, Robbie, where did you get that body?" she gasped. "It's magnificent!"

"I picked it up in the jungle," I answered, feeling quite pleased with myself.

Tracey winced and ran her fingers over the scars on my arms.

"So much pain," she observed. "Oh, you poor thing."

She turned as Mamooto stood up in the bath. With her petite frame and his being so very tall, her face was about six inches from his penis. Mamooto was a big boy. Her eyes widened to the size of saucers as she stared at his manhood.

Then she snapped out of it.

"Sorry," she said. "Sorry!" She went bright red. "I didn't mean to – you should have locked the door –"

She turned and ran out.

Chuckling, we dressed in our old clothes, which would have to do until we could buy some new ones.

Downstairs, Tracey was still pink with embarrassment.

"I am so sorry," she kept apologising, over and over.

"Tracey," I said, soothingly. "Don't worry – in the jungle, nudity is normal. It's no big deal, really"

Encouraged, she leaned over and whispered in my ear, "Are they all built like him in the jungle?"

"All except me," I grinned, and she laughed. "Tracey, could we get some new clothes? I could do with a haircut and shave, too," I added, feeling the scraggly beard adorning my chin.

"Of course!"

She drove us to a shopping centre where Mamooto encountered his very first escalator. He could not work out a moving floor – every time he got on it and felt it moving he turned right around and got off it again. I went back down and made him get on again, but halfway up he ran down again.

This time, Tracey went down and held his hand, walking him onto the escalator like a child. He stayed put right to the top, but had some problems getting off it again – when the escalator ended and the floor began, his feet stopped and his body kept going. He went crashing to the floor, taking Tracey with him. Fortunately, she landed on top of him.

She got to her feet and dusted herself off.

"I think we should go back down on the stairs," she suggested. "It's safer."

We quickly found a barber's shop, where I had a haircut and a shave. The aftershave burned like acid when it hit my skin, but it felt great. Mamooto, who had short curly hair and no beard, wouldn't let them near him with the blades, but he did want to try the aftershave.

"You won't like it," I warned him, but he wanted it anyway.

He was perfectly cheerful right up until it hit his face. He screamed and left the chair like a rocket. I thought he was going to kill the barber, so I stepped between them until the sting wore off.

Next, we went in search of new clothes. Luckily, they sold jogging suits in the clothes section, and one of them almost fit Mamooto. He accepted the garments gratefully, but he flatly refused to wear underpants or socks and shoes. I got fitted out and we went back to Tracey's house.

"You two wait here while I go and get a court order for you to see your children." Tracey told us.

"What about Mary?" I asked, worried.

"That will be a bit more difficult," she said. "She is in an institution, but I will see what I can do. You know where the drinks are," she said. "Help yourself – I'll be as quick as I can."

I poured us a couple of scotches and we sat in the living room, talking about Mary and the kids.

I glanced over at Mamooto: he had been taken from a jungle that he knew and loved into a civilised jungle he must detest, but he never showed it. He just carried on, calm and collected.

We finished the bottle and opened another, and we were just sitting back to enjoy our drinks when the door opened and in came Dave.

He looked a lot older than I remembered, balding slightly and quite tubby now. I was pleased to see him. He took one look at us sitting there, drinking his scotch and stopped in his tracks. His briefcase dropped from between his fingers and fell to the floor.

"I'm a police officer and I've got a gun!" he yelled, desperately, and ran back out of the house, where he ran into Tracey. "Run!" we heard him shout. "We've got burglars!"

"Calm down!" Tracey laughed. "They're our guests. Come in and meet them."

He followed her in, looking a little sheepish.

"Dave, I would like you to meet Mamooto," she said, introducing my giant friend.

Dave stared up at the massive man towering above him. They shook hands.

"And this is Robbie," she said.

Again, Dave held out his hand and I shook it, no flicker of recognition in his eyes.

"Robbie," she said, again. "You know, Robbie?"

Dave peered at me, clearly baffled.

"The last time we shook hands was a few years ago," I said.

"Twelve years ago, actually," said Tracey. "At the airport…"

"Robbie,,," Dave frowned at Tracey. "Robbie?" he squeaked, as the penny finally dropped.

"Yes," she said. "God, Dave, how many hints do I have to drop?"

"Robbie!" he yelled, throwing his arms around me. "Where the hell have you been? We thought you were dead! Tracey, why didn't you phone me and let me know?"

"I did," she said, smiling. "Your mobile was off."

"Oh yes… I'm out of credit, sorry."

He shook his head, as if trying to make sense of everything. Tracey made her way to the kitchen.

"I'll make dinner," she offered. "Dave, you go and get cleaned up and then we can all have a good goss'. Robbie, I've arranged for you to see your children tomorrow, but I'm afraid I had no luck with your wife. Once I can get her address I'll try again."

"So, Dave, when did you change jobs?" I teased.

"What do you mean, change jobs?" he asked, puzzled.

"Well, when I left you were a teacher, and now you're a police officer 'with a gun'."

"Sorry about that," he laughed, embarrassed. "It was a fear response. Literally the only thing I could think to say to give me time to run. I might be older and fatter, but I can still run fast when I'm scared."

He kept giving Mamooto sideways glances; Mamooto was sitting still and expressionless on the sofa. I suppose he did look a little threatening if you didn't know him.

Come to think of it, he looked threatening when you did know him.

After dinner I helped Tracey wash up.

"Just like old times," she smiled. "Let's get some more drinks poured and you can fill us in on your adventures."

We settled down in the living room and I told my story again, leaving out the gorier bits. Throughout this, Mamooto sat on the floor, drinking large whiskies.

"So," said Dave, nodding at him. "Where does he come into this?"

"He's my bodyguard," I told him, and explained how all that had come to pass.

After hearing the story, Dave stared at me, "You mean you fought that giant and won?"

"Do you remember Jenkins?" I asked.

"That little ruffian in your class," he said. "Yes, I do. What about him?"

"Well, if it wasn't for him I would be dead now, at the hands of a man who is now my best friend."

"Weird," he said, sitting back. "Weird."

Tracey was watching me.

"Your wife, Mary…" she began slowly, as though she wasn't sure how to phrase her next question. "If I remember rightly

279

you hated people with Down's Syndrome. That's why you moved out to Africa in the first place, to get away from them." She smiled slightly. "She must be a very special lady."

"Yes, she really is," I told her. "I am ashamed to say that I was a fool when I was younger, but if you knew what we had been through together you'd understand how we feel about one another."

Tracey nodded and I glanced at Dave, who was still watching Mamooto warily.

"He doesn't say much, does he?"

"No," I replied. "In all the years I have known him I doubt he has spoken more than a dozen words, and yet we are closer than brothers. As a penance for losing our contest the chief ordered him to guard my life, even at the cost of his own. He has risen to the occasion more than once. When we came back I tried to release him from his bond, but the chief forbade it.

"He worries me a little," I admitted. "He doesn't know our laws and if someone threatened me or Mary, or the kids, he would kill them without hesitation." I sighed uneasily. "I have told Mary to wait for me and stay out of trouble, but the children only know jungle law – that's what they grew up with. If one is ill-treated, the other will come to their defence and might do someone physical harm."

We talked for hours – there was a lot to catch up on. At about three a.m. Dave stretched and declared that he needed his beauty sleep.

"I've got a whole class of brats to teach in the morning!"

At the top of the stairs, Tracey put her arms around my neck.

"It's good to have you back," she said, and kissed me. Her lips were moist on mine. "Goodnight," she whispered. "I'll see you in the morning."

CHAPTER THIRTY-FIVE

The next day, after breakfast, Tracey drove us to the children's home, about fifteen miles away. The home was a massive Tudor building on a vast estate. With well-kept gardens around a huge lake, play areas were dotted about. From the outside at least, it seemed pleasant.

We climbed the steps to the door. Inside, Tracey went to the main desk.

"Mr Cross to see Jawana and Lani," she said to the receptionist. "We are expected."

"Yes," said the woman. "Down the hall, last door on the left."

As we entered, the children were sitting cross-legged against the far wall. They stood up when they saw us, but didn't make a move until I said, "Come here."

I held out my arms and they ran into them. We kissed and cuddled each other, desperately happy to see one another again.

"Where's Mummy?" Jawana asked.

"You will see her soon," I promised, hoping that this was true. "Hey, look who's here," I nodded behind me to Mamooto, who had followed me into the room.

Whey both smiled happily when they saw him, and ran into his arms. He picked them up as if they were light as feathers and held them tightly. Together, we went out into the sunshine. Tracey and I sat on a bench while the children took Mamooto to show him the swings, which they were clearly rather impressed with.

"When the children saw you they didn't show any signs of excitement," Tracey remarked. "I thought they would be over the moon."

"They were," I said. "In the jungle if they shouted too loud or made any sudden moves outside of the village they could be dead before we reached one another. It pays to be safe rather than sorry."

They played happily with Mamooto, but after a while Lani and Jawana ran back over to us.

"When will Mummy come?" they asked.

"Soon," I assured them. "Very soon, but until then I want you to stay here a little longer. We will come to see you as often as possible until we get things sorted out, okay?" My chest felt tight. The thought of leaving them here was heart breaking. "Promise me you will be good until then?"

"We promise, Daddy," they chorused.

"What did you say to them?" Tracey asked, when they ran off to be chased by Mamooto.

"Sorry," I apologised. "It's habit to talk in our tribal language. I asked them to try to be patient."

We all had lunch together in the cafeteria, which was lovely, and then went back out again to play with the children. This time, even Tracey joined in. Exhausted after hours of running around in the sun, the five of us sat on the grass, enjoying cool drinks.

The children, somehow still bursting with energy, took Mamooto down to show him the lake.

"For such a big man he is very good with the children," said Tracey.

"Yes, he is," I replied. "What about you?" I asked, after a moment. "No children, I notice."

"No," she said, a little sadly. "We can't have children – well, I can't have children."

"Oh, I'm sorry!" I exclaimed. "I didn't mean to pry."

"Don't worry," she said, gently. "It hurt to find out in the beginning, but I have got over it now."

I smiled at her, and then all hell broke loose.

Suddenly, children were screaming and parents were shouting. Tracey and I turned to look toward the lake. About twenty children were in the water, swimming madly towards the shore; Mamooto was standing up to his waist in the water, desperately grabbing children and throwing them onto the bank.

Teachers and parents were screaming at him, but of course he couldn't understand them.

"What on earth is he doing?" Tracey shouted, springing to her feet.

I shook my head, baffled – then it struck me.

"He thinks there are crocodiles in the lake and they will eat the children,"

We ran down to the lake's edge.

"Mamooto!" I shouted. "There are no crocodiles in the water!"

He clearly didn't believe me. He kept looking over his shoulders, expecting one to come up behind him, still throwing children onto the bank. When the last child was out I shouted again.

"There are no crocodiles in the water!"

Jawana and Lani were laughing so much that they nearly wet themselves. He came out, and I managed to explain everything to the bewildered parents and teachers. Eventually they saw the funny side, too, and laughed along with us.

The children were very disappointed when it was time to go, though they didn't cry. They gave all three of us hugs and kisses, and Tracey was moved to tears by their obvious warmth and affection.

On the way home she said, "I don't see why they can't be released into my care," she said. "They can stay in the spare room. After all, they haven't committed any crime and there's no suggestion that you've ever acted inappropriately towards them. I'll see what I can do tomorrow, I know someone who might be able to help."

"I need to see Mary," I told her. "She will be worried about me and the children."

Tracey sighed.

"I doubt the authorities will let you see her," she said, sadly. "To them, your marriage is a crime. I can go and reassure her for you if you would like me to."

* * *

The next day, Tracey tapped on the door of Judge Alistair Bates.

"Come in," boomed a deep, plummy voice.

Gently, she opened the door. Sitting at an antique desk was a man with pure white hair and a short, well-kept beard. He was studying some papers, but he looked up when she came in.

"Hello Tracey," he said, pleasantly surprised. "What brings you here? Come in, do, and sit down!"

She smiled.

"I have a problem you might be able to help me with," she said, taking the proffered chair.

Bates pushed a button on his desk.

"Miss Merton, can we have tea and biscuits for two, please?" he said, into the intercom. "And I don't want to be disturbed for an hour. Right now, if you please, my dear. Now," he said, returning his attention to his old friend. "How can I help you?"

Bates listened intently to her story, and for a while after she had finished speaking he sat looking at her, elbows resting on the table, hands together as if in prayer.

"There is no sign of Down's Syndrome in the children?" he asked, eventually.

"No," said Tracey. "They are perfectly normal, but very unhappy about being separated from their parents. With your help they could stay in my custody and live with their father in mine and David's house – at least until the trial."

Bates thought carefully for a moment. Tracey waited for his answer with bated breath.

"Alright," he said. "I will write to the proper authorities and have them release the children into your care. This is not very professional, but I trust you to make sure nothing happens that we might both regret."

"I will, Alistair, I promise." She rose from her seat and walked around the desk to give him a big hug. "Thank you, Alistair, thank you."

She left the judge's chambers feeling very pleased with herself. Next, she drove to the institution to see Mary. It was a fifty mile journey and all the way there she wondered what this woman was like. She would have to be someone very special indeed to change a man like Robbie, with his passionate hatred of Down's Syndrome sufferers, to a man with a passionate love for a woman with the condition.

* * *

Tracey frowned as she drove up the drive. The building loomed over her, shadowy and gothic, and faintly menacing. She stared up at it, wondering who in the hell thought that locking people with learning difficulties and mentally handicapped adults in a place like this was good for them. At the very least they would feel abandoned and depressed.

She parked the car and entered the main hall.

The ceiling was high, with wooden panels and arches coated in a black stain, as were the doors and frames. The walls were tiled in a brick-like finish, similar to the kind you might find in Underground stations in London. All the joints were grimy and black with dirt collected over decades of neglect. The floor was tiled in black and white, looking like a vast chess board. There were long cobwebs hanging from the ceiling, swaying gently to and fro in the draught.

Tracey walked towards a desk where a nurse waited impassively. Her uniform could have done with being burned, let alone being washed, but Tracey tried to keep her disgust off her face. The nurse didn't even look up.

Ding!

Tracey rang the brass bell on the counter, which was green with mould. The nurse turned around and Tracey stepped back in mild horror. The woman looked worse from the front than she did from the back: her hair was a matted cream colour that could have been dyed blonde about twenty years ago. It looked strangely faded. A brown nicotine stain from the fag hanging in her mouth.

Her skin was like parchment and covered in makeup, she had cupid lips with scarlet lipstick and shocking pink blush circles on her cheeks. Thick black mascara and bright blue eyeshadow completed the doll-like caricature. Tracey grimaced.

Her uniform dress was so short that she could easily see her knickers, riding up her thin, spindly legs, lengthened by her black, high heel shoes.

The bottom half of her looked like Olive Oil from *Popeye*, and the top half like a toy town soldier.

"Yes?" she snapped at Tracey.

"Oh," Tracey cleared her throat. "I've – er – I've come to see Mary."

"Mary who?" she asked, still puffing on her fag; the ash was longer than the cigarette.

Tracey stared at it, hypnotised.

"Mary *Cross*," she said. "I am expected."

The nurse examined her book, talking to herself.

"Mary Eves, Mary Gatland, Mary Kingdom… No, there's no Mary Ross. She doesn't live here, you must have the wrong home," she sneered.

"Mary Cross," Tracey repeated, frustrated. "Mary Cross."

She was mesmerised by the ash on the nurse's cigarette. With an air of finality, it fell off and landed on the bib of her uniform. The woman briefly looked down and rubbed it in with her hand.

Tracey shuddered.

"Ah, here she is," she said, after a moment. "Room 309. Wait here and I will fetch the doctor."

Tracey clutched her handbag close to her side, trying not to listen too closely to the sounds echoing through the halls. The noises sounded like something from a horror film: shouting, screaming, crying – doors slamming in the distance.

It was, hands down, the most depressing place Tracey had ever been in.

A man wearing a white coat emerged from a side door, carrying a clipboard under his arm.

"Tracey Reece?" he asked, approaching. She nodded and he extended a hand. "I am Doctor Joslin, come with me."

As he led her through the dank corridors and up endless flights of stairs, Tracey couldn't help but dwell on the general dinginess of the place. *It's so dark,* she thought.

"I am sorry, doctor, but this place is so depressing – it must make the patients feel worse, not better," she said.

"I know," he replied. "But it's all down to politics and money – bad politics and no money. Believe me, I would change it if I could." He shook his head. "You see, we are a charity and the government does give us some money, but owing to all the cutbacks they have reduced the annual amount by nearly half. We have a handful of people who try their hardest to raise funds, but we are fighting a losing battle.

"Once a patient has been placed with us their relatives seem to disappear from the face of the earth," he continued, sadly. "They want nothing further to do with us, or the patient."

"Your nurse, on reception..." Tracey ventured.

"Oh, Veronica," Doctor Joslin smiled. "She's not a nurse, she's one of our better patients who thinks she's a nurse. Apart from the way she looks she is pretty good on reception."

Thank God for that, thought Tracey.

"Here is room 309," said Doctor Joslin, and looked at her. "Would you like me to stay with you?"

"Why?" asked Tracey, suddenly wary. "Is she violent?"

"On the contrary," said the doctor. "She is very genteel – a perfect lady. She misses her husband and children terribly."

He paused.

"There is one thing we are concerned about," he said, seriously. "She is not eating properly or taking exercise, she just sits on her bed rocking backwards and forwards. If you could encourage her in some way I would be very grateful."

"Okay," said Tracey, glad that the man had Mary's best interests at heart. "I'll try."

He opened the door.

"Take as long as you like," he said. "I think you will find her a fascinating young lady."

Tracey entered the room. It was more like a cell than a bedroom, decorated in the same dark colours as the rest of the building, with a tiny, barred window looking out across the fields. Furnished with a little table and chair, a wardrobe, a chest of drawers, it was very grim. A bed was pushed against the wall, and sitting cross-legged on the bed, totally naked, was a young woman rocking backwards and forwards.

As Tracey approached, she couldn't take her eyes off her. She could tell immediately that Mary had Down's Syndrome. She was a little tubby, her skin bronzed like Robbie's, with a lighter line around her waist as though a narrow belt had been worn in the sun. Her hair was combed and she had put a flower over her left ear. Her breasts were pert and her muscles toned. Altogether, she looked a very fit woman.

"Hello, my name is Tracey," she said, gently.

"Ello," said Mary, without turning her head, still rocking.

"Robbie sent me to see you."

The rocking stopped immediately; Mary turned to stare at her.

"May I sit down?" Tracey asked.

"Yes," said Mary.

Tracey walked over and sat down on the bed. Mary had a face like stone, there seemed to be no trace of emotion there.

"Robbie told me to tell you that he loves you very much," said Tracey. "So do Jawana and Lani, and Mamooto. They will all see you very soon."

The effect was instantaneous. Mary's face lit up and she threw her arms around Tracey's neck, taking her completely by surprise. She gave her a kiss.

"Love them back," she cried, happily.

They talked, and after a little while Tracey realised that Mary never spoke a whole sentence if she could get her meaning across with fewer words. Instead of saying, 'I will pack my things and would like to go home now', she would simply say, 'Go home now'. Tracey found that once she had spoken a couple of words it was easy enough to fit the rest of the words in herself.

She would say one word, 'sleep', and then pat the bed to get her meaning across. Another time she looked out of the window and said, 'free'.

Then she said, "Married."

Tracey was stumped.

"Married?" she asked.

"Yes," said Mary, "married."

She put her hand under the pillow and pulled out a crumpled piece of paper, handing it to Tracey. Carefully, Tracey unfolded it and read the words.

This is a wedding certificate, she realised.

As she read, she smiled to herself at some of the promises: put him to bed when he is drunk, feed and water him'. She smiled and shook her head.

Tracey looked up at Mary.

"It's a bit one-sided, isn't it?" she laughed.

Mary sat smiling back at her.

"Love him," she said.

Tracey took her hand.

"I know you do and he loves you, too."

Mary stood up and went to the window. When she turned, Tracey could see the tattoo cut into her chest and stomach. There were other scars, too, and marks all over her body. Gingerly, she touched one of the scars.

"Painful," she remarked, looking at Mary, but Mary shook her head.

"No pain," she smiled.

Tracey noticed a larger scar on Mary's stomach and touched that, silently asking the question.

"Spear," said Mary. "Robbie."

"Robbie did that to you?" Tracey gasped. She thought for a moment and decided that there must be quite a story behind that, given how deeply in love Robbie and Mary were. "I will ask him about that when I get home."

Tracey found herself warming to this woman like a close friend.

"Mary," she said. "Robbie asked me to tell you to hang on for a little longer, but you must eat properly and exercise out in the sunshine."

Mary nodded her head, "Yes."

Just then, the bell sounded for dinner. Mary took Tracey's hand and walked towards the door.

"Mary, you can't go down to dinner like that, you are naked," said Tracey.

She rummaged in the chest of drawers and found a t-shirt and shorts.

"Put these on."

They didn't fit terribly well, but at least she was dressed now.

Dinner was being served in the dining hall. Mary ate three servings of dinner, three servings of pudding and a whole jug of water. Doctor Joslin noticed and came over to praise Mary.

"I see you have got her appetite back," he said to Tracey. "Thank you."

Taking Tracey's hand once more, Mary led her out into the grounds. In front of the house was a wide green, about a hundred yards square. Patients were playing with balls, moon bouncers, bikes and scooters. Most of them looked reasonably happy, despite the tall, metal fence surrounding them.

They sat on a bench in the sunshine.

Mary pointed and said, "Run."

"Who me, run?" Tracey asked. "No way, I can't run in high heels."

"Me run," Mary laughed, and set off at a steady pace around the green.

Just then, the doctor came out and sat next to Tracey.

"I see you have got her to exercise, too. Well done," he congratulated her.

"I only told her that her husband wanted her to, and that did it," said Tracey, thoughtfully. "Off she went."

"A strange situation," the doctor agreed. "She is obviously very much in love with him."

"And he with her, I can assure you," said Tracey. "They have a magical bond between them, you can feel it."

She bit her lip.

"Doctor, would you do me a favour?" she asked.

"I will try," he replied, smiling.

"If I ring you tomorrow morning at ten, would you get Mary to the phone?" she asked. "I know it's not entirely ethical, but if she could hear her husband's voice it might give her a bit of a boost."

"We have a patient's telephone on wheels," he said. "I can take it to her room and plug it in. She won't be disturbed in there."

"Thank you, Doctor." She looked at her watch. "God, is that the time? I ought to make a move," she said. "I'll give you a ring tomorrow. Bye!"

She stood up and waved to Mary, who ran over and embraced her tightly, and then kissed her on the mouth, much to Tracey's surprise.

"Love you," she announced.

"I love you, too," said Tracey.

It was the first time another woman had ever kissed her on the mouth, but it had felt so natural and innocent, like the kiss of a child.

Driving home, Tracey couldn't help but contemplate just what this young woman had been through in the past twelve years. Living in a hostile environment, deep in the jungle with a husband and two children, only to return to so called civilisation and have her life torn apart.

Who is really civilised? Tracey wondered. *The jungle, or us?*

CHAPTER THIRTY-SIX

When Tracey arrived home, Dave was cooking the dinner. Cremating it, more like! You could always tell when dinner was ready, because the smoke alarm would inevitably go off.

I jumped to my feet when I saw her.

"How is she?" I asked.

"She's great," Tracey smiled. "I will tell you all about it over dinner. I need a shower, first."

When she came back down, I was sitting on the floor, talking to Mamooto in our tribal tongue. He couldn't understand why we didn't just assault the places where Mary and the children were being held and rescue them, like we had with the Butata tribe.

Tracey sat a little way away and listened for a while. She didn't understand a word, but the language had a lovely ring to it and I think she liked hearing it. I noticed her watching.

"Sorry about the language," I apologised, "but Mamooto doesn't speak a word of English."

"That's alright, I'm not at all offended," she told me. "I like to hear you talking to each other."

Dave joined us, a plate of food in each hand.

"Good timing," he said, and gave Tracey a kiss. He went back into the kitchen for the other plates. "Okay, enjoy," he smiled.

Over the meal, Tracey gave us the news about the children and the doctor at Mary's institution, and how he would allow us to telephone her in the morning.

"What did you think of her?" I asked, curious.

Tracey looked at me and smiled.

"She is a lovely lady, and very quickly I felt like she was my best friend," she said, and I beamed. "She loves you dearly and misses you and the children terribly – Mamooto, too."

After the meal we sat down over a bottle of wine and talked about the outcome of the day; I translated for Mamooto.

"Robbie," Tracey said, finally, "I have a question for you."

"Oh? What is it?" I asked.

"Mary has two scars – one on her tummy and one on her back – and when I asked her how she got them, she just said 'Spear, Robbie'. Did you throw a spear at her?"

"No, no, no," I protested, and explained how it had happened.

"You mean it went right through her?" Tracey gasped.

"Yes," I said. "It's a wonder she wasn't killed."

Dave piped up, "All this *Tarzan and Jane* stuff seems a bit far-fetched, old mate – I mean to say —

"Shut up, David," Tracey snapped.

"Okay," he said, huffily. "That's my cue for bed. Good night all."

He disappeared upstairs.

"Sorry about him, he's an idiot."

Tracey poured two large scotches and gave the bottle to Mamooto, who took it upstairs to drink in peace.

We sat on the settee and Tracey looked at me for a few seconds.

"We don't do it anymore," she said, out of nowhere. "Dave – he's not the man he was."

Tears began to well up in her eyes; I stared at her, at a bit of a loss.

"Maybe he's tired," I suggested. "Teaching is a stressful job."

"Don't make excuses for him," she said. "He doesn't find me attractive anymore. God knows I try hard enough – sexy underwear, perfume, pillow talk – but he just falls asleep." She paused and looked hard at me. "I don't suppose you would consider…"

I put my hand on hers and she fell silent.

"I am flattered that you would even think about it," I told her. "Before I fell in love with Mary you were the most attractive woman I had ever seen, and I know I will regret not taking the opportunity, but I love Mary too much to cheat on her."

Dave needs a good kick up the backside, I thought.

Tracey put her arms around my neck and kissed me, her warm, moist tongue gently opening my mouth to find mine. My heart was pounding; I felt a stirring in my loins. I was about to give in and kiss her back when she drew away.

"I understand," she said, smiling. "And I still love you, Robbie. Goodnight."

She shut the door behind her.

Shit, what have I done? I thought. *I just threw away an opportunity of a lifetime and now I will never know!*

*   *   *

When I came downstairs the next morning, Tracey looked at me a bit sheepishly.

"Good morning," I said, cheerfully. "Today's the day I talk to Mary."

"Your breakfast is on the table," she said. "I'll bring you a cup of tea."

Gradually, as the morning wore on, all thoughts of the previous evening were gone and we could talk without feeling awkward. The wait for ten o'clock seemed to drag out for a lifetime. We all sat around the kitchen, not speaking, just waiting.

When ten o'clock finally came we all crowded around the phone. Tracey lifted the receiver and dialled the number. My heart was in my mouth – I was so excited to hear Mary's voice.

"Hello Doctor Joslin," she said. "It's Tracey Reece – is Mary there?"

"I'll put her on," he said. It was just loud enough for me to hear his voice. "Mary, I have someone here who wants to speak to you."

Tracey handed me the phone.

"Hello Mary, it's me," I said, feeling suddenly very lonely indeed.

On the other end of the line, Mary went mad with excitement.

"Robbie! Robbie! Robbie! Love you, love you!" she said, over and over.

"Now listen," I said, and she calmed down a bit. "I have been to see Jawana and Lani – they send their love. Soon they are coming to live with us here at Tracey's, and then we will come and get you."

"Okay," she cried, brightly.

"Until then you must eat properly and train hard," I said. "Will you do that for me?"

"Yes," she said. "Eat. Train hard."

"Mamooto is here, would you like to talk to him?"

"Yes!" she cried, happily.

I handed Mamooto the phone, but he had no idea what to do with it. I put it to his ear.

"Now speak," I told him. "Speak!"

He didn't say anything, but I heard Mary's voice say, "Hello Mamooto," and he dropped the phone jumping back in fear.

I picked it up again and held it to his ear.

"Mary, talk to him," I called.

It took him some time, but he finally understood and was soon chattering away with her, ten to the dozen.

"What is he saying?" Tracey asked.

"He's filling her in on past events and reassuring her that we will soon be together again," I told her.

After they had finished he handed me the telephone.

"Okay, my love," I said. "Be a good girl and we will see you soon," I said, missing her terribly. "I love you, bye!"

"Love you!" she cried into the phone. "Bye! Bye! Bye!"

"Right," said Tracey, when I hung up. "I must go into the office and check my mail."

"Before you go," I said, as she got up to leave. "What happened to Jane?"

"Ah, well," she said, wincing. "After you were missing, presumed dead, she met a man – Gordon. Gordon Stemp is his name. They live in a house on the Davis estate. We meet now and then for coffee, but he gives her a hard time. If he finds out she's been out with me he can get quite violent.

"They have three children, two girls and a boy, but they aren't married," she said, and I could tell that she didn't like that. "He's quite happy to take goodies, but without the responsibilities that go with them."

"Have you got her address?" I asked.

"Yes," said Tracey. "Are you really sure you want it?"

"Yes," I said. "I think it's only fair that she should know I am still alive. Mamooto," I said to the big man. "Stay here until I get back."

I called for a taxi, and when we pulled up outside the house I just sat there for a few minutes, staring at it. The front garden was a tip, completely overgrown with a wreck of a car and broken toys scattered all over the place.

At the front door, the bell push was hanging off, bare wires exposed. I decided to knock instead. I heard a girl's voice shout from inside, "I'll get it, Mummy!"

The door opened to reveal a young girl, who looked me up and down.

"Can I help you?" she asked, politely.

"I hope so, is your mummy in?"

She turned and shouted, "Mum! It's a man for you!"

"What man?" came the reply as Jane came out of the kitchen, wiping her hands on a tea towel. She opened the door wide. "Yes, can I help you?"

She was quite tubby now, with matted hair; one of her eyes was black and swollen and there was a bandage on her arm. Her clothes were grubby and unkempt, and the pair of slippers she was wearing had a hole in. I could see her toe poking out of it.

For all the changes time had wrought I recognised her straight away.

"Hello Jane," I smiled. "How are you?"

She stared at me for a few seconds before her expression changed.

"Robbie!" she exclaimed, and then fainted.

I caught her as she fell and carried her into the kitchen. I sat her in a chair as gently as I could.

The little girl was scared, shouting, "Mummy! Mummy!"

"Get me a glass of water, please," I said, and she ran to help.

She came back just as Jane was coming around. She took a couple of sips of water and regained her composure. She stared at me.

"I was told you *were* dead."

"I know," I said. "So was everybody else."

"I waited four years for you to come back, but you didn't," she cried. "Oh, look at me," she exclaimed, tears running down her

298

cheeks. "I must look such a mess! If I'd known you were coming
—"

"You would have baked a cake," I finished.

"You still have your sense of humour," she said, giving me a watery smile.

"I hear you have three children," I said, smiling at the little girl. "You've been busy."

"Yes," she replied, and turned to the little girl. "Robyn, go and get Jason and Erica."

"Robyn?" I smiled. "That's a pretty name for a little girl."

"Yes," said Jane. "I named her after her father."

"I thought her father's name was Gordon?" I said, confused.

"No, Gordon is Jason and Erica's father. Robyn's father is Robin."

I looked at her, puzzled.

"She's yours, silly!" she told me. "I was pregnant when you left."

"Mine?" I gasped, gobsmacked. "If I had known I would never have left!"

"I know you wouldn't," she assured me. "I didn't know then, either."

All three children came into the kitchen and stared at me, interested and a little shy. I couldn't take my eyes off this little girl. She did look a lot like Jawana – similar eyes, and that little button nose. Her hair was a shade darker and a bit shorter, but the resemblance really was striking.

Jane looked at the children.

"Robyn, take them back upstairs, please."

After they had gone I asked, "Does she know about me?"

"I told her you were dead – I believed you were dead."

While we were talking, Roby came back downstairs and stood

beside her mother, her arm around her neck and her smaller hand on hers. I could tell they were very close.

The distinctive sound of a key turning in the front door lock stopped Jane in her tracks.

"Oh my God, it's Gordon!" she exclaimed.

She was shaking like a leaf, a look of pure terror on her face. I had seen that look on the faces of men who knew they were about to die in the jungle.

The architect of her fear came in, slamming the door behind him. He came into the kitchen and caught sight of me.

"What's going on here, then?" he shouted. "Entertaining men behind me back?"

"It's not what you think," Jane protested, timidly.

He looked at me and shouted, "You! Get out of my house!"

Robyn put both arms around her mother, protectively.

He grabbed the little girl by her hair and threw her across the kitchen, smashing her into the wall.

"You slut!" he screamed at Jane, giving her a powerful backhander. It sent her reeling out of the chair and onto the floor.

She was crying, "Please don't – please don't –"

I ran across the room as he turned. He saw me coming and threw a punch, which hit me on the side of the cheek. I was so furious I didn't even feel it connect. He threw another punch. This time I blocked it and punched him full in the mouth. He crashed back against the wall, spitting teeth and blood.

Screaming abuse at me, he came at me again; I ducked and punched him hard in the stomach. As he doubled over, a swift uppercut to his chin lifted him clean off the ground. Another blow to his nose sent him crashing through the hall door and onto the floor.

I dragged the big man up by his lapels and pinned him against the wall with my left forearm across his throat. I drew back my fist.

"If you ever hurt any member of this family again I will come back and see you," I growled.

He stared at me, fearfully.

"Did you hear what I said?" I shouted in his face.

"Yes! I hear you!" he said, in a higher voice than before.

I dragged him to the front door and pushed him outside. He tripped on the top step and went crashing face down onto the garden path. The neighbours must have heard the commotion and some of them came out to see what was going on.

They cheered as Gordon got up and walked unsteadily out of the gate and down the pavement, still spitting blood. One shouted, "It's about time he got his come uppance!"

I went back into the house. To my surprise, Robyn ran up to me and put her arms around my waist, holding on tight. I lifted her up, held her close and kissed her. My emotions were going haywire.

Jane came through, her face swollen.

"He will kill me when he comes back," she said, with a certainty that frightened me.

I sat her down on the settee and cleaned her up.

"Do you love him?" I asked.

"What?" she said, still a bit dazed.

"Do you love him?"

"No, I hate him," she said, wearily. "But what can I do? I have the three children to look out for, and no money."

I put my hands on her shoulders.

"I want you to pack anything of value to you, bring the children

301

and come with me."

"Well I – I don't know," she stammered. "This is all a bit sudden."

Robyn ran up to her mother.

"Oh, please Mummy, please let's go!"

Jane tucked a loose strand of hair behind her daughter's ear, smiling painfully.

"Don't worry about clothes," I said. "We will buy you new ones."

"Have you got any pets?" I asked. No she answered not any more.

"Have you a telephone?" I asked.

"Robyn, take him to the phone," said Jane, and began to gather a few things together.

I dialled for a taxi and by the time it arrived Jane was standing outside the front door with her children, a sad collection of things – the only things that mattered to her – in a bin bag. I helped her bundle the kids into the taxi, feeing sad for her, and kind of responsible.

CHAPTER THIRTY-SEVEN

Back at Tracey's house, Jane burst into tears. She was shaking uncontrollably. Tracey quickly assumed command. She sat her down on the settee and gave her a tissue.

"Dry your eyes and calm down," she said. "You're safe now."

Mamooto stood up, frowning and the children backed up against the far wall, wide-eyed and mouths open. They had never seen a black giant before.

I told Tracey what had happened and all she could say was, "That bastard! Come on Jane," she said, angry on her friend's behalf. "Let's get you cleaned up."

Gently, she led her up to the bathroom.

Mamooto sat down on the floor again. The children just kept staring at him. After a while, Jason gathered his courage and slowly walked towards him.

"Are you a giant?" he asked.

Mamooto looked at me, questioningly.

"He's asking if you are a giant," I told him.

He smiled at the little lad and nodded his head. Jason ran back to his sisters and whispered, awed, "He's a *real* giant!"

When the women came back downstairs, Jane was wearing one of Tracey's dressing gowns. She was clean now, her hair washed and combed. She was still quite attractive.

"Now the little ones," said Tracey, kindly. "Come on, upstairs you three!"

After she had bathed them she wrapped them in warm towels and sat them on the settee. Jane and I put their clothes in the washing machine.

"Right, who's hungry?" Tracey asked.

"Me! Me! Me!" all the children shouted together.

"I don't want to be any trouble," said Jane, anxiously.

Tracey gave her a hug.

"You are no trouble at all," she assured her. "I'm just glad you're all here, away from that bastard."

Tracey explained everything to Dave when he came home and he agreed immediately.

"Of course, you can all stay as long as you like!" he said.

Dave ordered three enormous pizzas, which we all wolfed down as if we hadn't eaten in days.

That evening, after we had tucked the children up in bed, the rest of us poured glasses of wine or scotch and then sat down to assess the situation.

"Jane, what do you do for money?" I asked.

"I get my Giro every week and the family allowance – but Gordon takes most of it," she said, sounding exhausted.

"That *bastard*!" Tracey said, again.

"Okay," I said, looking at her tired face; her head was already drooping with sleep. "You go up and get some sleep, and we'll sort things out tomorrow."

After she had gone I gave her enough time to fall asleep before speaking.

"You two know that Robyn is mine, don't you," I said.

Dave and Tracey exchanged a look that spoke volumes.

"Well, she named her Robyn, so it was pretty obvious," said Tracey. "But she never let on."

"Look, I have a plan," I said. "But I will need your help."

"Consider it done," said Dave.

"Mamooto, where is your bag?" I asked, turning to my loyal friend.

I put it on the table and poured out the coins. Both Dave and Tracey gawped at them.

"Wherever did you get these?" they asked.

When I opened the packets of diamonds, Tracey nearly fainted.

"That little lot must be worth a fortune," said Dave.

Then I showed them the paper from Reg, saying that the contents were mine – paid for in exchange for the penis beads.

"Well, it's all legally paid for," said Tracey, reading it through with a laugh. "As long as we can confirm that this signature belongs to the last owner."

"I would like to do something for Jane and the children," I said. "You know, a house and a few shillings in the bank for their future, so she won't have to worry. First, though, I need to know that the government won't take the coins and diamonds away."

"Leave that with me," said Tracey. "I'll see what I can do. Tomorrow we will take them shopping for a new wardrobe. I will pay on my credit card and we can settle up later."

Dave nodded.

"Great," I said, glad to have such friends. "Job done."

*　　*　　*

The next day we all went to the shopping centre. We bought clothes, shoes, toiletries – everything Jane and the children might need. Tracey opened a new bank account in Jane's name so that Gordon could never get at it. Little Jason held Mamooto's hand and Erica clung to Tracey, who loved having a little girl to spoil.

We all enjoyed a fish and chip dinner before heading home, laden with bags.

"How am I going to pay for all this?" Jane asked worriedly, staring at the new things.

"Don't worry, it's all taken care of," I replied.

When we got in, the answer phone was flashing.

"It's my office," said Tracey, listening to the message. "Good news – the trial starts on the 30th – that's in three weeks' time. We can pick up the children tomorrow."

Jane looked up.

"What trial? Whose children?" she asked, bewildered.

We sat her down and explained everything to her.

"I thought everything was too good to be true," she said, with a wry smile. "But I rather suspected there would be someone else."

I didn't sleep a wink that night, I was so excited.

I rose early, and was dressed and ready to go when Robyn came downstairs, still in her pyjamas.

"Where are you going?" she asked.

"To collect my son and daughter," I replied.

"Can I come with you?"

I looked at Tracey.

"That's not a bad idea," she said. "But only if your Mummy says you can."

Robyn ran upstairs. By the time Tracey and I finished our coffee she came running back, fully dressed.

"Yes," she declared. "She said I can!"

We drove to the home, my heart racing with anticipation. Lani and Jawana were ready and waiting for us. When Robyn and Jawana met they took to one another immediately.

Tracey watched the two girls chatting away and gave a soft whistle.

"My God, Robbie," she exclaimed. "Apart from the hair they

could be twins."

By the time we got back to Tracey's the girls were jabbering away as though they had known each other all their lives. They ran into the house and jumped the settee without taking a breath.

It was Jane's turn to stare at them.

"I don't believe it," she gasped. "They look so alike!"

Tracey went to visit Mary again to keep her spirits up and I got to talk to her on the telephone. Jane phoned the Department of Work and Pensions and cancelled her Giro.

"That will upset him," she said, pleased. "He will either have to get a job or go without his beer and fags."

After a week of living with Tracey, Jane's cuts and bruises were healing nicely and the children all seemed a lot happier.

Tracey took a photograph of Reg's treasures, along with the bill of sale, and went off to Reg's old company. His partners were still there after twelve years, and were amazed to hear that he was still alive. They scrutinised the photo and the signature and confirmed that both were genuine. A time was set for Tracey and I to meet them and make a deal.

*   *   *

Early one morning, the telephone rang unexpectedly.

"May I speak with Tracey Reece, please?" the caller enquired.

"Speaking," said Tracey.

"I am Professor Jenkins, Mrs Reece. Could you come to the university? I have something to show you that might be of help in the defence of Robbie and Mary," he said."

"Shall we say next Thursday morning at ten?" Tracey suggested.

"I'll come with you," said Dave, when she told him. "It's half term next week and it'll give me something to do."

CHAPTER THIRTY-EIGHT

Thursday soon came around and Jane and I went to register her children in a new school. At the university, Professor Jenkins welcomed Dave and Tracey.

"Nice to meet you," he smiled, shaking their hands. "These are my colleagues, Mr Baines, and Miss Melanie Pointer."

"How do you do," said Baines, as they all shook hands.

"The reason I have asked you here is, while we were on our expedition we took photos and video film until the batteries ran out, and of course, Robbie, Mary and the children are in these images and videos. I was going to present them at court, but we thought you had better see them first."

He indicated a door behind which was a hall set up with a projector, video and screen. Several chairs had been arranged around it.

"Let's have a cup of tea, first," the Professor suggested. "Then we will show you the slides and then videos. After tea they settled down to watch the video's, intrigued?

The screen lit up in the darkness and pictures of the village going about its business appeared upon it.

"This next one should interest you," said the professor. "That's Robbie and Mary outside their hut with Lani, Jawana and Mamooto."

Tracey gasped.

"They're all naked!"

"Yes," said the professor. "I hope you are not offended."

"No," said Tracey. "It's just that I wasn't expecting it, that's all."

The professor nodded.

"I wonder if you know the meanings of your friends' tribal

names?" he asked, and Tracey shook her head. "Jawana means, 'Beautiful Flower' and Lani means, 'Handsome Warrior'," he explained. "Mary's tribal name is Jimaju, which means 'White Death', and Robbie's is Majumi, meaning 'White Devil Slayer'."

"Strewth!" Dave exclaimed, shocked. "How on earth did they get names like that?"

"I've heard Mamooto call Robbie 'Majumi'," Tracey observed.

The professor peered at them over his glasses.

"You don't know the full extent of everything that happened to them over the last twelve years, so we will try to enlighten you," he said.

He put a new slide up in the screen, this one showing a larger group of people: Lani, Jawana, Robbie, Mary, Mamooto and three other people. The professor introduced them as the chief, Mbata and the chief's daughter.

"There are two chiefs in this picture," said the professor. "One is obvious; which do you think is the other?"

"Mamooto," said Tracey, immediately.

"No."

"Mbata," said Dave.

"No."

"It's not Robbie," said Tracey.

"No," said the professor. "It's Mary."

"Never," Dave exclaimed, "but she is…"

He paused.

"Down's Syndrome," the professor finished. "I know. Don't underestimate her. It is said she is formidable in battle – which we witnessed first-hand – and she is so feared by the enemy that they flee from her sooner than face her in combat."

"I can't wait to meet this woman," Dave said, impressed. "She

310

sounds amazing."

"She really is," said Tracey, fondly.

"Now, take a look at this photo of Robbie and his family," said the professor. "With Jawana and Lani cuddling their dog – who, by the way – is called Jekyll. You will soon see that cuddly little dog in a very different light. Start the video please, Mr Baines."

There was a click and a whir, and the video flickered to life on the projection screen.

"We have cut out the boring bits," said Professor Jenkins. "So we will start where we were attacked by a nasty tribe called the Butata. We were camped in a cave near this clearing when they came out from the jungle. We ran and took shelter behind those boulders in the foreground. From that cover, our rifles managed to hold them off for a couple of hours, but still they kept coming. They were relentless.

"We were almost out of ammunition when everything suddenly went quiet," he continued. "You can see them completely ignoring us and looking to the other end of the clearing. As the camera pans around you can see what we saw then: standing in a line are Mamooto, Robbie, Mary, Mbata and that cuddly dog, Jekyll."

All their weapons were raised.

"What do you see?" the professor asked, pausing the video.

"Well," said Dave, "they are all naked except for coloured feathers around their upper arms, a waistband and those things on the men's penises."

"They are penis beads," Professor Jenkins. "All the men wear them. When a boy comes of age his father gathers small pebbles from the river bed and makes them into beads for him. Mary made one for Robbie because his father is dead. Apparently they give a whole new meaning to the word intercourse, if you get my drift."

He clicked the video back on.

"At this point the Butata regrouped at the other end of the clearing and the two tribes faced each other."

"What's Mary carrying?" Dave asked.

"It's a fire axe, salvaged from the crashed aircraft," the professor told him. "Robbie made his sword out of part of the fuselage."

Dave gave a low whistle.

"Now, sit back and watch the next few minutes," The professor told them. "It may shock you."

Robbie drew his sword and screamed, and the four warriors ran forward, Jekyll surging in front, snarling and snapping. Mary had her tongue out and her axe raised high above her head. The Butata charged from the other end of the clearing.

They met in the middle, and chaos ensued. Dave and Tracey sat speechless, their mouths fallen open in shock, watching the carnage unravel before them. When the dust was clearing after the battle the video ended and the professor called out, lights.

"Well, what do you think?" he asked.

Dave spoke first.

"I can hardly believe what I just witnessed."

"Nor I," said Tracey.

"What do you think of that fluffy, cuddly dog now?" asked the professor, with a little chuckle.

"I just saw it rip a man's face off," said Dave, flatly. "How can they possibly trust him with the children?"

"He guards the children with his life," said Jenkins. "He's very gentle with them. A real Jekyll and Hyde dog."

Together, they watched the rest of the videos.

Tracey frowned.

"Who's that man in the village, talking to Robbie?"

"Oh," said the professor. "That's Reg, the third survivor from the

312

plane crash."

"Is he the man who sold the treasure to Robbie for a string of penis beads?" she asked.

"Yes, that's him."

"Could I use the video to prove that Robbie is the legal owner of the treasure?" she asked. "I'm sure it would help to confirm Reg's survival."

"By all means," said the professor. "If they can help in any way you're welcome to use them."

After they had seen everything, Professor Jenkins invited them for lunch. Their little party spent the rest of the afternoon discussing the morning's shocking footage.

As they prepared to leave the professor took them to one side.

"There is one last thing I should mention," he said. "Mamooto."

"What about him?" asked Tracey.

"You know he is pledged to protect Robbie and his family to the death," he said. "He will carry out that pledge without question. When we left the village the chief released him from his pledge at Robbie's request, so that he could stay with the tribe. He told Robbie that the chief refused to release him from his bond and he had to go with them, or Robbie would never have allowed it.

"Robbie does not know this," he continued. "They are like brothers, but not only will Mamooto die for them, if he thinks any one of them is in danger he will kill for them as well. He doesn't understand our language, or our laws. If he perceives anyone as a threat to his family it could cost them their life. I would suggest you keep him out of the courtroom."

"Point taken," said Tracey.

Melanie approached her.

"Tracey, can I have a word, please?"

"Of course," she replied. "What is it?"

"Can I come and see you in private? I need to talk to somebody. You seem close to Robbie and I feel that I can trust you..."

Tracey gave Melanie her card.

"Ring me and we can meet up," she said.

"Thanks," said Melanie, gratefully. "I'll get in touch in the next few days."

On the way home, Dave asked, "Can you use the videos in court?"

"No, I don't think so," Tracey responded. "The prosecution would use it to say that they're barbarians and ought to be locked up. I will fight the case based on love, marriage and the welfare of the children."

She thought for a moment.

"I need to show Reg's partners the video to prove that he's still alive and get a settlement on the coins and diamonds," she said.

Back at home, everyone settled down for supper. Strangely, neither Dave nor Tracey wanted to talk about their meeting with the professor.

I phoned Mary. She seemed to be in good spirits, particularly when she spoke to the children and Mamooto.

CHAPTER THIRTY-NINE

The next day, Tracey and I went to meet Reg's former partners. When they saw the video they were convinced beyond doubt that their old friend was still alive. They took out the paper confirming the sale.

"You say the signature is genuine," I said, "but can you tell us what this number relates to at the bottom of the page?"

"What number?" Tracey asked.

The partners took the paper and scrutinised the six digits, then shared a look.

"I wonder," said one of them. "Reg has a combination box in our safe, and if this is the number then it would prove beyond doubt that your receipt is genuine because nobody but Reg would know the combination to open it."

They took the box from the safe, put it on the desk and turned the numbers to correspond to those on the receipt.

As the last number lined up the lock gave a loud click. They opened the lid and looked inside: it was full of all sorts of treasures and papers. One was Reg's Last Will and Testament, made before the fateful aeroplane ride. It stated that if anything happened to him then the contents of the box and all his worldly goods would go to his trusted friends and partners.

"Right," said the elder of the two men. "We will evaluate the contents and give you the going price – that is, if you will trust us?"

I held out my hand and we shook on it.

"We will send you a cheque and if you aren't satisfied with the amount, come back and I am sure we can work something out."

The telephone was ringing when they arrived home. It was Melanie.

"When can we meet?" she asked Tracey.

"How about tomorrow," Tracey suggested. "Here at the house at ten a.m.?"

Bang on time, the doorbell rang the next moment. Dave opened the door.

"Tracey!" he shouted. "It's Melanie!"

"Well, bring her in, you prawn," shouted Tracey.

She came through, took one look at me and threw her arms around my neck. Then burst into tears.

"Right," Tracey commanded. "Everybody out. Robbie, Melanie, go into the dining room. Dave, could you bring us three coffees, please? Then we don't want to be disturbed."

Once Dave had brought in the coffees and some biscuits, they settled down.

"Close the door on your way out," said Tracey.

She gave Melanie, who was still a little tearful, a couple of tissues.

"Now, let's have it," she said. "What's wrong?"

"I'm pregnant," she blurted out, "and I need to tell someone or I will go mad."

"Who is the father?" Tracey asked, gently.

Melanie looked at me.

Surprised, Tracey said, "Are you saying that Robbie is the father?"

"No," sniffed Melanie. "But he knows who is."

Tracey must have sensed something in the other woman because she shooed me out of the room.

"Robbie, leave us alone – this is women's talk."

It was some time before either one emerged. Tracey sat down beside me, looking shocked. She took my hand.

"Good God Robbie, that girl has been through hell," she said, in

316

a hollow voice. "She's just composing herself, then she wants to speak to all of us."

The door opened and we went back in, joining Melanie at the dining table.

"I want you to know I am keeping the baby," she said.

"Have you thought this out?" I asked, concerned.

"Yes, I have," she said. "I have made up my mind. We are the only three that know and when I get closer to my due date I am going to move away, where nobody knows me. That brings me to the other reason for seeing you. I want to hand over the Pointer foundation to Professor Jenkins.

"It is well financed and should last him for the rest of his life," she continued. "He won't have to go crawling to the universities for funding anymore. Tracey, could you draw up the paperwork for me?"

"Of course I can, leave it with me," she assured her.

Melanie turned her attention to me.

"You did the wrong thing, bringing Mary and the children back here," she said. It wasn't accusatory, just a plain statement of fact. "I lived with you in the jungle remember. You belong there, not here, in a society that will tear you apart because they don't understand your feelings for one another.

"Mary is a lovely woman and lucky to have a good man like you beside her," she went on. "In the jungle she is a chief in her own right and respected – here she is not understood and locked away in an institute that is really just another kind of prison. Take your family back to the jungle before it's too late, or you will lose everything."

After she had left, Tracey looked at me.

"Well," she said. "I didn't expect that confession from her."

"No, nor I," I admitted. "But I hope she feels a little easier, letting it all out at last."

Tracey nodded.

*   *   *

The next day, Jane took the children out to the park to give Tracey a chance to catch up on her work and I went for a walk to think about our future as a family. Melanie's words ran around and around my head: Go back to the jungle.

God, I thought, if we lose the court case, I will go to prison and Mary will be locked in an institution for the rest of her life. The children will be put into care. What have I done?

I arrived back at the house and let myself in. It was so quiet that I thought everyone must be out. I went up to my room to change and as I passed Dave and Tracey's bedroom I heard noises. The door was ajar so I looked in. The sight before me made me step back in shock.

Lying on the bed, flat on her back was Tracey, her arms around Mamooto's chest, legs locked around his waist by her ankles. They were both naked, sweat pouring from their bodies. This tiny woman, covered by this huge man in the throes of passion. She was whimpering like a puppy; he was groaning with every thrust.

I pushed the door to and beat a hasty retreat. I heard her scream as I reached the front door, Mamooto clearly taking her over the top. I went for another walk to clear my head and give them time to tidy themselves up. On my return, Tracey was sitting in the lounge as though nothing had happened, reading a magazine "upside down". Mamooto was sitting cross-legged on the floor, nearby.

Whoever would have guessed that a woman like Tracey would have given it up to this giant – my bodyguard, to boot. Mind you, he hadn't broken any law or taboo in his mind – the chief hadn't joined her in union to Dave even if a vicar had.

When Jane came home with the children we waited for Dave. After dinner and the children were put to bed. We settled down together.

"I have been thinking," I said, "and I've made up my mind. I should never have brought Mary and the children back to

England. We were happy in the jungle and I am taking us back whatever the court outcome. We are going home". Mamooto, I asked. "Do you want to live here or go home?"

"Go home," he smiled, broadly.

Tracey looked at me.

"I take it from that smile that he said 'go home'," she said.

"Yes," I answered.

"I don't know how you will get out of the country," she said, "but if you have a plan we will help you, won't we Dave?"

"Sure thing," he replied.

"Tomorrow I want you to go and see Mary," I said. "Tell her we are going home and to wait until I come and get her."

*   *   *

Tracey arrived at the institution early the next day.

Dr Joslin greeted her cheerfully, "Do you know, Mary runs about twenty miles every day? It sounds impossible, but it's true."

When Mary saw Tracey, she ran over and gave her a hug.

"Ello!" she beamed.

"Hello Mary, let's sit down," said Tracey. "I want to tell you something. Robbie told me to tell you to be ready. You are all going home soon."

"We go home!" she said, clapping her hands in delight. "We go home!"

"Shh," Tracey urged. "Don't tell anyone – keep it to yourself," whispered Tracey. "Just wait until Robbie calls you."

When she arrived home there was a letter for her from Reg's partners. She opened it and turned to me.

"Robbie, You have been made an offer here from the jewellers – do you want to accept it?"

"How much is it?" I asked.

319

She paused, and then said, "Four million, five hundred and sixty thousand pounds."

I blinked. Clearly I had been misheard.

"How much?"

"Over four and a half million," she said, again.

I just couldn't take it in. We were millionaires.

"Take it," I said, "and put it in your bank."

"Why our bank?" Tracey asked, surprised.

"Because if we disappear back to Africa without warning, you can keep the money," I explained. "All I ask is that you set Jane and the children up with a house and enough money that they can live on the interest – and you sew it up so tight that no one can ever take it from them."

Tracey smiled, a little overwhelmed.

"Of course I will," she said. "You're a good man Robbie, but how are you going to leave England if you get sent to prison?"

The date of the trial was fast approaching. Tracey and I spent hours preparing my defence.

"It's going to be a tough one," she said. "If we win the case it will open the floodgates for people with Down's Syndrome to cohabit legally and raise children. It goes against centuries of established prejudice. People seem to have a lot more patience for the physically handicapped than they do for the mentally handicapped. They don't understand, and what they don't understand they fear, lock away or destroy."

"But that's wrong!" I shouted. *"Wrong!"*

Tracey put her hand on mine.

"Robbie," she said, gently. "Think back – why did you leave us and go abroad in the first place? Because you didn't understand."

"But I do now!"

"Yes, you do now," she nodded. "But we have to convince a jury to understand, too."

CHAPTER FORTY

By the Saturday before the trial the press were yet to track us down – or perhaps they didn't feel our story was worth the effort. I hadn't really been sleeping, what with the trial looming.

With no warning at all, Robyn burst into the bedroom and pounced on me.

"Time to get up!" she screeched, joyfully. "Mummy is taking us out for the day – and you and Mamooto!"

"Where to?" I asked.

"It's a secret!" she giggled. "Come on, hurry!"

We got up, showered and dressed, joining the others downstairs.

"What's going on?" I asked, bemused.

"Jane is taking you all out for the day to unwind before the trial," Tracey explained. "It might be your last chance to be together for a while, so make the most of it. Go out and enjoy yourselves."

Three taxis were already waiting for us; they deposited us at the nearest underground station. We boarded a train and sped into the tunnel. For the first time since the incident with the bathtub, Mamooto was clearly unnerved. He sat bolt upright in his seat, his eyes as wide as saucers, trying to see out of the windows. He knew we were moving, but not which way or how fast. Each time we entered a station the bright lights made him jump.

Jawana and Lani took it all in their stride. They seemed to be getting used to the English version of civilisation.

Finally, the train pulled in at Piccadilly station and we came out into the sunlight. The relief on Mamooto's face was a picture. My mind drifted back to Mary, as it often did now we were apart. I missed her terribly. I would be glad when all this was over and I could hold her in my arms once more. I felt the desperate urge to reassure her.

To keep our minds occupied, Jane took us everywhere: the Planetarium, Madame Toussaud's (there was a wax figure of an African Prince holding a spear in there, and Mamooto went toe to toe with him, expecting him to speak), the Houses of Parliament, Nelson's Column, the Zoo in Regent's Park.

"Why are the animals locked up?" Mamooto asked. "They should be free."

I tried to explain, but he wasn't impressed.

Robyn held my hand all day; she never left my side. I knew I would miss this little girl when I left England – and I had so little time to get to know her.

We had a meal in McDonalds. To our astonishment, Mamooto loved it. He ate four cheeseburgers and chips, and washed them down with four colas.

We had a boat trip on the river. By then, the children were getting tired so we made a move for home. In the taxi, Robyn climbed onto my lap and fell asleep. Jawana and Lani fell asleep on Mamooto's lap, while Jane cuddled Erica and Jason.

We arrived home at about 6.30 p.m. The house was in darkness, which surprised me. The front door stood wide open, but the lounge door was shut. When I opened it to let us in, someone switched the light on and revealed a room full of people.

Everyone cheered as we entered. There were decorations hanging around the walls, the dining table was laden with food; someone put some music on and from out of nowhere came Tracey. She was wearing *that* red dress, the red lipstick and her scarlet high heels. Her perfume wafted up, taking me back twelve years. She was carrying a bottle of wine.

"Remember me?" she asked, beaming.

"I have never forgotten you," I smiled. "You are even more beautiful now than you were then."

"Flatterer," she laughed.

I looked around and there, smiling at me, was the captain from our high seas adventure, along with some of the crew. He introduced a tiny woman, who turned out to be his wife.

"This is Sue," he said. "Where is the big fella – she wants to thank him for saving my life!"

Just then, Mamooto stooped and entered the room. Sue looked up at him, almost vertically given her height; she was just under five-feet two inches, and Mamooto was nearly seven-feet tall. She walked over to him and held open her arms. He bent down and held her around the waist like a doll, and then lifted her up to his height. She cupped his big head in her hands and kissed him.

"Thank you," she smiled. Mamooto smiled back.

Jane took the children up to shower and got them ready for bed, but when they came back down all five of them were excited and not remotely tired anymore.

"Robbie, Mamooto, you stink," Tracey declared. "Go up and get showered and changed – and then come back down for the party."

While we were dressing I spoke to Mamooto, "Do you remember back home when we lit fires, at a big feast, got drunk and danced all night, and then chased the girls into the jungle," I asked him.

His face lit up.

"Yes," he said.

"Well," I said. "This is the English version – except we don't chase the girls into the trees."

Mamooto's face fell again.

"Don't worry," I told him. "We will be going home soon and we will be back to normal. Oh, and by the way," I added, with a smile. "Thanks for putting up with me. It must have been hard to leave the village and come all the way out here on the chief's orders."

"Yes," he said.

I held out my hand. He grabbed it, and instead of shaking it, pulled me into a hug. The feeling of loyalty and deep friendship I felt for this man would last me my lifetime, I just knew it. I know he felt the same way.

"Come on," I said. "Let's party!"

Back downstairs we mingled with the guests. There were some teachers from my old school who couldn't believe I was the same person.

"You were a wimp!" said one. "You didn't even like playground duty!"

The professor and Baines arrived with Melanie in tow, and the party got into full swing. Then I noticed a man staring at me with a wide grin on his face. He looked oddly familiar.

"'Ello, sir," he said. "You look a bit different from the last time I saw you," he said.

I knew I knew the face, but I simply couldn't place him.

"It's Jenkins, sir – my mother gave you a fat lip at school, but I don't think she would try it now, sir!"

"Jenkins!" I exclaimed. "How are you?"

"I just got out, three weeks ago, but I'm going straight now, sir," he grinned. "No more porridge for me!"

"I'm glad to hear it," I said, and told him how his advice on fighting dirty had saved my life in the jungle.

The professor excused himself after a while, saying that he had business with the captain. As the evening wore on and the children grew sleepy, Jane and Tracey took them up to bed. The telephone rang and Dave answered it.

"Professor, it's for you!"

"I'll take it in the dining room, thank you," he said. "It's a personal call."

I was really enjoying myself. The music was playing, wine was flowing and people were dancing all over the pace. Mamooto drank a bottle of scotch all by himself. He started swaying to and fro to the music, and when someone put on a record by a famous drummer Mamooto started bouncing up and down stamping his feet, oblivious to everyone. They all formed a circle around him, mesmerised by his rhythmic movements.

Jawana and Lani must have heard the drums because they quickly reappeared. They ran to the centre of the circle with Mamooto and danced with him. Jawana saw me and grabbed my hand. Pulling me onto the floor, too. Everyone cheered and clapped, and we showed them some real dancing – tribal style.

It must have been impressive because everyone joined in. That record was played at least a dozen times before everyone gave up, exhausted, leaving just the four of us dancing, revelling in the memories of our village.

The party carried on until well past five a.m.

Nearly everyone had left by then, leaving only a dozen or so diehards. We all sat around Dave and Tracey's living room, drinking and talking. Mamooto spoke more that morning than I had ever heard him talk in twelve years. I translated what he said into English and our friends sat, spellbound, wowed by his exploits – some gruesome, others quite funny.

Tracey asked him if he had family back home.

"No," he said. "My family is here. I would like to go back home with them."

We finally bid the stragglers farewell and crawled up to bed. I slept until lunchtime and then spent the afternoon and evening talking about the night before.

I wished Mary was there. I needed to hold her close and tell her how much I loved her. At least tomorrow I would be seeing her, even if I didn't get to touch her.

I barely slept a wink that night, my mind was so caught up in the trial the next day. If I was found guilty and imprisoned, how would I ever get my family back home?

I lay there listening to the night sounds of the urban jungle: a boy racer drove up the road, perpetrating a handbrake turn with screeching tyres and the smell of burning rubber. Dogs barked; cats wailed and fought; drunks shouted and kicked over dustbins. I thought back to the first night in the jungle when the animal noises scared me half to death. Mary had slept through the whole thing like a baby – bless her.

I looked over at Mamooto. He was stretched out on his back and the light of the moon glinted in his eyes.

"What are you thinking about," I asked.

"Home," he replied.

"Me too. I miss the jungle noises of the night," I said. "Do you remember that big old croc that used to lie in the water just off shore and growl?"

"There were two until you killed one of them," he chuckled. "Sometimes he would come out at night and tour the village, looking for someone to eat. I remember he nearly ate you once! That was the best dance I ever saw you do," he laughed.

"Mamooto, why did you let me think the chief made you come here and leave the village when he had released you from your bond?"

He didn't answer.

"I know it's true because the professor told me," I said.

He turned his head slowly towards me and took a deep breath.

"Before you came to our village I was known as Mamooto the Lonely One," he said. "I had no wife, no family – nothing. You came with your woman in child, and because you saved Mbata's life you were accepted into the tribe as a warrior. I was envious of the high regard the tribe held for you. I thought if I defeated you in combat I would gain that regard, but I failed and was ordered to be your bodyguard.

"It was the best thing that ever happened to me," he continued, earnestly. "Over the years you, Jimaju, Jawana and Lani have accepted me into your family. The battles we have fought side by side has gained me the respect of the chief and the tribe. Forgive me for not telling you that the chief released me, but if you had left without me I would have become nothing again."

"There is nothing to forgive," I replied. "In fact, I would have been disappointed if you hadn't come. It's been our pleasure to have you as a friend. I promise I will get us all home soon. We will hear that old croc again – mark my words."

For a long time we lay reminiscing and he admitted he missed Mary as much as I did.

"She is a fine woman," he said, "and she needs to be with her family."

"Soon," I said. "Soon."

CHAPTER FORTY-ONE

Everybody was up very early the next morning. Tracey had to go into the office.

"Jane will look after the children at court," she said. "Dave has taken a day's leave to support you. He will drive you to the court and I will see you later on for the briefing."

We arrived at court early and sat in the waiting for Tracey to arrive. She came in wearing her gown, wig and frills, looking very impressive.

"We are in court three, upstairs," she told me. "Judge Jordan presiding."

A man approached and shook Tracey's hand.

"Seen who's presiding he asked?"

"Yes, Jordan," she said.

"Sorry," he smiled, looking faintly apologetic. "Good luck."

After he left, Tracey nodded at his retreating back.

"That's Simon Story," she said. "Prosecution barrister – he's ruthless, but fair."

I instructed Mamooto to sit outside of the courtroom in the main hall. In court I was escorted to the dock, where I took my seat. It was a formidable place and I felt very humbled.

"Cooee!"

I looked around. Sitting on a bench behind me was Mary, waving and giggling at me. I waved back, delighted to see her despite the circumstances. She was a sight for sore eyes.

"Love you!" she shouted.

"I love you, too," I mouthed back. I put my fingers over my lips, "Shh."

Giggling, she took a handkerchief from her pocket and held it over her mouth. I smiled, surprised that she had remembered that from all those years ago. I don't know what the rest of the court thought about it, but I found it funny and it was very good to see her.

"All rise." Everyone stood up to the commanding voice. "Judge Jordan presiding."

A door opened behind the bench and the most miserable looking man I had ever seen entered the court. He was fat, nearly bald and had voluminous jowls that swung back and forth as he walked. He looked like a bulldog chewing a wasp.

Once everyone was seated he looked imperiously over the courtroom.

"Prosecution!" he barked.

"Story, your Honour."

"Defence!"

"Reece, your Honour."

The judge peered at Tracey over his glasses.

"We've met before, haven't we, Reece?"

"Yes, your Honour," said Tracey. "The Gershwyn case."

"Hmm, I remember," he growled. "You were trouble then, Reece, I hope you're not going to be trouble now."

"I'll try not to be, your Honour."

"The Crown versus Robin Cross," he announced. "According to my notes, Mr Cross and Miss Lane have been cohabiting for over twelve years, producing two children, Jawarner and Larnie."

"It's 'Jawana' and 'Lani', your Honour," Tracey corrected.

"Oh is it, indeed?" he asked, sending a glare her way. "We will begin with the prosecution, please."

Mr Story rose to his feet.

"Thank you, your Honour," he said. "Mr Cross is charged for having sexual relations with a mentally handicapped woman, namely Miss Lane, and did so knowingly taking advantage of her situation. I aim to prove Mr Cross guilty on all counts. I call my first witness, Doctor Barnett."

The door opened and an elderly, distinguished looking gentleman came in. He was escorted to the front of the court and sworn in.

"Doctor Barnett," Story began. "Will you please inform the court of your occupation?"

"I am a senior psychiatrist for the Crown, based at Harley Street," he said.

"Thank you," said Story. "Tell the court, have you had a consultation with Miss Mary Lane?"

"Yes, I have," he replied. "It is my opinion that Miss Lane's Down' Syndrome is severe and that she should be looked after in an institution."

"Objection," called Tracey.

"Overruled," said the judge, almost lazily.

"No more questions, your Honour," said Story.

Tracey stood up.

"Doctor Barnett, have you read Miss Lane's account of her life over the last twelve years?" she asked.

"No, I have not."

"Well, perhaps you should have, doctor," said Tracey, in a hard voice. In that time, Miss Lane has held together a family – which is more than many women deemed 'normal' can say. She has taken and cared for a husband, borne and raised two beautiful children, along with helping to care for numerous orphaned children in her village.

"She took care of herself and her family in a hostile environment and has learned a second language – that of the tribe that took her in," Tracey continued. "I would say that she's quite capable of making her own decisions, wouldn't you, Doctor Barnett?"

Tracey took her seat.

"No more questions, your Honour."

The judge glanced at the current witness, "You may step down, Doctor Barnett."

Mr Story called his second witness, Doctor Joslin.

"Doctor Joslin," he opened. "You have taken charge of Miss Lane at your institution over the last few weeks, have you not?"

"Yes, sir," he replied, and smiled up at Mary.

"Can you tell the court her state of mind and her physical state – in your own words."

Doctor Joslin nodded.

"When she first moved in I was concerned for her health," he said. "She would not eat or speak, she simply sat and rocked to and fro. I believe now that this was the stress of being removed from her family. Initially, we thought she was just another Down's Syndrome case, but when we got to know her she turned out to be quite an amazing young woman."

"In what way?" the judge asked, frowning over his glasses.

"We set her tasks," said the doctor. "Maths, reading and writing didn't interest her whatsoever, but when we put visual puzzles in front of her she excelled, solving each one with ease."

"What sort of puzzles?" asked Story.

"Three thimbles and a pea was one," he answered. "We must have tried it a hundred times and not once did she fail to find the pea. Miss Lane can memorise cards in the correct order, even if we changed them around she could put them back in the same order. We also have about twenty bent nail puzzles, and she can undo them in seconds. Surprisingly, she can put them back together just as fast. "She can speak two languages, English and another."

"What other language?" queried the judge.

"We don't know, sir, but it seems African in origin."

"What about her physical ability?" Story asked.

"Now that is unbelievable," the doctor replied. "She can lift over double her body weight. No one at the institute can best her at arm wrestling – man or woman. She runs twenty miles every morning before breakfast and another twenty miles before supper."

"That's forty miles every day!" the judge exclaimed, surprised.

"Yes, your Honour!" said the doctor, eagerly. "One morning she ran over fifty miles without stopping. She is incredibly fit."

"Doctor, you say that Miss Lane can work out children's tricks, but she can't read, write or do maths?" Story asked.

"That's right," said the doctor, "but –"

"Just answer the question, doctor," Story interrupted.

Doctor Joslin frowned.

"No."

"You say she is bi-lingual, but you don't know what the second language is," Story continued. "So for all you know she could be talking a load of twaddle, doctor?"

"Well –"

"Yes or no will suffice."

"Objection," Tracey called. "The prosecution is leading the witness."

"Sustained. Have a care, Mr Story."

"Your Honour, I merely wish to establish that this so-called second language could be a load of twaddle."

"Are you suggesting, Mr Story, that unknown African tribal languages are 'a load of twaddle'?"

"Of course not –"

"Miss Reece, that is quite enough," snapped the judge.

I watched Tracey's eyes narrow. That wasn't good.

"Thank you, doctor, that will be all," he continued. "You may stand down."

It sounded to me like the judge had already made his mind up.

CHAPTER FORTY-TWO

The case rumbled on. First the police were called, then customs. At a quiet moment I turned to look at Mary, who was staring at me. Her face lit up as our eyes met, that lovely smile of hers brightening up the whole courtroom. She waved at me and I waved back.

I sat watching my beautiful wife, who had the innocence of a little girl. The noise of the court meant nothing to me – I heard and saw nothing but the vision of the woman who held my heart. I wished I had never brought her back here to face this humiliation.

A sudden bang brought me back to the present as the judge's gavel came down on the bench.

"Court adjourned until ten am tomorrow ." he snapped.

Everybody got stiffly to their feet as he left the courtroom. I turned to Mary and mouthed, "I love you."

She blew me a kiss.

When we got back to Tracey's she told us that the judge didn't know we were living with them.

"If he found out he might take you to stay in prison for the duration of the trial, so keep quiet," she warned me.

The first witness the next day was Professor Jenkins. After swearing on the Bible, Tracey began her examination.

"Professor Jenkins, you have spent some time in the jungle actually living with Mr Cross and his family. Is that correct?"

"Yes, it is," said the professor.

"Would you say you ever saw Mr Cross take advantage of Mary?" Tracey asked. "Did you ever see him make her do anything against her will, or take advantage of her disability to gain, shall we say, favours?"

"Certainly not!" snapped the professor.

"Did she ever refuse his advances or push him away?"

"No, they are devoted to each other and live a natural, healthy, happily married life together," said Professor Jenkins. "They have two lovely children – a perfect family. They found one another in a hostile environment where our society had abandoned them for dead," he continued, sounding stern. "They found love and happiness, only to come back to a so called civilised nation and have to face this. It's humiliating."

"Thank you, professor," said Tracey. "Your witness."

The prosecution asked the professor their questions, trying to find a chink in his armour, but he stood firm. It was hard to find fault with the truth. At the end of the day we all trooped back to Tracey and Dave's house. Everyone was quite sombre, knowing that the end was coming soon.

Robyn came and sat on my lap.

"Daddy, Mummy says you might be going away soon," she said. "Can I come with you?"

"Well," I replied, knowing that I couldn't take her away from a mother that loved her. "If I am not here your mummy will need someone to look after her and Erica and Jason while I'm away – and I know you are the best one to do that."

"But I don't want you to go," she whined.

"I know," I said, soothingly. "I'll tell you what, look out of the window. What do you see up in the sky?"

"The moon," she said.

"That's right, the moon," I told her. "Now, every night when that moon comes up bright in the sky you can look at it and think of me. Wherever I am I will look at it and think of you, too. That's how close we will be for the rest of our lives – under the same moon."

"Promise?" she asked, tearfully.

"I promise," I assured her, swallowing the lump in my throat.

The next day we were back in court.

When Mary saw me she jumped up and down, waving like mad.

"Love you! Love you!" she shouted, waving frantically.

I blew her a kiss and waved back.

Today, the judge called Mary to speak on her own behalf.

"Now," he said. "I would like to meet the lady concerned in this case, Mary Lane. Bring her to the bench, please."

A court official took Mary's hand and led her forward. Judge Jordan smiled at Mary.

Well, I'll be blowed, I thought to myself. *Has she got through that hard shell of his and softened his heart? That's my girl.*

I clung to that glimmer of hope.

"Come and sit next to me, my dear," he smiled, benevolently. "I want to ask you some questions. Do you like living here?"

"No," she snapped, at once.

"Why not?" he asked.

"Go home soon!" she declared.

"You want to go home?" he replied.

"Yes," she nodded at him. Go home."

He smiled gently at her.

"It won't be long now and you can go home."

"Go home," she repeated.

"Do you like it at home?"

"Yes," she replied.

"You have lots of friends at home and people to look after you?"

"Yes," she laughed, bouncing up and down, clapping her hands together, happily. "I go home soon."

It was clear that the judge meant Doctor Joslin's institute, while Mary meant the jungle.

"Now Mary," said the judge. "Do you know anybody in this courtroom?"

"Yes," she replied, pointing right at me. "My husband."

"But he's not your husband," said the judge, still smiling. "You are not married."

Mary glared at him.

"Am too!" she snapped.

"No, you are not," said the judge, firmly. "You don't have a certificate of marriage."

"Do too," she snapped, louder this time. She pulled out the piece of paper that Reg had written out when he married us back in the cave.

The judge read it out to the court and everyone started laughing. I felt nauseous. Mary did not deserve this – even the judge was laughing.

"This is not a marriage certificate," he said. "It's a worthless piece of paper written by a man to pull the wool over your eyes so he could take advantage of you!"

Tracey was out of her seat before he even finished the sentence.

"Objection, your Honour!" she cried. "You are leading the witness!"

"Overruled!" he snarled.

The courtroom was in uproar.

I caught sight of Mary's expression. She was staring at the judge; I knew that look.

Uh-oh...

She had that same look before she went into battle – the only thing missing was the axe. She snatched her certificate back out of his hand and shoved it in her pocket. Then she pushed him hard, knocking him and his chair backwards behind the bench.

Sticking her tongue out, she grabbed the gavel and disappeared behind the bench after him. There was a resounding crack as it connected with his skull. I tried to run forward to stop her, but two police officers grabbed me from either side. Two more went to the aid of the judge, which was unfortunate for them, really.

She laid the first man out with a straight punch to the jaw; the second decided that discretion was the better part of valour and made a bolt for the door. He'd almost reached them when the great double doors bust open. A silence fell over the court as everyone turned to see Mamooto, Jawana and Lani, all looking pretty menacing.

When Mamooto saw me being restrained by two police officers and Mary still beating up the judge, he waded straight in. Out of nowhere, police ran in, holding their batons aloft. There must have been a dozen of them – more, probably.

Oh no, I thought. *I hope Mamooto doesn't kill anyone.*

His only thought would be to protect us, and he was picking up officers above his head and hurling them across the room. He brought a huge fist down on one officer's head, knocking him out cold. Even Jawana and Lani ran into the fray, stamping on toes and kicking shins. Mary looked up at me, smiled and waved.

Oh well, I thought. *In for a penny, in for a pound!*

I brought my arms forward, crashing the two officers holding me into one another. As they fell to the floor I ran forward. Mary jumped the bench and together we ran to help Mamooto. The place looked like a battleground, bodies lying everywhere. I held Mary tightly as Mamooto came over and cuddled us both, followed by Jawana and Lani.

Tracey stood behind her desk, staring at the carnage.

"Robbie," she said. "What the hell happened here?"

I looked at her.

"Mary got annoyed," I said. "People don't like Mary when she gets annoyed."

"FREEZE!"

We spun round, greeted by the sound of automatic rifles being cocked. We were surrounded by armed police wearing bullet proof vests.

I looked at Tracey again.

"Do you think I'll get a suspended sentence, or a few hours community service?" I quipped.

She smiled.

"If hanging was still legal I think you would be facing the gallows."

*   *   *

We were held at gunpoint while a string of ambulances took the injured to hospital, including the judge. Luckily, no one had been killed. When things calmed down, Mary was taken back to the institute – meek as a kitten under Doctor Joslin's escort. Jawana and Lani were taken into care and Mamooto and I were taken to prison.

Tracey came to see us.

"It doesn't look good," she said. "Roughing up a judge is considered bad form in these parts."

"If we were back in the village his head would have been separated from his body for the way he treated Mary," I told her.

Tracey smiled.

"I shouldn't laugh," she said. "But Mary took his front teeth out with his own gavel."

"Well, I said. "Every morning when he looks in the mirror to

340

shave he will remember Mary."

"So, what's going to happen now?" I asked.

"Well," she said. "You will have to stay in prison until another trial date is set."

"Will you go and see Mary to reassure her and tell her I love her?"

"Of course I will," Tracey smiled, "and the children."

* * *

After the preliminaries at the prison I was put into a cell with another prisoner. Mamooto shared a cell with an enormous man with skin the colour of ebony, whose name was Luther. He looked like he had had an argument with a shovel and lost.

As the guards locked him in I heard one of them say, "I doubt he'll last the night in there with Luther – no one else ever has."

To be honest, I thought to myself, *I feel sorry for Luther.*

My fellow prisoner kept staring at me, but when I looked at him he turned his eyes away.

Finally, I asked him, "Do I bother you, son?"

"I dunno mate," he said, in a strong cockney accent. "I saw what you and your missus did in the court 'house. I was wonderin' what annoys you, mate, 'cause I don't wanna go down that road."

"I am no threat to you, son," I said. "Unless you want to make a comment about my wife and family."

"No mate," he replied. "I got a sister that's Down's and I love 'er ter bits. She sees no wrong in me, mate, no matter what I does. I saw yer missus in court on telly. Jesus, mate, she can 'andle 'erself – and that big fella. 'e threw them coppers about like ragdolls. I wish I 'ad a mate like that, mate."

It turned out the lad was always getting in trouble defending his sister against idiots who would taunt her and call her names.

"I wish she were like yer missus, mate – no offence."

We got on pretty well for the next few days. I heard nothing at all from Mamooto and Luther, so I supposed they were okay.

CHAPTER FORTY-THREE

The following week, Tracey came to see us.

"I have some good news and some bad news," she told us. "The good news is we are back in court on Monday – the bad news is that Judge Jordan has managed to convince the authorities to let him preside again, despite the obvious conflict of interest. It appears that he wants to make an example of you, so there is no way you are going home. He will send you down for a very long time and there is nothing I can do to stop it."

"How are Mary and the children?" I asked.

"They are all okay, and they send their love," said Tracey. "I'm sorry, Robbie."

Mamooto and Luther got on well together. As luck would have it, Luther's ancestors had been taken as slaves from the same area our tribe was from, so he could speak a little of the language. Not much, but enough to communicate. This constantly infuriated the guards, who couldn't understand what they were saying at all.

On Monday we were taken back to court. This time, all three of us were in the dock. Mary sat between Mamooto and myself. She held both our hands and smiled up at us. I gave her a kiss; it felt good to be close to her again.

"All rise! Judge Jordan presiding!"

Everyone stood up as the door opened and admitted the judge. He was in a right state. He had a bandage around his head, two black eyes, a broken nose, swollen lips and no front teeth.

Now he really did look like a bulldog chewing a wasp – and the wasp was winning!

His left arm was in a sling and there was a bandage on his right hand. He must really have hated us to discharge himself from hospital to carry on with the case.

A low hum of laughter rippled through the courtroom as he sat down. He glared at every single person and the sniggering receded into chastened silence. If looks could kill, we would all have been cut down in one fell swoop.

The only person laughing now was Mary. She was pointing at the judge and crying with laughter, the tears rolling down her face – and the more he banged his gavel and shouted, "Silence in court!" the louder she laughed.

This, in turn, set off Mamooto. Jawana and Lani, sat with a social worker, joined in. I couldn't hold myself in any longer and I, too, burst out laughing. Soon, the whole courtroom was screaming with laughter.

The judge was frantically banging his gavel and shouted, "Silence in court! Silence in court!" but to no avail. Even Mr Story, the prosecutor, was doubled over in helpless mirth. Jordan gave up, humiliated and unable to be heard above the clamour. He stood up and disappeared into his chambers.

Shortly after this, the court room door burst open to admit twenty armed police officers.

I thought to myself, *I've seen this film before – this is where I come in!*

Eventually everyone calmed down (including the police officers, who were more amused than annoyed), and the judge returned, looking incensed.

"Another outbreak like that and I will send every last one of you to prison for contempt of court!" he bellowed. "Mr Story! Your next witness, please!"

"I call Mr Cross to the stand, please!"

"Mr Cross, when you first took advantage of Miss Lane –"

Tracey stood up.

"Objection, your Honour!" She shouted.

"Overruled!" snapped the judge.

Tracey stayed standing, muttering something that sounded a lot like, *"Now who's in contempt of court?"* but Jordan ignored her.

"I repeat," said Story, "when you first took advantage of Miss Lane, didn't you think you would ever get caught?"

"No, sir," I said. "I never took advantage of her, so I didn't think I was doing anything wrong."

"What?" he gawped at me. "Having sexual intercourse with a mentally handicapped woman seemed right to you?"

"Yes, sir."

"What made you do it in the first place?" asked Story. "I hear that you hated people with Down's Syndrome, is that not true, Mr Cross?"

"Well, I…" I stammered.

"Just answer yes or no, please Mr Cross," Story commanded.

"Yes," I replied.

"And yet now you want the court to believe that you didn't hate them, but loved them!" scoffed Story. "I put it to you, Mr Cross, that you took advantage of Miss Lane when she was in a vulnerable position, not even taking precautions and making her pregnant – not once, Mr Cross, but twice!"

"For your information, sir!" I snapped. "There are no condom machines in the jungle. Besides which, we were both very happy to have Jawana and Lani, and we love them dearly. And, sir, Mary is *not* mentally handicapped as you keep putting it. To me she is a perfect wife and mother, a strong woman and a friend."

I could feel myself getting wound up inside.

"No more questions, your Honour," said Story, looking smug.

Clang! Clang! Clang!

Everybody jumped out of their seats as the fire alarm went off.

The doors burst open for the second time today, and in ran Jawana and Lani, who had been escorted out as I took the stand. Thick grey smoke billowed in from the corridor.

Everyone started screaming in panic and running for the doors. The judge was the first to exit – he went out through his chambers like a bat out of hell.

We jumped up. Mamooto and I were still in handcuffs.

"Grab Jawana and Lani on the way out!" I shouted, "And stick together!"

Mary pushed her hand down my waistband, like she had in the jungle, and we headed for the door. On the way, Mamooto picked up the children, tucking them under his arms. Out in the corridor, the smoke was so think we were bumping into panic stricken people on all sides, all trying to make their way to the exits. We followed the flow until we hit the stairs.

"Keep together!" I shouted.

The police had opened the fire exits and we streamed out like ants from a nest.

On the pavement outside people were coughing and choking from the thick smoke, wandering about, not knowing what to do. We were all still together, and our family stood close, coughing and confused.

Suddenly, a blue Ford Transit van pulled up at the kerb; the side door slammed open and someone bellowed at us, "Get in, quick!"

Acting purely on instinct, we literally threw the children in and climbed in beside them. The door shut at some speed and the van lurched out into the traffic.

I looked at the driver, a little bit caught up in events. He wore a black balaclava, just his eyes and mouth were showing.

"Just sit tight, boys and girls, and enjoy the ride!" he shouted, without looking back.

And what a ride it was!

Weaving in and out of traffic, running red lights as we sped through the city – it was like something out of a Mafia film. Then, from behind us came the tell-tale siren: a police car – their blues and two's flashing – was close behind us and gaining.

We were driving through the suburbs of the city now, down narrowing roads. The driver took a sharp left into a side road with speed bumps every fifty yards or so. The road narrowed further to a single lane, presumably to prevent boy racers overtaking each other. There were trees planted down either side of the road, like an avenue.

I looked out of the rear window – there were three police cars behind us now.

As we approached the next narrow point I noticed a man sitting astride a motor cycle. We shot through the narrow gap and a second man pushed a tree trunk across the road behind us. Then he jumped on behind the biker, riding pillion, and they both sped off.

Whomever had organised this had clearly put some real thought into the exercise.

The first police car saw the tree trunk and instinctively swerved to avoid it crashing into a lamppost. The two other cars couldn't stop in time and crashed into the back of the first. Our driver laughed out loud.

"Suckers!" he shouted, plainly enjoying himself. He put his hand out of the window, middle finger extended.

We slowed down and drove back into the city traffic. Our driver removed his balaclava. It was Jenkins.

"I hope you enjoyed the ride, sir!" he grinned.

"Well, I'll be blowed," I laughed. "You young devil –you're a damn good driver!" I shouted, as we turned another corner at speed.

"I told you I wanted to be a stock car racer when I was grew up."

"You've certainly got the moves!" I called back.

"I have to," Jenkins grinned. "I'm the best getaway driver in south London!"

So much for going straight, I thought.

We all looked up, out of the windows. Above us we could hear the throb, throb, throb of a police helicopter; it was directly overhead.

"Hold onto your hat, sir," Jenkins declared. "Here we go again!"

I got the distinct impression that our driver was having the time of his life. Jawana and Lani cuddled up to Mary, who held them tightly. She was just happy to have them in her arms again.

Somewhere in the front of the van a radio crackled into life; it took a few moments, but then I realised we were listening to the police scanner.

"Be advised, this is Air Unit five – we have them in sight travelling south down East Talbot street, repeat, southbound on East Talbot street. Blue Ford Transit with a large number three painted on the roof – it's easy to spot, over."

"Okay five – stay on it. Be advised, we're dropping the ground units back – we don't want to panic them in the city. Pursuit too risky in the built-up areas, someone might get hurt, over."

"Acknowledged, over."

I stared at it. Jenkins had clearly done this before to have come so prepared. We sped through the suburbs, finally pulling into a multi-storey car park. The radio came on again:

"Be advised, suspect has entered Parkington multi-storey carpark, repeat, suspect has entered Parkington multi-storey carpark, over."

"Acknowledged, Air Unit five. Stay with them. Ground units are

closing on your position."

The moment we were under cover, the sound of engines revving up filled the air, echoing around us. I gaped as two dozen dark blue transit vans streamed past us and out onto the street. The helicopter pilot didn't seem particularly happy about this. He relayed the new information to the ground unit, sweating profusely.

"Calling all ground units, calling all ground units," came the strained response. "Anyone in the vicinity of the Parkington multi-storey carpark. Be advised, suspects fleeing in multiple dark blue Ford Transit vans with a number three painted on the roof. Stop and search every dark blue transit van. Repeat, stop and search every dark blue Ford Transit van!"

There followed a brief, but accurate, description of Mary, Mamooto, the children and myself, and a series of calls letting the control room know that various members of the Metropolitan police were suddenly extremely busy.

We pulled up in a secluded corner of the carpark and Jenkins told us all to get out.

"Thanks Jenkins." I said shaking his hand.

"No sweat, sir," he said. "Glad to be of help. Go through that door there," he said, pointing to a side entrance. "You will be met."

CHAPTER FORTY-FOUR

We watched him drive off, joining the other vans in causing chaos. Mamooto pushed the door Jenkins had indicated open to reveal a man dressed in full fire-fighting gear. He led us to a fire engine, of all things.

"Get in," he ordered.

Once we were inside the engine roared into life and one of the men in front turned on the blues and twos. The road traffic parted in front of us like the Red Sea.

Hanging up in the cab were fire-fighting tunics with helmets, axes, belts and boots.

"Put them on," said our new friend. "Keep the children out of sight."

He turned in his seat and cut our handcuffs off with bolt croppers.

Jawana and Lani sat wide eyed as we sped through the traffic. Police cars were everywhere, stopping every blue van they saw, too busy to give the fire engine even a second glance.

We drove away from the city centre and back out into the suburbs. After a few miles we turned into a wide road lined with tall Victorian houses. About halfway down stood a crowd gawping at a house that stood a little way back from its neighbours, set in its own grounds. Thick smoke was belching from an upstairs window.

A police officer moved the spectators away from the gates to let us in. My heart sank.

"It's alright," the driver told us, shouting over his shoulder. "He's one of us."

The fire engine roared up the short drive and around the side of the house and came to a halt where no one could see us.

"Everybody out!" he shouted. "Into the garage!"

I heard the children laughing and I turned to see what all the fuss was about. I grinned. Mamooto's helmet was so small that it perched on the top of his head like a pea on a drum. His tunic buttons were at least a foot from the button holes. He couldn't have done them up if he tried. He didn't even try to put the boots on.

Then I looked at Mary. She stood beside the fire engine with her helmet on back to front. The tunic hung over her shoulders like a sack, the fire axe dangling between her knees. She had both her boots on the wrong feet.

That sight will stay with me for the rest of my life.

If the public saw this motley crew turn up to fight a fire I don't know what they would think.

There was a people carrier in the garage; another man opened the rear door and ushered us over. Under the floor of the vehicle was a compartment.

"Take the fire gear off and slide in," he ordered. "Quickly! It used to be a hearse," he added. "It'll be a bit tight, but I think you can manage. Whatever happens, keep very quiet."

He pressed a button on a remote control and the garage door opened. The hearse slid out of a rear gate and out into the traffic again.

I thought to myself, *Whoever planned this escape has a brilliant mind. So far it has gone like clockwork.*

We rode in silence for about twenty minutes before the motor slowed down to a stop. I heard the electric window slide down, somewhere above us.

"Yes officer, can I help you?"

"Good morning sir," came a second voice. "Would you mind stepping out of the car, please?"

My chest tightened. This was not good. I tensed, ready for a fight. The car dipped and bounced as our driver got out.

"Open all the doors please, sir."

I could hear the policeman rummaging around in the back. He didn't find anything.

"Where have you come from, sir?" he asked.

I heard our driver tell him that he was transporting bodies from a dreadful road accident.

"Oh, it was awful," he said. "One was decapitated, the other disembowelled – and a little girl. The paramedics said every bone in her body had been –"

The rest of his sentence was covered by a mechanical whirring sound. I could feel the floor rising up, taking us with it. There was only a canvas cover over the five of us. I felt the driver take the corner of the canvas.

"I'll show you, officer. You won't see anything quite as gruesome as this for a long time."

The canvas moved a fraction; sweat was oozing out of every pore – I could feel Jawana and Lani trembling in fear, pressed between me and Mary.

"No, that's alright," said the officer, hurriedly. "I'll take your word for it. You can be on your way, sir."

I was shaking hard as we drove off. I had felt more fear in those few seconds than in any battle we had fought in the jungle.

We drove for another three or four hours, just long enough for it to get really uncomfortable in the hearse, before coming to a stop. I waited in tense anticipation. Was this another police check?

To my very great relief, the floor opened and our driver said, "You can come out now. Sorry it took so long. Better take the chance to stretch your legs."

The first thing I did was to take Mary in my arms and kiss her.

We held one another tightly and I became aware of something digging in my chest. I looked down as Mary undid her blouse and pulled out the fire axe and belt from our earlier disguise.

"Mine," she said, smiling.

I hugged and kissed our children and Mary kissed Mamooto. It was good to be together again as a family.

We're not out of the woods yet, though, are we? I thought.

I looked around. We had climbed out in a vast warehouse stacked with crates and boxes. At the far end was a toilet and a kitchen area, with five rooms housing fresh clothes and bunk beds. A table had been set up with a meal laid out upon in. There were soft drinks, wine and a bottle of scotch. Someone had obviously know we were coming.

After a shower and a fresh change of clothes we all sat down together to eat. It turned out that our driver was Professor Jenkins' younger brother Simon, who was usually an undertaker. The two men on motorcycles who had also driven the fire engine were his sons.

The transits had been 'borrowed' from a lock-up in Dagenham by my old mate Jenkins and his associates. The fire engine was on loan from a retained fire station in Sutton who owed the professor a favour.

They had even rented the empty Victorian house for the day and planted a smoke bomb upstairs to cause the necessary chaos to enable our escape. He assured us that no damage had been done, there or at the crown court.

All in all, it had been a well-planned and well-executed operation, all thanks to one man: Professor Jenkins.

"So, what next?" I asked.

"Well, tonight you will rest," Simon explained. "Tomorrow the next part of the plan comes into operation."

He wouldn't tell us what it was, so we gave up asking. Instead, we put the children to bed. They were so tired they fell asleep as soon as their heads hit their pillows. For the next few hours, the four of us sat and talked, Mary resting her head on my shoulder and one arm around my waist. Every now and then she would give me a gentle kiss on the cheek.

"We've had quite a day," Simon exclaimed. "One or two scary near misses, that's for sure. Edgar tells me by all accounts you have had quite an adventure yourselves for the past twelve years."

We finished the wine and the scotch while I told him some of our adventures.

"Blimey," he said. "That boat ride through the mountains…" he shook his head, chuckling. "I could never do that – I can't even ride on a rollercoaster without throwing up."

"Yes," I said, "But the way you handled that police officer when he opened the hearse…" I laughed. "I thought we were nicked for sure. We all handle situations in different ways, and I thank you for that."

Mamooto fell asleep on a blanket on the floor still holding the bottle of scotch. Mary insisted on sleeping with me, and in a single bed it was a bit uncomfortable. She went straight to sleep, of course. I swear she could sleep on a bed of nails and not feel a thing. I spent the rest of the night wide awake, wondering what the morning would bring.

In the morning we all showered and had breakfast. Simon arrived just as we were finishing, and he took us to a number of large crates.

"This crate has been designed with a double skin," he said, pointing at the nearest one. "There are engine parts around the outside walls so you can sit in the centre. Whatever happens you must all keep very, very quiet until someone lets you out."

Just then, the warehouse door opened with such suddenness that for a moment I thought we had been rumbled. Luckily, it turned out to be Professor Jenkins, Dave, Tracey and Melanie, all of whom were smiling.

"Well, my boy," the professor declared. "Everything has gone well so far." He shook my hand. "Just one more hurdle left: customs. They are watching the airports and docks for you."

Baines came in, next, followed by Jane and her children.

"You didn't think you were going without saying goodbye, did you?" she smiled.

"What time are the crates being loaded?" asked the professor.

"11.30 a.m.," Simon told him.

"Right, we have an hour and a half to say our goodbyes, and to get you packed and nailed in," said Professor Jenkins. "Everyone must be miles away from here before the lorries collect the crates or customs will get suspicious."

Jane was crying as she kissed me goodbye.

"I wish it were me you were going with," she whispered.

I kissed Jason and Erica, and Robyn threw her arms around my neck. I hugged her tightly.

"I love you, Daddy," she said, tears running down her cheeks.

"And I love you, too," I said. "Don't forget, we will both look at the moon and think of each other – and we will always be close. Someone has to look after your mummy, and Erica and Jason. Will you do that for me?"

She nodded her head, looking very sombre for a twelve year old. "Yes." She answered.

Dave came over.

"Well, Robbie," he smiled. "Whoever would have thought it would end like this when we were at teacher training college?"

He shook my hand and I pulled him into a hug.

"Good luck, my old mate," he said. "I wish you all well for the future."

Tracey gave me a hug and a kiss.

"Thanks for everything you have done for us," I said. "I will miss you. Did you bring it will you?"

"Yes," she smiled, opening her handbag and pulling out the funeral medallion I had found in the river on the way through the mountain. "There is one thing," she said. "Would you mind if I used some of the money to make a small donation to the institute?"

"Of course I don't mind," I assured her. "Please do!"

I approached the professor, who embraced me like a brother.

"Well, my boy, of all the adventures I have had, meeting you and Mary has been the best by far. I will be sorry to see you go. Mamooto and Jawana and Lani, too."

"I have something for you," I said. "To remember us by."

He gaped at me as I handed him the medallion. His eyes lit up.

"I will cherish this for the rest of my life," he stammered. "Thank you."

When we had finished our goodbyes, Melanie took my arm.

"I'm coming with you," she said. "Once I have the baby there will be nothing for me here – and with Mary's help I can start a new life in the village with no prejudice against me or the baby."

I turned to the professor, who shrugged.

"Don't look at me," he said. "It's her decision. She won't listen to anything I say. Everything has been taken care of," he continued. "Paid for by Reg's contribution. You'll get back to the village alright – give my regards to the chief and Manta and Reg"

He clapped me on the back.

"You saved us from your jungle, now it's our turn to save you from ours!"

We said our goodbyes and climbed into the crate. An inner lid was nailed down, leaving just enough space for air to get in, and polystyrene chips were poured in on top of us. We could hear the outer lid being screwed down and the sound of the warehouse doors crashing shut. Then, everything went quiet.

We waited patiently in the dark. Mary sat next to me with Lani and Jawana in her arms. Melanie cuddled up to Mamooto.

After what seemed like an eternity the doors of the warehouse opened and we heard the sounds of a low loader backing up. A forklift engine juddered into life; we could hear it loading the other crates onto the lorry. The crate shook and we guessed we were next. It was a very strange feeling, being stacked up as cargo. Once all the crates were secure, the lorry's engine started up again and we were off, presumably heading towards the docks.

About an hour later (though it seemed much longer inside the crate) the lorry ground to a halt. We heard the sound of our driver exiting his vehicle and the crunch of someone else's footsteps.

"Customs and Excise!" someone shouted. "What are you hauling, mate?"

"Engine parts, bound for Dubai," said the driver.

"Let's have your sheets, then." There was a pause, and then, "We're going to have to open all the crates and check the contents."

"What?" said a voice I thought I recognised. "We sail at five o'clock, if you open all the crates we will miss the tide."

"I can't help that."

"If you want to open them all, leave them on the dock and customs can pay for the storage until another ship is commissioned."

"You can't do that!" said the customs man.

"Oh yes I can – and I will, so make up your mind!"

"Alright," the customs man sighed, sounding harassed. "We will open three of the crates. That one, that one and that one. Leave them on the dock and load the others while we work."

I sat in the darkness, sweating. Had he indicated our crate?

I tensed every time a crate was lifted off the lorry and the vehicle moved on its springs. My heart was pounding fit to burst. The sound of men with crowbars opening our crate filtered through from above and my heart sank. Had all of this been for nothing.

"Come on out," a man's voice commanded.

CHAPTER FORTY-FIVE

I gasped as my eyes adjusted to the bright sunlight.

"Hello Robbie, it's nice to see you again!"

It was the captain.

An overwhelming sense of relief came over me and I burst into tears.

"Follow my man," he said, with sympathy. "He will hide you until we are out to sea."

We hid in the bilge while the three crates were opened, checked and repacked. Then the boat's engines started up and we moved gently away from the dock.

"You can come up now!" someone shouted down.

Out on deck, a man led us up to the bridge, where the captain was waiting for us, beaming.

"I think we've been here before," he said, as he shook our hands.

"I didn't think we would be here again," I answered.

"That was a close call with customs, but bullshit baffles brains," he laughed.

"How did you fare with the pirates and their ship?" I asked.

"I sold everything but the guns," he told me. "We still have them aboard in case we're ever boarded again."

"There was a price on their heads, wasn't there?"

"I collected that," he said. "I sold their ship and then pooled the money and divided it evenly amongst the crew. You remember the crewman we lost?"

I nodded.

"Well, we all put a quarter of our shares to his and made sure his wife and kids are set up for years to come. I took on his eldest son as a crewman," he added. "If he is half as good as his dad he'll do alright for himself."

About midnight we put the children to bed.

I was desperate to make love to Mary. It seemed like a very long time since the last time we had. I wanted her so bad I thought I would explode. She took my hand and led me to the prow of the ship. We lay under the stars talking, caressing and kissing, fulfilling each other's needs until the sun rose.

*   *   *

It turned out that the ship only had one stop, which was to put us off at Verno. Then it would carry on to Dubai to deliver the engine parts.

Melanie had quite a bump now, and was beginning to look radiant. She seemed more relaxed now we were away from England. I found her sitting on a crate in the sun the morning after we boarded the ship. I sat down beside her.

"Are you sure you're doing the right thing?" I asked.

"Yes, I am," she said. "There is nothing for me in England – especially with the baby."

"The problem could be with you adapting to jungle life," I said, carefully. "It will be dangerous at the very least."

"Mary did it," she said, looking at me."

"Yes," I said, "but Mary has no fear. She accepts everything as it comes – and she looks to me for guidance. There are no white men in the village, you know," I said. "Only Lani – and if you wait for him, he may not fancy the older woman by then."

I glanced sideways at her and discovered her giving me a sly grin.

"I was thinking more of Mamooto," she admitted.

"You little minx," I exclaimed. "Does he know?"

"No, I was hoping you would put a good word in for me."

"It doesn't work like that," I laughed. "My old Dad used to say, 'a man chases a woman until she catches him'."

Melanie looked puzzled.

"Think about it," I smiled.

The further away from England we travelled, the safer I felt. Each time we sighted a ship my heart would sink in case it was the coastguard. The days passed slowly.

*   *   *

One morning the captain said, "We should make Verno tomorrow at about noon."

With the next sunrise we could make out the coastline and by around midday we moored up at the dock. The last time we were in Verno I had hated it, but this time I simply felt a sense of relief.

We said our farewells to the captain and his crew, and I thanked him again for his help in our quest to get home.

Standing on the dock watching the boat pull away I wondered, *What now?*

"Oh no," said Melanie, a tinge of mild horror in her voice. "It's Lex… You're in for an experience you will not forget in a hurry. He's an idiot."

She gestured to a beat up old lorry about fifty yards up the road with a man leaning against it, smoking a cigarette. When he spotted us he pushed himself off and sauntered across towards us.

"How do," he grinned. "I'm Lex, your friendly driver and pilot. I'm here to escort you on the final part of your journey."

He looked at Melanie.

"Hello Honeychild," he leered. "I didn't expect to see you back here so soon. Just couldn't stay away from me for too long, eh?"

"In your dreams," she snapped.

"Right!" he barked. "The limo's over there. If you would all like to climb aboard we'll be on our way."

He looked at me.

"Robbie? you'll sit up front with me and I'll update you on the plan."

We shook hands.

We travelled through jungle and across small patches of deserts for three days, only stopping to refuel from jerry cans tied on the tailgate. We ate on the move and tried to time our toilet requirements to the fuel stops.

Once I got to know him I found Lex to be a real character, though I could see why Melanie couldn't stand him. Some years ago he had got himself into big trouble with the Mafia, running cocaine from Afghanistan to America and had had to disappear very quickly.

"I expect they will catch up with me one day," he told me cheerfully. "Until then I am quite happy here."

We finally arrived at the airfield in the late afternoon.

"The shower is over there," said Lex, pointing at a five gallon drum hanging in a tree. "After the first one has showered, they fill the drum for the next one, and so on. Then we eat. I erected the tents a fortnight ago, so choose which one you want and check inside them in case anything has moved in before you got here. Tomorrow, we start training," he added.

"What training?" I asked.

"Parachute training."

After a good night's sleep and a hearty breakfast, Lex took us to a tree where a harness hung from a branch.

"These," he said. "Are tandem harnesses. That means two people to a parachute, so sort yourselves out into pairs and let's get started."

"Okay," I said. "Mary with me, Mamooto with Lani and Melanie with Jawana."

Lex strapped us all in turn, starting with Mary and I.

"These are slow descent chutes," he explained. "You will all be jumping on a static line. That means your parachute pack is secured to the aircraft by a rope and when you leave the plane it will open the chute for you. You don't need to do anything until you land.

"When you are on the ground," he went on, "and not before you are on the ground, you undo the harness by turning the knob anti-clockwise on the front of the harness. This will spring open, revealing a button. Strike the button hard with the heel of your hand, and the straps will automatically release."

We practiced for hours until we all got it about right. I watched Mamooto practicing and wondered if he realised exactly what he was in for.

At about four pm. that afternoon, Lex said, "Well, that's about as good as you're going to get, so let's get airborne and get you home."

"Melanie," He said, as we approached the small plane. "Since you've jumped before, you jump first – so get in the plane last."

Lex had already removed the plane's starboard door.

"Mamooto, you go next," I said. "Mary and I will go last."

I climbed in with Mary and Lex tied our static line to a handle, before doing the same for the others. While Lex was preparing for take-off I asked Lani and Jawana if they were okay. They seemed more excited than anything else.

The engine roared into life and Lex peered back at us.

"Is everybody ready?" he asked.

"Yes!" we all roared.

He turned and pointed into the sky ahead of us.

"Wagons roll!" he yelled.

As the plane started moving and picked up speed we all held each other tightly. Faster and faster we roared down the runway, and then the nose lifted and the wheels left the ground. Melanie sat in the open doorway, holding Jawana. Their legs were dangling out into mid-air, but they both looked reasonably calm.

I looked at Mamooto, who did not. His eyes were as big as saucers; he was staring down onto the jungle as it rushed past below us, clinging onto Lani for dear life.

After several hours flying, Lex shouted, over the engine noise "We are nearly there," "I will try to find an open bit of ground, but you'll have to jump quickly or you might land in the trees."

He turned to look at us.

"Right," he shouted. "When I shout 'go', all of you have to get out as fast as you can."

He circled round. *"Go! Go! Go!"*

Without hesitation, Melanie slid out of the door with Jawana.

Mamooto was frozen in fear, staring out of the plane, terror etched into his face. Without thinking twice I put my foot in the middle of his back and pushed with all of my might. He shot out, arms flailing, trying to grab anything to stop himself falling.

Mary and I threw our legs out of the door. The last I heard of Lex as we left the aircraft, he was holding as steady as he could and wishing us all good luck at the top of his voice.

My heart was pounding in my chest as Mary and I dropped like a stone – I felt a sudden tug on my shoulders as the parachute opened. I looked up to see the canopy billowing open as our feet swung beneath us.

I looked down: below us were Mamooto and Lani, and below

366

them, Melani and Jawana. All three canopies were billowing.

So far, so good, I thought to myself.

We were falling towards a clearing just ahead of us. Mary was screaming with glee, clapping her hands together and shouting at the others below. The children were shouting too, having the time of their lives. Mamooto was screaming louder than Mary, but I think that was pure terror.

I watched as Melanie and Jawana landed. They stood up and waved.

Good.

They were safely down. Soon, Mamooto and Lani joined them, legs and arms waving like a windmill. They landed right on the edge of the clearing as we approached.

We sailed right over their heads and into the trees. We stopped with a jolt as the canopy caught in the branches. I looked down – we were still about ten feet from the ground. The others ran over.

"What are you doing up there?" Melanie called.

"Oh, just hanging around," I answered.

I turned the knob on the harness and thought to myself, *Oh well, shit or bust!*

I gave the button a sharp bang and the two of us dropped to the ground. I landed on my back, Mary on top of me. It knocked the wind clean out of my body.

"Mary! Are you alright?" I croaked, my voice much huskier than usual.

"Alright," she replied, standing up.

Everyone helped me to my feet.

"Wait a minute," I waved them off. "Let me get my breath back."

The sun was low in the sky now and we knew it would be dark in an hour or so.

"If we head towards the setting sun we should be going in the right direction," I said. "Then we will rest for the night and start afresh in the morning."

Then, in the distance, drums started beating. It sounded like we'd let the whole jungle know we were here.

CHAPTER FORTY SIX.

We hid the parachutes. Mary buckled the fireman's axe to the belt around her waist. "Right," I decided. "I will lead, followed by Mary, then Jawana, Melanie, Lani and Mamooto. bringing up the rear. You all remember the rules – if you see or hear anything, keep quiet and just raise your hand."

Mary grabbed the back of my waistband and we set off, the drums keeping a constant beat in the twilight. As the sun disappeared into the trees and darkness fell we found a hollow under a big tree. We slept there for the night, Mamooto and I taking turns to keep watch.

As the sun rose the next morning so did we. We found a stream where we washed and bathed. As we walked that day we picked fruit and ate as we went. We kept an eye out for likely looking branches in the forest and made spears with Mary's axe.

For three days we travelled in this manner, resting at night. We avoided any natives we saw on the off-chance they were hostile, and skirting around their villages. To get this close to home and die in the last few miles was not worth a confrontation.

On the fourth morning we were preparing to move out when something moved in the undergrowth. Mary drew her axe and Mamooto and I raised our spears.

Everything went quiet; then the thing moved again, getting closer.

Whatever it was came crashing through the undergrowth, heading straight at us. We stood in a line with our weapons raised. The bushes parted and into the clearing came a blur of fur. It was that damn dog!

He scared the living daylights out of us. He ran round and round our little group, wagging his tail so hard his whole body was juddering to and fro. He was ecstatic to see us – and we were pleased to see him, too. Everyone went wild, all hugging and stroking him. When he had calmed down a bit he looked at me. Jekyll sat down, ears back, tongue hanging out and his front paw raised. I have never been so pleased to see that mutt as I was that day.

"Good boy," I said, stroking him.

Then, out of the corner of my eye I saw a figure before us. I turned and there, standing in the middle of the path, was Mbata. For a second we simply stared at one another, then we walked towards each other.

"Mbata," I said.

"Majumi."

We held out our arms and hugged one another.

"It is good to see you back old friend."

"It's good to *be* back."

"We knew something was happening when the drums started," he told us. "Jawana's dog was restless – howling and trying to break his leash. I let him go and he led us straight here."

"I used to hate that dog," I smiled, rubbing Jekyll's head. "Let's go home."

After another few hours of walking I began to recognise familiar stretches of jungle. We were getting closer to our village with every step. More of our tribe came out to meet us, cheering and clapping when they saw who we were. They welcomed us home, shouting and calling.

Then we walked out of the jungle and into our village. The first person to greet us was Reg. He shook my hand vigorously.

"Hello, old mate!" he cried. "How was Blighty?"

"Dada!" shouted Mary, and ran into his arms.

They hugged and kissed, and then he scooped up Jawana and Lani.

"Look at you two," he laughed. "All grown up!"

The chief emerged from his hut.

"Welcome home, my son," he beamed. "I knew you would return." His gaze fell on Melanie. "You came back as well," he observed, surprised.

She nodded.

"You are welcome." He smiled.

Melanie had clearly been worrying about this moment because she burst into tears.

"Oh, thank you," she cried, tears rolling down her cheeks. "Thank you."

The chief turned his attention to Mary and smiled, holding out his hand. She completely ignored it and embraced him fully; he put his arm around her shoulder and held her close.

I doubt anyone has ever received a welcome like that from the chief before, I thought.

"Your hut is as you left it," he told us. "I expect you will want to refresh yourselves after your long journey. Tonight we celebrate your return!" he announced, and then disappeared back inside his hut.

Mary spent the rest of the afternoon with Melanie, cleaning our hut and making it liveable once more. For the time being, Melanie would be living with us.

Later that afternoon I went to see the chief.

"Come," he said. "Sit."

"It's about Mamooto," I said. "He has been a loyal bodyguard for years, but he had also become a great friend to me and to my family. I know you released him from his bond when we left and he refused, but now I think it's time he had the chance to settle down, take a wife and have a family of his own. I think he deserves that."

"What does he think about it?" asked the chief.

I laughed.

"He doesn't know I am here," I said. "I would like it to come from you – there's more chance of him listening."

"I will consider it," he replied.

That evening, Mary, Melanie and Jawana bathed, and when they returned to our hut to prepare for the feast, Mamooto, Lani and I bathed in the lake. We could hear our girls laughing and giggling in the hut. It was great to hear them enjoying themselves after the ordeals of the last few months.

Reg joined us in the water.

"I have something for you," he said.

I held out my hand and he dropped my penis beads in it.

"But they're yours," I protested, "in payment for your treasure."

"Well, as you don't have any treasure anymore, I don't need your penis beads," he said, with a smile. "Besides, I am far too well-endowed to wear such a small string of beads as that!"

"Cheeky sod," I said. Lani and Mamooto roared with laughter.

When we returned to the hut, Melanie shouted, "You can't come in! We're not ready yet!"

As usual, the fire was lit that evening with a massive spread laid out in front of the chief's hut. We sat cross-legged on the ground, waiting for everybody to arrive before the chief emerged.

Reg tapped me on the shoulder and pointed. Walking towards us were Mary and Melanie, both looking beautiful in the flickering firelight, their skin shining with fragrant oils. They were not alone. Between them walked Jawana. Our daughter had a crown of flowers on her head, her skin was oiled with little plaits of flowers at her wrists and ankles. There a necklace of beads at her neck and a gold chain around her waist.

For the first time it struck me that my little girl was a young woman now. I hadn't realised how grown up she was.

She smiled at me and I smiled back, nodding my approval.

Mary had made Melanie up to look like a goddess. Even with her baby bump she was stunning. Mamooto was staring at her; I swear he was drooling.

"What do you think of her?" I whispered.

"A handsome woman," he replied, not taking his eyes off her.

"She likes you, too," I said. "She told me so."

But the belle of the ball was my Mary. She stood at the edge of the firelight, holding a small posy of flowers and smiling at me. I rose and went to her, holding out my hand. She took it and I drew her close.

"You are beautiful," I whispered.

She went all coy as I held her in my arms. The smell of her perfume reminded me of the first time she had made herself up for me, all those years ago when we first arrived at the village.

We all took our places and waited for the chief. When he emerged he beckoned to Mary and Mamooto. First he spoke to Mamooto, and then to Mary.

Mamooto returned to us and sat down. Mary nodded at the chief as he spoke, smiling. Then one of the chief's wives came out, carrying a white toga with gold braid and a gold belt. Mary put it on and everybody cheered. The chief gestured for her to sit beside him; she looked at me and I nodded.

When the chief took his seat the feast began. Jawana sat at my side.

"You are a very beautiful young lady," I told her, kissing her on the cheek."

"I love you, Daddy," she smiled.

"And I love you, very much."

All through the meal, Mary was waited on hand and foot. She kept looking at us and waving, laughing contentedly, like a little girl. It was really good to see my family happy again.

Mamooto turned to me, about halfway through the meal.

"Thank you, Majumi," he said.

I guessed that the chief had released him from his bond. Nothing else was said; nothing else needed to be said.

Over the meal we told stories of our exploits. I told Reg that his partners back in England sent their regards. Mamooto could not stop taking about his amazing parachute jump.

After the food had settled and the drink began to kick in, the drums started. Melanie was among the first to get up. She started dancing right in front of Mamooto. The other women joined in and then the evening really got started.

Melanie was dancing seductively, throwing provocative moves in Mamooto's direction, thrusting her loins and juggling her breasts at him.

If he doesn't get the message now he never will, I thought.

I must have been staring at her for a bit too long, because Mary prodded me in the ribs.

"Naughty boy," she teased, her face stern.

"What?" I said. "I haven't done anything."

"You very naughty boy," she giggled.

She took Jawana's hand and I watched as they joined the dance. Jawana was a right little poser, clearly enjoying growing up. Lani was playing with the other boys. Girls hadn't turned his head yet.

I glanced at Melanie. Sweat was pouring from her body. She held out her hand to Mamooto, who took it lightly and joined her. It was the first time I had seen him let go enough to enjoy himself, and he was a pretty good mover – a jungle Fred Astaire.

I looked at Mary, who was smiling at me; she beckoned me over. Jawana was getting tired and told us she was going to bed. Lani was already asleep on the ground nearby. She woke him up and took him back to our hut.

I joined Mary on the dance floor. It may only have been made of earth, but it was the best dance floor I have ever danced on – and with the most beautiful woman in the world. The pace of the drums increased, pounding faster and faster until with jarring suddenness – they stopped. Screaming and giggling, the women ran off into the jungle.

Mary ran into our hut.

Well, I thought. *I won't have to search too hard to find her this time!*

I watched Mamooto as Melanie disappeared into the trees. He shot me a devilish grin and hared after her. I went to our hut.

Mary emerged, meeting me just outside with glasses of cool juice. We lay together on the shore, gazing up at the moon. I wondered if Robyn was looking up at it as well.

Mary lay on her back, her skin like liquid gold in the moonlight. She smelled like summer flowers and when I kissed her she tasted sweet, like honey. She was smiling up at me. I couldn't take my eyes off her.

"Love you," she whispered.

"I love you, too," I replied. "Always and forever."

The moonlight glittered across the silvery lake. Mary put her arm around my chest and pulled me to her. We made love to the noises of the jungle and fell asleep in each other's arms.

Mamooto and Melanie came back to our hut the next morning. She looked radiant and he had what looked like a permanent smile on his face, like he had a coat hanger in his mouth, upside down.

We all ate breakfast together and I felt we were a family, living exactly where we belonged: in heaven.

Over the next few years, we lost our chief to old age, but nobody mourned. Instead we rejoiced, celebrating the great man's life and giving him a proper send-off. Mbata was made chief after him, and a good chief he is, too. Mamooto and Melanie were joined in union and had five strong children. Her first born was a beautiful little girl who stole all our hearts.

Mamooto is still my best friend.

The tribes don't war anymore and we carry out trade in harmony Jawana has grown into a beautiful young woman and has one of the young men of the village following her around like a puppy. I think they will be joined in union soon.

Lani, the little ram, is a strapping young man now, and after the dances he chases the girls into the jungle as enthusiastically as any other man. I don't blame him for that at all.

Mary is still the greatest thing that ever happened to me.

When I reflect on my past I think how fate played its part in our lives. If I hadn't resigned my job as a teacher over my negative feelings for those with Down's Syndrome I would not have been on the plane when it crashed. I would never have met Mary, or Reg, or Mamooto, or Mbata – and I wouldn't have had two beautiful children.

I would never have lived this extraordinary adventure that some people would die for.

Each night, as we lie in our hammock we listen to the sounds of the jungle like a lullaby,

sending us to sleep. The last sound we hear before we drift off is that old croc' growl, rumbling across the lake. There used to be two you know?

The End.